W9-BUU-164

Ace Books by Chris Claremont

FIRSTFLIGHT
GROUNDED!
SUNDOWNER

SUNDOWNER

CHRIS CLAREMONT

ACE BOOKS, NEW YORK

To

Susan Allison and Ginjer Buchanan

*For all the faith and forbearance
a writer could wish for in his
publisher and editor.*

*As friends and colleagues, I
wouldn't have gotten here without you.*

This book is an Ace original edition,
and has never been previously published.

SUNDOWNER

An Ace Book / published by arrangement with
the author

PRINTING HISTORY
Ace edition / July 1994

All rights reserved.
Copyright © 1994 by Chris Claremont.
Cover art by Royo.
This book may not be reproduced in whole or in part,
by mimeograph or any other means, without permission.
For information address: The Berkley Publishing Group,
200 Madison Avenue, New York, NY 10016.

ISBN: 0-441-00070-3

ACE®
Ace Books are published by The Berkley Publishing Group,
200 Madison Avenue, New York, NY 10016.
ACE and the "A" design are trademarks
belonging to Charter Communications, Inc.

PRINTED IN THE UNITED STATES OF AMERICA

10 9 8 7 6 5 4 3 2 1

CHAPTER ONE

*Golden sun. Golden sky. Golden land. Rolling
country, a highland plain stretching along the seaward face of the continental spine, with good grass
and water to feed the great herds that wander from
north to south according to the dictates of the seasons. Good for prey, hard for hunters. Precious little
cover, and not much better for habitation. Too
much open space. Fast as you are, the prey is
faster, their bodies built for flight, mated to senses
designed to trigger them into action. They know
their safety lies in numbers: stay with the herd, stay
alive. Of course, that leaves the lame and the
sick and the old as meat, but there's no challenge
in that.*

Nicole sensed the boat's approach long before she ever saw it.
The wind was strong off her quarter and she had *Sundowner*
under full sail, genny and main trimmed to give her every
possible knot, the boat heeling so much she was almost
standing on the lower lip of the cockpit, tiller in both hands,
teeth bared in a grin of fierce delight. No thoughts to mar the
moment, no consideration of yesterday or tomorrow. Her
strength, her boat, all alone against the elements.

She knew she'd stayed out too long. Her skin had that
stretched taut feel that meant her sun block had given up the
ghost, and her muscles, especially across her back and arms,
were just this side of trembling. Her grip on the lines wasn't
what it should be and her concentration was worse. Not that she
was making mistakes. Not big ones, not yet.

1

By rights, she should have headed for the barn hours ago. Would have, had she been flying. In the air she was the consummate professional. She went to sea to goof off, cut herself some slack, no matter that the environment was potentially just as hazardous.

She was on a reach to Point Loma, at the mouth of San Diego Bay, when she suddenly looked back over her shoulder. She searched the water as she would the sky on a combat patrol, alert for the slightest sign of a hostile presence. Made a face and shook her head, wishing she had a third hand so she could rub her itchy scalp and possibly restore some semblance of order to her windblown salt-washed hair. She was thankful at least that she still wore it close-cropped, shorter in fact than a lot of men these days.

A glance westward showed the sun just three diameters above the horizon, dusk then before she was tied up at her slip. Way it went sometimes, couldn't be helped. The wind was great, the sea a match, the boat—her precious Bermuda Forty—an absolute joy. She'd gone so far out—too far actually for a solo sailor, even on a custom-rigged boat, experienced as she was—she'd been tempted to keep going. Almost as though she were testing herself, pushing the limit of how far she could go and still return within a day.

Lately, she'd been turning for home that much more reluctantly, hearing ghostly echoes in the cockpit of that last bitter conversation with Alex Cobri. He had challenged her to do just that: cut the traces that bound her to the Air Force and NASA, to a space program that had abandoned her, just as he would do with his father. The two of them would sail off together past the ends of the Earth, charting fresh destinies unencumbered by the past.

She hadn't made that break. Too many hopes, too many dreams, a faith that hadn't then been ready to die.

She'd gotten what she wanted, reinstatement as a full-fledged astronaut. For all the good it did her. Five years later, she was still stuck on the ground. Just as Alex was planted in it.

Another look, so sharp and sudden it caught her by surprise and prompted an acerbic mutter at instincts gone amuck. She'd also come to trust those instincts, so she eased off the main sheet to slow *Sundowner*'s headlong flight and ducked her head towards the radar repeater mounted beside the companionway at the front of the cockpit. Had to look twice to make sure she wasn't seeing things when the display flashed the contact's speed.

Awareness now of the other craft's engines, a basso rumble cascading across the wavetops, felt as much as heard, as a jet engine is on the flight line when it cycles towards full power. The boat was moving more slowly than she'd expected because the association in her mind was of an aircraft, and yet it passed her as though she were dead in the water, an expanded cigarette hull two-thirds out of the water, triple thrusters generating a white-water wake that rose almost as high as the bow. The boat was so beautiful it literally took her breath away, all sleek and streamlined, its power barely in check. It was almost Halyan't'a in its functional elegance, a form designed as much for aesthetics as practicalities, so much so that it would look more at home in the sky than on the sea.

She couldn't help but be impressed and was rewarded for her distraction with a slap of water in the face as *Sundowner* fell off a point. By the time she looked up again, the cigarette was out of sight, already rounding the point and heading into the harbor proper.

Autumn dredging was in progress at the yacht club, forcing members to relocate either to other moorings scattered around the anchorage or to other harbors entirely. Through a friend of a friend, Nicole had secured a slip at the shorefront hotel next door. She started furling her sails at the mouth of the bay, while there was still light enough to see, and kept a weather eye on lines and tackle as the automatic mechanisms tucked main and jib away. If *Sundowner* herself was a classic design, the systems Alex had incorporated to enable one person to sail her safely were a masterpiece, and gave Nicole the sense that there was nothing she couldn't do with the boat, nowhere she couldn't go.

The cigarette was parked at the end of one floating dock, as formidable at rest as in motion, almost predatory in its aspects. Nicole nodded to herself as *Sundowner* loafed past at finding her initial impression confirmed; there were Hal elements incorporated in its design. That was more and more the case these days, as contacts between Earth and the Hal Federacy broadened and deepened.

Much of it due to her.

Her own slip was on the same dock as the cigarette, halfway between it and the shore, amid a thicket of like-sized craft. She made the pivot perfectly, mind and body operating in sync with her boat; a touch or two on reverse throttle slowed *Sundowner* enough to bring her to rest with hardly a bump on the bow fender.

The boat securely tied, its equipment properly stowed, she dropped into the cabin for her gear, found herself slump-sitting on the bunk, then flat on her back, unable to move as though held in place by the G-forces of a high-acceleration lift-off.

She closed her eyes, figuring to open them again with the sunrise, but Alex's heartbreaker features got in the way. He'd left the boat to her, as well as his membership in the yacht club, giving her the option, he said in his will (and she could see the devil's grin on his face as he typed that, deliberately planting the seed of temptation), of changing her mind. She'd thought more than once of abandoning the boat—she couldn't sell it, that was one of the codicils—but the simple fact was she loved *Sundowner*. And couldn't help respecting Alex for the love and care and work he'd put into it. She'd done much the same herself rebuilding her own beloved Beech Baron; it was part of the heritage she'd drawn from her family's home on Nantucket—you want something, go out and earn it.

She swung her legs to the deck, sat a moment in what was now full dark broken only by abstract pools of light from the dockyard lamps shining through the cabin's curtained ports. Then grabbed for her kitbag and headed out the door.

Even tired as she was, she covered the distance to shore in long rangy strides, moving with deceptively effortless grace, noting as she did that the courtyard nestled between the hotel's twin towers was unusually crowded. From the sounds—boisterous songs, occasional squeals of delight and mock alarm, the splash of someone taking a header into the pool—a right royal party was in progress.

"Target acquisition," someone called from the dockfront bar. Before she'd gone a couple of more steps she found her way blocked by a half-dozen young men, cut at first superficial glance as though from the same cookie-cutter mold. Similar height, similar build, mid-twenties, close-cropped hair, details smudged by a lack of direct light that reduced them to silhouettes; they wore cutting-edge BoyToy civvies with the slightly self-conscious air of someone more used to a uniform, but were also possessed of the ballsy self-confidence of those who acknowledged no peer but their own breed. "Tachyon Topguns," they called themselves, the best of the best, standard bearers of the High Frontier. Young astronauts assigned to the ever-growing fleet of starships streaking outward from the Sol System. Nicole knew the type; not so long ago—and yet in many ways better than a lifetime—she considered herself one of them.

"Pretty lady shouldn't go unescorted," cried a voice from the shadows at the back of the crowd, to accompanying grunts of agreement and encouragement. Though the night was young, they were enthusiastically plowed, their behavior charmingly playful. Most of the crowd were American and military, but over the past few years—and especially since First Contact with the Hal and the passage of President Charles Russell's One World Treaty—the pool of talent had expanded worldwide, as well as into the private sector.

"And gentlemen," Nicole responded easily, matching tone to mood, "should be courteous enough to let a lady pass."

She followed her words with some forward motion, sliding through the group with an ease that surprised them, and set off along the promenade towards the relative security of the Yacht Club gate. She didn't think there'd be trouble but perceptions often got skewed at shindigs like this, one person's harmless horseplay coming across as someone else's premeditated assault. And while she could handle both, she was too tired to try.

The lads didn't take the hint and they brought friends. Probably considered this "rising to a challenge." Fighter jock mentality in a world where dogfighting—in the classical air combat sense—had become virtually obsolete.

"Except," said one of them, a head shorter than she but broader in the shoulders, "when the lady hasn't a clue what she's missing."

Point taken, sort of. Nicole had never attended one of these grand and glorious blowouts, since—while she'd gone through the course—she'd never gotten a starship slot.

That realization, and a sudden flash of envy that came from her fatigue, prompted her to reply with more of an edge than the moment called for. Even as she spoke, she knew she'd pushed too hard but it was too late for the words to be recalled.

"Give it a rest, flyboys," she said, putting a faint but distinct emphasis on the "boys." "Go play with someone else, okay, I'm really not in the mood."

"Hey, Rocky," called another among the crowd, "front and center, guy, we got a live one for you."

Nicole rolled her eyes, taking a reflexive step backward towards the edge of the walk, clearing just enough distance between herself and the crowd to give her full freedom of movement. She didn't think about it, her body was responding to the situation of its own accord. Of course, these buttheads weren't paying the slightest attention to her as an actual person—she was simply the object of their mass desire—so they hadn't a clue as to what was happening, of how far and fast things would get out of hand if someone put a foot wrong. Nicole needed a way to defuse the confrontation, but nothing came to mind.

Then her head snapped left as she caught the tang of a familiar scent mixed among the cologne and beer, the unique fragrance of high-country cinnamon common to the Halyan't'a.

The pilots were ushering someone new to the front of the crowd and at first glance a body'd be excused for assuming it was just one more of the same. Just as looped, just as rowdy, just as fixated on having a good time. Until he stepped into the clear and revealed himself to be an Alien.

He was taller than most of those around him, able to look Nicole in the eye, but not as bulky—which was a deception, she knew, because Hal tended to have more muscle mass than humans of comparable size. His coloring was hard to tell in the garish yellow light of the stanchions that lined the promenade; the basic coat appeared to be grey, with a scattering of black dots, differing from the patterns of stripes that marked most of the Hal Nicole had seen. Two arms, two legs, arranged bilaterally on a central torso, with a head up-top. Disconcertingly like humanity. Mobile and expressive features— although his, potentially quite handsome by any standards, were somewhat coarsened by all he'd had to drink. Alcohol wasn't an inebriate to them, but they had a fatal weakness for colas. The mix of sugar and caffeine hit their system as hard as hundred-proof liquor, producing an almost amphetamine high—which was at least superficially good-natured—combined with a near-total loss of inhibitions.

In earlier days that discovery had led to some amusing, and embarrassing, moments. And ultimately, a tragic one, as some bright boys—out to determine a Hal's ultimate capacity for indulgence—pushed past the cheerful facade and tapped into the warrior beneath.

This one was close. The others should have known the signs, although it was more likely that everyone—including the Hal—figured they could handle whatever happened, no problem.

He wore slacks under a wraparound tunic that had mostly pulled loose from its belt, rucked as well off to one side to flash a goodly portion of his chest. He had a can of soda in one hand, beer in the other, which he proffered sloppily to her along with what was meant to be a smile.

"Go get her, Rocky, you flyin', flamin' Tomcat!" yelled a voice in an encouraging cheer that was applauded by the others. The Hal turned to them, arms going up in a triumphal pose.

Nicole's voice brought him back around to her so fast he twisted over his feet and nearly tumbled, a couple of pilots on either side grabbing for him reflexively as he started for the pavement. They hadn't heard her, they weren't meant to. The subvocalized rumble had been pitched for Hal ears alone, although Nicole knew the effort would leave her throat painfully sore for days.

He recovered nicely, almost pulling off the deception that his stumble had been intentional.

"What did you say to me?" he demanded, speaking English with a careful formality that was very much at odds with the moment.

"*Voulez-vous coucher*, l'il Fuzz-buddy," offered one of the others, provoking a round of cheers and comments that went totally ignored by the two principals.

Nicole answered with equal formality, but in Hal. She wanted to defuse the situation, not make it worse by shaming him.

"This is not appropriate behavior," she said, again pitching her voice into its lowest register. "Either for a professional officer or a guest on this world."

"Who are you to judge? Or tell me what to do?"

She turned her head ever so slightly, allowing the light to catch the crystal stud she wore in her right ear. Even though its colors were distorted by the glare of the sodium arc lamp, the *fireheart* was still lit from within by its own unique radiance.

The Hal's face went slack with astonishment. The *fireheart* was the rarest gem known to his People, and represented one of their highest honors. Precious few Hal wore them and only one human.

"Shea-Pilot? Who bears Shavrin's name?"

"Who shares her blood and hearth," Nicole replied, letting him know precisely where she stood in the family, which also meant just how much he was about to screw up.

The Hal took a step back, only in his case it was a simple retreat. His friends caught the change in mood—about as difficult as recognizing an instantaneous shift from midnight to midday—and that threw the entire crowd momentarily off-balance. Nicole immediately pushed her advantage.

She singled out someone in the front rank.

"You got some clout with this bunch," she said, moving on without giving him time to reply. "Doesn't matter, you'd better assume all you can, right now. Put him to bed." She caught a flash of resentment from the Hal—"Rocky," they'd called him—the beginnings of rebellion against her authority, and quelled it with a look.

Around Rocky, a few of the pilots began to sense what was happening, responding not merely to her physical presence but to the unmistakable tone of command in her voice. Hotel babes didn't talk like that—indeed, hardly any civilians, men or women—and the kind of people who did were those that junior officers desperately didn't want to cross.

"I really couldn't give much of a damn about the rest of you," she said, "but I won't have this Hal's life ruined because his supposed friends were too flaming stupid to know what happens when they get looped. Take him to his room and make sure he stays." The threat was implied but distinct: there'd be real trouble otherwise, all from her and far more than they could handle.

Now, at last, they took the hint, gathering Rocky into the heart of the group—with those on the periphery drifting off so that its numbers visibly shrank as Nicole watched—and moving back towards the pool area. Rocky was in stalking mode, back a trifle hunched, the movements of his powerful form no longer relaxed. He was upset, equal parts anger and shame.

A hand on her elbow made her jump, automatically twisting into a defensive punch that she only barely managed to abort.

"*Jesus!*" cried an older man in uniform, his own hands having snapped up in an equally reflexive parry. He was slower, though, and less practiced. They both knew she would have decked him.

" 'Jesus' yourself, Julio," she responded, a small shudder of residual startlement in her voice.

"I saw you in trouble, Cap'n," the security guard said, "thought you might need a backup."

"Appreciate it. How rowdy do these boys get?"

"Ain't just guys, c'mon, ma'am, give our sex a break. Some'a those flygals can put on a pretty rude display themselves."

"That we can," she conceded. It wasn't so much a man thing or a woman thing, but a pilot thing. An astronaut thing. And at the peak of the pyramid, a starship driver thing.

She couldn't help looking up, ignoring the Moon—where she still had quarters, her home when duty took her all the way up the gravity well—for the few stars visible through the background clutter glare of downtown San Diego.

"You okay, Cap'n?" Julio asked gently, bouncing her out of her reverie. "You were standing there awhile."

"Just thinking, Julio,"—*About what I've missed*, she finished to herself—"sorry."

They strolled along the promenade to the yacht club gate, open wide enough for people to pass single file, with Julio's partner blocking the way. Julio—senior man on the shift, with an easy authority that came from twenty years with the city PD—gave him a quick update, then took his partner's cellular phone for a call to the local precinct. Not exactly calling in the cavalry, not officially anyway; just a conversation between old friends and former colleagues, meant to prompt a cautionary visit to the hotel in hopes that would be enough to cool down the night's festivities.

Nicole waved farewell and made her way up the walk to the club. She wasn't properly dressed—faded baggies over a one-piece swimsuit, with a long-sleeved pullover against the evening waterfront chill and boating sneaks that had long ago seen their best days—but after a day on the ocean clothes were the least of her concerns. Shower first, she decided, perhaps a soak in the Club's pool, to restore her to a fit state to be seen in public.

When she came upstairs, a half hour later, she'd changed as completely as was possible for her, into a sleeveless cotton sundress that left her tanned arms bare but covered her legs to midcalf. The skirt was full and loose to allow her a full range of movement. She hated the current tighter-than-skin fashions that left nothing about the body to the imagination and hobbled a woman, forcing her to walk in mincing little steps. She had her pullover slung across her shoulders, sleeves tied across her front, and had switched her sneaks for sandals. Nothing much she could do for her hair, it was short enough to have a mind of its own, even under an onslaught of mousse and hairspray.

She was intent on the dining room for a bite—it was in the tub that she suddenly came to the belated realization that she was starving—when a burst of conversation drew her the other way, toward one of the smaller private rooms just off the lounge. Another thing she'd forgotten. Poker night.

She ordered a burger and a beer while a place was made for her at the table. There was a new face opposite, the man rising politely to shake her extended hand.

"Bill Hobby," he said.

"Nicole," her reply, and then, to the others, "Sorry I'm late. To be honest, I think I lost track of the day as well as the time."

"Not hard to do," noted Reg Wallinski—who liked to say he tolerated the never-ending aggravation of a six-figure law practice because it allowed him the freedom to maintain a top-class race boat—"with a charmer like yours, Nikki." She hated the nickname, which was why he used it, always the cutthroat when it came to finding and exploiting an edge.

"There's a pool, you know." Larry Rodriguez, as elegant in

appearance as Reg affected blue-collar, with manners to match. He was Navy, commanding officer of a nuclear cruiser that was part of one of the two carrier battle groups home-ported here. "As to when you'll sail out and never come back."

"That's a vote of confidence." This was from Hobby, who was watching her.

Nicole sipped her beer and gave back as good a look as she got. Hobby was her height—average for a man where she was tall for a woman—with a physique that bespoke an athletic life. Square, solid features, the kind of bone structure that appeared put together by a craftsman rather than an artist. Within the broad parameters of handsome but nothing special. Alex Cobri, he had been one of a kind, a designer original in every respect. His was the kind of face and figure women dream of—at least Nicole dreamed of, probably more often (even these days) than was good for her—whereas Hobby was the kind they married. A distinctly African cast to his face, his dark skin fairly weathered, with a thicket of lines around the eyes that reminded Nicole of the ones she saw reflected in her own mirror. Stock in trade, and the cost, of a life in the air. She also had a sense that he enjoyed to laugh. His hair was close-cropped, a carpet of tightly curled salt and pepper. Academy ring marked him as Navy, like Larry, who was picking up on what Hobby and Reg were saying.

"Not like that, Bill. This isn't about Nicole getting into trouble. Good as she is, the way that boat's rigged . . ."

"Gimme a break, Larry," she protested.

"We just figure the day'll come when she'll want to see what lies beyond the sunset."

"Sailing an avocation then," Hobby asked, "not your occupation?"

"Just a hobby." She smiled. "Is this a game, gentlemen, or what?"

She couldn't relax in her chair, and indeed didn't much try to. The confrontation out on the promenade was still very much a part of her; she'd been so blitzed by her day on the ocean she hadn't really been able to control her response. Her body had reacted of its own accord, following training that went back to her first flight on *Wanderer*—and the seemingly never-ending hours of practice duels with the spacecraft's Law Officer,

Federal Marshal Ben Ciari—and instincts she'd possessed her whole life. She'd sized up the situation and dealt with it, in a Zen state that made her totally one with the moment, her conscious self along for the ride.

Much the same was happening now. It was as though she were flying a combat patrol, events occurring with such speed and complexity that taking the time to actually *think* about them was sheer, simple suicide. All the work—processing of input, formulation of response—was taking place a couple of levels below full awareness, so that there was no discernible lag between conception and execution.

She'd been playing with everyone here—save Hobby, of course—for nearly as long as she'd been a member. Good times and bad, some games sport, others deadly serious, evenings when they drew cards like bandits and others when they seemed not to care how much they lost. All the moods she'd seen, she'd shared.

Tonight was different. To the casual observer, there was nothing out of the ordinary; Nicole herself felt so charged with energy she was surprised she wasn't crackling, her concentration focused to an unbearably keen edge. Something had cut loose within her out by the dock; she had the sensation that she was riding the back of a tiger, as wild an experience as she could ever hope for but also one that had to be endured to the very end. No bailing out along the way.

Each man she assessed in turn, knowing with that glance their state of mind, the level of interest they brought to the table, which were credible players and which were goofing. And when the cards came, she knew exactly what to do with them.

By the time the deck had made its first circuit around the table, she'd won a small hand, folded three, lost three—once after pushing the bets to the limit. Two of those she'd quit had been won by Hobby, the unknown quantity and, she was starting to suspect, the closest in skill to herself.

She excused herself to the ladies' room when Reg called a break, filled the sink with cold water and dunked her face. No shakes when she lifted back up to reach for a towel. Scary how calm she was. More so perhaps because of the raw intensity of her anger. She was eager for what was to come, part of her regretting that none of the crowd on the promenade had struck the spark that would have ignited a fight. She was as good a pilot as they, with kudos in her personnel jacket they couldn't hope to match. Hell, the fact that the Halyan't'a had made it to Earth at all—much less that the First Contact had gone successfully—was due in large measure to her. Yet they all had starship berths, and she was still stuck on the ground.

Someone was going to bleed for that.

Second round, three wins, four folds—twice before they'd gotten anywhere near serious bets.

"You active service, Bill?" she asked Hobby as he dealt a six of clubs to complement the pair of sixes she had hidden. Starting off with three of a kind, not bad.

"Not so's you'd notice," Larry answered with a laugh, "not the last couple of months."

"It's my design, for Heaven's sake," Hobby protested, in the same good humor, "of course, I'm going to have a hand in the sea trials."

Seven of clubs, she raised once, then asked, "You don't mean that magnificent piece of work parked next door, do you?"

"One and the same," Larry said proudly, raising her right back on the basis of a royal pair he had showing. She knew he was bluffing, but all she did was match him.

"I nearly fell over when I saw it on radar."

"She can do better," Hobby said. "This close inshore, I decided to hold her back."

"How's her stability in the open ocean, in any kind of serious sea? Any problems with the propulsion system?"

"Better by far than you'd think to look at her. The Hal aren't much for open-water cruising . . ."

That isn't the half of it, Nicole thought, *they don't sail at all.*

And Nicole had a sudden flash of memory that put her atop the Memorial Mount on s'N'dare, the Hal homeworld, overlooking *T'nquail*, the Great Western Ocean. Her eyes were open but what she saw before her wasn't the poker table; instead, a vast expanse of shoreline stretched away to the north, under a sky accented in warmer hues than Earth's comfortably familiar blue. Sweeter air, as thick with salt as what she'd smell from the porch of her parents' Nantucket home. In the near distance, disturbingly close to shore, where pale shallows abruptly gave way to the darker cobalt that signified deep water, a huge, streamlined shape broached the surface, body arcing almost completely into view—like a Terrestrial orca or a dolphin—before disappearing without a splash. Behind the body trailed a network of great tentacles and when they struck, the water exploded into froth as though struck by an artillery shell. A lot of teeth in that head, Nicole remembered, and an appetite to match, a combination the Hal had long ago learned to respect. Top of the food chain, as dominant a predator in its own environment as the Hal were on land.

Nicole wondered how much of her own world's history would have had to be rewritten if only the great cetaceans had been as aggressively territorial.

". . . but the principles they've evolved of aerodynamic design," Hobby continued, as Nicole's awareness returned belatedly to what he was saying, and to the game, "can be applied just as effectively to naval architecture. Basically, it's doing the same with a boat that NASA's been doing up at Edwards with that advanced shuttle project. Taking the best of both worlds and trying for a whole greater than the sum of the parts."

True enough, as Nicole knew better than most since she'd been Project Manager on the shuttle virtually from its inception.

Eight of diamonds, busting her potential flush but still building a straight. She bet as though that was what she had, figuring Reg held two pair and Larry was aiming for a flush of his own. Hobby was the unknown quantity, with nothing coherent showing among his face cards, yet the mix gave him a considerable potential depending on what was hidden.

Two folds came this round, as the betting turned a trifle rich for some of the others present. Her last up card was a nine, four to a straight. A dangerous moment. If she didn't fill out the straight, she still had trip sixes, three of a kind. Enough to beat Reg, if all he had was two pair, which she was certain was the case even though he was betting as if he held a full house. The faintest of tightness about the lips, the way he held his hands close to his cards, gave him away; barring a miracle, what he had was as good as he was going to get. Larry, however, had his flush and wasn't about to be chased by anybody's bluff. Hobby was pure ice, as cold as he was unfathomable.

Over the past few hours, Nicole had been gathering a sense of the man, gotten to know the way he thought. Just as he had been doing with her. The trick was, who had come up with the more accurate assessment and who could put it to best use?

Reg had the dominant cards showing, so he led off the bets. By checking. Hobby checked as well, leaving Larry the honor of the first bet. Nicole hadn't looked at her card yet, she kept her eyes on Hobby—the others, as far as she was concerned, were irrelevant—and moved some chips to the center of the table. Reg shook his head disgustedly and threw down his cards, finally bowing to the inevitable. Larry's features tensed ever so slightly as Hobby saw Nicole's bet and raised it; he merely saw the bet. Nicole took a cursory glance at her final card and raised Hobby right back, to the limit. Now, the man grinned as his friend breathed a stunned and painful "Jesus!"

And matched her bet. Larry did the same. She was called.

She flipped over the last card, a six. And then her hidden pair of sixes, dealt at the start of the game. With the six already showing, she had four of a kind.

"*Jesus!*" Larry said again, more audibly now with feeling to match.

"Very good," Hobby conceded ruefully as she pulled the pile of chips towards her.

"I have my moments," she said, matching his predatory smile with one of her own, while thinking, *And the best, chum, is yet to come.*

By the time the cards came around to her for a deal, the table was down to herself, Hobby, Larry, and Reg, and everyone sensed this would be the last hand. There were no gifts for her in the deal this time, just an abstract scattering of cards that had potential. The others were deferring to her, keying their own play off hers. She obliged by pushing much the way she had earlier when building the straight, creating the deliberate impression that she had far more than met the eye. And because the last few times she'd followed that pattern, such had been precisely the case, the others quickly became seriously gun-shy. Larry was the first to go, when Hobby drew the third card to a flush, and Reg a card later, when Hobby got the fourth. It was essentially the reverse of the other game. Hobby with a strong hand showing, Nicole with seemingly nothing. He thought, long and hard, before he bet; she responded without a moment's hesitation. The contrast couldn't have been more striking. A crowd had gathered but Nicole ignored both the people and the commentary swirling about her, focused entirely on the man opposite. It had been a long time since she'd felt so relaxed, so totally one with the moment. She had no doubts, because she knew she was going to win.

Hobby sensed that confidence and it sparked in him a tiny smidgen of doubt. He looked at the cards, looked at the pot, looked at the pile of chips remaining in front of Nicole and finally at his own. At best, this game would hurt; at worst, it could get bloody. And he couldn't help the question, was it worth the effort?

Nicole sensed that inner exchange and permitted herself the tiniest of smiles, barely a quirk at the corner of her mouth. Whatever happened with the cards, in the way that mattered she had already won the game.

Hobby caught the smile, and when he stepped back inside himself and looked over the last minute or so, he also realized what had just happened.

He flipped his cards. She'd won.

"That was a bluff, wasn't it?" Reg demanded incredulously. "You didn't have shit."

But she'd already mixed her cards in with the whole of the deck; the winner didn't have to show her hand if the opposition folded. Better by far to leave everyone guessing. Give her an edge next time.

"I told you she was a cutthroat," Larry said with a laugh, clapping Hobby on the shoulder.

"To see is to believe, *compadre*. Nicole"—he held a hand across the table—"that was most impressive. I can't remember when I've had as enjoyable—albeit expensive—an evening."

She took his hand with a gracious nod of the head, then called out to the club steward who'd been looking after them all evening.

"Put all the damage on my account, Luis, okay?" She meant the evening's expenses of food and drink. In the same gesture, she indicated the chips she'd won. "And would you make sure these get credited?"

"With pleasure, Ms. Shea."

"Don't be ridiculous," Hobby protested. "I thought this was dutch."

"Most nights, it is," she conceded, "but big winners always pick up the tab. This is a friendly game, we're not out for blood."

She pushed up to her feet, surprised at the effort it took. Her body felt cast from soft lead, incredibly heavy and able to move only with tremendous difficulty.

"May I walk you home?" Hobby asked.

Nicole shook her head, "I'm fine, just tired."

"Exhausted is more like it."

"I don't have far to go, and I know the way. But thanks for the offer. Perhaps some other time."

"I look forward to it.

She said her "good nights" and made her way along the foyer, face twisting in dismay as she blearily focused on her watch and discovered how late it was. *Another round or two*, she thought, *we could have had breakfast.*

There was an unseasonable chill to the air, enhanced by a breeze blowing off the water. It took a bit of a struggle but she managed to pull on her sweater, the thick-weaved cotton falling bulkily to her hips. From the lack of activity around the hotel pool as she walked along the promenade, it sounded like all but the most lovelorn rocket jocks were back in the barn.

At the entrance to the dock, she paused a moment to clear her head. The prefab, modular jetties were normally safe as could be, and as well lit as the shore. But they still floated on the water and there were always plenty of opportunities to put a foot wrong.

She was almost to *Sundowner* when she sensed another presence close by, in a flash of prescience disturbingly similar to the one that had alerted her to Hobby's boat. Under other circumstances that inner warning might have been enough to save her. But Hobby had been right, she *was* exhausted; her reaction came with the speed of cold molasses, and she was only partway through her turn before she was blindsided. The impact spun her completely around, the smooth leather soles of her sandals finding no decent purchase on the dock; one foot went over the edge and the rest of her followed.

The water shocked her awake, but that wasn't much help. Her sweater dragged her down as effectively as diver's weights—she couldn't seem to muster the coordination necessary to wriggle out of it—and her skirt kept tangling up her legs, so she had to work twice as hard to keep afloat. She tried to call for help, got a mouthful of oil-tainted salt water for her trouble that triggered a bout of choked coughing. No sign of whoever had bodychecked her; somehow, she doubted he'd run for help.

There was no grace to her as she floundered towards her boat, just a steely determination that she was damned if she'd drown in her own berth. She lunged for the toe rail, couldn't find a handhold, fell back with force enough to dunk her head under. She had no chance to grab a breath of air and for the few interminable seconds it took her to break the surface she danced along the edge of panic. There was no strength left in arms or legs, and she was rapidly losing what little mental focus remained.

Rage made her try again, and this time she caught a cleat. She hung there a long moment by both hands, gathering her strength, trying to do the same with her wits. She had no idea where on the boat she was. From the stretch, more likely forward than aft. She tried to picture in her mind the location of the cleats, came up empty. The logical move would be to make her way along the hull and pull herself aboard by the cockpit, where the deck was closest to the waterline. But logical wasn't always smart. She had a suspicion this was her only shot and that one more immersion might prove her last.

She cursed herself for not accepting Hobby's offer of an escort, but she was far more angry at how completely she'd been taken by surprise. That was grounder carelessness; astronauts were supposed to know better.

Gritted her teeth, wasted a breath—from lungs already burning hot with strain—for another call for help. She wasn't surprised when it wasn't answered; it hadn't sounded terribly loud even to her own ears.

Pulled. Nothing happened. Tried to swing an ankle over the toe rail, couldn't even lift her leg all the way into the air. Damn skirt. And she couldn't risk letting a hand go to pop the waistband buttons and try to get rid of it; hard enough for two hands to keep a grip, she had no faith in one alone, even for a minute.

Kicked up once more, cried out as she barked her ankle, ignored the pain because she'd managed to catch hold. Now all that remained was to drag the rest of her onto the deck.

She lunged for a stanchion, but her fingers slipped off the smooth metal, and she had to scramble to keep from losing her purchase. Even so, in the momentary confusion, her leg slipped, and she found herself back almost where she started, hanging from the lowest lifeline, the plastic-wrapped wire cutting into her fingers.

Suddenly a hand closed over one wrist, then the other. A strength that put hers to shame hauled her waist-high into the air, while a familiar voice called on her to make one last effort.

"Damn it, Nicole," a woman, in a tone used to instant and pretty much unquestioning obedience, as she pitched herself backward, angling Nicole's torso over the deck, "I can't do this by myself, you're too bloody heavy!"

"Not my fault," Nicole mumbled, managing to catch a foot on the toe rail and heave herself finally aboard.

She lay sprawled facedown on the weatherworn teak, thinking absurdly that *Sundowner* was about due for a refit. Her impromptu swim had been one adrenaline rush too many, with a crash to match. Simple thoughts were all she could manage, actual movement was utterly out of the question. No matter. It was a nice night, she'd stay where she was and let the sunrise wake her. She'd feel awful but that beat the alternative.

Her rescuer, however, had no patience with such intentions.

Hands hooked under her arms, rolled her over on her back, then lifted her to her feet.

She didn't want to see the face of the woman who held her, but the slip lights didn't allow much choice.

Judith Canfield shook her head, expression speaking more eloquently than any words, then ducked slightly to tumble Nicole over her shoulder in a fireman's carry. That was when Nicole decided enough was enough, the hell with fighting the inevitable.

By the time Canfield straightened to her full height and turned towards the cockpit—and the companionway down to *Sundowner*'s main cabin—Nicole was blissfully and completely unconscious.

CHAPTER TWO

*She's young, barely more than a kit, with a young-
ling's invulnerability born of arrogance, striking her
own trail off from the family, ignoring bared fangs
and open claws at this open defiance of law and
custom as she follows the sun westward to the
edge of the world. She hadn't believed such a wonder existed, this Great Water that beggars experience and imagination both, stretching up and down
the coast and off into the distance as far as she
can see.*

The first time she opened her eyes, the world was doing a
passable imitation of a runaway carousel. She knew her boat
couldn't spin so fast, if at all, but that was what it looked like
so she went back to sleep in hopes things would improve later
on.

Smell woke her next, tea steaming hot and close at hand. Her
vision was smudged like a windshield smeared with oil and
rubbing the heel of a palm across her eyes made only a
marginal improvement.

She thought of sitting up, tabled the notion almost immediately. No will, less energy, and a conviction that her present
horizontal state was the safest for her.

She heard someone bustling behind her in the galley,
managed a cough to let her know she was awake.

Canfield came into view, mug of coffee in one hand,
half-eaten bagel in the other.

"You've seen better days," she said.

"Kind of you to notice," Nicole grumbled in reply, adding an automatic "ma'am," because even though Canfield was dressed casually in slacks and a polo shirt, she was still a full General and Nicole's boss.

"Here," Canfield said, laying down her own mug to indicate the one she'd set by Nicole's side. "Herbal tea," she explained, "the taste isn't half-bad and it shouldn't put too much strain on your stomach. Can you sit up?"

"Give it a shot."

She winced as she wriggled her elbows underneath herself and used them as a lever. The pain in her chest was something fierce, so intense it left her short of breath. Canfield had to help her the rest of the way.

"Where does it hurt?"

"Where doesn't it?" was Nicole's rhetorical whine in reply. "Lungs mostly. My mouth tastes like a refinery."

"Not the cleanest water I've ever seen, I'll grant you that."

"About par for an anchorage, actually." Her words were broken by a bout of coughing, followed by a longer pause as she took some tentative swallows of the tea. "I just wish I hadn't tried to swallow so much of it."

"No major bumps or bruises that I could find. I have a car, though; I'll be happy to run you over to the hospital."

Nicole bent her left leg at the knee, bringing her foot as close as she could, using eyes and fingers to probe her sore heel. Found a patch of gauze taped professionally in place.

"Scraped skin mostly," Canfield told her, "but you'd drawn blood so I thought it best to wrap the wound."

"Thank you," Nicole said.

"I'm glad I was here."

"Makes two of us."

"I didn't see whoever dropped you."

Collage of shape and scent, bouncing helter-skelter out of memory, so intense a barrage of images that it made Nicole dizzy. Across the cabin, Canfield turned sharply as Nicole subvocalized a growl, the fingers of her visible hand flexing as though to extend a set of claws. It was the smallest of gestures, a reaction so quick and reflexive it could easily have gone unnoticed. Only it wasn't, by either of them.

"Probably for the best," Nicole said, and let her body slump partway down the headboard, as disturbed by her reaction as by the attack itself. And as unsure how to respond to both.

She heard the sudden sound of feet on the dock outside, three or four people, nervous—from the way they kept shifting their weight, unable to stay still.

"Ahoy, *Sundowner*," called a young woman with a pronounced Scots accent.

"She's asleep, Jen," a man's voice said, looking for any excuse to slip away, "leave her lie, we'll come back later." Nicole couldn't make out the details of the woman's reply, only that it was clear she wasn't about to give him the chance.

"I'll talk to them," said Canfield, but Nicole waved her to a seat, grateful for the interruption.

"My boat, General. My life."

Admirable sentiments, put immediately to the test as Nicole swung her legs over the edge of the bunk. This wasn't a hangover—she hadn't drunk more than a beer all evening, which in a way was part of the problem—but the residual effects of her day on the water. Behind her eyeballs, where no one but she could see, Nicole made a rueful face and shook her head. Totally sun-fried. She'd let herself become dangerously dehydrated.

She had all the sensations of a fever without actually running one. A headache right up across her forebrain, stapled in place with baby railroad spikes, plus the feeling that some parts of her body were held together with barbed wire—while others had been flooded with helium. Her skin felt flushed, almost glowing, and her stomach rumbled demands for food while the very thought of eating made her nauseous.

No two ways about it, she was a mess. If she had half a brain, she'd take Canfield up on her invitation. Of course, if she'd had half a brain when it really mattered, she wouldn't be in this state to begin with.

And she felt she had something to prove.

Somehow, after getting her below last night, Canfield had managed to strip Nicole of what she'd been wearing and get a T-shirt onto her. Nicole gave it a cursory tug as she fumbled up the companionway steps, hoping to achieve a modicum of decency.

Another glorious day; midmorning, she decided, from the sun's position overhead. For those first moments though, after she emerged, she was blind with the glare; the railroad spikes inside her skull, oh-so-exquisitely sharp, immediately doubled in number and size. But they didn't kill her, so she merely waited for all the various elements to sort themselves out. Which they did, in surprisingly short order.

Arrayed on the dock was a quartet of rocket jocks, three men and a woman, part of the crowd of baby astronauts that had commandeered the hotel. None of the faces looked familiar but Nicole assumed they'd been part of the crowd she'd encountered. The men looked appropriately shamefaced. From the way they'd arranged themselves, Nicole knew immediately they were here because of Jenny and they really didn't like it.

She said nothing. Just stood and watched and wished for the mug of tea Canfield had made her. As if the General had read her mind, a hand popped up beside her, holding out the mug. Nicole took it, indulged in a solid swallow, gazing disdainfully at the four below.

"Nicole Shea?" the woman hazarded at last.

She took another swallow, thankful that her insides were behaving themselves, and answered with a cursory nod, refusing to cut the delegation the slightest slack.

"I'm Jenny Coy, Flight Leftenant Coy, a blue suit like yourself," the woman went on in the face of Nicole's determinedly minimalist response, while Nicole tried to reconcile Jenny's Asian features with a strong Highland Scots accent. The Lieutenant gave the man next to her a pointed, prompting glare, and Nicole amended her initial assessment; Jenny was far beyond annoyed, she was actually angry.

"About last night . . ." Jenny prompted.

"We were out of line," the man finished, and Nicole suddenly realized they had no idea what had happened on the dock, they were talking about the earlier encounter on the promenade. "If we'd known . . ."

"Who I was," she finished. "That's the difference? Otherwise, what? I'm a piece of meat?"

"It wasn't like that."

"Fine," she said. *Bullshit*, she thought.

She made a dismissive gesture with her free hand, no longer interested in prolonging the conversation.

"You've made your apology. I accept. Have a nice day." And she started to turn away.

"You got a hell of an attitude, lady," snapped one of the others, bridling at her acid demeanor. "Especially for a sublight driver."

"Damn it, Axel," Jenny cried with a slap to his bicep. Not a playful blow, either, for all that she was shorter and slighter than the men. "Will you put a lock on your damn mouth!"

"Back off yourself, Jen. If she's so hot, how come she spends most of her life on the ground? No offense, ma'am," said to Nicole in calculated insult.

"In case you hadn't noticed," Nicole said quietly, "this is a private dock." Her own blatant subtext, *get the hell off my porch.*

They got the message—Jenny Coy was furious and not bothering to hide it, this hadn't gone at all the way she'd planned—but before they could act on it, Nicole sensed a presence behind her. Shock stamped the astronauts' faces and Jenny snapped an altogether unnecessary, "Atten-*shun!*"

"Captain Shea may be willing to overlook last night's . . . activities, gentlemen," Canfield said, stepping around Nicole and all the way into view, "I am not feeling quite so charitable. Especially since someone blindsided her into the anchorage here not long afterward, nearly drowning her."

Nicole spared the quartet a look. They knew who was responsible, as did she. And possibly, she suspected, Canfield in the bargain. But none of them were about to offer a confirmation. Nicole wondered where Rocky was, and if the Hal was aware of what his friends were doing on his behalf.

"We didn't know," one said.

"Things last night," this from Jenny, "they sort of got a little out of hand."

"A somewhat misplaced use of understatement, Lieutenant," said Canfield, without mercy. "Try some of this kind of behavior out along the Frontier, you could very easily find yourself breathing vacuum."

"No real harm was done, General." Another of the men, not comprehending that safety lay in silence.

"Consider that, Lieutenant, your great good fortune. As Captain Shea said, this is a private facility. I'm sure you can all occupy yourselves to better purpose elsewhere."

There was an awkward moment, where the realization that

they'd been summarily dismissed vied with their pride's need to make a graceful exit. Nicole's eyes met Jenny's, and she hoped the younger woman understood this wasn't the way Nicole had planned things, either. The guys were already on their way, and with a small gesture of apology, Jenny turned to follow.

"That wasn't necessary," Nicole said to Canfield.

"From your perspective, no," Canfield conceded. "From mine, absolutely." A gently pointed reminder that their relationship, however close and even heartfelt, was not between equals.

"No offense, General," Nicole asked as she dropped past the General into the cabin to refill her mug, "but why are you here? I mean, I'm grateful for the timing . . ." She let her voice trail off.

"Variation on a theme. Since Mohammed was unable to come up to the mountain . . ."

"Very considerate. But all you had to do was ask. There's nothing in the test program at Edwards that can't absorb a few days absence on my part." Subtext thought, *How the hell else did you think I could manage this?* Meaning the boat. "And truth to tell I would have welcomed the flight time beyond low Earth orbit."

"This had the virtue of being less . . . official. I wasn't planning a royal summons, Nicole, I just wanted to see you."

Nicole looked up from the nav station, where she'd just tapped in a request for the local weather. "Well," she said, "this is too spectacular a morning to waste; d'you feel up to a taste of open-water sailing?"

"Are you able to handle it?"

Nicole grinned, her first genuinely cheery expression since she'd surfaced. "After yesterday's overindulgence, you mean?"

She rummaged in a locker, came up with a pair of battered baseball caps emblazoned with the boat's name, tossed one to Canfield.

"Only one way to find out."

As Nicole motored over to the harbor market to top off the fuel tank and grab provisions for the day, she asked Canfield—belatedly, a reminder to herself that she wasn't yet firing on all cylinders—if the jaunt was safe.

"For my bionics, you mean?" was the reply. Before Nicole had been born, Judith Canfield was one of NASA's premier astronauts, part of the first cadre to fly the Baumier/Cobri starships. As signal a group in their own way as the original seven Mercury pilots had been a generation earlier, when the farthest anyone had thought to travel was the Moon.

Towards the turn of the century, with the Soviet space program collapsing along with the Union itself, and its American counterpart floundering in search of a true mission, a French-Canadian physicist named Jean-Claude Baumier wrote himself a chapter in the history books with the discovery of a means to push matter beyond the speed of light. An expatriate Soviet rocketry engineer, Emmanuel Cobri, was the only one to see the potential inherent in Baumier's theories—which most of the establishment scientific community had debunked as being one step removed from science fiction—and the two men, working like galley slaves, took the equations and translated them into schematics for a functional, practical stardrive.

Somewhere—and there were rumors galore about that, mostly centered around the Odessa Mafia—they found sufficient funding to bankroll a prototype and sufficient clout to persuade NASA to test it out of the atmosphere. One spectacular success spawned another until the moment at last came for a manned flight. By all accounts, the raw suspense—as much for those aboard the vehicle as those left behind waiting for its reports—was akin to what had been felt by those watching Chuck Yeager's legendary flight aboard the Bell X-1, during his attempt to break the sound barrier. Only that had been a flight of mere minutes; this turned into one of days.

Once the *Challenger*—named in tribute to the lost shuttle—returned, events tumbled one after the other like a line of falling dominoes. Humanity literally exploded out into the cosmos, with the pent-up energy of a race who'd begun to believe there were no more frontiers to conquer. Plans, long dormant, for bases on the Moon and the outer planets were hurriedly pulled from archival data bases and brought into being. The Patriot space station became obsolete within a couple of years of its launching as demand grew for a far larger and more extensive facility. And after Sutherland in near-Earth space came Hightower, the first L-5 colony.

Meanwhile, the first generation of Cobri starships was blazing trails outbound from the Sol System. Canfield hadn't been part of the initial *Challenger* flight, but she'd been the one to chart Faraway, the first habitable planet discovered outside our own. Then, disaster. A shuttle crash that left her a multiple amputee, so badly maimed that any semblance of a normal life was considered out of the question, much less the continuation of her career as an astronaut. But there'd been advances in the fields of bionic prosthetics to rival those of spaceflight, and she was fitted with artificial limbs that matched perfectly what she'd lost. With the aid of Nicole's father—who pled her case all the way to the Supreme Court—Canfield won reinstatement to the astronaut corps. All that, before Nicole had been born.

"They're sealed systems," Canfield said, gazing down at the sleek legs stretched out before her. She'd cheated a bit when they were made, designing herself an extra couple of inches of height, as well as sleek, muscular curves. "Proof against water, fresh or salt. There's swimming on the Moon, Nicole, it's excellent cardiovascular exercise."

Nicole knew that, she'd simply forgotten.

She took *Sundowner* down the harbor first, a ways below Coronado Bridge, before reversing her course and making for the open sea. She wanted to work the kinks out of her own body and see how she and the boat and Canfield all handled themselves under sail. The General's ignorance was near total, but she only had to be told what to do once.

The sun was already fierce, the occasional marshmallow dots of cumulus providing only brief and scattered protection as the wind pushed them merrily along. Nicole handed out sun block and smeared lotion liberally on her bare skin.

"That tan safe?" Canfield asked as she did the same. Even with the block, Nicole had spent enough time in the open to turn her skin a moderate bronze. It made for a striking complement to her jade eyes and dark russet hair—although the sun had bleached that color more red than black.

"I'm screened every quarter, as well as a Class-A medical each year. So far, no cataracts, no cancer."

"You can't be too careful."

"I know."

"Do you?"

"I'm human, General."

"Is that an excuse?"

"I don't see the need for one. Merely an explanation. What happened yesterday was an aberration." Although, even as Nicole said that, a small voice deep inside her thoughts wondered, *Was it?* "I want to fly," and both women knew she meant far more than simply in the atmosphere or local space. "I'll do whatever's necessary to fulfill that. Even wait," she finished pointedly.

"You're a valuable asset, Nicole—you find that amusing?" Canfield asked, responding to Nicole's derisive snort.

"Sorry. Couldn't help myself."

"You haven't answered the question."

"I suppose that depends on the relative perceptions of value. Yours and mine are different."

"You've been spending a lot of time on this boat."

"My own time, ma'am. On no occasion have my duties or responsibilities suffered." Nicole's back was up and she didn't bother hiding it.

"Agreed. Your evaluations have been first-rate."

"Then what's the problem?" Nicole demanded, both of them very much aware of how insubordinate she sounded.

"I could ask you the same," was the counter, in the same conversational tone Canfield had used from the start, refusing to rise to Nicole's provocation.

For a time, there was silence between them as Nicole headed away from land until the shore was a low smudge on the horizon. In the middle distance, even farther out, they saw a plume of spray, then another, marking the presence of a pair of humpback whales broaching the surface for a breath. Nicole altered course to run parallel to them, and keep her distance.

"They're beautiful creatures," Canfield said, standing by the mast, shading her eyes with a hand for a better look.

"And territorial, especially when they're traveling as a family. Spook 'em, we could get ourselves bumped, and worse."

"That happens, every so often, doesn't it? Sailboats being sunk by whales."

"It's the ocean, General. Everything happens here."

"Profound."

"Want a drink?" Nicole offered.

"Beer, please."

Nicole thought a moment about taking one for herself, then settled on a bottle of water spiked with lemon.

"I'm very impressed with your work on the new shuttle design," Canfield said, joining Nicole in the cockpit.

"It's a team effort, General."

"Don't sell yourself short. The project wouldn't have gone as smoothly and quickly without you."

"Thanks."

"That was a compliment, Nicole, not an insult."

"And it's appreciated."

"But it's not enough."

"No," Nicole said flatly. "It isn't. Not anymore. It's been five years since I won back my wings, and I'm still stuck on the high desert. Some of those wannabe hotshots back at the hotel had barely started at the Academy back then; they've got starslots, why don't I?"

"I don't recall seeing any guarantees on the oath you swore."

"That's not what I mean."

"We don't always get what we want."

"I've done everything asked of me, General, and more. I've earned my shot."

"It's your great good fortune—as well as your curse—to possess unique qualifications."

"Give me a break! I'm not the only blue suit who speaks Hal. Hell, I *taught* most of 'em!"

"Precisely. *You* taught—us how to deal with them and them how to deal with us. Gallivanting about the galaxy may be more personally satisfying, Nicole, but I submit it is also of infinitely lesser value, to your service, to your *world*."

"Is that it, then? I mean, is this what I have to look forward to? At least when I was grounded, General, I didn't have the option of flying. Now, I have the skills, the training, the ratings—I could step on board a starship tomorrow, into damn near any position—but I'm not allowed to go."

"Are you asking me to change that?"

"Is that what it takes? Hell, I'll even beg."

"We're awfully far out," Canfield said, looking aft towards the horizon. There was no sign of land, the shore hidden behind

coastal haze, plus some smog that had strayed south from the
Los Angeles basin.

"Yeah."

"What?"

"Hmnh?" Nicole asked, confused by the General's suddenly
sharp question.

"Something in your tone."

"Nothing. I was woolgathering."

"I don't believe that any more than you do, Nicole."

"Watch your head," Nicole told her as she pulled on the
tiller, "I'm coming about."

There was a momentary loss of headway as *Sundowner*'s
bow broached through the oncoming swell, and then the big
main boom swung across the boat with a crash and clatter. In
those same moments, Nicole switched sides herself, monitoring
the automatic winches as they reoriented the jib; she did the
fine adjustments manually—pulling on one line, easing a
couple of others—refining the trim of the sails just as she
would the control surfaces of any aeroplane.

"To be honest," she said, plucking a water bottle from its
holder and taking some hefty swallows, very much aware—as
was Canfield, she knew—that she was stalling, "I'm not
altogether sure. Just a feeling—some feelings—I've been
having lately. To use one of the twins' equestrian metaphors, I
am chafing at the bit. I'm angry, I'm frustrated, I'm scared; I
feel boxed and I don't know why."

"For a long time," said Canfield, "it looked like the closest
Alan Shepard would get to true space was his fifteen-minute
suborbital aboard *Freedom 7.* And until *Apollo-Soyuz,* Deke
Slayton didn't even have *that* much. How d'you think they felt?
Not to mention all those third and fourth generation sky-pilots
whose chance for a ride crashed and burned with the original
Challenger. Think of it, they'd all but resigned themselves to a
space program that was in permanent retrenchment. Returning
to the Moon was becoming a pipe dream, much less anything
more ambitious. Then, along came Baumier and Cobri. And the
stars were at last well and truly our destination. Only they were
a shade too old, just that fateful little bit beyond the performance curve.

"Me, folks like me, we were in the right place at the right

moment in history. But we were always aware of those who got left behind. Thing is, now I'm one of 'em.

"I stay and watch youngsters like you blaze trails across the galaxy, when all I really want is to be flying along by your side."

Nicole took a long breath, let it out in a huff, painfully aware of how childish she sounded.

"I know it's unprofessional, feeling sorry for myself," she said.

"You're not alone. As you said, we're only human. We all have missed opportunities and regrets."

"You and my dad?" The words were out of Nicole's mouth before she could stop herself, yet while part of her was aghast at her temerity, another was cheering herself on—*Way to go, woman, it's about bloody time.*

"What has Conal said?" Canfield asked, taking the question totally in stride.

"I'm asking you, Judith," Nicole said, deliberately using Canfield's first name to put them on an equal footing. Canfield's initial response was a sharp, assessing look—almost hawklike in its intensity—capped by a shallow nod, accepting Nicole's terms.

"He saw me through a fair chunk of my therapy, physical and emotional. Two years of court battles. Hard under those circumstances *not* to form any emotional attachment. Probably impossible. Was it love? I like to think so. We were lovers. And grew from that into best friends."

"But when it was all over . . . ?"

"I wasn't fighting for a principle, Nicole, although that was what my victory established. I wanted my slot back, same as you did five years ago. I wasn't about to give that up, for anyone or anything. And Con couldn't follow me up to the Frontier."

"Arrythmia. He can't even fly suborbitals because of ascent/descent G-forces."

"One of life's ironies. Medical technology rebuilt me better than before, but it couldn't do a thing for him."

"I don't think he would've gone anyway," Nicole said. "He loves all this too much." And she waved an arm wide to encompass the sea and sky about them.

"Did it hurt, Nicole, walking away from him? More than anything, and that includes being maimed. Do I regret my decision?" Canfield shook her head. "Not for a moment."

"So you won't begrudge me the same ambition. And determination."

"Are you satisfied with the performance of the *Swiftstar*?" Canfield asked after another small silence.

"Access the program files, they'll tell you everything."

"I have."

Nicole let her active concentration slip for a few moments, confident in her boat and body's ability to handle themselves on automatic, imagining herself on the flight deck of the sleek, wedge-shaped spaceplane.

"Atmospheric tests were all we'd hoped for and more," she said at last. "The prototype handles like a dream, with so few glitches we're starting to get a tad nervous."

"You don't trust perfection?"

"More like, don't believe in it. We're waiting for Murphy's Law to kick in. It's sort of a perverse inverse-square relationship—the better that beast behaves, the bigger the backlash when it comes. And perhaps less prepared the flight crew'll be to cope. We're a superstitious lot, test pilots."

"And in low Earth orbit?"

"On profile, the whole way down the line. But there's only so much you can simulate; eventually, you have to try her for real, that's the acid test."

"That's next, correct?"

"Yes, ma'am. A standard mission, launching from a platform in high orbit, making an unassisted approach to a landing stage here on Earth, then a lift-off and return to origin. All inertial systems, no refueling."

"You sound confident."

"I know the beast, she'll do fine."

"You're flying left seat?"

"Unless somebody tells me different."

"There's a lot riding on the *Swiftstar*. The one absolutely critical inhibiting factor in our—and by that I mean us and the Hal together—exploitation of known space is our ability to transit from vacuum to atmosphere and back again. Not simply exploratory landers but heavy-duty cargo lifters. Standard STS shuttles require a whole launch complex to get off the ground, and suborbital ScramJets don't have the full range of capabilities we need. *Swiftstar* has."

"You'll get the best we're capable of, ma'am," Nicole said, about spacecraft and crew both, "that's all I can guarantee."

"From you, Nicole, I've never expected less."

For all the good that's done me, Nicole couldn't help thinking sourly, and wondered how much of the thought showed on her face. The General's eyes narrowed, lips thinning, as though she wasn't happy with what she saw. *Well, screw that,* Nicole thought, *and with all due respect, General, screw you! I am what I am, and a lot of that's what you made me; you don't like it, that's your problem.*

"You're still living with the Hal at Edwards, yes?" Canfield asked out of nowhere, and Nicole wondered why, because she had to know the answer.

"Pretty much."

"How's Kymri?"

"Fine, last I heard." Although, based on the last video he'd sent her, she'd seen him looking better. And told him so herself in her reply. She'd heard nothing since.

"Which was when?"

Nicole shrugged, certain this, too, was a question to which Canfield already had the answer. "Not in a while, actually."

"You and he kept a fairly close correspondence after his recall to s'N'dare."

"We went through a lot together." Up to and including an attempt on President Charles Russell's life. Nicole and Kymri prevented the assassination, but the Hal Commander came away from the incident critically wounded, so much so that he never fully recovered. His return to the Hal homeworld was prompted in part by the realization that there were limits to how much help Terrestrial medicine could be to him, and the hope that his own people would be able to accomplish far more.

"What's this all about, General?" Nicole demanded. "Has something happened to him?"

"Not that I'm aware of. I was just curious."

"Excuse me for stating the obvious, ma'am, but Generals are *never* 'just curious.'"

"I've assigned you to starship berths four times in the last five years."

Nicole stared, thunderstruck.

"Each time," Canfield continued in the same flat tone, "the order was countermanded by higher authority."

"What are you talking about? You're a four-star General . . ." Nicole's voice trailed off as pieces clicked neatly into place.

"The White House?" she asked.

An imperceptible nod.

"Why should they care? I mean, okay, I helped save the President's life but other than that I'm really just a junior blue suit, a dime a dozen around the Beltway, barely worth the time of day."

"They care, youngster, because somebody made them."

"Emmanuel Cobri? The closest he could come to revenge over what happened with his son?" Even as she spoke, Nicole knew she was wide of the mark. Canfield's reply confirmed it.

"Just because Russell felt he couldn't officially acknowledge what you put in your report—that Amy Cobri was responsible for the Wolfpack you encountered during your first . . ."

"My *only*," Nicole couldn't help commenting, sotto voce.

". . . *Wanderer* mission and that she may well have been behind the assassination attempt on the President—doesn't mean he didn't believe it. The Executive Branch has cut Cobri, Associates, very little slack this term. So much so that Cobri opposition to your appointment would be a sure guarantee of its approval."

"Then *who*—?" Another insight, so obvious that Nicole chided herself for taking so long to realize it. "The Hal?" she asked quietly.

"Very back-channel. Very unofficial and off-the-record. A favor, one government to another. Both sides have gone to great pains to keep this private little codicil buried. And, professionally, you along with it."

"Why?"

"I don't know. The only surety is that they've gone to the greatest of trouble to keep you out of the interstellar service."

"That's nuts."

"Could it have something to do with your being Shavrin's adopted daughter?"

"I suppose." Shavrin commanded the Hal expedition that

made First Contact between her species and humanity; Nicole—on her first deep-space mission for NASA, with her spacecraft blasted to so much derelict junk by a marauding raider Wolfpack—had been her opposite number. The whole experience had been scary enough at the time, but the passage of years hadn't softened the impact. Quite the opposite. Now, looking back, Nicole still couldn't believe where she found the gumption or sheer dumb luck to do what she'd done in that first critical encounter.

"But you're not sure."

"General, I've been living next door to the Hal at Edwards ever since they arrived. I probably spend more time with them than I do my own kind. Hell, there are moments when I find myself wondering which species *is* my own kind."

That brought her up short, and Canfield too from the looks of things; it was a thought—a realization—she'd never voiced, never before admitted. Yet, when spoken aloud, one that was immediately recognized by them both as true. She spoke the language as well as a human could; indeed, when she was with the Hal, she thought in their tongue, no longer needing to transliterate their speech into English and back again. She favored their style of dress, their sense of fashion suiting her far more than what passed lately for Terrestrial haute couture. And was as comfortable with their customs, and cuisine, as with her own.

At Edwards, that didn't seem at all strange. The differences between species didn't appear so marked, because they were all pilots and astronauts, a fraternity that transcended lesser cultural details. The laws of physics, of aero- and thermo- and spatiodynamics, applied equally to Hal and human; the same benefits, the same costs. More than once, these past years, the Hal had stood by Nicole at the funeral of a fellow test pilot. And General Sallinger and his staff had joined her and the Hal in singing the spirit of one of their own to rest, who'd fallen from the sky.

Only on the outside, apart from the moments and the people, did she see how strange that must look.

"For all of that, though, I've barely scratched the surface," she said quietly. "The Hal at Edwards are specialized folks in a specialized environment." She laughed ruefully. "I mean, try asking your average aeroplane driver about socio-anthropological tribal customs, or governmental policy— except where they directly relate—and see how far you get."

"Point taken. You're smiling?"

"Just a thought. Am I being coddled for my own protection or in some way held hostage? I'm not learning anything special for humanity that isn't being duplicated in universities and cultural exchanges across the globe, and I doubt I'm teaching the Hal anything revelatory. I suppose I could ask Shavrin directly, I have the right of access."

"Where do you fit in her hierarchy?"

"Pretty near top of the family pyramid, I think. Although every time I've tried to press the Hal—including Kymri, in my letters—on precisely what that means, they get infuriatingly oblique. Very much like the Chinese. Lots of explanation, precious little enlightenment."

"Have you asked Ben Ciari?" Ciari was a United States Marshal, who'd served as Law Officer on Nicole's *Wanderer* flight. Shavrin's own mission had been intended from the start to make contact with humanity, only her ship, *Range Guide*, had suffered a catastrophic event in the early stages of its journey. Nicole had never been able to determine whether the explosion had been a true accident or sabotage, but the consequences had been devastating. Fully a third of Shavrin's crew were killed, including the Speaker, a Hal who'd been genetically engineered to communicate with any Terran they came across. Among the Hal, Speakers were phenomenally rare, treasured as diplomats and mediators; Shavrin had just the one aboard.

Soon after Nicole and the other three *Wanderer* survivors— Ciari, and civilian mission specialists Andrei Mihailovitch Zhimyanov and Hana Murai—had come aboard, *Range Guide* was intercepted by the same raiders who'd attacked *Wanderer*. In Shavrin's eyes, that made finding a replacement for her Speaker imperative. She already knew she had no candidates among her own crew, so she surreptitiously had the four Terrans tested. Ciari was deemed most compatible, and was infected with the genetic virus necessary to give him a Speaker's knowledge and abilities.

It worked, too well for Nicole's taste. By the time they'd

won free of the raiders' base—destroying the asteroid in the process, an experience which at long last had finally stopped giving Nicole nightmares—he was more Hal than human. Even though the process was successfully reversed, he was left with sufficient residual knowledge and awareness to make him the ideal liaison between the first Terran Embassy to s'N'dare and the Hal themselves. He'd been there ever since.

In the early days, he and Nicole had corresponded regularly. Actually, he did most of the communicating, goading her to improve her command of the Hal language, spoken and written. They'd had a flashfire romance aboard *Wanderer*. It might have turned into something more lasting, given time and opportunity, but their careers took them farther and farther apart— *Much like,* Nicole realized, *Canfield and my dad.* He never came home and she never got the chance to go to s'N'dare after him. She hadn't heard from him in a longer while than from Kymri, and was a bit chastened to discover that she wasn't bothered anywhere near as much. Somewhere along the line, the Hal had eclipsed him in her affections, Ciari becoming almost like a ghost.

"No," she said flatly, unwilling to voice anything more. And then, because she was thinking about letters and her old crew, Nicole suddenly asked, "Hana and Mikhail are both interstellar-rated, aren't they?"

Canfield nodded.

"Have they gotten starship berths?"

Slowly the General shook her head.

"So," Nicole mused. She adjusted her course slightly to correct her approach to San Diego Harbor, keeping a weather eye on a hulking commercial vessel a half-dozen klicks off her port beam, heading in roughly the same direction. "Be interesting to discover if the same restriction applies to them?"

"It would indeed. I'll see what I can learn. To be honest, I hadn't thought of checking that."

"Course, if it does, the next question is why? What's so special about the three of us that the Hal want to keep us locked in this solar system? And if we find out—what then?"

CHAPTER THREE

The water is a fascination to her, and the life she finds stranded in tiny pools amid the sand flats deliciously sates her hunger. Catching them is a whole new game in and of itself; their bodies are impossibly wriggly and their slick, smooth skin proves a formidable challenge to hold on to. She tries the water, too, finding it salty, like fresh blood, but nowhere near as palatable; a good drink makes her violently ill.

As always, the *Swiftstar* took her breath away.

Nicole hovered in midair in one of Sutherland's flight bays, gazing down along the magnificently sleek form of her hyper-space plane. Where the original Rockwell Space Shuttle had been an aerodynamic box with wings, roughly the size of an old DC-9 commercial airliner, the *Swiftstar* was all smooth curves and easily three times the size. The bulk didn't register at first, because of the way the design elements blended artfully, almost elegantly, together. That was her Halyan't'a hallmark, a dynamic form crafted as much for aesthetics as practicality. Her handling fulfilled the promise of her looks; the *Swift* was a dream to fly, surpassing expectations throughout every test regime.

The plane was a fully "Fly by Light" system, controlled as much by her on-board computers as by her pilots; indeed, in many respects they were far more essential to the plane's survival. The *Swift* could fly without Nicole, but Nicole was helpless without them. The spacecraft was too big, there was too much to do, to depend on purely mechanical linkages.

Where in the old days, wire cables ran from the flight deck to the control surfaces, the *Swiftstar* was laced through with fiberoptic lines, carrying those commands along strings of light.

She'd spent the better part of the past hour making her examination of the plane's exterior, the traditional pilot's "walkaround" inspection. In gravity, with aircraft this big, that was confined to the bottom of the vehicle: the engines, the wings, the wheel assemblies. More for reassurance than anything else; the days were long gone when the flight crew could check to make sure the mechanics had done their work properly. She had to trust that the people assigned to her knew their job. The difference in zero was that she wasn't restricted to the deck, and so her survey had taken her over the upper half of the plane as well. It was a giddy feeling, swimming through the air, and Nicole never tired of it. That was always one of the harder adjustments to make when she returned to the World, losing that ability to fly.

She'd actually know the plane's status for sure once the Chief Line Mechanic presented the results of his far more comprehensive diagnostics exam, and after Nicole ran a comparative series of her own from the flight deck. There was always a possibility of error; the trick was to make it as small as possible. This wasn't a foolproof system by any means; it seemed, no matter how hard everyone tried, that once every generation or so there had to be a catastrophic accident to remind people how complicated these machines were, how dangerous and unforgiving was the environment they worked in, how awful the cost of a mistake. The launch pad fire that had claimed the lives of the *Apollo 1* astronauts just past the dawn of the Space Age, the *Challenger* disaster two decades later, the loss of the starship *Hermes* a month before Nicole's graduation from the Air Force Academy. That last had cut both ways: one of her professors had been killed among the crew, and another had been court-martialed for contributory negligence. He'd been project officer on the C^3 software— Command, Control, and Communications—and had certified the material fully tested to NASA specifications when it wasn't. The result was a cataclysmic systems crash that reduced the *Hermes* to sparkling dust during her first transition to warp.

"She is an impressive piece of work," Ramsey Sheridan called, using his hand-held thruster pack to propel him up from below the nose, pivoting as he came close for a better view of the *Swift*. He expertly bled his velocity away to almost nothing, so it took only the touch of Nicole's hand on his shoulder to bring him to a full stop. Like Nicole, Sheridan was in shirtsleeves—the casual day uniform of slacks, shirt, and military sweater in Space Command blue-black, with Colonel's eagles on each epaulet and command pilot wings on the patch over his left breast—because the Curtains were down, massive steel shutters that could be cycled out from the primary "walls" to seal off sections of the flight bay, enabling a breathable atmosphere to be established and thereby create a far more comfortable place to work.

"And then some," Nicole agreed.

Sheridan was just closing out his tour as a test pilot at Edwards when Nicole arrived five years ago. Afterward, he'd moved on to command a line squadron for a year, then Air Force War College, passing up a high-visibility Pentagon appointment for a chance to fly suborbital ScramJets; a little over six months back, sporting a pair of bright shiny silver eagles, he'd won the slot of Operations Commander aboard Sutherland, the primary Earth-orbit space station. Scuttlebutt had him being groomed as the station's Commander, with an eye to moving him farther out, to join Judith Canfield's staff on the Moon, all of which Nicole thought would be a good thing.

He certainly looked the part of a rakehell pilot, his classic Tuscan features—*Hell*, she thought, *the man has a profile straight off an Imperial Roman coin*—providing an incongruous but somehow fitting contrast to his quintessentially WASP name and background. Sheridan was a top-notch pilot, who'd forced himself to learn to deal with the paperwork that comes with rank and responsibility, but whose primary forte was dealing with people. Nicole had never seen the person or situation he couldn't handle. And with the growing internationalization of NASA's facilities—both on the ground and here in space—that had become an essential talent. Especially when the term "people" embraced those not born anywhere near the Earth.

"Enjoy your tour?" he asked.

Nicole tried a smile, but ended up having to stifle a yawn instead. She stretched her eyes wide, then rubbed her face with her hands to flush some animation into her sleep-stiff features.

"Well, young Captain, your weekend on the waters certainly seems to have left you tanned and rested."

"Burned and brain-fried is more accurate."

"True, but why belabor the obvious?"

She gave him a look. "Taking no prisoners this morning, Colonel?"

"Prerogative of rank." Problem was, his bantering tone was belied by a steady, assessing gaze. "I gather you had something of an adventure in San Diego."

"I won at poker, if that's what you mean," she replied, knowing full well it wasn't.

"That, too."

She shrugged dismissively and told him, "It was nothing."

"You're sure?"

"It was dark, Ramsey," she said quietly, "and I was exhausted. Probably more than a little looped in the bargain. I didn't see who decked me." Which was true, but she hadn't needed sight to identify her assailant. "It could have been an accident. Whoever it was may have panicked after I went in the water. But I came out okay. No harm was done."

Now it was his turn to shrug, as he faced away from her, looking down the length of the spaceplane, as though he could see through the very fabric of the station itself to the Earth, five hundred miles below.

"Your call, Captain," his tone making clear that while he understood and respected her position, he also thought she was wrong. "I note from the log that you had Ch'ghan fly the ascent phase from Edwards."

"He's my Hal counterpart," she said, "as knowledgeable about the *Swift* and as well rated as I am. Besides, boss, another night's sleep and I'll be fine."

Nicole heard a hailing *beep* in her ear and adjusted her headset to improve the reception.

"*Sundowner* Command," that was her personal call sign, "this is Sutherland Flight Operations, over."

Another aspect she liked about space, they still used living controllers; on the surface, most of the routine communications were handled by computers. The artificial voder voices were pleasant enough—some were even being programmed with a semblance of personality—but she preferred the real thing.

"Sutherland," she replied into the tiny boom mike, "*Sundowner* Command, reading you five-by, over."

"If you've completed your inspection, *Sundowner*, please exit the flight bay. We're preparing to commence vehicle fueling. Over."

Her brow furrowed. "Say again, Sutherland . . . ?"

"Acknowledged, Sutherland," Sheridan broke in. "We're on our way."

"What gives, Ramsey," she demanded as he indicated the main hatch. "I thought the flight wasn't scheduled for another couple of days, at least."

The *Swift*'s primary fuel was hydrogen, loaded in liquid form at close to absolute zero. It was also extraordinarily volatile. As their thrusters pushed Nicole and Sheridan towards the exit, a trio of figures in full armored pressure suits, solid enough to survive all but the most tremendous of explosions, lumbered into view, anchored both by MagnaSoles on their boots and LifeLine tethers. Once the bay was fully cleared of unprotected personnel, the atmosphere would be evacuated to establish a full vacuum. The Curtains stayed closed and sealed, to confine the effects of any mishap and thereby minimize the risks to the flight bay and station as a whole.

"Circumstances have changed," was his taciturn reply.

Nicole watched the start of the fueling process from an observation blister, then pushed away as a blast shield slid shut across it. Behind her, a VideoWall was subdivided into a score of monitor windows, some showing data displays, most a multiplicity of images of the *Swiftstar*. A more comprehensive view, in fact, than she'd had from her vantage point in the bay itself or from the blister.

Nicole's crew was present, her Hal co-pilot Ch'ghan, and two systems specialists, Simon Tyrrel and Dan Fahey, respectively responsible for flight dynamics and engines. Plus one new arrival, another Hal, a face and form she recognized from the waterfront.

"What's this," she demanded of Ramsey.

"Flight Officer Raqella has been assigned to your crew as an observer."

"The Hell you say!"

"The decision was made by Higher Authorities, Captain," he said in a formal tone edged with warning frost. He wasn't happy, either, but there wasn't anything they could do about it. "Hal *and* human. And is not subject to appeal."

"Te*rrif*fic."

"You have a problem with that, Nicole?"

She met his gaze. "No," she said. Then, after a slight but deliberate space to make her protest plain, "Sir."

Raqella sat off to the side, a definite distance from the others, and from the furtive, darting glares he tossed towards Ch'ghan, and the way their collar fur was ever so slightly bristled, Nicole knew there'd been words and more between them.

Since this was crew business, she turned away from Ramsey and slipped on her headset.

"Something I should know about?" she asked Ch'ghan, on a private com channel, keeping the conversation exclusively between themselves.

"The youngblood had some thoughts of sitting in my place. If my behavior warrants my removal, Shea-Pilot, that is your prerogative."

She sighed and shook her head, breathing a subvocalized and heartfelt, *"Shit!"*

"Nicole?" Sheridan prompted, stepping close beside her.

"Raqella struck an attitude. Ch'ghan responded accordingly."

"Can you cope?"

She raised an eyebrow. "If I can't, Colonel, I've no right to be here."

She changed channels on her com and Raqella visibly started to hear her. They were across the room from each other and Nicole had pitched her voice so low that Sheridan was hard put to hear her; Raqella didn't have that problem, Nicole came through his headset as clearly as if she'd been standing right in his face.

"Do you acknowledge me as commander of this vehicle?" she demanded.

"So I have been told." He didn't look at her. In fact, he

turned his face even more away from the body of the room and the others. His answer wasn't wholly satisfying but Nicole decided to let that slide.

"Do you acknowledge me as Shavrin's cub?" This, she spoke in Hal, and allowed herself the smallest of smiles—barely a crease at the tip of her lips—as his spine straightened.

"So I have been told," he repeated. This, she wouldn't ignore.

"Do you acknowledge me as Shavrin's cub?" she repeated, no louder than before but with an unmistakable edge.

"I so affirm," he said, after a deliberate pause that he'd run out to just this side of an unforgivable insult.

"You have been named to my crew," she continued, still in Hal, "I am therefore responsible for your life. In fulfillment of that responsibility, if I don't have your word that you'll behave yourself—now and for the duration of this mission—I'll abort the test. Is that understood?"

"I give you my word, Captain," he said in his exotically accented English.

She was tempted to pull the plug. Ramsey knew it, without more than an idea why, simply from the set of her shoulders and jaw. Nicole also saw when he deliberately caught her eye that he was fully prepared to back her. He didn't understand Hal, not the fully colloquial and idiomatic way she was speaking it, but he trusted her judgment. That faith tipped the scales.

"By Hearth and Home," she growled, casting down before Raqella one of the Hal's most sacred oaths. "By the blood of She who bore you, and the claws of those who have fought to preserve that life—since you are not yet of an age to do so in your own behalf. By the Waters of the WorldSoul."

Raqella reacted to that, springing to his feet with such force that he shot straight to the ceiling, so upset that he couldn't react in time to prevent a solid impact. It took him a moment to recover; that plus the shock of the collision itself blunted his immediate, instinctive response to hurl himself at Nicole's throat.

"You shame me with such words," he spat, full-voiced, turning heads throughout the room, although only Ch'ghan guessed the reason.

Nicole breathed her reply into her mike, keeping the conversation as private as possible to avoid precisely that.

"You shame yourself," she said, "with your acts. We are here to work, as professionals. If you would join us in that spirit, you will be welcome."

To his credit, and Nicole's frank surprise (because she didn't think he had that in him), Raqella mastered himself and brusquely nodded his head.

"I would," a hitch in his voice, as he made sure his emotions were properly under control, "join you, Shea-Pilot."

"I want your word, Raqella."

"You have it. By Hearth and Home, by blood and claws. By the Waters of the WorldSoul."

"No trouble, Colonel," she told Sheridan.

She scanned the room, belatedly noting that one figure was missing.

"Where's Gene?" she asked. As in Gene Hardesty, the *Swift*'s electronics systems specialist.

"On the monitor console, here at Main Mission," was Ramsey's reply.

Nicole was aghast. "This isn't funny, Ramsey. You screw around with the flight schedule, then start strip-mining my crew. You trying to guarantee failure or what?"

"You have so little faith in what you helped build?"

"Be real. The crew's as integral an element as the machine itself. We're a team."

"I'm afraid you'll simply have to adapt. It's no reflection on his capabilities, Nicole, he's a good man. But circumstances warranted the assignment of someone better qualified to take his place."

"There is no one!"

"Such a vote of confidence," said a new voice from beyond Nicole's shoulder. "Does a woman's heart proud, y'know what I mean?"

"Damn," Nicole said, surprise giving way to delight as she saw who'd spoken, "oh, damn!"

"Is that a good cuss, d'you think," Hana Murai asked Ramsey, "or a bad cuss?"

Nicole gave her a mock punch on the arm, then gathered the other woman into a bear hug of an embrace. Momentum sent them spinning in slow circles, rising at the same time until Hana raised a hand to keep their heads from bouncing off the ceiling.

"What the hell are you doing here?" Nicole demanded as a gentle shove settled them back on the floor.

"Glad to see you, too, Ace. You want I should leave?"

"Get stuffed, Murai. What I mean is, from your last letter, aren't you supposed to be chasing rocks around Saturn or something?"

Hana was about to reply, but offered a dismissive shrug instead.

Nicole stared long and hard at her best friend, then turned her gaze once more on Ramsey.

"The point was made," he said, "that since Dr. Murai designed most of your vehicle's electronics—hardware and software—she might be a valuable addition to your crew. Not to mention your history." That, he had pegged perfectly; there was no one Nicole would rather have at her back. But she'd thought only *she* knew that.

"What's this all about, Colonel?" she asked quietly.

Sheridan shifted position, so that everyone could see him.

"An announcement has been made by Earth First that an attempt would be made to disrupt the test."

Comments were immediate, and mostly dismissive—"Are you serious?" from Dan Fahey, "Are they?" from Simon. And, upon seeing Sheridan's reaction, a collective groan. "Fucking terrorists. Give us a goddamn break!"

"Spookshow's checking it out," he told them, "CIA, FBI, the United Nations Intelligence Service, the rest of the Intelligence alphabet. As yet, neither Langley nor the Bureau nor Turtle Bay can offer any definitive corroboration of the threat. They could be blowing smoke, they could be serious, nobody really knows."

"You knew about this?" Nicole asked Hana.

"I'm here," she replied.

Nicole turned to Ramsey. "What about capability, can they actually carry out such a threat?"

"Nobody really knows."

"Ter*rif*fic."

Newton's laws applied as much to politics as physics; that

Nicole learned early, at the feet of her lawyer father and journalist mother. Every action had its opposite reaction, the distinction being that in politics—unlike physics—that response wasn't always equal.

The world had been having a hard enough time coming to grips with the new realities of space, and Earth's place in the scheme of things, even before contact was established with the Halyan't'a. In the span of a generation, humanity had gone from its first hesitant steps exploring its local solar system— with barely one active space station and no installations at all on the Moon—to active exploitation of this galactic neighborhood, and a steadily growing fleet of FTL cruisers reaching hungrily out across the neighboring stars, much as the early explorers and mountain men had across the North American continent two centuries before. In the lifetime of Nicole's father, new worlds had been discovered capable of supporting human life, and colonies established. Human perspective on the Universe had widened immeasurably. A generation had come to maturity that owed allegiance to Earth as the motherworld only in the abstract. It was Future Shock in top gear, every morning bringing some new change. And not everybody liked it.

Then, humanity discovered they weren't the only players on the board. The Universe had to be shared, not only with the Hal, but with a far nastier species—who they'd encountered but Earth had not—from farther down the spiral arm towards galactic center. This brought even more cries of alarm from concerned and agitated pundits, pointing back at Terrestrial history and the catastrophic encounters between the so-called First World—Europe—and the less technologically advanced societies of the Third, with repercussions still being felt to present day. No matter that the Hal and humanity seemed to stand at comparable levels, or that the Hal approached Earth as potential allies and equals. The fear was that somehow, some way, the human species would be subverted and ultimately overwhelmed, unless the same was done to the Hal in reverse.

Earth First was born from that xenophobia, pushed along in no small measure by the passage—midway through Charles Russell's second term, as the keystone of his foreign policy—of the One World Treaty, essentially binding the nations of the Earth into a global confederacy centered around the United Nations. The individual governments retained autonomy over their internal affairs, but in matters relating to the world as a whole, especially diplomatic relations, the Secretariat held sway. Nobody really liked the arrangement; indeed, more than a few grumbled that it was merely a ploy by the United States to maintain its hegemony over interstellar exploration. But a majority had grudgingly, eventually, come to accept Russell's core argument: that standing alone would only bring about a balkanized and terminally conflicted political structure that would in turn guarantee the exploitation of Earth by the Halyan't'a that everyone most feared.

Unfortunately, passage of the Treaty didn't end the debate; quite the contrary. The counterargument was made—passionately, persuasively—that humanity was being sold down the proverbial river. In the four years of Russell's second term, aided and abetted by a couple of spectacularly disastrous incidents between human and Hal, that opposition had coalesced into the Earth First movement. However, while there was sufficient support to make them a credible force, there was nowhere near enough to change basic policy. That perceived impotence—along with the fact that time could well work against them, as positive ties between the two species became stronger and deeper—only made matters worse. It wouldn't be the first time a political movement with no hope of victory working within the system took to armed struggle to achieve its ends. And thereby perpetuated that conflict from generation to generation, so that it seemed to take on an inextinguishable life of its own.

"For political reasons," Sheridan said, breaking Nicole's train of thought, "it's been decided that the test cannot be postponed."

"Like hell!"

"I beg your pardon?"

"I'm Spacecraft Commander *and* Project Manager, and I will not put my vehicle and people in jeopardy simply to serve somebody's political agenda."

"I hate to state the obvious, Captain"—his use of Nicole's rank instead of her name was deliberate—"but that's precisely what donning these uniforms means. And I would hardly dismiss President Russell as 'somebody.' He was fully briefed, by General Sallinger among others, and communicated his decision to me directly. With the full concurrence, I might add, of General Canfield—both as C-in-C Space Command and NASA's Director of Manned Spaceflight. Occasionally, we have to fly in harm's way, no matter what, and charge the guns at Balaclava."

"So we're launching early to throw them off-balance, assuming there's any 'them' waiting out there?"

"Precisely. A day ahead of the original mission profile and three ahead of the revised flight schedule I released yesterday."

"I'd feel happier with some harder data, one way or the other."

"Wouldn't we all. Anything turns up, we're supposed to hear."

Nicole made a face, and Sheridan nodded reluctant assent.

"Granted, Nicole, I know how the bureaucracy works, same as you. Executive Branch—in DC *and* New York—needs this test to fly, and do so perfectly, for a whole host of reasons. No one's going to raise a red flag for anything less than a battery of active antimissile launchers. Perhaps not even then."

"It's unlikely we'll encounter any threat during the descent phase," she mused aloud, as much to herself as the others. "We'll be under power, with near a full load of fuel, and at a fairly hefty speed. We'll be deaf and blind during the ionization period, but that should be too high an altitude for any opposition to reach—unless they've orbital capability and they're up here already."

Sheridan shook his head: "Nobody's in near-Earth space who isn't supposed to be. And we'll be closely monitoring everything that lifts during your flight window."

"We have the advantages going down; they'll have 'em during our ascent. Our fuel will be limited and with it, our options. If we fail to achieve orbit, we'll be forced to glide home, just like the original shuttles; won't leave us much room for maneuver. Also, since we'll be climbing to a known rendezvous, we're committed to a specific trajectory." She had an inspiration, and looked sharply across to Sheridan.

"I want authorization to change that, as circumstances dictate," she said.

"Come again?"

"If there's trouble, I want to be able to switch insertion trajectories out of the standard West-East corridor."

"Nicole, all the support facilities are geared along that route. You go haring off in some other direction, we could lose you in every sense of the word."

"I'm prepared to accept the risk, Colonel. Pilot's discretion."

"I'll consider it, and give you my decision before you board."

"Ter*rif*fic," she grumbled again, and then heard the familiar growl of Ch'ghan's voice as he wrestled with words that still came hard to him, even though he was wholly fluent in the language.

"Is the likelihood of attack so great?" he asked.

"You couldn't ask for a more ideal opportunity," Ramsey answered sourly as he indulged in a mug of coffee. Because the flight bay was zero gravity, the container was sealed and he had to sip the liquid through a straw. No fun, especially when it was piping hot. "The first human/Halyan't'a joint venture, with all that's riding on it for both cultures, it's almost too tempting a target to resist. On the other hand, this could be nothing but a PR bluff. If Earth First is serious, though, it represents a quantum increase on their part."

"You, too, can be a world-class terrorist."

"I wish it were that funny, Hana. It isn't simply the threat itself, but the capability behind it. We're talking about something a whole lot more sophisticated than driving a truck full of explosives into somebody's barracks."

"Somehow," Nicole said, "that doesn't make me feel any better."

"Me, neither. Cliché notwithstanding, young Captain, I'm afraid we'll just have to play the hand we're dealt. I know this makes for a lousy reunion," he said to the pair of them, "and for that I'm truly sorry. Briefing in an hour, people, you launch in twelve."

Insertion was magic, *Swiftstar* sliding through the transition from vacuum to atmosphere—more properly known as the Entry Interface—as though it were riding rails, with a supernal smoothness that made Nicole grin delightedly. On her main panel display, the course ahead curved off and away around the rim of the world, reaching across the dark Pacific towards the coast of California. They were still well beyond the Terminator and wouldn't see daylight until just before landing. The plane was so high their altitude was measured in miles—even in a mostly decimal society, aviation was where some old traditions yet held fast—and their speed such that their passage through what passed for air created sufficient friction to warm the leading edges of the wings and lower hull to a bright cherry and leave a trail of fire in their wake. Nicole felt some mild buffeting, more of a tremble actually, which would increase with their descent. Nothing unexpected, and well within operational parameters.

A fast, reflexive glance at the secondary displays, flanking the larger main screen, assured her that ship systems and flight dynamics were at nominal levels. She flexed her shoulders against the snug fit of the four-point restraint harness and waited for the growing G-forces to push her into her seat. There was a wide-angle mirror mounted above the canopy; that gave her a view of Ch'ghan in the right seat beside her, as well as the two stations directly behind. Hana was behind him, while Raqella backed Nicole. The last two crew members, Simon and Dan, were farther back and out of her sight. If necessary, though, she could switch one of the displays to a visual of them.

"Ionization peaking," Hana reported, "we're in Shadow." As atmospheric drag on the vehicle generated friction, the heat buildup stripped electrons from the air surrounding *Swiftstar*, enveloping it in an ionization field that effectively inhibited all external communications, both radio and telemetry. Normal duration of the "Shadow" was about twelve minutes.

"Simon," Nicole called.

"Systems nominal," came his immediate reply, with confirmation from the raw data on the appropriate display. "Skin temperature at twelve hundred degrees Centigrade, rising along predicted curve. Heat exchangers are handling the load nicely."

"Dan?"

"Engine status nominal, skipper. Ready to take the mains off-line and cycle the Scrams up to speed. Fuel status at eighty-seven percent."

"We'll glide for now. I want to touch down with as much in the tanks as possible."

"Affirmative."

"I mark external atmospheric pressure readings of ten psf," Simon again, "four hundred eighty pascals; confirm automatic disengagement of reaction control system roll thrusters."

"Confirmed. Primary responsibility shifting to aero-control surfaces."

That didn't mean terribly much at this point. The RCS—tiny rockets located at strategic points about the hull and wing structure of the plane—allowed her to maneuver in a vacuum. In atmosphere, those responsibilities reverted to the traditional, mechanical elements—in this specific case, the main wing elevons. Nicole swung her yoke, mounted on the left arm of her chair, fractionally from side to side. The display indicated movement in the control surfaces but there was no response from the vehicle itself. That would change in fairly short order.

There was a stir to her right and she saw Ch'ghan's reflection turn slightly towards her. He had as little play as she, thanks to his own restraints, and the snug-fitting crash helmets only made matters worse.

"You anticipate a need for the additional propellant, Shea-Pilot?" he asked in his raspy voice; it had the timbre of an old back-lot pulp movie thug, slum sidekick to the likes of Humphrey Bogart or Jimmy Cagney. Raqella, by contrast, was more cultured and European. Her favorite Hal voice, however, belonged to her favorite Hal, Kymri, Sharvin's second-in-command and her oldest friend among their delegation to Earth. His was an almost Highland burr, as raw and rich and resonant as a malt whiskey.

"We'll know that when it happens," she replied matter-of-factly. "I'd just rather not be caught short, is all."

"Understood."

"Maximum heating, Nicole."

"So I see, Simon." Through the canopy in fact, with narrowed eyes against the white-hot glow leaching around the sleek boundary curve of the *Swiftstar*'s nose.

"Within tolerance specs at fourteen hundred seventy-nine degrees Centigrade. Altitude a quarter mil, velocity fifteen thousand."

"Eighteen minutes to landing." That was from Ch'ghan.

"External pressure now at twenty psf," Simon, calling out the pounds per square foot, "nine hundred fifty-eight pascals. RCS pitch thrusters deactivated."

"Confirmed," said Nicole.

They emerged from the Shadow at two hundred thousand feet, a little higher than normal, their speed cut in half to eight thousand miles per hour. They were five hundred miles west of the coast, with a dozen minutes left before landing.

The approach ended as it began, smooth as silk. Everyone did their job, just as they'd all rehearsed more times than any of them—save, of course, Hana, who was fitting in with an ease that didn't surprise Nicole at all—cared to remember, and the *Swiftstar* responded like an old campaigner, as though she were a proven design, and this a run she made often.

The sun was well clear of the horizon as Nicole turned their back on it and lined up the *Swift* for an east-west approach to Rogers Dry Lake. Ahead stretched mile after mile of hardpan, as firm and dependable a surface—except on the rare occasions when it rained—as the concrete runway beyond. Hashmarks had been etched into the surface of the ancient lake bed, giving her the necessary reference points to properly line up her approach. They weren't using the autoland system, that would violate the operational parameters of the test. The idea was to duplicate—as much as feasible—the conditions of an outworld descent, where none of the usual landing aids would be available. Which meant that Nicole was making the touchdown manually.

She flared at threshold, as the *Swift* flashed over the first set of marks, letting the plane settle naturally towards the ground, holding her steady through the ground effect created by the aircraft's own bulk compressing the air beneath it, waiting for the bite of the main gear as rubber struck dirt. In quick succession, Ch'ghan deployed the speed brakes while Nicole did the same with the thrust reversers—the brakes themselves would be used only in the final stages—slowing the spaceplane in a matter of heartbeats from better than two hundred miles per hour to a brisk walking pace.

"Edwards Tower," she called, and then gave them her call sign, "*Sundowner* flight, down and dirty."

"Looking good, *Sundowner*." Nicole raised her eyebrows as she recognized the voice: Brigadier General Michael Sallinger, Commander of the flight test center. "Textbook approach."

"Pity, sir, that's only half the battle won."

"Acknowledged. Switch over to Ground, *Sundowner*, they'll direct you to the evaluations bay we've set up for you. Figure an hour there, two tops, to flush your telemetry, and you'll be cleared for launch."

Nicole was about to reply when she felt a hand on her shoulder. It was Raqella, reaching forward from his seat, but as she caught his eye in the mirror he indicated that it was Hana who wanted her. Hana had her helmet off and motioned for Nicole to do the same.

"What's up?" she asked when she'd done so, loosening her straps as well so she could turn in her seat.

"I'm monitoring a Guard transmission," Hana said quietly, referring to the Air Defense Command alert frequency. "Lots of chatter, all of a sudden. Seems they've tagged a ghost in the high atmosphere."

"Details?"

"Nobody's sure, they can't get an accurate skin trace on the bogie."

"Stealth configuration?"

"Good bet. Or it could simply be a glitch in the system. Hardware error, software error, operator error."

"Christ, why don't they simply dump the esoteric hardware and open their damn eyes? From orbit, they've got height on the bastards, find them with enhanced optics."

"The contact was so fleeting it almost went unnoticed, and in orbital opposition to Sutherland. Nobody's placed properly for a visual search. I think that's the reason they haven't called us, nobody's certain."

"Sutherland's overhead, yes?"

"Yes. Beyond the Edwards horizon in seven minutes."

There was a tiny bump as Ch'ghan guided the spaceplane over the boundary between the dry lake bed and the concrete taxiways of the base proper. He turned the nose towards the hangar facility, a couple of miles distant at the South Field Complex, but Nicole laid her hand lightly on his arm, holding him back from the throttles, keeping the plane where it was.

"Main HUD, please, Hana," she said, and the heads-up display burst to life across the canopy in front of her, far larger and more intrusively than it would be under normal circumstances. The image stretched across the width of the flight panel, a glittering, magical lattice of multicolored light.

"Orbital schematic, God's-eye perspective," was Nicole's follow-up command, and an image appeared of a Mercator projection of the globe. Hana had anticipated Nicole's next request. There was a flashing blip next to the dot that indicated Edwards, and two more better than halfway around the world behind them.

"Those aren't hard contacts on the bogies," Hana said, "simply my extrapolations from the initial tag."

"You're assuming a standard suborbital loop?"

"Only for the sake of argument. I'm tapped into the Guard network; they get any data updates, I'll hear, and believe me they're trying. There's a consensus growing that this ghost is nothing more than it appears."

"You buy that?"

"Can't say, I didn't catch the initial contact. But even our best stealth fighters aren't invisible, not to the level of scans they're flashing upstairs."

"If they are hostile and we go park ourselves, we'll be an awfully big target."

"You think they'd try to take us out on the ground."

"Lot easier than an airborne intercept. It's what I'd try in their shoes. Don't even need to come in close, just lob some over the horizon smart munitions in our general direction and let the targeting computers do the rest."

"*Sundowner*, Edwards Ground," interrupted the Tower, "we have you at Alpha Intersection. Make a left turn, please, and proceed to docking facilities via taxiway Golf. Do you copy?"

Ch'ghan acknowledged the transmission, but when he looked to Nicole for clearance, she shook her head, fingers steepled before her face, as she absently chewed on the tips of her thumbs and wondered if the prickling she felt had the same meaning for her as for Macbeth's witches.

"Shea-Pilot?"

It was Raqella, who'd slipped loose of his restraints and stepped into the space between Nicole's and Ch'ghan's seats, for a better view of the display. He'd removed his own helmet as well.

"Would it be possible to see any recording of the initial contact?" he asked with a deference that surprised all three who heard.

Hana opened a secondary window in the display and gave them what she'd secured from the Guard net.

Raqella snagged his lower lip between his fangs, a disconcertingly human gesture, and asked to see it again.

"I am not totally familiar with your scanning systems, Shea-Pilot," he said, "would they be effective at detecting Hal configurations?"

"Ch'ghan?"

The burly Hal shrugged, a learned human response adopted by many of the Hal during their duty tours on Earth, and shook his head.

"In deep space, certainly; as you and Hana did when you first detected our StarShip *Range Guide* . . ."

He broke off because Nicole was shaking her head.

"What about purely combat vehicles, designed for close atmosphere work?"

"Possibilities, perhaps . . ."

"You have another opinion?" she demanded of Raqella.

"Only possibilities, like Ch'ghan. Similarities to some Hal equipment I have flown."

"Not even close, youngblood," growled Ch'ghan. "I know what you're saying, but it is almost totally unsupported by the data."

"With respect," and Nicole looked at him sharply to hear the determination in his voice. The boy was on a steep and slippery slope and knew it but was committed to standing his ground regardless. "This vehicle is a hybrid of Hal and human technology. Could not someone else do much the same?"

"*Sundowner*, Edwards Ground, is there a reason for your hold? Do you require assistance, over?"

"You," Nicole snapped, pivoting the spaceplane towards the main runway and pushing the throttles forward to move the *Swiftstar* into place on the end stripes, "take Ch'ghan's place. Ch'ghan, you're my RIO"—Radar Intercept Officer—"Hana, light up his board and tie it into the gunpod."

She reached out to the main console and tapped a sequence of numbers into the command keypad. Off to the side was a row of newly installed candy-striped guarded switches; one after the other, she flipped up the covers and threw the toggles.

"Combat security systems on-line," Hana acknowledged. "Weapons systems on-line."

"Edwards Tower, *Sundowner*," Nicole called, but didn't give them time to answer. She was already cycling the engines to full power, holding the huge aircraft in place with both feet pressing hard on the brake pedals. It was no easy effort and she indicated to Raqella to do the same as he hurriedly fastened his restraints and reconnected his pressure suit's umbilicals.

"I am declaring a pilot's emergency and going for an immediate turnaround."

"Negative, *Sundowner*, that decision is not authorized. You are to power down and taxi to the test facility. Over."

"My authority as Vehicle Commander, Tower. My responsibility."

"Nicole," a different voice, General Sallinger, replacing the controller. "Explanation."

"Call it a hunch, General. I don't think those 'ghost' contacts are phantoms. And I don't intend sticking around to find out the hard way."

"Cleared to launch, *Sundowner*." And she thought, *Bless you, boss!* "I hope you're wrong."

When they'd left Sutherland, and begun their descent into the atmosphere, all had been supernally, unnervingly silent. Just the whine and hiss and beep of on-board servos and monitor cues to herald the occasion; not the slightest hint, save for a shudder in the airframe and some lively action on the appropriate displays, of the awesome power being unleashed behind them.

This was different.

A terrible roar echoed across the desert hardpan, filling the sky like a palpable, physical force, so raw and powerful that it wasn't so much heard as felt. The air hammered against the skin of those who watched, leaving them a little at a loss for breath as the engines spat speed cones of blue flame out their exhausts.

Nicole pushed the throttles to their stops and that little space beyond that marked the—crucial—difference between full power and full *military* power. A hundred percent of rated thrust and more. Only then did she and Raqella release the brakes.

There was no gradual acceleration, as there'd been during their initial takeoff a couple of days earlier for the ferry flight up to Sutherland. This had more in common with a catapult launch off a carrier's flight deck. Their speed seemed to increase at an exponential rate, the force of the acceleration pressing them deep into their chairs, prompting the G-bladders of their pressure suits to fill in response so they wouldn't black out from the strain.

In a matter of seconds they reached and passed their commit speeds. The plane wanted to fly but Nicole held her on the ground a little longer, letting more and more velocity build up until, when she finally pulled back on the yoke and cried "Rotate," they literally shot into the sky.

As soon as they were off the ground, Raqella—without being told—raised the landing gear, and then he held on to the arms of his chair as Nicole set a climb angle more reminiscent of a vertical gantry launch.

"Talk to me, Ch'ghan," Nicole grunted, the G-forces she was subjecting them all to making it an effort to speak.

"Nothing to report, Shea-Pilot. My screens are lit and scanning, and empty to the horizon."

Shit, she thought, but it was really no more than she'd expected. "Can you search on Hal bandwidths?"

"Your equipment lacks the necessary refinements."

"Well that's of precious little use. Make a note, patch it into the Mission Control telemetry stream."

"Easier said than done, Nicole," Hana reported. "Someone's walking all over my signal paths in seven-league boots. We have no external contact, voice or data."

"Naturally occurring phenomenon?" Nicole asked rhetorically, trying to make a joke of it and getting the response she deserved.

"If anyone wants my opinion," Hana said, "not that there's any point since nobody ever listens to me anyway, I say bingo back to the deck. Whatever's out there may be cloaked but we sure as Hell aren't. We drop back into the five-figure regime"—that is, flight levels below one hundred thousand feet, within the operational parameters of frontline Air Force interceptors—"at least we can count on some backup."

"A logical suggestion, Shea-Pilot," Ch'ghan echoed formally, "I concur."

"Shea-Pilot," this from Raqella, a thread of concern in his voice, "we are well beyond the point for turnaround. If we continue along this trajectory, we will achieve orbit in total opposition to Sutherland's track and at too great a velocity to achieve rendezvous."

"Same rules of physics apply to whoever's coming for us, is that it?" Hana asked. "Create so extreme a rate of closure that he won't have a decent shot."

"In part," Nicole agreed, eyes scanning from panel to canopy to her infuriatingly clean HUD. "If they're playing this smart, I'd say we're facing a minimum of three bogies, descending in a long echelon. When the first emerges from Shadow, his partner'll still be inside, with the third waiting up-top as high cover. We'll have a decent chance of dodging the first pair. Number three's the trick, and the problem."

Dan Fahey came on-line. "We're nearing the upper limit of the Scrams' effectiveness, boss," he told her. "We'll need to light off the mains, especially if you want to maintain this rate of climb."

"What's the worry, Dan?"

"You're pushing awful hard, Nicole. It won't take much to drain us dry."

"They must be having fits on Sutherland," Hana noted idly.

Suddenly a shrill warbling filled Nicole's headphones, followed by a frantic cry from Ch'ghan.

"*Tone!* I have a tone!" They'd been acquired by the interceptor's targeting radar.

"Screw that," Nicole bellowed, "tell me what's coming and from where!"

"Missiles," was the quick reply. "Three. Twelve o'clock high"—straight ahead that meant, and above them—"range twenty kilometers."

"Burn 'em, Hana. Full Spectrum ECM!"

"Electronic CounterMeasures systems active," Hana ac-

knowledged. "Little buggers seem to be well and truly hard-
ened. No change in their approach; no joy, Ace."

"Hang on then, everybody."

There were cries of alarm and protest from everyone save
Hana, who merely smiled grimly and locked her gloved hands
around the ends of her armrests, as Nicole slammed her yoke to
the side, the *Swiftstar* responding as violently as any classic
hardwired airframe. By rights, the maneuver should have been
impossible; inhibitors built into the flight dynamics software
were designed to prevent the pilot from engaging in any
maneuvers that took the vehicle beyond its established operational characteristics. Which was why Hana had spent—at
Nicole's request and with Sallinger's grudging approval—the
better part of six months crafting a subroutine to disengage it.
Nicole could do anything she wanted with the plane, including
fly it into the ground.

They rolled left, to right angles of their original heading, the
cabin bucking and shaking from the tremendous stresses. For a
few seconds, the G-forces went to the top of the scale, and
Nicole heard a basso grunt erupt from deep within her, of real
pain, as her suit bladders swelled so tight she thought they'd
crush her bones. Her lips peeled back from her teeth, to such an
extent she thought they'd tear free, and her vision turned into
fog, shot through with splotches of red and purple. Even in a
centrifuge, she'd never felt anything so awful; it was beyond
endurance. But the moment that despairing thought surfaced in
her head, her last she assumed, her gamble gone for naught, the
pressure eased.

She'd have collapsed if the restraints hadn't held her in
place. She didn't want to imagine the sight of her shoulders
where they'd bitten into her; the bruises, she knew, would be
spectacular. Almost as much, in fact, as the notion of living to
see them.

Her breath hurt, as though she'd just sprinted through a
thousand crunch sit-ups, and she had to force her voice to be
heard, even by her microphone's sensitive pickup.

"Missiles," she gasped. "Where are the missiles?"

"Hostile . . . ordnance." Ch'ghan had to pause for some
breath of his own, his own voice soft and thick with pain. A part
of Nicole noted, automatically, analytically, that the intercom

amplified his speech and cleaned it somewhat, to make it better heard and comprehended. "No longer . . . a factor," he continued. "One attempted to follow. Stress tore it apart." His speech was improving with use. The hurt was still there, in full measure; he was simply determined not to let it matter. Nicole wondered what Raqella thought of that and if the boy would try to match him.

"The other two," he finished, "burned in the deeper atmosphere."

"Where . . . are we?" Raqella asked. Another surprise for Nicole, as he didn't bother hiding his own pain. Almost as though bravado was for lesser moments, when nothing but pride and status were at stake.

"Heading south," she replied.

"Outstanding," Hana grumbled. "Nowhere to set down for over a hemisphere but water and icecap. And in midwinter, too."

"The vote of confidence is appreciated," was Nicole's retort. "I'd rather not be surprised again," she said to Hana and Ch'ghan both, "either find a way to hide us from them or for us to pick them up. Somehow!"

"They cannot disguise their heat signatures as they maneuver in atmosphere, even up here on the fringes," Ch'ghan said. "I have negative contact to the limit of my scanning range."

"We running or fighting?"

Nicole's eyes went to the mirror but her friend's features were hidden by the faceplate of her helmet.

"You got a preference, Hana?"

"I don't like being shot at."

She heard what passed among the Hal for a chuckle from Ragella and guessed he was baring his fangs ever so slightly in agreement with Hana's sentiment.

"They will expect us to run, Shea-Pilot," he said. "Unaware that we have teeth."

"Are you guys serious?" came Simon's cry from aft.

"Operational hazard when you fly with Nicole, fellas." Hana grinned. "Better get used to it."

"This is a shuttle, damn it!" This was Dan's contribution. "We're not rated for combat!"

"Well, actually," Nicole replied, "we are." Thinking, *Be real,*

Fahey, how the hell else d'you think we pulled through that high-G turn?

"Fuel status, please, Daniel."

"Forty-one percent on the Scrams, skipper, eighty-three point six on the Roks. Better than eighty-five percent on the maneuvering thrusters. We're in a substantially ballistic flight mode"—which meant they were gliding—"and, in case no one else has thought of this, probably leaving a fairly intense kinetic signature in our own wake."

"We still being jammed, Hana?"

"Negative signal acquisition on any orbital station, but that's hardly surprising considering how far off normal flight paths we've traveled."

"I thought the TDRSS network was supposed to guarantee constant contact regardless of position." Simon was referring to a brace of communications satellites—initially launched in the 1980s—arranged in a geosynchronous orbit about the Earth, to serve as relay points for transmissions anywhere within the Earth-Moon system.

"No joy," Hana said. "Might as well open a hatch and yell for all the response I'm getting. But I don't think it's jamming per se, at least not in the classical sense."

"Explain."

"Makes more sense to feed an invasive program into the satellite's C^3 software, designed to chop us out of the loop on command. We're transmitting fine; it's just that all the local receivers aren't listening. Same applies in reverse, except that their transmitters can't get a definitive lock on us to establish contact." Nicole heard a shrug in her voice. "Everything's sourced and tasked and cycled through solid-state chips; compromise the software, the hardware's rendered useless."

"I have a signature," Ch'ghan, "very hot, a hundred kilometers behind us and pushing hard to close."

"Shea-Pilot," Raqella, "could our own Command software have been corrupted?"

"Now there's a cheery thought."

"If this were Amy Cobri's doing, Hana, she'd be more likely to rig the controls so we'd fly ourselves into the ground. There'd be no need for the interceptors."

"The flight is still young, Ace."

"It's not her style."

"Blitzing software? That's *precisely* the little bitch's style; it's how she tried to get to you before, only she killed that Secret Service agent instead."

"Seventy kilometers, still closing," noted Ch'ghan. "I have a second trace flying wing position on the first. I have no contact with the third. I have establishing emissions from a fire control radar but negative lock at this time; the range is still too great." But not, his tone made clear, for much longer.

"Prime the guns to my stick," Nicole said. "Ch'ghan, you handle any missile attack. I plan to fire at ten."

"Ten?" squawked Simon. "Ten kilometers?"

"Depleted uranium shells, Simon, ground-attack tank killers. At the speed they're flying, they'll barcly have time to realize the danger before they're hit."

"If they don't zap us first."

"I'm open to suggestions, Hana."

"You always say that."

"It's always true."

"I wonder who they are?"

"If we're lucky, we'll probably never know." Unbidden memories flick-flashed across her mind's eye: a young man spinning silently in zero, eyes wide with surprise, one hand clutching behind him for the arrow Nicole had shot through his heart; and a Hal, small and lean, lunging for her with fangs and claws, driven mad by an assassination indoctrination program intended for Nicole, staggering in midair, the sleek symmetry of her body broken by the impact of the bullet from Nicole's gun. The boy had been a stranger; Matai, the Hal, genetically engineered to be Nicole's psychic twin.

Her hand began trembling and she moved it clear of the yoke, so as not to disturb the plane's flight. *Strange*, she thought, *how some memories stay with you, the bad more easily than the good, acid etched in crystal for perfect clarity.*

They still haunted her, those deaths, she suspected they always would.

She heard Hana mutter under her breath. She couldn't make out what was said, but it seemed to strike a subconscious chord, because it brought her back to full alertness.

"What?" she demanded. "Hana, what did you just say?"

"God, I hate these open circuits. I was just talking to myself, Nicole."

"Talk to me, now. What?"

"It's those guys behind us. They're making a helluva lot of electronic noise for folks so far back."

"Maybe they want us to know they're there."

"Precisely. But why? They may be the active threat but they aren't coming *that* fast, we've got plenty of time to respond, they have to know that."

"They want us so intent on them, we'll forget all about Number Three!"

"The thought had struck my mind."

"Find him for me, Hana. Ch'ghan, you too! Flash me when pursuit closes to within twenty-five kay; until then, the third bogie has absolute priority." She opened the circuit to the entire crew. "Everybody make sure you're strapped snug and secure, things may get lively."

"What was that before, skipper?"

"But a prologue, Simon, to our play. Number Three's got to be coming from above and behind," she said, thinking aloud, "we'd better swing to meet him."

She nudged one of the pickle-switches on her yoke, firing the appropriate attitude thrusters, and the horizon rose up to fill the canopy as the nose dropped; while the plane pitched literally head over heels, she rolled it on its long axis so that when she fired a braking counterburst, the *Swiftstar* came to rest flying backward, in a moderate nose-up attitude.

"Eyes peeled, campers," Nicole called, "be nice if we could see the bad guys first."

That honor went to Raqella, as he pointed and cut loose with a hoarse cry of excitement—tinged, though he'd deny it vehemently, with the stress of fear. Nicole tried her best, but Hal eyes were better.

"Two missiles," Ch'ghan reported.

"Jam 'em, Hana!"

"Working on it. They're locked on our configuration, internal guidance, we'll have to burn them!"

Which is precisely what Ch'ghan did, with the laser that was part of their weapons package. Two split-second bolts of light that ignited the onrushing warheads with eye-searing brilliance.

He tried to acquire the launching platform as a target, but the hostile was streaking too fast down the gravity well; there was simply no time to lock and fire their own missiles.

Nicole thumbed up the safety switch on her yoke, freeing the trigger, a squib of data on her HUD confirming that she had control. Around her was a cacophony of sound and activity, everyone seemed to be talking at once, a storm of voices— some human, most electronic—feeding her an unending torrent of data, all of it essential. She wasn't listening, in any active sense of the word, she'd gone far beyond that; she let the information flow directly into her subconscious, which allowed her to make decisions on an extra-rational basis without stopping to actually think about them. In effect, to act from "instinct."

All this happened in less time than it takes to tell—a matter of seconds, really—from the moment Raqella sighted the hostile to Nicole's pulling her trigger. A one-second burst, a hundred shells from the Gatling gunpod mounted flush with the fuselage.

Think of it as strewing a handful of gravel in the path of a speeding car. The faster the car's going, the more damage the impact causes. When the target's traveling at better than seventeen thousand miles per hour, even a single hit can be devastating.

At first, though, it looked like they hadn't been that lucky. The hostile ripped past them, too far away for Nicole to get a decent look at its design—she hoped the hull cameras had more success—and with no indication of any debris.

Nicole didn't have any opportunity to worry about that, she'd already shifted her focus to the other two spacecraft, which had accelerated over the past few seconds and were coming into fighting range.

"Boundary layer, Nicole," Simon told her, doing his level best to keep the strain from his voice. "We're starting to get some friction heating on the hull. We should restore our proper flight attitude."

She smiled at his deadpan delivery of that last line. He knew as well as she that she wasn't about to do that with a pair of hostiles on their tail.

"Make a note, Hana," she said, hoping this would sound funny, "we need a way of shooting backward. Ch'ghan," she continued, in a more serious vein, "can you tag the bastards?"

"Negative target acquisition," he growled in frustration. "They are as hard to catch as mercury, even with a ranging laser."

"I want that design," Hana breathed and Nicole nodded. So much for their fond belief that *Swiftstar* was state of the art.

Then, suddenly, "I have tone," Hana cried, "they're locked on us!"

Nicole's hands moved of their own accord, to the bank of throttles on the console between her and Raqella. It was like being bodychecked in pro hockey, as her body was hammered back into her chair, while the main engines went to full thrust. The cabin shook violently and a couple of displays hiccoughed from the systems overload as they tried to keep track of what was happening.

"Jesus Mary and Joseph," she heard bawled in her headset, Dan's voice. There were red flashes all over her panel—she assumed his own dedicated console probably looked much worse—as she once more pushed the *Swiftstar* beyond its operating tolerances.

At the same time, as their speed dropped markedly—and their altitude as well, the sudden, savage deceleration dumping them like a stone into the atmosphere—she swung them through another roll, worse than any roller coaster. Somebody retched but drowning in their own vomit was the least of their worries.

It was Simon, she could tell from the hoarseness of his voice as he called her.

"We're *inverted*!" Upside-down, with the magnificence of the world filling the whole of the canopy, the clear Lexan already taking on a roseate fringe from the rush of air molecules over the hull. The entire fuselage was intended to handle a modicum of reentry heating, but the bulk of the insulation was along the belly. There was no way they could survive the way they were, an opinion emphasized in no uncertain terms by Nicole's flight telltales.

She ignored them.

She had eyes only for the targeting grid on her HUD as the two hostiles, caught unawares by her sudden maneuver, popped past, unable and unwilling to break off their own descent into the atmosphere. They'd lost their chance to fire, she wasn't about to do the same.

The act was simplicity itself. With Nicole at their Six, the hostiles' radar-deflecting configuration didn't matter; they were pumping so much residual heat from their own engines, not to mention what was being generated by the friction of their own reentry, they'd become perfect targets for a heat-seeker.

But the hostiles surprised her. As she fired, the two space-planes split formation, one going into a spinning corkscrew loop that made her gasp—with awe and admiration, both for the pilot nuts enough to try such a maneuver and the vehicle capable of surviving it—while the other increased the velocity of its own descent. Some might argue that it was trying to outrun the missiles, or gambling that they'd burn up before reaching him, but Nicole knew better. One plane was providing too juicy a heat signature for the missiles to ignore, sacrificing itself so its wingman could escape.

It succeeded.

Nicole didn't bother trying to follow the other one down; as the first plane exploded, she rolled the *Swiftstar* right side up, adding a couple of microbursts from the nose thrusters to restore them to proper attitude. That took longer than she liked; the plane was wallowing, the controls unresponsive. She had no idea where they were at this point, somewhere along the way they'd slipped past the Terminator into the Earth's nighttime shadow, denying her any ground points she could use for reference. The inertial plot would tell her eventually, once it unscrambled itself, but she wasn't sure they had the luxury of waiting. If she committed to reentry, there wouldn't be fuel for another orbital insertion; and, she had a suspicion, not much more for cruising about in the atmosphere. Going for the Black would likewise demand all their remaining fuel; if the third bogie—or any others that might have been missed along the way—chose to reenter the fight, they'd be sitting ducks.

"Dan," she called, "fuel stats."

"High or low?"

"High."

"It's dicey, Nicole. We blew off a lot of delta-V and sky, I don't know if we can get them back."

The data flashed on her display and she considered it a long moment. The plane was shuddering as it encountered denser air, but that was no more than they'd experienced on earlier reentries.

"Plot me an insertion window, Raqella," she said. "Let's get back where we belong."

They were ten seconds into the burn, clawing through the transition from hundreds of thousands of feet to miles, Nicole's eyes flicking—nervously, she had to confess—from the fuel bars to the course display, where the *Swiftstar* appeared to be disconcertingly close to the lower edge of their flight path, when Raqella pointed again. Down and to the left.

It was the third hostile, the one that had jumped them from on high. Ch'ghan managed to swing a camera around and bring up a close-in view on the main screen. Nicole wished he hadn't.

It was obvious from the first that the hostile was doomed. Some of the shells had hit home after all. It was in Shadow, its flight crew opting for reentry rather than orbit and realizing too late they'd made a fatal mistake. From the heat signature of the engines, Nicole knew they were trying to echo the *Swiftstar*'s ascent. But they were going too fast. Their passage through the deep atmosphere had enveloped the spaceplane in an articulated teardrop of fire. A window was open on the main display, presenting an infrared view of the vehicle. Across one wing and the fuselage—just aft of the flight deck—was a scattering of hot spots, dull red pinpoints against the darker—cooler—upper surfaces of the hall. Impact points. As Nicole and the others watched, those hot spots grew brighter—red shifting up the scale to white—until at last they became visible to the naked eye on the main display. The shells had cracked the hostile's shielding, and now friction was burning holes right through its skin.

A piece tore off the wing, tumbling away behind as it blazed to brilliant incandescence. The hole on the hull became a tear, reaching back towards the fuel tanks. And then, as all had known it would, the entire wing folded in on itself. In the blink of an eye, the vehicle twisted broadside to its line of flight, tumbling through every dimension for the few terrible seconds it took the tanks to rupture and that awful heat to consume the remaining fuel.

It was an ending a Viking would be proud of.

"For what it's worth," Hana said softly, "I have TDRSS acquisition. Both Sutherland Mission Control and Edwards are back on-line, voice and telemetry."

"Nicole," Dan's voice, "permission to give Simon a hand? I'd like to unseal his helmet. He's a mess."

"Set up the vacuum cleaner first," she told him automatically, only a little bit of her mind concentrating on the job at hand, "I'd like to keep the cabin clean, if possible."

"My sentiments exactly, boss." Hardly a surprise, since nobody wanted to breathe air scattered with floating globs of weightless vomit. "Will comply."

Nicole sensed movement to the side, and looked around to see Hana motion Raqella out of the co-pilot's seat. She took his place, strapping herself in with enough slack so that she could face Nicole. She held out a communications patch cord, one end already plugged into her own suit. Nicole did the same, guaranteeing them a private line.

"You okay?" Hana asked.

"I guess I keep forgetting how good I am at this."

"Ben Ciari said you had that knack. He also said you were one of the best."

"It's not a skill I'm proud of."

"It's saved our lives, Nicole, more than once."

She twisted to look at her friend. "I didn't join the Air Force—or become an astronaut—to kill people."

Hana shrugged. "Sometimes, Ace, desire and destiny, they don't always match up the way we like."

CHAPTER FOUR

*She's tired from her run, and a full belly takes the
edge off her concentration. There are some flat
rocks along the shore, an inviting perch to bask in
the glorious sun, watching its light sparkle off the
nearest pool and off the skin of the glittery shapes
swimming within it. She doesn't mean to doze but
also doesn't believe there's anything at hand to
threaten her.*

They were met at the reception hatch (still archaically called
the "gangway") by a distressingly young-looking—and,
Nicole had to confess, even though she hated the term,
fresh-faced—Lieutenant, Junior Grade.

"Welcome aboard the U.S.S. *Constitution*, ladies and gentlemen," he said proudly as she returned his salute.

He was brand-new, the ship itself was brand-new, they were
of a piece.

As he motioned them toward the exit, Nicole couldn't resist
a backward glance over her shoulder to reassure herself that the
Swiftstar was in good hands. The plane had already been
shackled onto a tow truck and, while she watched, was started
on its short journey off the ramp and towards the hangar bay.
She frowned at the sight of scorch marks along the upper
fuselage, where the skin had taken too much heat while they
were inverted. Their own survival hadn't been guaranteed
during the flight, by any means; their safety margins measured
in a handful of seconds. She wondered if the hull panels would
have to be replaced and made a mental note to swing by for a
chat with the maintenance chief.

She couldn't help a reflexive bounce on the balls of her feet before falling into step behind the Lieutenant, a tiny little stretch to ease the kinks in her muscles as they found themselves once more in gravity. She wanted to roll her back as well; she could already feel a tightening between her shoulder blades as her body belatedly protested the treatment she'd subjected it to during the dogfight, but couldn't think of a discreet way of managing it.

He was giving them the Cook's Tour along the way, pointing out first thing a clear display plate mounted shoulder high on the wall beside the doorway. A spoken request presented a schematic of the giant starship, showing this specific location—in relation to the immediate neighborhood and the ship as a whole—and then directions to any requested destination. The plates were as ubiquitous as they were evidently essential; if the Lieutenant was to be believed, even experienced crew personnel occasionally found themselves lost as they tried to navigate the three-dimensional maze that comprised the starship's innards. Small wonder. Big as the *Constitution* appeared on the outside, that was no comparison to the almost inconceivable amount of usable space within.

Imagine a ball, a gleaming man-made sphere better than a mile in diameter. Not a perfect circle of course, the globe was faceted—shaped and flattened—in all manner of places to accommodate sensor and tracking arrays, launch and recovery platforms, access hatches of every dimension. The Shell—the primary hull—served as shielding; a hundred meters thick to begin with, it was comprised of reinforced steel bonded to asteroidal rock, to form an extraordinarily resilient amalgam, proof against both physical impacts and most significant wavelengths of radiation.

Within was a world.

Level upon spherical level, descending to the heart of the spacecraft, its Baumier Core, the *Constitution* represented the grand experiment in starship design philosophy, the ultimate expression of the doctrine that said "bigger was better." Previous classes of spacecraft had been mission specific: exploratory vessels, combat units, transports, what have you. The *Constitution* was intended as a jack-of-all-those-trades, plus quite a few more—capable of breaking new trails, fighting battles along the way, founding settlements and then supplying them with sufficient means to give them a decent shot at survival. To that end, the intent was to mix its complement of actual crew with dependents to a degree never before attempted by NASA or any of the military services. Which created, ultimately, a fair-sized traveling town in space, with all the benefits of a community-based environment, and all the attendant liabilities.

The first indication of that came when they emerged into one of the main transit corridors to find a couple of young teenagers scrubbing glumly and purposefully away—under the supervision of an appropriately stern Proctor—at a wall they'd evidently "tagged" with spray paint. Nicole and Hana only gave the scene a cursory glance, however; they were more taken aback—to the extent that they both forced themselves to take a long and deliberate pause—by the sight of the road ahead, and behind, curving *down* and away from them.

"Takes a little getting used to," the Lieutenant said so smugly that Nicole was certain he must have been equally freaked himself the first time he turned this particular corner.

Circular floors in and of themselves were no problem for spacers. The arc of Sutherland's torus was far more extreme, as was the carousel of any standard In-System spacecraft; the critical difference came in orientation. On Earth, the sheer bulk of the planet prevented a body from seeing the surface curvature from ground level; to get a decent sense of it required an altitude of better than twenty kilometers. Here, it was disconcertingly evident.

In the artificial environment Nicole was used to, a semblance of gravity was created by rotating a ring about a central hub; the speed of that rotation determined the outwards inertial force with which a body was pushed against the deck. Ideally, one G. In effect, you were standing on what might normally be considered the ceiling, which curved *upward* along the line of rotation. Not so on the starship.

As an operational by-product, the Baumier Drive generated a gravity field all its own, to the extent that designers felt challenged from the start to determine the best means of incorporating that feature into their creations.

Until the Halyan't'a came along, the *Constitution* globe configuration had seemed like the ideal solution.

They'd come aboard just above the ship's "equator," and once they'd made their way to a mainline slidewalk, the Lieutenant led them north, towards what he referred to—being Navy—as the "Bridge." Primary Command was at what had been arbitrarily designated the top of the starship—its own equivalent of the North Pole—with an identical backup installation (SecCom, Secondary Command) at the opposite end.

A quartet of armed Marines stood watch at the main entrance, and carefully checked Nicole's and Hana's IDs—CardEx, plus hand and retina prints, the entire ritual—before passing them through.

It was surprising to Nicole how prosaic everything looked, just like any Main Mission complex on the Moon or Earth itself. In the center of the room were a half-dozen circular step platforms, three meters deep, rising in layers like a cake. Each tier was ringed with consoles, and at the apex of the modest pyramid was a thronelike dais with a high-backed chair and console all its own. On the level immediately below were arrayed four subordinate command stations, each at what Nicole assumed were the cardinal points of the compass.

Dominating the room, in every sense of the word, was an enormous video display, that swept all the way up in a perfect hemisphere from the deck to the peak of the ceiling overhead. At the moment, it projected the view directly outside, the complete one-hundred-eighty-degree sweep that might be visible were one looking outward from the surface—which, Nicole had to remind herself, was the other side of the Shell. The Earth floated majestically in the moderate foreground—still better than a hundred fifty thousand klicks distant—with the celestial starscape beyond.

She couldn't help herself. The sight took her breath away.

"Wow!" Hana breathed.

"Right up there with the real thing," nodded Nicole.

"Actually," Ramsey Sheridan said, making both women start at the sound of his voice, since he'd come up unnoticed behind them, "the technology comes out of a joint venture with Hollywood."

"We're suitably impressed," Hana said, absent her usual tone of jaded irony.

"You should see it from the Throne," Ramsey indicated the Command Console and its attendant chair, "complete with a dedicated holographic HUD."

Nicole didn't say anything. Ever since she was a kid, she'd devoured all there was to consume about the space program, and most especially starships. It was a hunger that had only sharpened after she'd joined the Air Force. She'd studied them in every way possible—books, videos, sessions in Virtual Reality—but none compared to the actuality of *being* here, even if only for a visit.

"I believe, Captain Shea," Sheridan continued, with a smile to voice and face that belied the formality of his phrasing, "you've already made the acquaintance of the *Constitution*'s Commanding Officer." A new figure stepped down off the bottom platform and more clearly into view, as Nicole automatically straightened to attention. "Nicole Shea, may I present Captain William Hobby, United States Navy."

"Sir," she said, taking frantic refuge in the proprieties.

He took his cue from her and returned her salute in kind, as crisply as if they'd both been on the Annapolis parade ground, and then gave way to a smile that matched Sheridan's. He held out his hand.

"Welcome aboard, Captain. And you as well, Dr. Murai."

He indicated a nearby doorway.

"If you'll both follow me, we'll get this show on the proverbial road."

The two women exchanged a quick look of puzzlement as they made their way past another couple of sentries and into a two-room suite that functioned as the Captain's Alert Facility—so he'd have somewhere to catch some sack time while remaining immediately accessible in any emergency.

Judith Canfield was waiting.

The General waved them all to seats around the circular table. There was a Marine officer by the door. At a nod from her, he stepped smartly over the threshold and cycled the hatch shut. A status light on the display plane embedded in the table told Canfield that the room was secure against both intruders and eavesdroppers.

As the two women settled into their chairs, one of the walls blinked to life with a myriad of displays that mixed multiple video records of the *Swiftstar* dogfight with schematic telemetry.

"I guess we weren't as out of touch as we thought," Hana commented.

"Totally, as a matter of fact," said Canfield. "Whatever the hostiles used to take you off the air was entirely too successful, so much so that we still haven't been able to isolate the cause."

"Hana hypothesized a virus, designed to disable the communications software," Nicole said.

"We're leaning in that direction ourselves," Canfield agreed, "but the bloody thing hasn't left a footprint we can tag."

Nicole felt the tap of a fingertip faintly against one of her hands where it rested on the table, flicked her eyes sideways to be met by Hana's. Her friend mouthed the word "Cobri," but Nicole only shrugged, accepting the judgment without agreeing with it.

On the main screen, the display had cycled back to the beginning of the dogfight. Sheridan and Bill Hobby stood close by, Ramsey echoing the maneuvers on the screen with his hands, Hobby shaking his head as they watched the *Swiftstar* roll over onto its back.

"My heart liked to stop when I saw that live, Ms. Shea," Hobby said.

"Mine, too," Hana deadpanned, prompting an appreciative chuckle from the Captain.

"Ah, Nicole," sighed Sheridan with exaggerated patience, "what is it with you and new toys? The minute we put you in the air, somebody tries to blow you to bits."

"Is that a serious question, Colonel?"

"Let's hope not," interrupted Canfield, calling the meeting to order in no uncertain terms, "since the *Constitution* is a considerably more valuable asset than all of Captain Shea's previous assigned vehicles combined."

"I beg your pardon," Nicole asked, feeling an absurd sense of déjà vu, to the moment—years gone now—when she sat in the Oak Room, the best restaurant on Luna, listening to Canfield tell her she was getting her first Ride.

Canfield slid two packets along the table, one for Hana, the other for Nicole.

"Effective immediately," the General continued, "you are both assigned to the crew of the United States StarShip *Constitution* for the duration of its current mission tour."

"Why?" Nicole asked, before she could stop herself.

"A number of reasons," was Canfield's reply, as though the question had come from a peer and not a substantially junior officer. "For one, to get you 'out of town.'" She tapped commands into her computer pad and a window opened in the main display, presenting an overhead still photograph of the pursuit craft that had flamed in the atmosphere.

"Nobody on my staff, nobody we've queried among the various spookshows, nobody on the Hal embassy, has ever seen anything like that."

"Forgive me, General," Hana interjected, "but not a chance."

"Quite so. Somebody's lying. My people, I think I can vouch for, although nothing is absolutely certain in life, least of all loyalty. Can't say the same for any of the Terrestrial intelligence services or, for that matter, the Hal. Clearly, though, we're up against an opposition with considerable resources—both of matériel and information and, I suspect to no small measure, influence.

"Those ships didn't just magically pop into being. They had to be designed and built, pilots had to be trained, the intercept had to be rehearsed. To do all that and maintain absolute secrecy betokens a force to be reckoned with. Dedicated, it appears, to driving a wedge between humanity and the Hal."

"Is that possible?" Sheridan asked.

"Yes." Canfield paused a moment to let the implications sink in, then continued. "Nicole, for various reasons, serves as a flashpoint for these anti-Hal sympathizers. I for one would prefer to see her taken off the bull's-eye for a while. Also, that dovetails neatly with our need for ongoing trials on the *Swiftstar*. Nicole is Project Manager, it's only logical she oversee the field evaluations.

"And there's a third reason—in my estimation, a compelling one—which you, Bill, as Commanding Officer, need to know." Hobby didn't move much in his chair—to the casual eye he looked as relaxed as ever—but Nicole sensed the line of tension along his body as he came fully alert.

"It was recently brought to my attention"—and Nicole couldn't help but think of their conversation on her boat—"that none of the surviving personnel of the *Wanderer* flight crew— save for Marshal Ciari—have been posted to interstellar duty, even though all three are eminently qualified and Dr. Murai for one has repeatedly requested it. Dr. Zhimyanov chooses to stay close to home for personal reasons. Captain Shea and Dr. Murai were removed from the assignment pool, by Executive order."

"Does the White House know you're doing this?" Ramsey asked.

Canfield slid another, thicker envelope across the table to Hobby.

"That's a complete dossier of my observations, assessments, assumptions, conclusions," she said. "To be opened once you've cleared the system. Quite frankly, I'm not at all sure *what* the Hell is going on; this is sort of an ad hoc attempt to shake the tree a little and find out.

"The coalition—the consensus—in support of the Alliance is very fragile, on both sides. It's early days in our relationship, yet because of the nature of the times and our technology we're rushing headlong into a future we have to take substantially on faith.

"Make no mistake, I believe in the Alliance. Like President Russell, I want it to succeed with all my heart; I think that's imperative for the survival and prosperity of both worlds. But I am also, and foremost, a serving flag officer in the United States Air Force, sworn to preserve and defend my homeland—and by extension my homeworld—if need be with my life. I want to know what's out there, Bill, good *and* bad. We know what the Hal have committed to Treaty. I want you—and Nicole and Hana—to tell me what's in their hearts."

"So we'll have Hal among the crew as well," Hobby said flatly, making no bones about how little he liked the idea.

"Ch'ghan and Raqella are integral to the *Swiftstar* project," Canfield countered, brooking no argument, "we haven't even a prayer of answers—to a whole host of questions—without them."

"Your people, Ms. Shea," Hobby told Nicole, "your responsibility."

"Yes, sir."

"Won't this be fun," Hana muttered under her breath, for Nicole's ears only.

"You'll love every minute," was the equally muted retort. But Nicole's mind wasn't on the exchange. She was staring across the table at the main display, still running the intercept on a perpetual loop, her eyes on the surviving plane as it corkscrewed back to the safety of the deep atmosphere, fading from sight with disturbing speed despite the best efforts of the high-resolution scanners to keep it in frame.

"Do you want the pilot's ass, or a shot at flying the plane?" Hana asked her.

Nicole smiled. "Can't I have both?"

"Is he good?"

"He's okay. It's the plane that makes the difference. High-thrust, low mass, configured for combat maneuvering across the full spectrum of the operational envelope."

"What are you thinking?"

"It's where our own design philosophy might have gone if the Cold War relationships had lasted."

"How so?"

"When the Soviet Union collapsed, so did the cutting-edge technological threat. Conceivably, an ongoing Washington-Moscow military rivalry could have pushed the potential theater of confrontation over the top of the atmosphere; we'd need vehicles that could actually *fight* in near-Earth space."

"What, you figure this is an attempt to start the same kind of rivalry between us and the Hal?"

Nicole shrugged.

"You keep looking at the video, Nicole," Canfield noted from her chair. "See anything we may have missed?"

A shake of the head, not so much a demurral really as an attempt to order her thoughts. "It's the structure of the attack," she said finally. "I can't put a finger on it, but . . . I dunno, I guess it looks familiar. Feels familiar. But from nowhere I remember."

The ComPlate inset in the table before Canfield beeped imperatively. The display was angled—and the surface of the table itself glossed—so that no one but Canfield could see who was calling. It was clear, though, from the set of her mouth that she wasn't thrilled. She nodded her head, and a few seconds later, the doorway hissed open.

Nicole heard a gasp from Hana, but she herself wasn't at all surprised when Amy Cobri strode in as though she owned the place.

Considering her father's company had built the *Constitution* and could buy it, fully equipped and crewed, without suffering more than a minor and transitory financial strain, the kid probably had some justification.

Hobby didn't bother masking his own reaction to her arrival. With a curt nod to Canfield, he excused himself and strode out to the Bridge, to find out no doubt who'd allowed Amy aboard and why he hadn't been notified the moment she'd arrived. It didn't help his mood that the alert call had gone to Canfield instead of him; she may be Director of Manned Space Flight and C-in-C Space Command, but this was *his* ship. He clearly didn't like having his place usurped, as much, Nicole could see, as Amy enjoyed doing it.

"It's my understanding," Amy said without preamble, taking a seat opposite Canfield as though they were the only two present, "that Captain Shea is about to undergo a major duty reassignment."

Canfield didn't bat an eye, but the announcement brought Ramsey Sheridan straight up in his chair. On the corner of her vision, Nicole saw Hana react much the same way.

Canfield said nothing, which Amy decided to take as confirmation. She'd dressed corporate for the meeting, in a knee-length designer suit, with elegant gold earrings and a necklace of asteroidal crystal that Nicole knew cost more than the General earned in a year. Her hair was pulled back in a sweeping chignon intended to give her an air of maturity, but it really wasn't needed. Even as a girl, when Nicole had first known her, she'd carried herself with an air of personal *gravitas* that compelled those around her to pay attention. Over the years, that natural talent had been shaped and honed to the point where Nicole couldn't help thinking—sadly—that Amy had very much become her father's child.

"Under the circumstances," Amy went on, "I can't think of a more devastating course of action."

"To who?" Hana growled. Amy ignored her.

"My personnel," Canfield replied easily. "My prerogative. My decision."

"I've come to ask you to reconsider."

Now Nicole cocked an eyebrow, very much impressed. The Amy she remembered would have gone ballistic, thumping the table with her demands. But Nicole also knew that couching her desire as a request was merely a convention; Amy fully expected to get her own way. She invariably did.

Again, Canfield said nothing, leaving the ball in the young woman's court. Amy fielded it without missing a beat, raising Nicole's estimation of her a notch higher.

"The *Lamplighter* Project has moved from a theoretical to a practical stage," she said. "Captain Shea's participation, as you well know from the briefing caches we've submitted, is essential to the project's viability. In effect, without her there *is* no project. Yet, at this critical juncture, when she's needed most at home, you propose to send her haring off across the galaxy."

"What the hell are they talking about?" Hana demanded sotto voice in Nicole's ear, but only got a terse shake of the head for an answer. Nicole hadn't a clue and didn't like it. The expression on her face hadn't changed but Ramsey, who could see her straight on, as could Amy, spotted something in Nicole's eyes that prompted him to try to relay a warning to his boss.

"I was assured," Canfield said icily, "that an alternative would be found."

"I was wrong."

"That is unacceptable."

Amy flumped back in her chair, body collapsing into a boneless slouch that totally undermined all her attempts to look and act grown-up—so totally teenage a gesture that Nicole, despite her growing fury, couldn't help a sniff of amusement.

"Tough," Amy said, flinging her hands into the air in a dismissive gesture. "What d'you want from me, anyway? I know Nicole and I have a history, okay? What happened, happened."

The girl pushed herself up again, flinching neither from

Canfield's basilisk glare nor Nicole's, almost as though daring them both to strike out at her, just to prove she could take the hit.

"I'm not exactly zipped at the turn of events either, okay? But *I* have put too much time and sweat into *Lamplighter* to simply flush it because of someone else's attitude."

"Hardly that, Ms. Cobri."

"I have a green light, okay?" Amy was out of patience and didn't bother hiding the fact, the offhand delivery of her line casual notification that the gloves were off, and all pretenses dropped. She'd walked through the door knowing the outcome. "From DARPA and NASA both, signed off on by the White House."

She plucked a thin business envelope from an inside pocket of her jacket and slid it across the table. The letter barely made it halfway and Nicole reached out, taking a fast glance at the Executive monogram in the corner and the heavy wax seal on the back before handing it to Hana, who passed it on to Canfield.

"I need Nicole on Earth," Amy said, throwing down her gauntlet. "By rights Nicole shouldn't even have flown the *Swiftstar* test. She's too valuable a commodity; the moment you had word of any threat, she should have been replaced."

Hana leaned close by Nicole's ear. "Nice of Her Highness to care," she whispered, "or is it simply a guilty conscience?"

"If it's not too much to ask," Nicole broke in, ever so softly, "what exactly are we talking about here?"

Canfield didn't give Amy the chance to answer as she pressed the letter flat on the table. "This is indeed an unqualified statement of support," she said. "Which affirms your statement of Captain Shea's value to the project. However, her actual assignment to *Lamplighter*—which, I point out, in no way guarantees her cooperation—is at my discretion."

"That's not what it says!"

"It's how I choose to interpret it. I think you'll find the specific phrasing sufficiently ambiguous to allow me that latitude."

"Fine. I'll come back with an order that can't be questioned."

"The *Constitution*'s already on the flight board. By the time you dock at Sutherland, much less return to Earth's surface, she'll be on her way. And unfortunately, people these days travel far faster than radio waves. You might persuade the Executive to launch a pursuit cutter to try to catch up, but I suspect the bureaucratic consensus will be to simply wait 'til Captain Shea returns home. And cross your fingers, of course, that she does so safely."

"You can't do this. She's not supposed to go *anywhere!*"

The room got very still. Nicole noticed that Hobby had returned, but was staying back by the door, out of immediate notice.

"And how is it, young lady," Canfield said softly, "you know that?"

"We're Cobris, we have sources."

"Captain Shea," Canfield said, in a voice that had gotten not a whit louder but which carried an air of implacable command, "would you and Dr. Murai excuse us a moment? Colonel Sheridan, Captain Hobby, if you please?"

It was the last thing Nicole wanted, far too much was being left unsaid and she didn't at all like the turn the meeting had suddenly taken. But Canfield was just as clearly in no mood for argument. So Nicole took her cue from the two men and strode towards the doorway without even a glance at Amy.

Outside, she watched as both doors cycled shut and a couple of armed Marines stepped into place, while the display panel obligingly informed them that the room was fully screened from all forms of external monitoring.

"What the hell is this all about?" Hobby wondered.

Hana, characteristically, took the low road response. "Maybe we'll get lucky, and Canfield'll rip the little bitch's heart out. Or better yet"—her grin widened at the images—"the poor dear might slip on a conveniently wet patch of deck. Oops, she hit her head on the table, what a terrible accident, how tragic that a life of such youth and promise gets so suddenly cut short, tough break."

Ramsey couldn't help a snort of laughter, made worse because he was sipping coffee at the time. While he tried to keep from choking, an orderly offered Nicole a mug. To her surprise, it was tea, brewed the way she liked best.

"Any ideas, Captain?" Hobby asked.

"I wish, sir. This is a new one to me."

"There've been a fair share of rumors about *Lamplighter* the past year or so," Ramsey said. "Very 'black' project, very esoteric, totally off the books. No mainstream, public sector funding as I recall, pretty much a private, in-house operation, and a sidebar one at that. The scuttlebutt consensus was that it was something Amy was doing to amuse herself. That's why nobody paid much attention."

"How come you know so much, Ramsey?"

Sheridan shrugged, "Cobris ain't the only folks with sources, Bill."

"What d'you figure's going on in there, Colonel?"

"For truth, Nicole? Hana's fervent yearnings notwithstanding, I suspect the boss is cutting a deal."

"If the kid gets her way," Nicole said, with an implacable strength to her voice that was eerily reminiscent of Canfield, "the minute I set foot on the ground, her precious *Lamplighter*'s dust. I'll resign my commission before I become a part of it."

"Relax, Nicole," Sheridan told her gently. "You box yourself away from your options, you'll find yourself with no choice but to go nuclear. Is that what you want?"

"What I want, Colonel, is that family out of my face."

"I'm afraid, Captain," Canfield said from the doorway, which had cycled open unnoticed behind them, "in that regard, you're somewhat doomed to disappointment."

Amy was with her, but the young girl didn't look especially triumphant. There was an eerie mingling of child and woman, and a haunted shadow to her countenance that reminded Nicole of what she occasionally saw reflected in her own. Any other time, she'd have felt sorry for the girl; today, she couldn't care less. The more misery, the better.

"Captain Shea flies this mission, that's final. Yet Ms. Cobri is equally adamant about proceeding apace with *Lamplighter*. After exploring various options, we believe we have arrived at a mutually acceptable solution. She'll continue working on the project aboard *Constitution*. You'll have a full list of her requirements before departure, Captain."

"Do I have a say in this, General?" Hobby asked, before Nicole could ask the same question, in a far less rational tone of voice. Her temper was flaring like a solar storm and it took an effort to hold on.

Canfield allowed herself a small sigh. "If you insist, Bill." Clearly, she'd rather he didn't. And he got the message. Nicole sensed the same restriction applied to her, and followed the Captain's lead, even though what she really wanted to do was scream, or better yet punch Amy's lights out.

"Ramsey," Canfield said, "I have a job for you."

"You had that look, boss. This is a good news/bad news joke, am I right?"

His tone was light and bantering, intended to ease the mood. Only Canfield smiled in response and that was a tiny one.

"I want you to oversee *Lamplighter* as Project Manager. You have authority over all phases of the operation. You review everything. Your decision's final." She looked to Amy. "Those terms are non-negotiable."

Amy nodded. Nicole knew she figured that when the time came she'd find a way around the restrictions and Ramsey.

"I didn't pack," Ramsey said to Hobby.

"We'll find you something, ol' buddy, not to worry."

"You'd better explain this to my wife, boss."

Now, Canfield permitted herself a genuine smile. "Your wife, Ramsey, the President, and Emmanuel Cobri. All things considered, gentlemen and ladies, I think I'd much rather be flying with you. Godspeed, Bill," she said, holding out her hand. Her parting words were ostensibly for them all, but when she spoke she looked straight at Nicole.

"Come home soon, and safe."

CHAPTER FIVE

The touch of water changes that assumption. She comes instantly awake, fighting the drowsy residue of her nap as she takes stock of scene and situation. Both are dire. When she came to the beach, there was land in every direction; now, it's mostly water. Even as she looks around, a fresh wave sends its upflow swirling over her rock, covering her to her ankles. The backwater leaves the rock exposed, but she knows that won't last much longer. She leaps shoreward, and finds herself immersed almost to her belly. Each surge pushes her inland, but it also lifts her feet from the ground, leaving her floundering helplessly to keep her head above water and make further progress. Worse, the outflow wipes away any gain. And the longer this takes, the deeper the water grows about her. Her eyes open wide, with exertion and an atavistic terror she defiantly refuses to acknowledge, and she redoubles her efforts, with the same fierce, indomitable determination that allowed her to stand up to the family Elders.

"What'll you need, young lady?" Hobby asked Amy as Sheridan and Canfield stepped out of earshot and Nicole simply glared—at the ceiling and the stars, at the people around her, anywhere but towards Amy Cobri. "Can your equipment be transshipped up from Earth?"

Amy grinned personably, as deliberate and calculated a response as Hobby's choice of words. She could charm with the best if that helped her get her own way. She didn't mind if people knew what she was doing, either, it made the challenge that much more delicious.

"Isn't any, Captain, not in the sense you mean. I can facsimile what hardware I need from your own stores. The key to *Lamplighter* is the design schematics and the software. Those, I carry with me. As far as I'm concerned, you can rock and roll when you like."

Hobby turned quickly to Canfield.

"In that case, General," he said, "I'd like to launch through our original window."

She nodded.

"Approved, Captain. Light up the Runway as soon as my shuttle's clear."

"Thank you, sir."

Canfield stepped close to Nicole, and the others obligingly shifted away to give them some privacy. Nicole wanted to go herself, but there were some things Captains simply did not do to full Generals, regardless of the perceived provocation.

"This isn't what I wanted," Canfield began softly. "Quite."

"I've no reason to complain, sir. I'm getting my Ride."

"For a whole host of reasons, Nicole"—fractional pause, acting as a bridge for Canfield's thoughts and a break between them—"I wish I were going with you."

Nicole paused herself before answering, letting her gaze roam the room, almost as though she were the one about to take her leave, trying desperately to imprint the scene on her memory.

"Actually," she conceded, a little surprised with herself at how she felt, "so do I."

"Bill Hobby's a good man and a good Commander."

"Don't doubt it. Was that what the poker game was all about?"

"More to do with the *Swiftstar* test, actually. You have a certain . . . reputation. And this is Bill's ship. He'd read the reports, he wanted to see for himself what kind of officer he'd be dealing with before making a final decision."

"That was only for a visit. Now he's stuck with me."

Canfield nodded.

"I don't blame him for being gun-shy," Nicole continued, "it's how I feel. The Air Force teaches you how to play well with others, General, but not this many. I mean, *Wanderer* had a crew of seven, and since I've been at Edwards, I've worked pretty much on my own. It won't be like that here."

"No, it won't. If you're that concerned, Captain, come with me. You have that option up to the moment I leave."

Nicole faced her. "You don't think I can hack this?"

"If I didn't, you wouldn't be here. But I've always respected *your* judgment, Nicole. You accepted being grounded because you knew the Medical Evaluations Board was right; at that time, you were unfit for astronaut's flight status. Afterward, though, when you'd won back your wings, you never pushed as hard as you could have for a starship assignment. You asked, but you didn't seem to mind being turned down. I had to wonder about that."

"I guess I was . . . comfortable where I was."

"I have no use for comfortable officers, Captain. Nor for those who are afraid of their own potential."

Nicole matched Canfield's hawklike glare with one of her own.

"I'll send you a postcard, sir."

A twitch at the corner of Canfield's mouth that may have been a smile was echoed by an even slighter one from Nicole.

"You do that," Canfield told her. There was a nod, and a shift in expression around the eyes, and Nicole knew that if they'd been alone, the General would have embraced her. Then, Canfield turned on her heel, took formal leave of Hobby and his staff, and was gone, with Ramsey Sheridan hustling along behind as she gave him the last of his marching orders.

"Nicole!" It was Amy. Before Nicole could respond—when what she wanted most to do was ignore the girl—Captain Hobby demanded her attention.

"Ms. Shea," he said with a slight turn towards Amy to forestall any protest at the interruption. "If you'll go with Lieutenant Braeden, Ms. Cobri"—he indicated the JayGee who'd escorted Nicole from reception—"he'll see you settled in your quarters."

Amy had other ideas, but Braeden took his cue from Hobby and put himself between her and the Captain. She couldn't object without staging a scene and decided instantly to let this pass.

"Interesting girl," Hobby mused, watching her go.

"You got *no* idea," growled Hana.

"It's a big ship, Dr. Murai, and a bigger service," he said, "but ultimately we're all part of a surprisingly small community."

Hana shot a glance to Nicole, wondering if he was fishing for information or telling them he already knew, but got no response. This was Hobby's turf—in effect, Hobby's game—Nicole would leave the active gambits to him.

"Lot more ship and people than I've ever been a part of," Nicole said, halfway musing, "sir."

"They'll take some getting used to, true. But that's what we do in space, yes? Adapt. NASA is a combined service—in this case, a crew that comprises not simply the entire spectrum of the American military but of over a dozen other countries as well. Plus civilians. To avoid confusion, we arbitrarily operate under a specific organizational hierarchy."

"Naval?"

"Precisely. Tradition dictates there be only one Captain. So, for the duration of your term aboard, you'll hold a temporary increase in grade to Major. All of the authority and responsibility"—he grinned suddenly—"but none of the pay."

"Doesn't seem quite fair."

"What's the old saying, Dr. Murai, 'TANJ'?"

"'There ain't no justice.' Typical military mentality."

"My self-appointed mouthpiece notwithstanding, sir," Nicole said, "I have no objection."

"Didn't think so, Major."

Nicole couldn't help herself, she liked the sound of the new rank.

Hobby held out a hand, and a small jewelry box, for Nicole. Inside were a pair of gold oak leaves.

"The rest you can get from Stores," he told her, "but these should get you off to a good start."

"Were they yours, sir?"

"No." He smiled, his expression shadowed, as though touched by a surprise memory. "But they have a history. I hope you do well by them."

"I'll do my best, sir. Thank you."

Hobby turned towards the pyramid and called to the Officer of the Deck.

"Mr. Rossmore, status?"

The Commander bent over his console, scrolled through its main sequence displays, spoke into his boom microphone.

"PreLaunch Checklist in progress, Captain," he said when he'd seen and heard what he needed to know. "Telemetry nominal, flight systems green across the board. Ramp reports that General Canfield and party are aboard and her vehicle is cycling for lift-off."

"Thank you." His attention returned to Nicole. "I want you in SecCom when we light up the Runway. You're familiar with the procedures?"

"Fully rated, sir." *But—Mary Mother of God,* she thought desperately, *only in a bloody simulator!*

"You'll be running a parallel checklist, monitoring the Bridge. You'll have no active linkage with the C^3 systems unless we go off-line but you're expected to yell blue murder if you spot a glitch."

"I understand, sir."

"Then what are you waiting for, Major? We don't go without you giving us the green light."

Nicole and Hana were assigned a Marine to show them the way. The Sergeant set a brisk pace and even Nicole's long legs felt the beginnings of a burn as she hurried to keep up.

"Wouldn't it be easier cutting straight across the globe," Hana wondered aloud as they made their way along the main corridor, "than going all the way around like this?"

"In distance, probably so, ma'am," the Sergeant replied, the cadence of her words as sharply clipped as those of her feet, "but a lot more effort."

"Think about it, Hana," Nicole said, a trifle daunted herself by the realization. "Climbing down a half-mile flight of stairs, then climbing up."

"They don't got elevators, they don't got slidewalks?"

"We do indeed," the Marine told them, "but they get jammed up more often than the skipper likes. And new crew, he prefers they learn to find their way around on their feet. Like that test the London taxi drivers take, y'know . . . ?"

"The 'Knowledge,'" Hana said.

"Is that what they call it? Well, same difference, I guess. If all you know are the lifts and rollers, and the Directory FlashMaps, how you gonna cope when the system crashes?"

"The system crashes?"

"Not for real, not yet. But the skipper, he does love to pop his drills. This bucket's his, ma'am, heart and soul, but I don't think he'll ever be comfortable aboard her. Too many conflicting elements—y'know, dependents and the like. Add the fact that we're the first ship of a new class, with all the attendant teething troubles. Add your 'Fuzzies.'"

"I don't like that term, Sergeant," Nicole said casually, but with a ghost of frost that let the Marine know she was utterly serious.

"Meant no disrespect, Major. We're jarheads an' proud of it, we got insults for everybody."

"Among your own, that's your business. Just use some discretion elsewhere."

"Aye-aye, sir."

"You ever serve with a Hal, Sergeant?"

"Never *seen* one, sir, except in pictures."

"They're very proud and their sense of humor isn't at all like ours."

The Marine stopped and faced them. Nicole kept her face expressionless but she was grateful for the break. She hadn't been marched so fast since the Academy.

"Is the Major suggesting that we establish some ground rules, the Hal and us, before we get to raggin' on 'em?"

"They give as good as they get, Sergeant. I understand about learning that the hard way. Just be careful nobody gets hurt."

"Captain Hobby wouldn't like that at all."

"Goes without saying. Nor me, neither."

The Sergeant spared Nicole a long look, then straightened to attention and snapped a parade ground salute.

"Understood, Major. This is SecCom, sir, we've arrived."

They were expected—Nicole suspected their progress had been monitored the whole way and wondered if the surveillance had included their conversation as well—but they still had to submit to the full security regime before being admitted through the massive airlock.

The two chambers—Primary and Secondary Command—

were twins, from the vaulting display overhead to the layout of the consoles. Nicole spared a quick glance at the "sky" when they entered; the stars were different, the view that which you'd see from a true world's South Pole rather than a replication of what was being screened up-top. All the stations, she noticed, were occupied. As she and Hana approached the pyramid, a bluff-bodied figure—shorter and much stockier than the two women, especially clad as he was in an armored suit— descended to greet them. Emblazoned on the biceps, right below the national flag, were the two and a half stripes of a Lieutenant Commander, the naval equivalent of Nicole's new rank.

"Welcome to the back brain of the dinosaur," he announced cheerily. "I'm Tom Pasqua."

"Nicole Shea," she replied, in kind. He had a firm grip. Hana introduced herself and Pasqua waved them up the steps to the Throne.

"What's with?" Hana asked, about the suit, while Nicole noted that the personnel seated at the four Second Tier consoles, a step below the Throne, were in fully sealed pressure suits.

"Never can tell what'll work and what won't," Pasqua replied, "hope for the one, prepare for the other. Can't assume there'll be time to jump into one of these if we have a catastrophic event."

"But not everyone here's wearing a suit."

Pasqua shrugged—or at least tried to, as much as his armor would allow. "Wouldn't be practicable, for operating the consoles or wear and tear on the gear. A cadre in Damage Control stands each watch in full suits; during major maneuvering, we expand that to the Systems Managers here in SecCom. By rights, Major, you sit the Throne, you wear what I'm wearing. This time, I'm here to cover, just in case."

"And I thought *Wanderer* was a beast," Hana muttered.

Pasqua laughed. "No comparison, Dr. Murai."

"I'm Hana."

"Tom." He looked over to Nicole. "Got to sit sometime, Major . . ."

"Nicole."

"Nicole, then. Especially when you're keeping the skipper waiting."

She shook her hands, to snap some tension out of them, then took the proffered chair.

It was comfortable, and got more so almost immediately, as its sensors shaped the bellows cushions to the contours of her back.

"This is very nice," she couldn't help noticing, buckling the four-point restraint across her torso.

"Considering how long some folks have to sit there, and what they have to do, creature comforts are an absolute necessity. If it feels a little big on the flanks, remember that's because it's also intended to accommodate someone dressed like me. Lay your arms on the side panels, would you, where they'd naturally fall."

Nicole did so, and the chair continued to adjust itself to her, sliding the control pads along their track until they rested under her fingers.

"Satisfied?" Pasqua asked, a couple of minutes later, after completing the last series of adjustments.

"Pretty much perfect."

"Not quite. You'll need to make modifications, we all do, but that comes through usage and experience. You can swing the chair two ways, either manually"—which Nicole did, by a light touch on the appropriate toggle—"or automatically, which is to say the chair will orient itself towards whatever you're looking at. Better take a couple of steps back, Dr. Murai," he cautioned, and Hana followed his suggestion, "the ride on auto can be a little wild, until you get used to it."

Nicole wasn't sure what he meant until, at Pasqua's suggestion, she looked towards her friend. Immediately the chair spun right to match her line of sight. She looked up at the ceiling, and the chair tilted and flattened obediently to make that easier for her. None of this happened at any ferocious speed, for which she was thankful, and she suspected that was solely for her benefit.

"Anyone ever get sick doing this?"

"Sooner or later, everybody."

"I wondered about those bags clipped to the side, plain old-fashioned barf buckets, who woulda thought?"

"Your turn will come, Hana," grumped Nicole.

"What we'll do now," Pasqua said to close out the briefing, "is imprint the configuration in the chair's memory and in the ship's main data nexus; that way, every time you come on watch, this'll be ready and waiting for you.

"*Constitution,* Pasqua," he called, pressing the com switch amid the bank of controls imbedded in the left forearm of his suit.

Nicole didn't hear any reply but there must have been one because Pasqua pointed at her.

"Headset," he said.

She tucked the earphone in her left ear and plugged the jack into the chair.

"State your name, please," she heard the ship's neutral, vaguely female computer-generated voice tell her. "Family name, first." This, she knew, was to establish a baseline record of her voiceprint.

"Shea, Nicole."

"Service and status, please."

"United States Air Force, Space Command, brevet Major, on assignment to the United States StarShip *Constitution.*"

"State personal security password, please."

She spoke without thinking, letting instinct dictate the answer.

"Sundowner."

"Access code approved. Access to C^3 nexus approved. Network coming on-line."

She couldn't help a gasp of astonishment, mingled with outright surprise, as a glittering holographic HUD field popped into being right in front of her. It was starting from scratch, a basis systems boot, and she had to suffer through the display of its pedigree, hard- and software, before finally being released to the main menu.

"Very nice," she heard Hana murmur from over her right shoulder. A glance backward showed her friend leaning on the chair. Pasqua flanked her on the other side, standing near the edge of the dais. He'd donned gloves and helmet, life support courtesy of a ROVER backpack. There was a yelp of surprise from both women as the chair began to swing, Hana jumping back almost to the safety rail like a startled cat.

"Shit, oh, *shit!*" Nicole tapped the selector back to Manual, then asked Hana, "You okay?"

Hana looked down at herself, to see the HUD splayed around and across her midsection, then back to Nicole as she deadpanned, "Shall I move?"

"Allow me," Nicole said with a weak grin, and pivoted the chair clear. She couldn't see Pasqua's face behind his visor and for that she was supremely glad, even though she was sure the story was already making the rounds. *Probably laughing themselves sick up in PriCom,* she told herself, *not to mention wondering what the Captain could be thinking of giving me this chair.*

"One of the benefits of the Alliance," Pasqua said over the radio, as though nothing untoward had happened. "The Hal are a generation or more ahead of us in optical technology, especially holographic imaging."

"Our stardrive's better." Hana, for Nicole's ears alone.

"More powerful," Nicole agreed, without transmitting back to Pasqua, keeping this exchange private, "but I'm not sure we're as good with secondary applications."

"Hey, cut the Race some slack, Shea! I mean, we've only had the damn thing for less than half a century."

"Bugger that, Murai. A half century after Kitty Hawk"—and the legendary first powered flight of the Wright Brothers—"we'd broken the sound barrier and were on our way to the Moon."

"On your toes, Ace, your HUD's blinking."

It was a small red bar, at the bottom of the display, alerting Nicole to an incoming call. She opened the channel.

"SecCom, Bridge." It was Commander Rossmore and he didn't sound the type who liked to be kept waiting.

"SecCom, acknowledged," Nicole replied.

"We show you on-line, Major, any reason for the continued delay?"

"Just sorting through my systems, sir."

"We don't have an unlimited window, Major."

"Understood, Commander. If you'll give me a moment, we'll be ready."

"We'll be waiting."

"Not a happy camper," from Hana, a comment which Nicole didn't need right now, or much care for.

"Tom," she called, clearing a parallel line to him, "how do I address the ship?"

"By her name, of course."

Of course, Nicole thought sourly. Nothing like missing the obvious, even if she wasn't used to ships that talked back.

"*Constitution,* SecCom," she said formally.

"State access code, please."

"*Sundowner.*"

"Acknowledged, *Sundowner.*"

"Display launch sequence main menu on my station, and light up the Runway."

"There is insufficient graphics capability at your station to comply with your second request, *Sundowner.* The Runway can only be presented on the main overhead display."

Nicole closed her eyes and sighed—frustration mingled with a pinch of anger at herself for once more missing the obvious, forgetting what she already knew.

"Slave-link SecCom main display to the Bridge, please, and light up the Runway."

"Compliance."

It was like watching magic. Before their eyes, the stars came down off the ceiling to float in midair, aligned about the images of the Sun, the Earth and Moon, and the *Constitution* herself. The details appeared perfect: off in the distance, the Sun formed a bubbling globe of raw fire, casting prominences off its surface with wild abandon, while in stark and absolute contrast, the Earth's dayside glowed a cool and glorious blue against the darkness. The Moon was in opposition from Nicole's perspective, masked from sight by the bulk of its mother planet. The *Constitution* was closest to her, the false perspective of the display making the ship appear as large to Nicole as the planet and star beyond. A few inches out from the surface, and moving farther every moment, was Canfield's cruiser, identity confirmed by a floating data window right beside it.

She felt the beginnings of a smile tweak the outer edges of her mouth and gently thumbed the control toggle, rotating the orientation of the display—prompting a cry of pure delight from Hana behind her—to bring the Sun around until it was floating right overhead, just beyond her reach. It was the size of a beach ball, about half a meter in diameter, and for a long few seconds all Nicole could do was stare in wonderment. She'd worked with holographic displays her whole career— most initial training these days was run through Virtual Reality—but somehow, and very much to her surprise, this moment had a quality to it she'd only felt once before, when she and her *Wanderer* crew boarded the Hal StarShip *Range Guide*.

A magnificent prominence exploded from the surface, a curling whip of fire that in reality was climbing better than a hundred thousand miles from the solar surface. Here, it merely flicked the air a hairbreadth beyond Nicole's nose. The flare was so sudden, so fast, so close, Nicole couldn't help jumping in her chair, but at least she managed to stifle any outcry.

"Wow," she said simply, mostly to herself, forgetting that her microphone was picking up her every word.

"State of the art," agreed Pasqua, "and then some."

"Are these the only two outlets for the system?" asked Hana, who sounded equally chagrined at how easily and completely she'd been entranced.

"On this scale, I'm afraid so. There are smaller imaging chambers scattered about the ship, but they can't match this for sheer impressiveness. The other drawback is that imaging— especially these LiveTime displays—eats a tremendous volume of computing power. That's why the system has its own dedicated sensor and cybernetics array."

Nicole restored the scene to its default perspective. A second window had opened on her HUD, listing the navigational waypoints of their outbound course. In the air above her, following the computer's dictates now, the display compressed as an arrow of light speared up and away from the *Constitution* and the Solar System, indicating their initial departure vector. When the ship was actually ready to go, the scene would back away to reveal the course in its entirety—too large a scale at that point to show the Sun as more than one dot of stellar light among many and the Earth not at all.

"Departure checklist, please," Nicole requested from the

computer and was immediately obliged, via a subordinate window in her HUD.

She began with Master Systems Review, which presented the starship's operating status in broad brushstrokes: Engineering, Life Support, Personnel, Structural Integrity. For the better part of the last day, the SysTechs seated at the lowest ring of consoles (the Fourth Tier) had been checking off each of the individual component elements and subroutines, performing a manual backup check of the computer's own examination. Now, Nicole was using a different element of the system to overview the entire procedure, one computer watchdogging the others. If she wanted specifics, she could isolate them on a display menu or request it verbally.

She saw the status with a glance, but made herself take the time to be sure, remembering a time sailing aboard *Sundowner*, not that long after Alex Cobri's death and before she'd properly gotten to know the boat. She'd thought she knew what she was doing—arrogantly assuming her own skill plus the adaptations Alex had made to the gear would allow her to handle this cruising yacht designed ideally for a crew of six. She was a half-dozen klicks off Hanecgar, on a glorious reach with both wind and speed in double digits; she was stretched full length in the cockpit, luxuriating in the warmth of the afternoon sun, a disk of rich autumnal gold against the sky its radiance had bleached to a pale cream. The sea was dark, sunlight scattering the surface and spray with flashes of golden fire, so brilliant it hurt the eyes. It was a rare moment and it made her careless. She wasn't paying attention to sea or sky and was caught totally off-balance when the wind shifted. In barely a heartbeat, the boat's deck had tipped near vertical, pitching her sprawling across the cockpit, dunking head and shoulders underwater as a wave broke over the rail.

She lost hold of the tiller and the boat swung clumsily out of control, righting itself; she flopped backward this time, coughing and sputtering from the salt water she'd swallowed, cracking her head painfully hard on the opposite coaming. There was no time to worry about how badly she'd been hurt, however; the mast had been set to the wrong tension and the violent torquing motion collapsed a set of spreaders two thirds of the way up. She cursed, grabbed for the tiller, but the blow to the head had scrambled her perceptions and she missed. *Sundowner* wallowed in the swell—all the elements that made the day's sail such a treat now conspiring to make a bad situation significantly worse—and Nicole had to duck to avoid being clobbered by the boom as it clattered past to the limit of its traveler with what sounded like a tremendous crash.

She manhandled the tiller around, bracing it with one foot and herself with the other while she hauled desperately on the sheets. Unless she could bring *Sundowner* into the wind, and take the strain off the gear, she would very likely lose the mast as well.

It was a very hairy few minutes—in no small measure because a Bermuda Forty was *way* too much boat for a single sailor—and she had the goose egg just behind her right ear and the cuts and bruises to show for it. Fortunately, that proved to be the extent of the damage, to herself and to her boat. She was luckier than she deserved. After that, for the better part of the year, she never left the harbor without a crew, until she'd come to know the boat as intimately as she did her Beechcraft Baron or, later still, the *Swiftstar*.

Everything had its learning curve, the trick was coming through intact.

She blinked, frowned, reran the memory in her mind's eye, trying unsuccessfully to find the aspects of it that bothered her. She shook her head finally and forced her attention back to business.

"PriCom," she called, "SecCom."

"Bridge, aye," replied Commander Rossmore.

"Stage One MSR complete. I have a clean screen at this station."

"Affirmative. Proceed to Stage Two."

Now they'd assured themselves the ship was all right, it was time to see about getting her safely under way. This involved accessing a vast sensor web encompassing the entire surface of the hull, whose function was not only to tell them where they were in the celestial firmament, but how best to move through it. Baumier maneuvering wasn't like standard spaceflight. Nicole's *Wanderer*, for example—or the *Swiftstar*—propelled themselves in the classically old-fashioned manner: thrusters, either chemical or nuclear, fired in one direction, thereby provoking an equal and opposite reaction in the other. Essentially, sublight In-System spacecraft were giant, inexhaustible firecrackers, no different in their basics from the finger-sized— and altogether illegal—bottle rockets Nicole used to celebrate the Fourth of July. The Baumier Drive by contrast manipulated gravimetric fields, sliding through the fabric of the Universe like a bar of wet soap.

One by one, the consoles on the Third Tier completed their responsibilities towards the checklist and posted the data to Nicole's HUD. While they worked, she opened yet another window to monitor the progress of the Second Tier, the starship's combat systems.

A tiny flash caught her eye and she froze her screen, scrolling carefully back through the entries until she found one tagged with scarlet. Obligingly, the name and face of the relevant SysTech appeared beside the list.

"Talk to me, Chief," she said, after paging him.

"Nothing much to say, I'm afraid, Major," was his reply. "I have no clear explanation for the glitch. Matter of fact, it only appeared on your display because the system hasn't updated itself yet. Diagnostics routine is giving me a green light, has been from the start. In my opinion, sir, what we got here is a hiccough in the network. I read no fault on any of my telemetry."

"Ter*rif*ic," Nicole muttered, biting ever so lightly on the inside of her lower lip as she stared at the HUD, and the data that confirmed what the SysTech had just told her. "But something had to trip an alarm."

"I can't see too clearly from this angle, Ace," Hana said, leaning forward to place her head by Nicole's, "what section are we talking about?"

"Communications, the tertiary C^3 nexus."

"Not a frightfully essential system, then?"

"Only if the primaries and secondaries crash."

"Which, as we all know, is supposed to be impossible."

Nicole bent the microphone arm away from her mouth and covered it with her hand.

"Damn it, Hana, don't act coy, and don't play dumb. I've got the whole countdown on Hold for this. I don't flash the Bridge in fairly short order, they're going to be wondering what the Hell's the problem."

"Communications is where we got zinged aboard *Swiftstar.*"

"You think this could be a replay?"

"A variation, perhaps? Want to lay odds Little Miss Wonderful has already tapped into the system?"

"Give it a rest, willya?"

"You saying you haven't considered the possibility?"

"SecCom, Bridge, acknowledge please."

Nicole shot Hana a glare. "I have a fault indication, Commander," she told Rossmore.

"We don't see it here, Major."

Nicole shook her head in frustrated agreement. "Nor here either, sir, since the Chief recycled his board."

A new voice came on-line, Hobby himself. "Could be a short in the monitor system. Had a problem like it in a car once, turn signals and hazard flashers kept quitting on me for no apparent reason. Then, a while later, they'd kick back in, fine as can be."

"The Chief labeled it a 'hiccough.'"

"Same difference."

"Captain," Hana interjected, "this is Dr. Murai, suppose it's in the software? You have an unimaginable number of data algorithms running around in there . . ."

"You suspect you have something, Doctor, all the evidence to the contrary?"

"With respect, sir," Nicole said, "this system is 'Command, Control, and Communications.' Even though it's the backup to a backup, it still interfaces with the primary operating networks; a bug here could well spread throughout the entire C^3 infrastructure."

"You have a recommendation, Major?"

"Unplug it, then run a full-range diagnostic on the hard- and software."

"And hope we won't need it in the meanwhile?"

"Yes, sir."

"I don't think such action is called for in this situation, Bill," Rossmore protested, deliberately into his open mike.

"So noted. You've got yourself a job, Ms. Shea. Pull the tertiary nexus, but leave it in stand-by for the departure phase, just in case. Once we're under way, and you and your people are comfortably settled, you can begin your inspection. I want it thorough and I want it fast, understood?"

"Yes, sir."

"We're in vacuum, Major, instead of on the sea but we're still sailors at heart; we prefer the term 'aye-aye.'"

Nicole shook her head ever so slightly, her reaction belied by an equally small, equally instinctive smile. "Aye-aye, sir," she said, and released the Hold, allowing the countdown to continue.

A moment later her screen confirmed the Chief's report that the tertiary C^3 nexus had been removed from the active network and isolated.

"Billions and billions of bits," Hana muttered, "won't that be fun. How d'you want to work it?"

"Software actually should be the easy part. Pull the program from the Master Archives and run a spectrum comparison, see if the raw numbers match. Your portable have enough capacity to handle the load?"

"Should do. Why?"

"I'd like to have at least one computer available I'm absolutely sure of."

On her HUD, the remaining elements of the checklist fell neatly and speedily into place. Her voice lost none of its calm, professional intonation—indeed, the casual observer might well assume Nicole had done this scores of times before—but there was a brightness to her eyes, a sharpness to her manner that spoke all too eloquently of the growing excitement of the moment. Hana was much the same; only as a pure observer, she had the luxury of being able to show it.

"Ever wonder what it must have been like in the old days," she mused aloud, Nicole paying only marginal attention as she acknowledged one item on the checklist after another, "sitting on top of a million kilos of thrust, waiting for someone to light the candle and send you on your way. Knowing that once you fire a solid fuel booster, you can't shut it down. It's a little like that here, I'm thinking . . ."

"Thinking too much, sounds like to me," Nicole said.

"Probably so. But even if we abort the instant we leave the Runway, it'll still be the better part of a light-year before we fully reintegrate with Normal Space."

"True fact. Baumiers are great for zipping around the galaxy, miserable for local flying. Just like a hypersonic transport, just like a Ferrari or a Jag. But what a helluva way to fly."

Nicole reached the end of the list, and split her HUD into five windows, one for each of the Second Tier Manager consoles. She called them in turn.

"Power, final status for launch."

"Engines on-line, performance telemetry nominal across my screens. Primed for warp insertion."

"Life?" The one oversaw all aspects of the ship's power plant, the other its life-support systems.

"Atmosphere, nominal. Gravity, nominal. Environment, nominal. Biologicals, nominal." This last related primarily to the crew and basically meant that everyone aboard was healthy. It also applied to the stores—food and water—necessary to sustain the crew.

"C^3."

"Runway's clear, scanners register open space to the hundred and a half mark." A hundred fifty million kilometers, a shade under one astronomical unit, the distance from Earth to the Sun, that would be disrupted by their passage, in much the same way the movement of a vessel through water creates a wake, only these swells were made of energy. That's why all approach and departure vectors were perpendicular to the plane of the ecliptic, moving at ninety degrees difference from the orbital track of the planets. On one hand, that minimized the danger of running into anything along the way, but it also reduced any interaction between the Baumier wakes and the planets themselves, not to mention the Sun. Theoretically, the backwash of even the largest starship shouldn't have even the slightest deleterious effect, but aviation and space history was replete with disasters—the DeHavilland *Comet* for one, the *Challenger* STS shuttle for another—that came about when the outside of the operational envelope was pushed wide open and "theory" slammed up hard against reality. No one wanted to make a similar mistake here.

"Final data and communications updates from DaVinci Flight Control logged and loaded," the Manager, a Lieutenant, Senior Grade, reported.

"Nav?"

"Waypoints tagged and entered, outbound course locked in. Helm free to navigate."

"Combat?"

"Local space clear to ten kay," ten thousand kilometers. Normally, *Constitution*'s "local space" was a globe around the ship a hundred thousand kilometers in diameter, but this close to the Earth-Moon system that wasn't practicable, there was simply too much traffic. "Runway clear to the Outer Marker. Weaponry systems, enabled. Targeting systems in active acquisition, no contacts at this time. Vessel is at Condition Two readiness."

Nicole swung her chair towards Pasqua: "Tom?"

"Got no comments, no complaints, Nicole. Make the call."

She did, and told Rossmore the consensus at her end was "go."

Pasqua tapped her shoulder and pointed. Her eyes followed his arm, and she swung her chair to follow her gaze. From opposite sides of the great curved imaging shell, a pair of brilliantly colored bands of light stretched off into the distance, reminding Nicole of nothing so much as the marker beacons of an actual runway. Her HUD elongated into a skinny rectangle before her, to show the starship's Runway in its entirety.

She felt a small tug at her midsection, a grab at the back of her chair from Hana, who'd felt it, too, and immediately an overlay window appeared to tell them what they'd already guessed, that the *Constitution* was under way. It was a steady one-G acceleration, ten meters per second per second; every second the ship went ten meters per second faster—by the one-minute mark their velocity was six hundred meters per second, better than thirteen thousand miles per hour. The stars ahead changed color ever so slightly, taking on a marginal bluish tint as the spacecraft's perception shifted the value of their light higher up the visible spectrum.

The dominant window of Nicole's HUD was a projection of their course schematic, while the others informed her of velocity, vector, ship's internal and external status, and the condition of the Baumier Drive as it projected its field around and ahead of the ship—focusing on the still-distant Outer

Marker—acting on the physical fabric of space itself and
creating the functional equivalent of a black hole.

The overhead display showed no true sense of what was
happening other than that they were moving fast enough to
actually notice. With good reason, if the HUD visuals were any
indication. It was as though space had become the velvet
curtain imagined by ancient philosophers and someone had
twisted it violently to form a crude spout. The *Constitution* was
racing along the curve of that spout in a nauseating motion that
tested even Nicole's storm-weathered stomach.

The Outer Marker, when it finally came, was disconcertingly
anticlimactic. In the back of her mind, although intellectually
she knew it wasn't so, Nicole had always imagined, hoped, the
Transition to warp space would be the way it was portrayed in
the movies she'd devoured as a girl. Lots of sound and fury and
brilliantly spectacular special effects.

"Drat," she groused, before she could stop herself, as her
HUD quietly announced the Transition, and the blip that
represented the *Constitution* left the Runway far and fast
behind. The only real difference, so far as she could tell, was a
quantum increase in velocity, from miles per second to parsecs
per day.

"Not what you expected?" She was startled to hear Pasqua's
voice for real, instead of in her earphone. He'd removed his
helmet and was rubbing his scalp in a gesture Nicole found
painfully familiar.

"To be honest, no. Anyone ever taken a look outside while a
ship's in Transit?"

"Not me. Not anyone I know. Not sure, as a matter of fact,
it's ever been tried."

"Come on," Hana scoffed as Nicole released herself from her
harness and stretched to her feet, giving small voice to her
aches as her body vehemently protested its confinement,
"somebody must have. What about back in the beginning, the
initial test flights, before we had these wonderful toys?"

Pasqua shrugged. "What do you want from me, Doctor? If
anyone has, it's a secret. But I've got to say, if it's anything like
what the Universe looks like when we're on the Runway, then
I got no complaints about missing the view."

"You've watched Transition live?"

"On a bet. Big by-God mistake, that I can tell you. Typical kind of wager, who can hold out the longest. Pretty fair kitty, too, as I recall."

"You didn't win, I take it."

"No, Nicole, I sure didn't. An' I got no desire to be that sick again, either."

"Excuse me," a new voice, faint but definite Scots burr, from a couple of tiers below, a woman Nicole recognized—from Earth, she realized—but whose name totally escaped her. She was too far away, especially in the chamber's muted light, for Nicole to make out her ID tag.

The woman raised her right hand flat to her forehead in a British military salute.

"Flight Leftenant Coy, sir, Royal Air Force."

"I remember you—Jenny, isn't it"—a nod in reply—"from the dock in Hanecgar."

"San Diego, sir."

"What's Hanecgar?" Hana asked.

Nicole shook her head and frowned. "Haven't a clue. Something I was thinking about, I guess. I must've transposed the name."

"I've been assigned as your dog's-body," Jenny said.

"Say what?" This, from Pasqua, who'd stepped off the Throne to make way for his replacement, in shirtsleeves instead of armor.

"Britishism," Nicole told him, "their equivalent of a gofer." She looked towards Jenny. "I thought you just got your starflight wings."

"I did. But my assignment to the *Constitution* was set fairly early on—assuming, o' course, I didn't wash out—so I've a quite comprehensive knowledge of the ship an' its systems."

"Nearsighted leading the blind," came a comment from Hana, along with a chuckle, "this should be interesting."

The officer who'd passed Pasqua—another light Commander—offered Nicole a salute, which she automatically returned.

"I relieve you, Major," he said.

"I stand relieved," she replied with equal formality, and made way for him in the chair.

When they made their way outside, after a round of farewells and a last, appreciative look at the overhead display—now presenting a simulacrum of what they'd see were they still in Normal Space, derived from the computer's inertial plot of their course—Nicole wasn't at all surprised to find the Marine Sergeant patiently waiting for them.

"Let me guess, Sergeant," Nicole said, "you're here to make sure the officer sent to make sure Dr. Murai and I don't get lost doesn't get lost herself, yes?"

"If you ladies will follow me," was the reply.

This pace, thankfully, was considerably more relaxed than the one the Sergeant had set earlier, more of a brisk stroll than a race. They hadn't gone far before Hana decided to state the obvious.

"Funny," she said to Jenny without preamble, "you don't look Celtic."

She got a big grin in reply. "Not bad, Doctor. Not half so tactless as some I've heard."

"I'll take that as a compliment."

"I'm an island Highlander, off Skye."

"Whereabouts?" Nicole asked.

"Portree, that's the main town. My dad's a teacher, my mum's a nurse."

"And you're a pilot."

"Not so great a leap as y' might think. Dad was RAF, too, for a bit. Flew ground attack until he caught some antiaircraft in the Balkans. Mum looked after him in the casualty ward. One thing led to another."

"How long've you been on Skye?"

"I'm the fourth generation. Great-granddad was highland Vietnamese, Air Attaché at the Embassy in London when Saigon fell. Asked for asylum. I think he'd done some work for MI-6—that's our Secret Service—because Whitehall let him stay without a fuss and helped get whoever else in the family wanted to come into the country as well."

"Never thought of going back?"

Jenny paused before answering, as though every time she heard this particular question it had to be given proper consideration. "No," she said, finally and flatly. "Wherever my family may have come from, Major, Skye is my home—is something wrong?"

Truthfully, Nicole couldn't say, any more than she could understand the sudden and inexplicable pang she felt at Jenny's reply. As though the same sentiment no longer had meaning for her. She was a boat, adrift and becalmed, with neither wind nor current to move her on her way, but that didn't matter—because even if she had the means, she had no destination. She was where she always wanted to be, with no idea of where she was going. Or, worse, of where she belonged.

CHAPTER SIX

The tide is too fast, the beach it covers too large, and she's quickly caught in the surf, as waves that had originally broken far in the distance now break on top of her. It's like being caught in an avalanche, she's hammered to the sand hard enough to make her lose most of her breath, then tumbled head over heels as one comber quickly yields to another. She can't find her bearings; she has no idea where to find the air, as bands of fire tighten around her chest and her heart feels as though it's about to explode.

It was a long time before Nicole slept, she was so jazzed. Hana crashed right off and Jenny soon after, but Nicole stayed in the sitting room of their duplex apartment, clad in singlet and running shorts, feet tucked tight under her as she scrunched herself into a corner of the couch and wished for a hearth fire. She tried for the next best thing, calling up a representation of one on the DisplayWall, but erased it after a few seconds, switching instead to a starscape. A subordinate window flashed all the relevant information about the ship's speed and status. Nicole held her breath for a short five-count and watched tens of millions of kilometers flash by, so significant a velocity that their progress could be noted simply by the movement of the stars. She snuggled deeper into the pillows, cradling her mug of tea against her breast, luxuriating in its warmth, and shuddered imperceptibly with a mixture of awe and raw delight.

The com beeped, demanding attention, using the Wall to tell her that Amy Cobri was on the line. Nicole ignored it, and the com obligingly shunted the call to its memory buffer. Amy'd been trying to get through since Nicole came off-watch, but Nicole was in too good a mood to deal with her.

Be a pleasant change for the girl, she told herself and the others, *to discover she can't get her own way in everything.*

"Library," she called suddenly, as another thought struck home.

"Accessing," replied the computer, in its neutrally female voice.

"Do you have any information on the word 'Hanecgar'?" And spelled it as well, as best she could.

"Pronunciation suggests a Halyan't'a derivation."

"Damn!" She sat a little straighter on the couch, and a furrow appeared between her eyes as her attention focused; she should have been aware of that from the start, and wondered why she wasn't.

"Anything beyond that?" she asked.

"Hal referents are limited; this term is not included among them."

Inspiration, since she'd somehow transposed it with San Diego: "It could be a seaport, or perhaps something relating to the ocean, does that help?"

"Hal referents are limited; this term is not included among them," it repeated. "Nor can the term be found among any Terrestrial data bases."

"If you come across anything, let me know."

"Will comply."

She craned her neck a little, and rolled her eyes towards the gallery overhead, the upper level of the duplex, where the Hal were quartered. It was common procedure to bunk members of the same operational team—or flight—together. In this instance, that policy served a double purpose, allowing Hobby to semiquarantine the XTs—as the Hal had come to be called, in a more socially acceptable alternative to "Fuzzies"—among those humans who knew them best. Conflict would be inevitable, that was assumed from the start, the idea here was to minimize the opportunity.

There was an ache beneath her breastbone, a hollowness of longing that struck her as sharp and deeply as a knife, and she found herself thinking of Ben Ciari. Five years and more since she'd seen him in the flesh, since they'd shared a bed, and that memory prompted a wicked little smile. They'd been very good together, more than a match for each other.

But the smile turned almost immediately to a frown and she shook her head angrily as images blurred in her head, details smearing and merging, the sleek smoothness of bare skin giving way to a shape that was just as lean, just as hard, but covered with a fine, silken fur.

"Christ," she breathed, crossing her arms to hide her face, half afraid to take a decent look for fear of what she'd see. "Mother of Christ! What is happening?"

It wasn't Ciari who had changed in her mind's eye, it was Nicole.

Sleep wasn't the comfort she'd hoped for but at least she had no dreams—that she could recall, anyway—until all of a sudden she sat bolt upright on the couch, heart racing with an adrenaline surge, fully awake, completely alert without knowing why. That answer came a beat later as perceptions caught up with senses and she heard the two-toned, short-long burst of the alarm klaxon. The entire DisplayWall was radiating a scarlet background and pulsing the word ALERT in letters larger than Nicole herself.

Her first thought as she kicked off the couch, springing for the bedroom doors in a single giant step, was that the suite's primary environment was still stable. No discernible change in either atmosphere or gravity, which by implication meant the power plants were still okay. Beyond that, though, they seemed to be out of luck, as she slapped a switch to turn on the lights and nothing happened.

"Everybody up," she bellowed, hammering on the door to Jenny Coy's room. Hana's opened before she could hit it, Hana yanking a T-shirt over her head as she demanded an explanation.

"No details yet," was Nicole's hurried reply, "just that damn horn. Check upstairs, Hana, find out what happened to the Hal." As a species, their hearing and visual acuity were more sensitive than human norms; this noise that was painful to Nicole would be brutal for them. Ch'ghan was an experienced spacer, he'd know what it meant even if Raqella didn't. Nicole was surprised they hadn't reacted to the clamor already.

Hana's call from the gallery told her why.

"They're both gone," she cried, "the rooms are empty!"

Nicole was at the desk, typing commands on the keyboard in an attempt to get more information on the alert.

"Shit," she snarled as the screen filled with garbage, "shit shit *shit!* Total systems crash, I can't access!"

The door popped wide, swinging inward so hard it bounced off its stops. The moment she heard the locks disengage, Nicole grabbed for a handhold against a possible decompression, but all that occurred was that the foyer filled with a trio of armored Marines. Their helmet lamps were blinding, like staring into a set of aircraft landing lights, and the troopers moved with practiced efficiency to collect the three women and hustle them into the corridor outside.

It was a struggle to keep from being panicked or disoriented as they were rushed along. The air was thick with noise, different kinds of alarms assaulting the ears along with the shouts of the Marines, exhorting them to pick up the pace until they were moving at close to a dead run. The halls were in total darkness, the only illumination coming in random splashes of brilliance from the Marines' helmet and hand lamps, and that did more harm than good since each dose of light left the victim dazzle-blinded, vision splattered with opaque spots and rendered virtually useless. The dominant impression was one of tremendous urgency but even as Nicole and her flatmates— plus quite a few others, all looking like they'd been rousted from bed, their confusion and growing apprehension almost physically palpable—were gathered together, she began to suspect there was less to what was going on than met the eye. The harder she looked, the more deliberate the pandemonium began to seem.

She heard a cry, calling her name in genuine terror: "Nicole! *Nicole!* What's *happening?*"

The girl lunged for her, but it was like trying to move across a subway platform at rush hour, the only sure way to make progress was to go with the flow, two or three steps forward, one to the side. Amy—characteristically—just plunged in, expecting the crowd to make way. Someone's foot snagged on someone else's, she was bodychecked by a Marine, and before she'd taken a decent step she was falling. Nicole realized all this immediately and began reacting even as Amy tumbled underfoot. The Marine made matters worse by trying to keep from trampling her, thereby setting up a chain-reaction collision with the people following. Nicole threw her own body into the mix, gathering Amy into her arms to shield her, but fast as she was, the Marines shepherding her and Hana were a match. She and Amy were caught before they hit the floor and even though they were both jostled and bumped and bruised a little they quickly found themselves upright once again and back in the pack.

"They *hurt* me," Amy wailed, purest adolescent, without a care for her normal air of grown-up self-possession.

"Wasn't intentional, kiddo," said Nicole, keeping an arm protectively about Amy's shoulder and the girl herself held close. Her mouth was set, her eyes flashing her anger at this increasingly helter-skelter situation; she was convinced now that there was nothing really wrong, this was some elaborate performance. Inside, though, she was smiling at how she and Amy were relating to each other. Given a moment to regain their normal equilibrium, she knew they'd both be back at sword's point, but this was a pleasant change. She wondered if Amy felt the same—or if she'd even noticed.

"Simply what happens," she continued, a glance over her other shoulder satisfying her that Hana and Jenny were together and close at hand, "when bare skin collides with body armor. If they were serious, we'd be busted all to bits."

"This doesn't feel right," Hana told Nicole, and Nicole had to laugh.

" 'Right,' who knows? It's certainly bogus."

"No emergency?" from Jenny, holding tight to Hana.

"I'd bet serious money on it."

They were bundled en masse through a final hatch, into what Nicole assumed was a cargo bay, a space easily big enough to handle the crowd pouring through the single entrance. The Marines took a fade at that point, most staying outside in the corridor, while the few that remained took up stations along the periphery. The mood was still primarily one of confusion, as folks looked for people they knew—friends, colleagues, family—and tried thereby to get their bearings. Nicole used her height to good advantage, going up on tiptoe to try for a

look over the surrounding heads, but the room was too dimly lit
for her to see anything useful. The illumination was so poor, in
fact, that she couldn't make out the other walls from where she
stood, nor the ceiling. The floor at least was delineated by
softly iridescent GlowStripes.

"Interesting," she said to no one in particular.

"What?" Hana replied.

"There are no kids here."

"I saw some along the way."

"Me, too. Rents are asking and looking, though—see how
the Marines are singling some couples out, pulling them aside
for a quick talk?"

"Would there be a protocol for evacuating kids separately?"

Nicole shrugged. "Even if there was, I suspect it doesn't
apply here."

"The floor's cold," Amy complained, gathering arms and the
body of her cotton nightgown close about her.

"I think somebody stomped on my foot," Jenny echoed with
a grimace, Nicole acting as a brace while the young Scot lifted
her leg to gently probe for broken bones. Jenny favored
pajamas, the sheer silk material at odds with the ostensibly
respectable design.

"WELCOME," boomed a huge male voice, catching everyone off-guard, the omnidirectional speakers giving no clue as to
the origin of the broadcast.

Simultaneously, the darkness overhead was banished by a
glorious explosion. Every face looked upward to behold an
indescribable wavefront of energy—a glowing, growing
sphere of radiance that expanded in mere seconds to fill the
entire viewing surface.

Nicole couldn't help but be impressed, this was a level of
display technology on a par with the imaging system in the
Command Centers. Around her, she heard cries of awe and
delight mingled with those of outright terror.

That explains about the kids, she thought; *they'd be scared
stiff already from the rush through the halls. They find
themselves in what appears to be naked space, the poor
things'd probably go berserk.*

Some of the adults weren't handling things that much better,
and Nicole reassured one nearby couple that this was only an

illusion; appearances to the contrary, they were all still safe and sound, deep within the starship's hull.

There was a shout from down front and a scattering of appreciative applause, plus an outbreak of nervous laughter to break the tension everyone felt, as the wave front swept past them and away, leaving in its wake a sky filled to bursting with stars. It was as though they'd all been privileged to eavesdrop on the moment of Creation, a billion years of genesis compressed into a few wondrous moments.

"In the Beginning," she remembered and as always thought about what that meant: *The more we learn, the less we know. The more completely we seek to comprehend the elemental, fundamental nature of Reality, the more it comes to be seen as magic.*

Which neatly closed the circle on what was happening here, a spectacularly orchestrated and produced magic show.

Forms were slip-sliding through the firmament, wriggling salamander streamers of fire that coalesced into a multitude of shapes and figures, the most spellbinding being the last, a majestic raptor with a crested plume of solar gold and a body of autumnal flame. It was approaching with wings and claws outstretched, as though descending for a landing, but at the last possible instant, another metamorphosis occurred, from bird to man, illusion to reality, as Bill Hobby stepped out onto an invisible dais.

The special effects took Nicole's breath away, she didn't mind admitting that in the slightest—albeit only to herself—as Hobby's amplified voice once more filled the room.

"I bid you welcome," he announced formally but with a smile, tone and manner intended to ease the residual tension among the crowd. He wore a terrific costume, the shape of his body defined exclusively by the same fiery salamander streamers that had romped earlier across the sky. They never let the audience get a decent, definitive picture of the man; instead, they cast him in a succession of highlights, all keyed to make him look as impressively godlike as possible.

Worked, too.

He wore a crown and staff as well, an ebony Zeus presenting himself to his mortal congregation.

He wasn't alone, either. Another figure had materialized

from the background shadows to stand a step behind him and to the side, an appearance that prompted a collective gasp from the gathering.

"Ch'ghan," Nicole heard Hana breathe, and she nodded acknowledgment. She'd never seen the Hal in full formal regalia, only the attire they'd adapted for use on Earth. She hadn't realized he stood so high in Shavrin's Household. He wore many of the same insignia as Kymri and carried a baton, she noted, topped with a rubylike gem that seemed to carry a miniature star within its depths.

Not quite the real thing, she thought, fingers going to the stud in her right ear to lightly touch the silver chased shard of crystal hung there. It was a *fireheart*, a jewel as prized by the Hal as it was rare, in no small measure because of its unique properties of luminescence. A virgin crystal would imprint itself on a simpatico wearer, that person's natural electrical field setting up a resonance within the gem that in turn sparked a unique radiant glow. The bond, once forged, could be broken only by death and never be transferred.

For Ch'ghan to carry a facsimile on his baton meant he had a true crystal at home, a mark of singular status that moved him up a few notches more in Nicole's estimation.

"Since time immemorial," Hobby was saying, "it has been the special province of Ship's Masters to mark the passage of their vessels. On the sea, those signal moments were the crossing of the Terrestrial equator and of the one hundred eightieth meridian, what's referred to as the International Date Line. The details evolve, the tradition remains. Aboard this new, proud spacecraft, we sail an ocean of wild energy. And the boundaries we cross are those between the stars.

"Our gathering tonight is to celebrate that moment, and invest those among us who are making their maiden voyage into the not terribly ancient but nonetheless sacred Order of the Phoenix."

"This," grumbled Amy, "is ridiculous."

Nicole gave her a *look*, and the young woman responded with an exaggerated face of resigned tolerance. Her act said she wasn't about to put up with such foolishness, but she quieted down and stayed put. She'd gotten Nicole's message.

"Let the Lesser Host come forth," Hobby boomed on, like

something out of a biblical epic, "that they may bring before Us those who crave admittance to this most august assemblage."

On which cue, matters began to turn decidedly, gloriously silly.

Before the echo of the Captain's voice had faded, the audience discovered what had happened to the kids, as hidden doors burst wide to admit a shrieking, howling, deliriously madcap horde. Picture "Never-Never Land" gone coed, every-one done up in rags and war paint, romping through a crowd of grown-ups who still weren't sure how to react. The kids were carrying sparkler sticks and every so often somebody would point theirs at the ceiling and pull the trigger. There was a pop and an initial modest spray of sparks. But a moment later came a vastly more impressive sequence of secondary explosions overhead that went on and on, one triggering another seem-ingly spontaneously, in a cascading fireworks display of breathtaking color and variety. The audio system added to the splendid artifice, conveying the force of the multiple reports as well as the raw noise. Nicole knew it was all a projection but found herself swept up in the illusion regardless; moreover, she found she didn't care. Even Amy, beside her, found it impos-sible to hold on to her usual air of jaded ennui. The girl let fly with some whoops of her own and a couple of cheers besides after a particularly stellar sequence.

As Hobby proceeded to call the roll of those to be inducted—that is, those making their first journey out of the Solar System—the Lesser Host scampered to collect each and every one and usher them, none too decorously, up to the dais.

Hana elbowed Nicole—none too gently—in the ribs and pointed towards the walls, where more of the crew had made their entrance, in costumes of their own. Nicole crowed her own delight and the two of them began comparing notes, giddy as the schoolchildren, in an attempt to catalogue all the various creatures who were gathering around them. It was like attend-ing a cast reunion of every space opera that had ever been filmed; the most cursory glance tagged Imperial Storm Troop-ers, a Cylon, Klingons and Metalunans, somebody Nicole tried to place but couldn't looking altogether bemused in pajamas and a bathrobe with a towel draped over his head, plus a score of wildly baroque creations that had to come from Japanese animation. Hana amazed even herself at how easily she named the lot. A couple of robotic types that most resembled upside-down trash cans with a gun barrel sticking out their domed lids roamed through the crowd, electronic voder voices ominously intoning, "*Exterminate, exterminate*," but no one appeared to take the threat seriously.

In hardly any time at all, Nicole was laughing so hard she ached, and her eyes were blurry with tears.

"Do you *believe* this?" she cried to her companions, voice hoarse from projecting over the background hubbub.

"Outstanding!" was the reply.

"You guys are so easy," muttered Amy, who defiantly refused to be swept up in any more fun, after her initial lapse during the fireworks.

"A cross we're glad to bear, Ms. Cobri," responded Jenny.

"I've worn a blue suit nearly ten years," Nicole said, "I never heard a whisper about anything like this. Not at the Academy, not at DaVinci, not at Edwards, not anywhere, from anyone! How the hell could they keep this a secret?"

"Some secrets are worth keeping, I guess. Check it out at your ten o'clock, Ace, looks like Ramsey Sheridan's number's up."

A child grabbed each of the Colonel's arms, while a third gave him a hearty shove in the backside to get him moving—Sheridan stumbled, off-guard and off-balance, and only some fancy footwork kept him from sprawling full length on the floor. Nicole heard a snort of amusement from Amy, which figured, and hoped wickedly to see what happened to the girl when it was her turn.

The kids danced around Sheridan as he was ushered to the dais, wrapping him in strands of glittery rope before prostrating him at Hobby's feet.

"How is this supplicant named?" the Captain asked, and Nicole struggled to keep her face appropriately straight.

"Ramsey Sheridan," piped one of his escort.

"Why hast thou come before us, base creature? Dost crave admittance to this most sacred and august company?"

She couldn't hear his reply, since he wasn't amplified, but assumed he said yes.

"Hast thou the courage to slip free of the bonds of Earth and cast flesh and heart and soul before the cosmic winds. To blaze new trails and brave new worlds with an open mind and open hand?"

And after presumably another affirmative response: "Wilt pledge to keep to thyself all that thou hast seen and heard this night, as one of the Fellowship of the Phoenix?"

She saw him nod.

"Then arise, and stand before us."

There was a scattering of applause, led by those who knew Sheridan best. Nicole offered a cheery whistle, a bad attempt at what her father did so well whenever he needed to hail a taxi. She took a big gulp of air afterward, to mostly catch her breath, and caught a strong gust of tangy cinnamon in the process. Almost immediately, there was a protesting yelp from Amy as Raqella spun her from the safety of the crowd, dancing her towards the dais while a couple of youngsters scampered under his arms to wrap the rope around her body.

Nicole shook her head. Raqella had been working hard, just like the kids, sheer exertion and the excitement of the moment had made his scent especially pungent.

Another salvo of fireworks, no brighter than before yet suddenly Nicole found the light so intense it hurt. Closing her eyes was no help, the awful radiance seemed to burn through the skin of her eyelids. Imagination took her out of herself, cast her back through memory to the *Wanderer* gunship. Paolo DaCuhna was sitting left seat, as pilot; Cat Garcia sat beside him, with Chagay Shomron behind. They'd just detonated an antimatter warhead, sacrificing their own lives in a desperately improvised attempt to save *Wanderer*. It all happened so fast, but in space even the minimal distances were so vast there was a perceptible passage of time between act and consequence. They saw their success, and knew what it meant, watching death come to claim them.

Cat had flown starships, Paolo never got the chance.

"Yo, Ace," Hana said quietly in Nicole's ear.

Nicole blinked, a veil of confusion shading her features as she sought visibly to reorient herself and make proper sense of the world about her. She blinked again, a couple of more times, each one marking the restoration of a little more of herself to her expression. She tried to say something, but couldn't manage. Her skull was crammed to bursting with words; it was simply that she couldn't manage to shape them in coherent sounds.

She let her breath out in a deliberately heavy sigh. She knew she was awake, but she felt as though she'd just been roused from a fitful slumber, where her body was roaming about almost completely disengaged from her conscious mind. Her head felt logy, synapses firing through cushions of cotton wool that disrupted some circuits and slowed down them all.

"The skipper just called your name, Nicole," Hana continued, as though nothing whatsoever was wrong. "Time to get humiliated like the rest of us. It's no big deal," she continued, seeing Nicole's hesitation, "whatever he asks, you answer enthusiastically in the affirmative. Just watch out for the kids with the cream pies."

"Ter*rif*fic."

"You'll love it. Go!"

The children had found them by then, a quartet descending on Nicole with their ropes to drag her before Captain Hobby and Ch'ghan. Their eyes met—hers and the elder Hal's—for the briefest of moments before the Lesser Host sent her sprawling (in a pratfall that looked far more serious than it actually was) at the foot of the dais.

His expression shook her. Partly because it seemed so much at odds with the celebratory nature of the evening. But mostly, she realized, even while she responded appropriately to Hobby's inquisition and took the initiation itself in great good humor, because it was directed right at her. At first, she'd thought it was sadness, though she couldn't imagine why. But as she considered further, as his scent mixed with the residue of Raqella's, the combination somehow opening doorways in her brain to resonances and associations that were as strange as they were comfortable, the more certain she became that it was far more.

Not simply sadness, but sorrow.

As though for the dead.

"Why are you doing this to me?" Nicole asked of Hana a little later, stepping from the shower and wishing for a robe, shivering slightly with a chill that had nothing to do with being cold.

Hana stood with her back to Nicole, buttoning a high-collared blouse of peacock silk, whose rich cobalt matched the blue of her eyes.

"I would have come a lot sooner," she said, "if the damn job hadn't kept me so much on the road." She pulled on a pair of pleated trousers, black wool, an elegant complement to her shirt. "To be honest, I'd have chucked the job—considered it more than once, y'know—if I thought it would have made a difference." Now, she looked up at Nicole, from where she sat on the end of the bed. Nicole had her back to the wall by the bathroom, towel clutched about her like a coat of chain mail.

"That's a nice outfit," Nicole said finally.

"It's what everyone sees as your style. That's why I figured I'd find you something else."

Nicole fingered the dress laid out on the bed.

"This?" she asked.

"What's the matter? You worried about what folks'll think, or is it that you don't want to break the mold, even a little?"

"Get off my case, Hana."

Nicole grabbed at the clothes but found, once she had them, that she couldn't seem to decide what to do next, and ended up folding helplessly to a seat on the bed, around the corner—at right angles, back to back—from her friend. There was a meter between them. It might as well have been a mile.

"A starship came for me," Hana said finally when the silence became intolerable.

"What?"

"You heard. Dropped down off the plane of the ecliptic from half a light out, to a perfect rendezvous. No mean feat, I'll tell you, with us on final approach to Saturn. They matched trajectory and orbit, exchanged a replacement mission special-ist for me, then bounced through another point-to-point trip back to the Moon. I wasn't even given time to visit our flat before I was sent on my way to Sutherland." She chuckled with the memory. "It was a longer flight by shuttle down the well from the Moon to Sutherland than from Saturn to the Moon. And when I walked through the door of that briefing room, I was wearing literally everything I had with me. Fortunately"—

and she waved a hand to indicate both what she wore and what Nicole was uncomfortably holding—"the *Constitution* here has a more than respectable rental outlet; they were able to supply what I needed."

"Canfield," Nicole said flatly. "She brought you back."

"Nobody said. But she certainly has the juice. And, foolishly, I suspect, she cares about you."

Nicole twisted to face Hana. "I didn't ask for that."

"Nope. Defiantly solo, if it kills you. No matter that such an attitude goes against everything we stand for out here, everything you—as a blue suit—are supposed to believe."

Nicole wanted to answer, but nothing came save another awkward silence.

She plucked at the skirt she held and said, "I can't wear this."

Hana, putting on her makeup, was clearly out of patience and didn't bother hiding it. "Fine," she said with some asperity, "go naked. Wear your damn flight suit, if that's what makes you happy, I don't care. Just get off your ass."

"What the hell's the matter with you?"

"Wrong question. What the hell is the matter with *you*? You like playing the hermit, be my guest. But it takes two to be friends, and I'm tired of doing all the work."

"I never meant . . ."

"Nicole, I don't want to hear it. I want to go dancing. I want you to come with me. I think you'll have fun. I know that's a scary and alien concept, but give it a shot. Who knows, you could surprise yourself."

"You've made your point, Hana."

"Hey, don't do me any favors."

"I've never worn anything like this in my life."

"You're an astronaut, you're supposed to be open to new experiences."

Slix went on first. They were a little more than tights, a little less than pants, that fit as snugly as a second skin, creating the illusion of bare skin while remaining thankfully opaque—ideal fashion wear for zero gravity. Nicole was thankful the material was heavy enough that she didn't have to worry about tearing holes in it.

"Here," Hana said, as Nicole smoothed the *Slix* along her legs and over her backside, "I'll give you a hand. The top's pretty tight, I don't think you can manage on your own." As she started hooking the bustier into place—ignoring the occasional odd noise from Nicole—she said, "So what'd you wear when you were growing up? Jeans, I'll bet, and khakis, and mostly polo shirts."

"They had the virtue of being comfortable, what can I say?"

"Probably spent all your time sailing or flying, right?"

Nicole looked back over her bare shoulder. "Yeah, right," she replied. "And how about you, cramming like a bandit since you were old enough to read to pass the entrance exams into the right junior high, and the right high school, and the right college."

"That's how I started, but I broke the profile. Got myself accepted to CalTech. You've no idea how liberating that bunch of loonies can be."

"I've met my share, I can imagine."

"The first semester, I wore my Japanese school uniform, same as I would've at home. Nobody made fun, they accepted it as my own individual fashion aesthetic. Mind you, they took every chance they could to offer alternatives. To look and life-style. By sophomore year, I began to let myself blossom."

"Me, I joined the Air Force."

"I know. You like being told what to wear, and when, and how."

Nicole zipped up the tiny skirt and settled it into place around her waist.

"Pink is not my color," she said sourly, but that wasn't the line Hana was looking for. "It wasn't something that I thought much about. It didn't mean a whole lot."

"Dressing up? Looking good?"

"I wanted to be judged on my abilities, Hana, not my tits."

"Are the two mutually exclusive?"

"Gimme a break! How many guys you figure we'll see tonight wearing illuminated codpieces?"

"In this crowd . . . ?"

"Okay," Nicole conceded, "special case. Maybe a few. I guess you could say it's an area of expertise, of"—a hesitancy now more than a real pause, as though Nicole was just considering the thought and all its implications—"competition, where I don't feel altogether comfortable."

"You the best pilot in the world?"

"No."

"The worst?"

"No!"

"But you're good."

"I'm very good."

"This is the same."

"Not from where I stand."

"That's why you're wearing the dress tonight, to force you to stand somewhere else."

Even Nicole had to admit, when all was said and done, that the effect was as impressive as it was startling. They stood before the room's WindowWall, its video elements displaying multiple images of the two women so they could see their reflections from every angle. Nicole hadn't hoped for much getting dressed, the image of her own body in her mind's eye was made up of too many angular bones and muscles, as though she were some unfinished piece of sculpture that was mostly rough edges. Hana, on the other hand, she always considered the finished, fully realized product. But the effect surprised her, far more smooth and sleek and nicely dramatic than she'd anticipated.

She'd thought the pink too pretty-precious when she saw it on the bedspread, but the color nicely offset her tan, itself something of an exotic fashion accessory on the Frontier. The bustier was satin, overlaid with polka-dot tulle; the lace was pink, the dots tiny and black. The skirt reversed that arrangement: here was satin on the outside, with the lace polka-dot petticoat underneath, so short it barely qualified as a skating skirt. She wore a black bolero jacket on top, velvet, with an upstanding collar; it could be buttoned under the breasts—which made the initially striking effect even more so—but Nicole left it open, to allow for more freedom of movement. For all their snug appearance, the clothes had a surprising amount of give, which they'd need if the party turned out to be anything like the Initiation that preceded it. Thinking about that, Nicole wondered if she wouldn't do better outfitting herself with a crash helmet and safety pads. Earthside, the final complement to an outfit like this would have been ankle-breaker stilettos, but nobody wore those kind of shoes in space,

even in a full gravity section. Instead, she wore classic black
high-top sneaks, whose flexible soles would give traction on
smooth surfaces. For a final accent, the laces had been replaced
by electric pink ribbon.

It was a very feminine effect. To Nicole, it looked and felt all
wrong.

Hana stood by the door, ready to go, her expression
deliberately neutral. Nicole knew that if she decided to stay
behind, her friend wouldn't try to talk her out of it.

So she pulled on her gloves—pink Dotted Swiss netting,
with frilly lace cuffs, totally club couture and so precious she
could just *die*—and led the way.

Because the ship's one-gravity environment was artificially
derived from the energy field generated by its Baumier Core, it
was possible to customize conditions in certain compartments.
For the most part, those areas were confined to the docking
facilities, where the ability to shunt heavy masses with minimal
resistance was most useful. It hadn't taken very long, though,
for folks to figure out the practical possibilities from an
entertainment standpoint as well.

They were far from the first to arrive and Nicole took the
time after they entered to give the bay a proper once-over.
Imagine a cube, fifteen meters by twenty by twenty—
essentially a four-story building in one direction, and a six in
the others—lit like a bordello and moderately filled with flying
bodies, whose interaction with the ceiling projection made it
look as though people were soaring among the very stars.

The music came from all around, far richer and more
all-enveloping than a live band would have been—jazz, with a
dominant beat that gave the dancers their physical cues. There
were refreshment stations in each of the room's corners, half
for food, the rest for drink, although this crowd wasn't here to
get themselves plastered or fed. They came to dance, in a
manner unlike almost anywhere else in the Solar System.

There was no floor. Dancers kicked themselves out into the
open air and used the other dancers as their platform. It wasn't
so much dancing per se as a form of acrobatics. Each action
triggering an equal and opposite reaction, ideally sending a
body from the arms of one partner to those of another. Thing

was, movement never occurred simply along a single plane. On the ground, there was forward or back, right or left; if a dancer threw their partner into the air, gravity dragged them back down. Here, they kept going, until contact with another dancer spun the pair of them off into new and unexpected directions. It demanded close to the ultimate in concentration; not only did each dancer have to remain aware of their own position but of those of everyone else. Think not only of the effect any movement might have on one's own trajectory, but how it might interact with the rest. It was like playing chess, at breakneck speed and living pieces, bounding through a board that encompassed every physical dimension.

The nice thing about the chamber was that it was big enough to accommodate dancers of every proficiency, novice to master. The novices stayed close to the bulkheads and hand-holds, giggling and whooping like teenagers out for their first stint on fresh ice, with skate shoes tied so loose their ankles collapsed right from the start. For them, the fun was as much in the pratfall as the successful turn around the rink. Much the same here, as Nicole watched one young man go into what would have been a sublimely elegant turn in gravity only to have it go sidesplittingly awry as an unsuspected secondary motion started spinning him head over heels. A spacer would have turned the move to his advantage, kicking a leg up and over to impart some more velocity, while throwing the body into a rolling twist to change orientation so that he could reach the bulkhead. The young man lightly panicked, flailing about with arms and legs, actually making things worse until a couple of companions caught hold and brought him safely to rest. Nicole heard some profane and shaky oaths and a lot of nervous laughter.

But the comic relief wasn't what interested her. And her eyes turned to the center of the room, as far from the walls as a body could go, and a wickedly mobile mass of figures whose only anchor was to each other, and that often only for the most fleeting and phantom of moments. They spun, rolled, twisted, jackknifed, somersaulted, split-kicked, ran the whole magnificent gamut of acrobatic possibilities, in solo and combinations. The truly breathtaking aspect of the event, what kept all but the bravest and most skillful—and, some would say, and rightly so, most foolhardy—on the sidelines, was that it was all improvised. People and movement and music, coming together on the spur of the moment, with equal opportunities for disaster or magic.

Tonight, Nicole knew from the first, was magic.

And without a second thought, or the slightest hesitation, she knew she had to be a part of it.

She gave Hana a smile that must have been a wonder, judging from the one she got in return, and launched herself with a gentle push off the wall. Plenty of time to get silly, what mattered first was sliding themselves in sync with the music. It was Native Australian jazz, freeform, horns and guitars mated to didgeridoos, not as emphatic a beat as was heard in clubs stateside this season, but far more sensual. Nicole caught Hana's hand and pulled her close, momentum turning them into a spin before Hana let go and threw an arm wide to pull her away from Nicole with a little more speed. The trick was to remember as second nature something that had been learned the hard way a century ago, with NASA's earliest ventures into space. Objects in zero gravity had no weight, which meant they were susceptible to the slightest physical influence. One hearty shove could easily send a multiton satellite spinning on its way. But at the same time, those objects lost none of their mass. Which meant that once they started moving, they became annoyingly difficult to stop. As importantly, they could do a fearful amount of damage to anything—or anyone—who got in their way.

Same applied to people. Getting them moving in zero was nothing; the trick was controlling each move so that everyone ended up precisely where they were supposed to. Challenging enough for a couple on their own. In concert with a few dozen more, all doing pretty much the same thing, it could get quite exciting.

A new hand caught her on the periphery of the cluster of dancers, pulling her away from Hana. Nicole went with the flow, pulling a reverse jackknife into a rolling twist that sent her cascading off along a totally different orientation. She found herself becoming one with the music in a way she hadn't enjoyed for far too long, letting it soak into muscles and bones, and slowly, inexorably established herself as the core about which this system of fellow dancers began to revolve. As naturally as the movement of the spheres she fashioned the structure of the dance; she was such a wild talent, imbued with such strength and grace that the others couldn't help but gravitate towards her, to be cast out along the pathways she defined. She didn't do this intentionally, she wasn't aware it was happening, that required an objectivity of perception she didn't possess right then.

The music built to its crescendo and then broke, and with it the dance.

Nicole spun gently about the long axis of her body, like a dancer pirouetting on toe, joining the others in their applause, not realizing yet that most of it was directed at her. She was looking about for Hana—the press of bodies and the lousy light didn't make that task any easier—and consequently, not where she was going, when someone's arms reached out to gather her in.

"Excuse me," Nicole stammered automatically, in the moment of collision, "I really am sorry, I should have been paying better attention—!" Then she recognized the other, shorter but broader, figure, and her voice cut off.

Amy Cobri regarded her eye to eye—zero being that rare environment where that was easily accomplished—and smiled.

"Fancy meeting you here, Nicole," she said.

Five years ago, she'd been a child just beginning her awkward transition to adulthood, a darkly handsome girl possessing her father's brute strength cast in a much sleeker mold. Now, that promise was substantially fulfilled. She had a swimmer's physique, with powerful shoulders and superbly sculpted muscles, a big girl maturing into a big woman. She wore her hair long, in defiance of spacer custom, a thick mass of elegant waves the color of aged mahogany that fell to her shoulders and somehow stayed obediently in place despite the lack of gravity. On her own, she was quite pretty, with her father's Catalan olive skin and dark eyes; the expert application of makeup—which like her hair had survived the rigors of the dance substantially unscathed—made her beautiful. She wore slippers and a black dress that verged on scandalous. In her wildest mood, Nicole doubted she'd risk anything so short or tight, and she also had to confess that she doubted she'd look as good in the bargain. No jewelry, though, nothing on her person to indicate that Amy was heir to the richest private fortune in human space.

Nothing in the young woman's eyes to indicate that five years before she'd tried her best to have Nicole killed.

"Likewise," was Nicole's still reply.

"You're a hard person to get ahold of. Except, I guess, in an emergency." She offered a shy smile at the memory of the pandemonium earlier tonight in the hallway. "You figure that's what gazelles feel like in the middle of an elephant stampede?"

"You came through okay."

That wasn't the response the young woman had been looking for, but she hid her reaction well.

"You look good," said Amy.

"As do you."

Unaccountably, Amy threw back her head and laughed, that small act sending her drifting ever so slightly up and away from Nicole. She braked herself automatically, with an unconscious skill that impressed Nicole—*As*, Nicole thought in that same moment, *it was no doubt meant to*—but remained in the slightly dominant position.

"God," the girl crowed delightedly, as though she'd just aced an Olympic downhill, "the look on your *face*, it's *priceless*! I'm sorry, I shouldn't make fun, especially with all the history between us—but, Nicole, give me some credit willya? I'm not going to bite." She flashed a grin that was meant to be knowing and wicked. "Unless I'm asked."

Nicole couldn't help a smile in return, thinking back to the night they'd first met at a reception Earthside, shortly after Nicole's assignment to Edwards. Amy was thirteen, and Nicole had just been grounded, stripped of her astronaut's flight status. Amy'd set out to win Nicole's friendship, overjoyed that Nicole and her older brother Alex had crossed swords from the start. Too late, Nicole came to understand the genesis of their sibling rivalry. By then, Alex was condemned, even though Nicole tried her best to save him.

The last time Nicole had seen Amy was not long after that, at the Cobri compound on Staten Island. The girl stood at the top of the mansion's main stairway, shrieking "You killed my brother!" over and over again, her voice spiraling ever upward into an out-of-control falsetto.

The two images always came side by side whenever Nicole thought of her.

Residual momentum had scattered the mass of dancers, a rough analogue to the dispersal of celestial bodies, Nicole and Amy moving a small ways off by themselves. Eventually, they'd reach the wall, but the only way Nicole was going to get anywhere fast was to work in tandem with Amy, which was no doubt what she intended. Nicole kept that realization to herself, and her face relaxed, and resolved to wait for Hana to find her.

Assuming, she thought suddenly, concern betrayed by the smallest tightening of the lips and the return of combat tension to her arms and legs, *she's able to*.

That day with Emmanuel Cobri, she'd warned him off in no uncertain terms: attempt even the slightest harm to her family and friends and he'd regret it. Even though his resources beggared her own—Hell, they beggared those of most of the nations on the globe—he paid her heed. Because she had assets he couldn't touch. By adoption, she was Hal, and High-Born, and they played by different rules. It was the most basic of business equations: any satisfaction derived from revenge against Nicole simply wasn't worth the potential cost.

Amy, though, didn't think like that—or rather the Amy Nicole remembered. She bore grudges, and didn't care a damn how high the price would be to pay them back.

The music caught her by surprise, a harsh, driving, modern beat, far more emphatic and demanding than the jazz piece that preceded it. She caught a flash of movement from Amy, almost too fast to follow, and let her body handle the parry, spinning aside and around in an aikido deflection, aborting her counter-strike only at the last second as she realized this was no attack but merely the invitation to another dance.

Nicole wanted to pull away, but Amy proved surprisingly adept at controlling the space between them. She kept herself in Nicole's face, and the pair of them separate from the others, challenging Nicole to prove how good she truly was by getting past her. Nicole refused to take the bait. She met Amy on the girl's own terms, seized moment and situation and made both her own, content to let her lead but always ready to act should matters slip out of hand.

A new shape slithered between them with the sinuous charm of an otter. Nicole thought it might be Hana to the rescue— *About bloody time, woman*, was her thought in that instant of mistaken identity—until scent and the briefest of touches, flesh on fur, and ultimately sight told her it was Raqella, the young Hal flight officer.

To flout Nicole, he twisted away with Amy, who let him, quickly disappearing from sight below the main mass of dancers.

Nicole wanted to breathe a sigh of relief and return to enjoying the party.

Instead, she arched into a cartwheel that brought her into an arm's-length interaction with another couple, which in turn imparted sufficient delta-V—an increase in forward velocity—to propel her across the crowded heart of the room. She danced, because that was what was expected, but in reality she was hunting, sliding through the air as a dolphin would through water, playing people like currents to help her on her way. As she flew, never at rest, each movement flowed one to the next as though choreographed, Nicole totally aware of the others around her, taking care that her physical intentions never impacted negatively on theirs.

Jenny Coy popped out of nowhere to try to partner her, but Nicole was here and gone before the young woman could properly get her bearings and she had to content herself with a very nice systems analyst from Lockheed. An astronaut managed to pace her for an entire sequence, gaining a round of spontaneous applause from the small clutch of onlookers watching near the entrance after Nicole left him flat.

The room was big and crowded, and everyone was moving every which way—but it was still a finite number of objects in a finite space, and so Nicole finally caught up with Raqella and Amy. The Hal tossed Amy into Nicole's arms, but Amy would have none of that, using a variation on Nicole's own aikido parry to twist herself back the way she came towards Raqella.

What had come before, it was quickly realized by everyone else present, had been but prologue. This was the main event. The three of them were poetry, in sync with themselves, the space, the music, so much so that the other dancers instinctively deferred to them, pulling gradually closer to the walls to give them more and more room. They didn't need it; none was ever more than an arm's length from the others, and only out of contact for the heartbeat it took to fly from one hand to the next. In a way, it was like watching eels, they moved with an almost boneless magic, bodies seemingly inextricably intertwined. And with such speed that the slightest misstep or hesitation would have meant disaster. They were utterly dependent on one another, operating on levels of trust that went far beyond conscious thought. There simply wasn't time to rationally evaluate the danger of each action, each had to assume the body would be there to catch them, as they would be in return. More than once, there were gasps from the audience, as some thought the dance would come shatteringly to an end, a few spacing themselves out along the walls in hopes of being able to stop a collision if that was the case.

But they never missed.

There was a drumbeat undertone to the music, a pulse Nicole's body responded to long before her mind caught on. Her heart seemed to pound in tune, with such force that she was flushed, as though her skin were a garment grown stiflingly, unbearably hot.

Raqella turned, and she crooked legs and arms, head tilted *just so*, in a pose that meant nothing to her but struck him like an almost physical blow. Amy tried to interfere, but he set her aside with a force and look that effectively quelled any more protests—though her expression spoke eloquently to Nicole that this little confrontation was far from settled. Nicole noticed, but couldn't care less. She was watching an altogether different show.

Raqella answered her pose with a similar one of his own, resonant to the crane stance in tai chi.

They began to move. Nicole wasn't sure who initiated things, nor if that mattered; from that moment, the two of them were a perfect match. The drumbeat was louder, more demanding. She responded, hearing as well the wild *skirl* of a Hal reel, unsure now which was real and which imagination. Both struck with equal force. Very little of their music was contemplative; their preference was passion, raw and untamed. Music and dancing were ways of unleashing the beast within, of hearkening back to the ages of tooth and claw, before they'd embraced the necessary strictures of civilization.

Nicole grinned, swept up by music and movement and yet at the same time seizing control of both. The dance between her and Raqella was evolving as they went, each becoming an extension of the other, interacting with increasing confidence in a duet that was as much about war as love. He lashed out, too fast to see, and she felt the brush of surface tension across her cheek as she flinched just enough to make him miss by a hairbreadth. She in turn spun 'round behind him, hands flowing down his back, following the curve of his spine without ever touching, as he curved forward, then arched his body to full extension.

Each moment fed on the one before. Each movement inspired another even more passionate. She would lead one measure, then let Raqella have the next. Her body knew precisely what to do; her head was just along for the ride.

She lost all sense of where she was and with it of who. A small part of her awareness answered to the name of "Nicole" but it was a label without meaning. She didn't think much about that, though, she was centered totally on her partner and the dance.

Suddenly Raqella rushed in close and caught her hand. She started—up 'til now, there'd always been at least a fractional separation between them—baring teeth in anger at this breach of protocol. He took her by the chin and held her head fast, the barest hint of claws on skin insuring that she wouldn't move. She couldn't speak, she was so outraged, as his golden eyes flicked back and forth between hers.

"Ach'snai!" she finally managed to snarl, *"back off!"* In a tone that mandated instant obedience.

He didn't pick up his cue.

Her free hand slapped up and outward, breaking his hold on her jaw; then she shoved hard at his chest to complete the disengagement. Didn't quite work, though, his grip remained tight about her wrist.

"Let go, Raqella," she said icily in English, the *glamour* of their dance irretrievably broken.

"Shea-Pilot," he began, as though about to offer an explanation.

She didn't want to hear it. *"Let go!"* she repeated, in Hal.

He did. But neither of them moved any farther apart. Nicole floated with feet apart, a combat stance, eviscerating him with her eyes, body primed to go for his throat. Common sense as much as pride kept Raqella where he was, as he realized that any gesture he made would most likely be misinterpreted.

"You," Hana, to Raqella, with a sharpness Nicole had never heard from her before as she pulled up beside them, "take a hike." When he didn't respond quickly enough, she turned to Amy, who was fuming in the background. "You! Get him out of here. Keep him the hell away from Nicole, is that clear?"

Amy nodded, took Raqella by the arm. The Hal allowed himself to be pulled away, with a stumble to both step and attitude that was a pale echo of how Nicole felt.

Hana took Nicole's head in both hands, her palms splendidly cool against Nicole's fevered skin.

"Nicole," she said quietly, "look at me. Listen. Can you hear me? Do you understand what I'm saying?"

Of course I can, she thought, *don't be absurd.*

But somewhere between conception and execution, the reply got sidetracked. Nicole felt her mouth trying to form different words, recognized them for what they were, grabbed her friend by the wrists as though she were a life preserver.

"Hana . . ." she forced out.

"That's right, Ace. I'm here, I've got you, everything's okay."

"Easy . . . for you to say."

"Complete sentence, and a joke. There's life in the old broad yet!"

"I ain't no broad." Pause for breath and a little reflection. "Wow."

"How d'you feel?"

"Like I pulled too many G's in a dogfight. Greyed out. Eyes are open, body's functioning as though I'm awake, brain's totally gone."

"Part of it, anyway."

"What's that supposed to mean?"

"You don't remember?"

"I was dancing with Raqella. It was fun. It was wonderful, actually. Then he grabbed me and . . . everything went sour. Christ"—she looked at Hana, suddenly stricken—"am I nuts?"

"If you are, I'll never tell."

"If I am, woman, you'd better."

Nicole was sodden and breathless, as she let herself be towed to the sanctuary of the wall, as weary deep down in her bones as she was after a hard day's sailing.

Hana held out a drink. Nicole took it—in a hand that trembled, the reaction as much emotional as physical—placed the nipple in her mouth and drained it.

"Grapefruit juice," Hana told her, "to replace your keytones."

"I'll take another, please."

"Way ahead of you, Ace."

"Bravo, miss!" someone clapped her on the back—an Earthside gesture that bounced her off the padded wall and prompted an immediate embarrassed apology from the man. "Absolutely wonderful," he continued, trying to make up for his gaffe with compliments, "I've never seen anything like it. I wish I had a video."

"Thanks," was all she could manage in response.

She looked around, letting the head movement pull her body along after in a gentle turn. She was at her limit and done with dancing for the night. *For my lifetime*, she thought.

"Cobri Minor is at ten o'clock high, just along the seam," Hana said casually, meaning Amy.

"Thanks for spotting," Nicole told her as her own eyes picked out Amy on the wall, attended by a couple of eager lads. "And Raqella?"

"Youngblood's right and low, just around the corner."

Alone, and deliberately so.

"Since when did you start using Hal slang?" The term referred to Hal males and females who hadn't achieved their majority—which involved undertaking the ritual Hal equivalent of an Australian walkabout combined with an Amerindian vision quest. There wasn't much call for the Ordeal these days, in its full and ancient form; as with the forms of Terrestrial religions, it had been modified and streamlined to make it more acceptable to a society that felt it had more important concerns. Still, it was the Halyan't'a rite of passage, the point of transition out of the nursery and into the House proper.

"Long time now."

"And, what, I haven't been around to notice?"

"Something like that. She's grown some," Hana commented further, meaning Amy.

"Haven't we all." Nicole spoke in a tone meant to change the subject, but Hana refused to take the hint.

"Her old man took her out of circulation right after her brother died."

"Is this any of our business, Hana?"

"Considering our history, Nicole, absolutely. She's been in therapy, you know."

"She was a screwed-up kid, I'm glad her father realized that."

"She's been in virtual seclusion 'til this past year. This is the first time she's been off the surface. To be honest, I'm surprised they're letting her out alone."

"She isn't alone, not even close. I can spot at least four bods who read as security, which means there's probably triple the number present."

"Way to go. Little Ms. Nutcase is well and truly protected. Where does that leave the rest of us?"

"Why are you so angry?" Nicole faced her friend, who'd pressed herself back into the crease where two bulkheads came together, a position that not only covered her back but gave her a much wider field of possible escapes should trouble come her way.

Hana sighed in disgust, but Nicole couldn't tell whether it was for Hana herself or Nicole. "D'you have the slightest *fucking* notion"—deliberately emphasizing the profanity for shock value—"what it was like watching the three of you? What could have *possessed* you to put yourself in that bitch's hands?"

"Actually, I was concerned, about her and Raqella both." She wanted to explain about the incident in San Diego but Hana didn't give her the chance.

"Well, I'm sorry, Nicole. I was concerned—about *you!*"

"I can take care of myself."

"So you say!"

"Hana, if I'm willing to accept the risk—whatever, wherever, whyever—then you'll have to accept the decision."

"Blood's coming," was Hana's clipped response.

"Greetings, Shea-Pilot," the Hal said in English, his voice possessing only the promise of the rich thrill that would come with full maturity.

"Raqella."

"I commend you on the dance. I had been told of your skill, but confess I did not believe. I stand corrected, and humbled."

Very pretty speech, Nicole thought, *well rehearsed and with just the right touch of sincerity.* He'd have said the same, she knew, if she'd been awful. A charmer certainly among his own kind, with all the right instincts, lacking only practice to work on Terrans.

"Kind words. Good as I am, though, Dr. Murai here is better." Which Nicole believed to be true.

"Then she should have joined us. Will you come again?" This directed pointedly at Nicole, as people drifted into the air for the next set.

"I'll pass, thank you."

Without an acknowledgment, he was gone, flashing up and over in a madcap series of acrobatics that scattered anyone in his way and brought him straight to Amy.

"Show-off," Hana muttered.

"What's he trying to prove?"

"Y'ask me, Ace, it's that NASA's star flight selection process ain't all it's advertised."

"He came with a full rating, from the Hal. The tour through NASA was icing."

"Then the Hal should know better."

The next set kicked off and with it Amy and Raqella, as fresh as when they started and even more daring.

Nicole watched and as she did her expression grew increasingly somber. The two youngsters were quicksilver together, flesh made mercury, impossible to hold. It should have been a spectacular display. But to Nicole, it was scary.

"The question is," she mused, "why didn't they?"

CHAPTER SEVEN

At last, miraculously, the water smooths and she manages to find enough of a footing on the bottom to leap straight up. Nothing in her life ever tasted sweeter than this first breath. But that's all the triumph she's allowed as she's slapped in the face by another wave and swallows a heavy mouthful of ocean. She struggles to get her bearings, fighting panic as she realizes there's no solid footing beneath her, no matter how she stretches her long, lean body, even taking the risk of ducking her head under the surface. The shore is as far in the distance as the water seemed when she first came onto the beach.

Earth to Faraway was seventeen days. Eight in warp, the rest spent decelerating through the system to achieve final orbit around the planet itself. So easy to take for granted, Nicole told herself, a journey that didn't exist barely a generation before.

This was a much younger world than Earth, mountains newly formed, their sharp, sawtoothed profile relatively untouched by the wind and weather that would eventually wear them down. Because of the violent interaction of the crustal plates, the coastlines of the existing land masses were mostly demarked by walls of towering cliffs that Nicole found achingly, disturbingly familiar.

Life-forms were as primitive as the world, grassland plains with minimal forestation, insects being the highest order of animal existence. The soil was rich, however, and easily adaptable to Terrestrial biomes. A quarter century's hard work had expanded the initial settlement at Hart's Landing to better than a dozen communities scattered across the single huge continent, plus various research stations established on a score of attendant islands in the Northern Ocean. Despite this, immigration wasn't anywhere near as extensive to Faraway as to the other colony systems—Paradise, Last Chance, and Nieuwhome—basically because the world remained geologically active. Its surface was still meshed together into a supercontinent that strongly resembled Earth's Gonwondaland, the proto-land mass from which all the modern continents derived. The tectonic forecast here was for some fairly violent—and to a certain extent unpredictable—epochs in the future, as tectonic evolution reshaped the planetary plates into new configurations. The saving grace being that this "future" was measured in tens of millions of years.

Throughout the flight, Nicole found herself kept far busier than she'd imagined—indeed, than she could ever remember, on the ground or in space. As a field grade officer, she had watch-keeping responsibilities, alternating between SecCom—where she sat the Throne—and the Bridge, where she shared the Second Tier Systems Manager role with three others. They switched consoles every tour, which in fairly short order gave Nicole a comprehensive working knowledge of the *Constitution*'s central systems. In addition, she was assigned a division of the crew, roughly three hundred people all told, including dependents; they had problems, they came to her. If there was trouble, it landed on her doorstep. This job, thankfully, she shared with Tom Pasqua, who proved as adept at handling personnel as he did paperwork.

And, of course, there were the Hal.

Both had kept their distance since the Initiation ceremony. In Raqella's case, the explanation was simple: off-duty, he was hanging with Amy. It was Ch'ghan who had Nicole stumped. They'd never been close, in the way she'd been with the first Hal she'd met—Shavrin and Kymri—but now their relationship was defined by a formal reserve that he wouldn't explain and which nothing would break. After a couple of days, Nicole quit trying. So long as it didn't interfere with their work, it was a state she'd learn to live with.

However, those tasks barely began to fill the dance card of

her working day. There was the *Swiftstar* to see to, and the investigation of the C^3 glitch Nicole had reported during the prelaunch checklist.

They were a day past Approach Transition, blue-shifting velocity in the braking phase along a huge cometary parabola around the sun that would bring them up on Faraway from behind, when Hobby asked for a status update.

"Nothing really to tell, sir," she told him, seated with Hana and Pasqua in his Alert Facility off the Bridge. "We pulled the archival software from the vault and ran a comparative evaluation; perfect match, top to bottom. Hardware looks clean, too—although those are only preliminary indications. We specced a random sampling of the circuitry boards and registered nominal function on every one." Nicole glanced at her DataPad. "This isn't to say there may not be a fault, but based on the evidence at hand, especially the fact that the system has passed every test we've thrown at it, I don't think we're justified in looking further."

"How about the monitor subroutines?" asked Hobby.

"Clean bill of health there, too, skipper." It was Pasqua who replied. "Major Shea even pulled the console to trace the fiberoptic wiring."

"In line with what you'd said, sir," was Nicole's follow-up, "about your car's electronics. I was hoping to find a loose connection that'd explain everything."

"Would've been nice," the Captain agreed. "I gather that wasn't the case?"

Nicole shook her head. "The problem is the sophistication of the system. We're talking about boards whose control paths are etched onto chips on a molecular and even atomic level. The manufacturing process is totally automated; likewise, any inspection. Ultimately, all we can tell you is what our machines have told us."

"You tried a blind replacement?"

"Twice, using randomly selected replacements from stores—including a generic, all-purpose CRASH board."

"Very thorough. I'm impressed. Tom, Dr. Murai, I assume you concur in Major Shea's conclusions."

Pasqua, enthusiastically so. Hana offered a slight tilt of the head that Hobby chose to construe as agreement.

Nicole wasn't so sure, as she said, "I'm sorry it turned out to be a waste of time."

"Hardly that, Major. It gave me an ideal opportunity to watch you in action. All in all, I'd rather deal with false alarms anyday." He consulted his own notes.

"Before we adjourn—what's this from your Hal about modifications to the *Swiftstar*?"

Not my Hal, sir, she thought, uncomfortable at being frozen out of their company. Aloud, she replied, "A project we initiated back at Edwards. We want to mate a warp generator to the plane, to give it localized jump capabilities."

"Is that possible?" Pasqua asked.

"Given the size/mass ratio of the plane, you don't need that big a Baumier cell. The Hal have come up with a self-contained module that they feel will do the job. Preliminary tests have been quite encouraging."

"Live or Virtual?" from Hobby.

"All computer models so far. The requisition is to fabricate a mock-up of the *Swift* from ship's stores, and see how the gizmo works for real. We'd like to try some In-System runs during our layover at Nieuwhome."

"I'm not sure I see the point," Pasqua again.

"I do," said Hobby. "There are occasions when I'd love to be able to slide into a system aboard something significantly smaller than the *Connie*. Especially something with atmosphere operating capabilities. I'll green light your tests, Major; keep me abreast of results."

Nicole nodded assent and started up from her seat, but a raised hand from Hobby sat her back down again.

"Not quite finished, Nicole."

"I was afraid of that, sir."

"Tom, if you'll excuse us, I'm afraid this discussion is confidential."

"Understood, Captain. See you later, Nikki."

Hana rolled her eyes; she liked the nickname as little as Nicole herself did and radiated a lot less tolerance for Pasqua's frequent use of it. The man simply refused to take the hint.

After the Commander's exit, Hobby activated the security screen to isolate the room.

"I understand your ambivalence, Major."

"Sort of hard, Captain, to work with someone who's tried to kill you."

"Dr. Murai," and he offered Hana a look to give due emphasis to his words, "without the deal Judith Canfield cut with Ms. Cobri, we wouldn't be having this discussion at all. She gave her word. By extension, so did the pair of you."

"We've been busy, sir."

"I know, Nicole. I'm responsible for a fair measure of that. But none of us can stall any longer. Ms. Cobri's played the game as well—with a lot more grace than I'd been led to expect from her—however, she's not about to be put off any longer, either. I have a formal request to initiate work on the active phase of *Lamplighter,* and I haven't a blessed reason to deny it."

"How 'bout she's psychotic?"

"Hana!" Nicole snapped. "Give it a rest!"

"She passed a class-one astronaut's physical," Hobby told them pointedly, "including a psychological evaluation, both Earthside and here aboard ship. She's as qualified to be here, on those grounds, as the pair of you. And, I might add, she isn't the one who spends an hour or more a night jogging around the circumference of this ship. Or the one who watches her go and sits up worried sick until she comes home."

There was a long and awkward silence, neither woman willing to be the first to break it.

"I appreciate you're only human," Hobby continued finally, "we all have problems, some great, some small, welcome to the club. And I appreciate that whatever is concerning you is having a negligible impact on your professional performance. But the pair of you also occupy a fairly sensitive position, both on this ship and in NASA itself, and I'm afraid that makes you somewhat special cases. You're more under a microscope than most, sad but true; on the other hand, you get cut a fair degree of slack as a result. In this instance, ladies, that slack's run out.

"Schedule a start-up meeting with Ms. Cobri and Colonel Sheridan. I'd like a progress report within forty-eight hours and a viable schedule before planetfall. Clear?"

"Aye-aye, sir." Nicole rose.

"Then we're adjourned."

As they emerged onto the Bridge, Nicole tried a joke to mask her flash of apprehension. "Ah well," she sighed, "I was hoping if we simply ignored her, she'd forget all about us."

"That'll be the day."

Nicole looked at her friend. "You were awfully quiet in there."

"Nothing to say."

"Oh."

"Look," Hana grumbled in exasperation, "sometimes this 'Big Brother' side of the job gets to me. Being under perpetual surveillance makes me hinky."

"On a flight, we're *always* part of a telemetry stream; that comes with the territory, has from the start."

"I'm not a complete dim, Nicole, I *know* that. In-System, though, you're talking about a half dozen, maybe a dozen people in the crew; the . . . intimacy makes it easier to take, because everyone's in everyone else's face. And after the first few days, you forget about the data link with DaVinci. They're sort of too far away to matter. This bucket, though, it's so damn *big!* Someone's always peeking, only I never know who."

"I think I know the feeling."

Hana bridled visibly. "I worry about you, okay? But more often than not you're so damn *solitary!* Bad enough that makes it pretty near impossible for people to offer help, you don't offer a whole helluva lot of encouragement when it's needed in return."

"What's that supposed to mean?"

"You're the rocket jock, figure it out."

Hana turned on her heel and strode away so suddenly that Nicole had to sprint to catch her. Her pager beeped, but she ignored it.

"What's wrong?" she demanded, refusing to back off as Hana shook her arm loose of Nicole's grasp.

"A great many things, my friend. And not all of them can be addressed by a belated acknowledgment of concern, no matter how heartfelt."

"I'm sorry."

"I know you mean that. I know you care. When you're reminded. It doesn't help." Suddenly Nicole felt as cut off from Hana as she was from the Hal, and as equally unsure of the reasons for it.

"Look," Hana said brusquely, seeking refuge for the both of them in a change of subject, "about the C^3 glitch."

"You still think there's a problem."

"Just as much as you, I'll bet."

Nicole shrugged and shook her head. "All I've got to go on are instincts, which I'm not sure I trust anymore."

"If that's the case, we may be well and truly doomed." Nicole looked up sharply. "I've seen you operate, Ace. I'll go with your instincts over the empirical data more often than not. Especially when the data's bogus."

"You got proof?"

"Instincts of my own. Plus a small advantage: I wrote a fair chunk of the software. Something about the program doesn't feel right, but it's going to take a while to be sure."

"Be careful," Nicole said.

"Always."

"I'm serious. Assume your suspicions are justified, Hana; consider the implications. If there's a flaw, it has to be in the archival files as well or in the diagnostics software. That makes it real unlikely that it exists by accident—*shit!*"

The pager had begun warbling a continuous peremptory summons that would not be denied. Whoever wanted her was serious. Nicole cast about for a WallCom station and accessed the message. When she turned back towards Hana, she didn't bother hiding her anger.

"We're wanted back at our quarters," she said flatly. "There's trouble."

"Now *this* is cute," Hana noted dryly as they surveyed the damage.

Someone had been busy with a few cans of spray paint. Multicolored block lettering, cast at an angle across the doorway, big and garishly bright enough to be as impossible to ignore as easy to read.

The Cathouse.

"Did they get inside," Nicole asked the woman who was waiting for them.

"Didn't bother to try," was her reply as she held out her hand. "I'm Rose Guthrie," she said, "Chief of Security." She didn't much look the part, standing a full head shorter than

Nicole and Hana, which made her pretty much average height. She had a trim figure, cast along the lines of a ballroom dancer. Wheat-colored hair and dark hazel eyes on an oval face that still retained much of the prettiness of youth. She was in Navy khaki, but she wore a skirt instead of trousers—a rare exception in the blue water fleet and far more so in space— with the silver leaves of a full Commander on her shirt collar. The ready smile was genuine, but her gaze was the true measure of the woman; it missed nothing.

"Only the doorway was tagged," she continued. Square-cut nails and a firm grip, a woman who balanced appearance with the practical necessities of the job. Nicole suspected that more than one person was so taken in by the "Mom" facade that they missed the cop underneath. "And only your doorway. They left the Hal entrance alone."

"So what comes next," Hana wondered aloud. "You round up the 'usual suspects'?"

Rose grinned. "No need. We got who did it."

"Anyone we know," asked Hana.

"Not one of my division," from Nicole, as Rose led them along.

"No, and not quite," they were told.

"Don't take offense," Hana said, "but you don't come across much like the other naval types."

That got them a laugh, unrestrained but still ladylike.

"Perish the thought. I'm a Marshal. What you got here is a small town, what you need to keep the peace is a Sheriff. They got the Marine detachment for busting ass in combat."

"Is there really that much need?"

"You take the world into space, Major, you take its problems with. But while you can haul some Seaman Striker up before the Captain's Mast for discipline, or convene a general court-martial, the same doesn't necessarily apply for that same Seaman's"—she shouldered open the entrance to a Security substation, in effect the local precinct—"fourteen-year-old kid."

He was skinny and scared, growing faster than his clothes could keep up—even if they were the right size, he hadn't time to get comfortable in them, any more than in his own skin. His hair was blacker than Hana's, the color out of a can, parted to the side in the style of classic Japanese *anime*, so that it swept straight down to mask half his face to the chin. He was slumped over, hands and elbows on the table, as they entered the interrogation room, but as soon as he had an audience, he flipped his hair up and away and tilted back in his chair, the picture of total insolence.

"You got no right to hold me," were the first words out of his mouth, with a sneer in place of outright profanity. "I didn't do nothin'."

Rose took a chair opposite and motioned for Nicole and Hana to join her. She was smiling, but there was nothing pleasant to her expression.

"Paint residue on your fingers," she said.

"I was doin' some decorating. I didn't like the color the housebox came in. Figured I'd pretty it up, make it more a home. Got a problem with that?"

"You got some mouth, kid."

"What, you didn't hear of 'Freedom of Speech'? First Amendment to the Constitution, go look it up. Figure this stupid ship's named after the fuckin' thing, oughta have some respect for it."

"We have you on tape," Rose said.

"Bullshit."

"Oh, that's right, I forgot, you disabled the ScanCams for that entire subsector. Nice piece of engineering. Unfortunately, not quite as comprehensive a job as you may have assumed."

"So, what, I haveta scrub it clean?"

"That an admission of guilt?"

He twisted in his chair, body language striking resonant chords in Nicole of how Amy Cobri still occasionally behaved. He plucked a cigarette pack from under his vest.

"You light it," Rose said quietly, "you eat it. Hot."

This time, he paid attention. He started to put the pack away, but Rose snapped her fingers. His lips pursed, he looked ready to argue the point, but then thought better of it and threw the cigarettes across the table. Another snap and the lighter followed.

"I know you," Nicole said, having snuck a glance at the boy's file on the DataPad in front of Rose. "Your father's in my division."

The boy said nothing, his sole acknowledgment a slow blink of the eyes. Nicole felt her arm tingle and flexed the fingers of her right hand to bleed off some tension. Problem for her was, she'd much rather do it by punching the kid in the face.

"He's got a good record," she said, pulling the information from her own memory, "but this is his first ops on the Tachyon Highway. You want to mess it up for him."

"He lives his life, I live mine."

"Listen to the Major," Rose said, "cause she's being nice and cutting you some major slack. Right now, sonny, what's saving your skinny pale ass *is* your old man. We're tryin'—*real hard*—to keep the sins of the child from being visited on the parent. But if you want to cut yourself loose"—and the smile she gave him this time was purely predatory—"fine with me."

He was sweating now, little beads on his forehead and upper lip, as he bounced his eyes from one to the other of the three women across from him.

"Hey. It wasn't any federal crime or nothin', it was just a 'tag.'"

"We'll talk about that in a minute. You bounced the ScanCams off-line. It was very nice work. Those systems are there for a purpose. You do them harm, you do the ship harm, you put lives at risk. *That's* a Federal offense. You want to think different, we'll find you a nice little compartment up-top and open a door to outside, see how *you* like it when you're screaming for help into an inactive screen."

"It was a *joke*!" He was whining. If anything, Rose's smile got even more dangerous.

"That's why we're having this little talk, Louis. To establish ground rules as to what is and is not funny. Or acceptable.

"You got a problem with girls?" she asked, abruptly changing tack.

"Hey," he said dismissively, clearly not.

"How about with lady officers? Maybe you, maybe your old man, you still figure they got no rightful place in the Navy, or space, or whatever?"

"Hey!" Again, from tone and gesture, clearly not. He could see where this was going, though, and he didn't like it.

"How about the Hal?"

"Hey!" A clear protestation. "Don't I get a lawyer or nothin'? Or a lousy phone call?"

"You haven't been charged, Louis, we're just having ourselves a friendly little talk."

"So I'm free to go then, right?"

"You want to make this official, Louis?"

"I got zip against the Fuzzies, okay? I never even met any of 'em. Christ, gimme a break."

"Just Major Shea, then?"

"Hey. There's talk, y'know?"

"What kind?" Nicole asked.

The boy shrugged. "Talk," he said, as if the single word explained everything. "Y'know, 'bout how you're a Fuzzy in all but fur."

The interview didn't last much longer. It was all recorded but because the boy hadn't been charged, or even read his Miranda rights, none of it was official. Putting him in the brig wouldn't accomplish much at this stage, Rose told them, better to try to warn him off and hope he'd learn from the experience.

"Nice attitude," said Hana. "The boy, I mean."

Rose shrugged. "Surely it's one you've heard before."

"Not really," Nicole confessed. "Not that much."

"The virtues," Hana said, "of the monastic life at Edwards. Folks there know you, know the Hal, they have what we'd consider the 'right' perspective."

"You saying you *have* heard it?"

"In bars. Bull sessions. The Moon. The Belt. Where who we are, you and me, and what we did is more story than truth."

"And you know kids," Rose said, expanding on Hana's comment, "always go for the jugular, especially when you're dissing somebody. Louis may not even believe most of what he said, it's simply what would get the biggest rise out of you."

"So what's the next step," and then, Nicole answered her own question. "Talk to the father, I suppose."

"You and me both," agreed Rose. "This ship isn't a playground. And the next time, his targets might not be so forgiving. He'd better realize I wasn't altogether kidding. This is a closed social system. Problems can't be exiled to prison. Unfortunately, they can be disposed of. I don't want that kid, or his old man, or anybody, to find themselves breathing vacuum.

"We'll hold him overnight, to give him a taste of what's in store for him if we ever have to get 'official,' then send him over first thing tomorrow to clean up his mess."

Nicole nodded.

Hana didn't want to go straight home, however, striking a path instead towards the starship's equator and the hangar bay where the *Swiftstar* was parked.

Before boarding, Hana pulled all the umbilicals that plugged the spaceplane into the *Constitution*'s power and life-support grid. Then, as Nicole settled herself on the flight deck, she sealed the hatch behind them. Nicole thought the precautions were a little extreme, but kept those feelings to herself.

"This is not good," Hana said finally, sitting herself across the aisle from Nicole after plugging her PortaComp into the adjacent console and scanning a page of data.

"It's a kid with an overabundance of attitude and hormones, Hana, not a federal case."

"Nicole," and she took a breath to master herself. "Nicole, I've been on the Frontier these past five years. Trust me, it's different from Earth. From the Stations. From DaVinci," this last referring to the primary starport, and Manned Space headquarters, on the Moon. "There is fear. There is a lack of trust. There is hatred. Earth First is an extreme, but that kid's tag is partly where it starts. As far as we're concerned, our specific situation," she went on, "I know three people on this globe well enough to trust implicitly—myself, you, and Ramsey Sheridan."

"Go on," Nicole prompted, when Hana fell silent.

"The probability is that I'm simply being paranoid—believe me, I know how weird this all looks, the way I'm behaving here—but the fact is we're a long way from home, aboard a ship where we pretty much don't know a soul. And I mean *know,* Nicole, as in you'd bet your life on them without a second thought, the way we both would with each other or Andrei or Ben Ciari.

"Part and parcel of the ambush on the *Swift* was an attack through the C^3 software. Not the on-board programs, mind you, but their mainframe counterparts on Sutherland and DaVinci. We were totally incommunicado with those on whom we depended most. Now, those nexuses are supposed to be inviolable. Only somebody got to them, with a target-specific routine so well masked that the only reason it was spotted at all was because we survived. *Constitution* could hear us fine, along with a half-dozen other ships in local space, plus Hightower and Hawking," Earth's two L-5 colonies. "We even got picked up by a ham operator on Mars, for Heaven's sake! But not the Moon and not Sutherland. To me, that betokens a capability as formidable as the fighters.

"I don't believe in coincidences, Ace."

"You could be making a mountain out of the proverbial molehill, Hana."

"That'd make my day, believe me. But think about it—suppose you hadn't been in SecCom? Who'd know about the glitch?"

"You suggesting there's an Earth First cell on this ship? You saying Tom Pasqua's part of it?"

"I'm suggesting that any organization determined enough to mount a military operation in the high atmosphere, with what appears to be cutting-edge equipment, has to be taken seriously.

"We're totally isolated here, Nicole. We're'e a long way from home, and we've no access to independent—and secure—sources of data. Other than, perhaps, what we brought with us."

"Your PortaComp."

"At the moment," Hana waved her hand over the little computer. "It's scanning for 'bugs' and generating a 'snow' field to disrupt any tape recorders that might happen to have been left aboard. You'll be happy to know we're clean."

"I'm so pleased."

"You're the one who said 'be careful.'"

Nicole slouched in her chair, chewing on a thumbnail while her focus gradually turned inward; she was staring straight at Hana, but had lost almost all awareness of her. Hana let her think like that for a couple of minutes.

"Your hair looks awful," forgetting herself and muttering aloud a comment she'd intended to keep to herself.

"I beg your pardon?" Nicole blinked, centering once more on her friend.

"You don't take care of yourself."

"Last physical says different." She still wasn't wholly tracking, responding to the words while missing the subtext that held their true meaning.

Hana threw up her hands, as if to say, *why do I bother?* "Fine," she snapped. And then, "More precisely, you don't seem to care much about yourself. Very neat, very presentable, totally regulation; the only thing about you that's *you* anymore is that damn flight jacket. The rest is all camouflage."

"I haven't your flair, but we've both known that from the beginning."

"No, Nicole. You don't have the will anymore to *try*, unless someone puts a gun to your head. It's like you've crafted an image of yourself, inside and out, that you're determined to hold on to—like an icon or some talisman—for dear life."

"That's way out of line, Hana."

"Probably. But where we're concerned, I don't figure I've got all that much to lose."

Nicole stood, turning away from the other woman to brace her hands against the curved ceiling overhead. Hana watched expectantly, and then her mouth opened in a silent gasp as she heard a subvocal growl that raised the atavistic hackles at the base of her skull and set her nerves to buzzing. She had goose bumps, she knew from fright, her back-brain sending a frantic series of primordial cues for her to run for the nearest tree. For her life.

Nicole wasn't even aware of what she'd done as she looked back over her shoulder, acting as though the previous exchange hadn't taken place.

"Have you told any of this to Ramsey?"

"You're the one and only."

Nicole nodded. "The software's the key. Proof, one way or the other. If this glitch exists, can you find it?"

"Yes."

"Make it sooner rather than later, okay?"

"Do my best. Course, you know who my prime suspect is."

"No offense, but that's too damn convenient."

"Want to bet she had a hand in instigating Louie's little stunt at our door? Most likely provided the means to disable the ScanCams."

"Let's worry about suspects when we have some evidence."

"I merely mention it in light of the *Lamplighter* conference we've got scheduled."

"We're stuck with that, Hana."

"Tell me about it." Hana faced Nicole, started to reach out a hand and then thought better of it.

"It's just . . ." she tried to say, and then thought better of that, too.

Outside the hangar, they went their separate ways.

To Nicole's surprise, when the meeting convened, Ramsey Sheridan brought along Jenny Coy. Amy challenged her presence, citing security; the Colonel replied flatly that Jenny was part of the team on Judith Canfield's direct orders—which prompted an exchange of intrigued looks between Nicole and Hana—and there was the end of it. The young woman backed off.

There was a set of grim determination to Ramsey's features Nicole had seen only in some wartime photos of him, one in particular, after three days of almost nonstop combat. The picture showed the face of a young man but the eyes of an ancient soul, with a haunting, hollow stare that Nicole had never forgotten. Ben Ciari had it as well, and she'd seen it in her own reflection, albeit to a much lesser extent, after the *Wanderer* mission.

She knew then that whatever *Lamplighter* represented, it was bad.

Amy, by stark and absolute contrast, was enthusiasm personified.

"*Lamplighter* is a revolutionary C^3 network," the young woman said. She favored her corporate look again today, attempting to present a demeanor that belied her age. "Command, Control, and Communications. Our goal is to establish a full-spectrum biological interface between pilot and vehicle."

Nicole couldn't help herself; she sat back in her chair, thunderstruck.

"Are we talking about some kind of plug-linkage," Jenny asked, to everyone's surprise, "hardwiring the brain to the ship?"

Amy shook her head, trying to gauge Nicole's reaction.

"Something completely different, along the lines of a software adaptation, using genetic engineering."

"On *me*?" snapped Nicole, making Amy jump with the violence in that last single word.

"I'm not exactly thrilled by this either, you know," Amy protested, an unexpected blitzkrieg of nerves cranking her up to motormouth mode and stripping away a significant layer of her grown-up veneer. "I know what you're thinking, I know what people will say, especially if something goes wrong. I also think we're on the verge of something really important here. But *Lamplighter*'s subject specific. Without you, Nicole, we've got nothing. We'll have nothing. All the work, all the hopes, all the possibilities, will have been wasted."

Then, kiddo, came the automatic response in Nicole's thoughts, *you are flat out of luck.*

Aloud, she said flatly, "Tell me," and Amy obligingly rushed on.

"We use a variation on the Hal genegineer virus to synchronize your nervous system with the C^3 network of a spacecraft." Her eyes—and Hana's as well—flicked to Nicole's hand on the table as the fingers arched and flexed in a slow, deliberate, totally unconscious movement, almost like a cat stretching its claws. "The idea is to have both sets of circuitry—biological and mechanical—resonate on the same frequency. You'll have livetime, ongoing access to all ship systems. You'll instinctively—consciously and unconsciously—know the status of the vehicle and its components. You can actuate them as well, literally control the spacecraft with your thoughts. In essence, you become the craft, the craft becomes you. A gestalt biotechnological organism."

"A wireless linkage, then?" asked Jenny.

"In theory, it'd be more like the ship becoming an extension of the pilot's body. Not so much asking specifically, 'Tell me, ship, the status of the secondary lateral sensor array,' but having an almost empathic awareness that your mind automatically interprets as the status of that particular system."

"Can you disconnect?"

"I beg your pardon?"

"Shut it off, Amy," interrupted Hana brusquely. "Disengage. Remove yourself from the network."

"Yes!" Amy snapped, responding to the acid in Hana's tone.

"And the effect?" Jenny again, as devoid of passion as Hana was brimful of it.

"I'm not sure what you mean," she replied, which nobody else at the table believed for a moment. Nicole set her teeth and hid behind her best poker face.

"If I understand correctly," Jenny posited in the same casual manner, as though this were some abstract academic forum, "your interface in effect makes the pilot the organic CPU of this cybernetic system—let's say, for the sake of argument, we're speaking of the *Constitution* here. Nicole has total access to the Network, and total control over it. Everyone else in Primary and Secondary Command becomes her redundant system. That means she's processing a tremendous volume of information."

"No," Amy explained patiently, feeling herself on more secure ground, the surge of confidence reflected in a calming of both voice and manner. Nicole couldn't help wondering if that was precisely what Jenny had intended. "The ship processes the information; Nicole taps into it as and when needed. There are enhancements built in to the genetic program to allow her to handle the additional capacity, plus buffers to prevent overload."

"But how does she—fuck this," Hana almost snarled as she went entirely the opposite direction from Jenny, and tried to depersonalize the focus, "how does the *pilot* deal with the *loss* of that access, Amy? We're not talking about a transient circumstance, like melding with a Virtual scenario. You're making the person part of the ship, and the ship part of the person, as integral as any element of the organic physicality. How do you sever that? How do you deal with the emotional consequences? Does damage to the ship impact on the pilot? Or the reverse, if the pilot's injured? Where the hell does one begin and the other end?"

"Why me?"

Nicole's voice made some of the others jump; the conversation had gotten so heated, so quickly—and she had remained so supernally still—that they'd nearly forgotten she was present.

Amy paused, and let her shoulders slump as she leaned a little forward onto the table.

"You . . ." another pause, as she struggled with the words, "are the primary component of the core data base. To a comprehensive degree we've been unable to match elsewhere. And believe me, we've tried."

"Where'd the information come from?" It was a pro forma question; Nicole had already intuited the answer, but that was a small horror compared to what she'd already heard.

"My brother. The research project he ran on Virtual Reality. In going back over his notes, after he died, I suspect that this may've been where he was heading all along."

"Son of a *bitch*!" hissed Hana.

Nicole thought much the same as she added: "And you just had to carry on the family tradition."

"You don't know what's at stake!" Amy cried with surprising passion.

"Where you and your family are concerned, should I care? Alex is dead and buried, the same should go for his research."

"It isn't about me, Nicole. It isn't even about you. It's about ships like this and how safely they get where they're supposed to go. Columbus knew the principals of sailing and navigation when he headed west across the Atlantic, but he'd never seen a hurricane. Suppose, that first trip in 1492, he'd run into one, a rip-snorter of a Cat 5 storm, with winds in triple digits and wave tops higher than his mainmast. Want to lay odds on his survival? Or how eager the Spanish Court would be to bankroll the next sailor who wanted to follow in his wake—assuming you could even *find* such a guy."

"So?"

"So. Here we are, jaunting helter-skelter across the stars— only we don't have a clue what it's like outside while we're in warp. We don't even know if that word applies. Think about it. We are traveling through an environment about which we know *absolutely nothing!* And none of our instrumentality can tell us. It's designed and built to function in the 'real' Universe; it's limited by its programming. It can't tell us what actually *is* out there, only a marginally applicable Normal Space analog, because that's the only language it knows.

"We're no better. The environment is so fundamentally *alien* to any of the concepts that our evolutionary biology is grounded in that we can't comprehend what we're looking at, even if we do something as seemingly obvious as looking out a damn window!

"Think of us as autistic children. We function within a perfectly consistent solipsistic framework; the problem is, it bears no relation to the external reality we live in. We're unable to comprehend the input or make our own actions or speech comprehensible to others.

"We need a Rosetta Stone. A way to perceive the raw data of this alien environment in terms and a context that make sense. The capacity to adapt, to evolve, to apply inspiration and imagination. Not Artificial Intelligence, but true sentience, mated to the storage and processing capabilities of a CyberNet. The hope is that *Lamplighter* is it."

"Which was essentially the argument that was made to General Canfield and the President," Ramsey added quietly, "when the project was initially proposed. Given the nature of your . . . history with the Cobris, Nicole, all concerned were predisposed to reject the submission out of hand. But it made too much sense.

"Step outside and talk to Bill Hobby. Or better yet, assuming you get the chance, take a look at the Memorial Cenotaph in Challenger Plaza. Every year, on average, we lose a couple of starships. Still. We don't know why. Accidents happen. A crash in Normal Space, more often than not there's wreckage. We can analyze the debris, the flight telemetry, ultimately determine what went wrong. Aside from the logistics—which I grant you is no small difference—it's very much like an accident investigation on Earth.

"But a warp crash is by its very nature a catastrophic event. There's nothing left, the vessel is wholly—we assume, instantly—vaporized. We don't know whether it was a design or construction flaw, hostile action, or the poor bastards simply ran into something. We have to find a way to expand that data base.

"One of the fundamental presumptions behind the *Constitution*'s design philosophy," Ramsey said, "is that size begets survivability. Of course, much the same was said about the *Titanic*. If there are icebergs, we need to be able to see them."

"So does that make Nicole a guinea pig or a sacrificial lamb?"

Ramsey faced her. "Your fundamental attitude is noted, Dr. Murai, there's no need to press the point. If you're unable—or unwilling—to make a positive contribution to these proceedings, I'm more than prepared, however reluctantly, to go on without you."

His expression softened, but you had to look really closely to tell. "That's as formal as I want to get, Hana, and it's the last time I want to have to mention this particular subject. Is that understood?" His gaze swept the table, to encompass them all in turn.

"I'm still intrigued," Jenny offered, "by this notion that Nicole's the *only* viable test subject . . ."

"I told you, Alex established a unique data base for her."

"Aye, that I ken." There was a shyly embarrassed little grin, and Jenny flushed ever so slightly. "Sorry. You'd think a proper university education would pummel the hometown dialect out of me long ago." It was a deliberate attempt at humor and it didn't work as well as she'd probably hoped; nobody even smiled. But there was a perceptible easing of the tension.

"I've reviewed the data encompassing the entire run of the test program . . ."

"You had no right!" Amy snapped. "That's proprietary information!"

"I have proper clearance." As earlier, Hana and Nicole exchanged intrigued looks, asking silently, *Who the hell is she?* "And the fact is, miss, your brother was implicated in an attempted presidential assassination. His work at Edwards was considered evidence in that investigation. My focus is more on the human side of the equation, rather than the electronic— that's Dr. Murai's domain—but"—she shook her head for emphasis—"I don't think I saw anything that couldn't be replicated with another subject."

"Learn to know what you're looking at, then," Amy responded nastily, "before you go around passing judgments." She tossed her head in a scoffing motion that took a crucial five years off her age and reminded Nicole of the girl she'd been at Edwards.

"We ran Alex's profile. On a score of subjects, all told. Duds, every one. The computer models wouldn't even come close to matching. Nicole is it."

"As Jenny said," from Hana, "tech is my domain. I want your specs, Amy. Everything Alex did, everything you learned. And, please, spare me the 'proprietary information' bullshit, okay? You hold back, we're done. In that, I think I speak for us all."

Nicole nodded and said, "I have enough on my board with the test regime for *Swiftstar*. I assume that has priority during our visit to Faraway." This last was directed to Ramsey Sheridan.

"It's one of the reasons you're here, Major."

"We'll use the Faraway stage of the mission to analyze the background data—myself, Hana"—she offered a pointed, questioning look at Jenny—"and Jenny. We'll reconvene after departure for Nieuwhome and determine where we go from there."

"I have no problem with that," said Ramsey. "Ms. Cobri?"

"If you want any help . . ." she offered haltingly.

"Give us the data," Nicole told her flatly. "Answer our questions. We'll see."

The three women stayed in the facility after Sheridan and Amy left. Nicole arched back in her chair, tilting it all the way as she stretched her arms full length behind her head. Hana rummaged in a pocket, slid a packet across the polished surface of the table that plopped onto Nicole's lap. Nicole peered past her chin, smiled, unwrapped the gum, and chewed contentedly.

Then she blew a bubble.

Jenny kept her distance and just watched, until Hana tossed her a piece of her own. The Scot's reactions were better than her skill; she made a game try but bobbled the catch, and the gum fell to the floor.

As she ducked underneath the table, Nicole asked casually, "So, Jenny, who the hell are you anyway?"

"Little too old to be a Loot," noted Hana.

"My comparative rank's the same as Nicole's," Jenny retorted. "At least, when she was a Captain. And we're all pretty much of an age, thank you very much."

"I have six years active service," Nicole said, after a bubble popped prematurely. "You've only just come through your astronaut's qualification courses. What came before?"

"University," mused Hana, when Jenny didn't reply right away, "Canfield. Human equation. On the *Lamplighter* team."

"Don't mind her," Nicole said while Hana was speaking, "she thrives on mysteries. A detective at heart."

"The answer's obvious."

"Yes?" Nicole prompted.

"Doctor, am I right?" Hana challenged. "Flight surgeon. Shrink in the bargain, I'll bet."

"Aye. On all counts."

"To keep an eye on me?" Nicole asked.

"That's the general idea."

"Fucking Canfield."

"That's uncalled for, Hana."

"That's what *you* say. Does that make you Canfield's pet spook, then?" she demanded of Jenny.

The other woman bridled at the question and the way Hana put it to her.

"Firstly, I'm nobody's 'pet' *anything*. I've no notion *why* I'm here—in any context you mean—except perhaps for the fact that I'm bloody good at my job and the General thought I might be of some use. And possibly because I felt it would be an honor to work with the pair of you."

"I am not comfortable with being thought of in those kinds of terms," Nicole muttered.

"Get used to it, Ace," grinned Hana. "The worst is probably yet to come. Speaking of which—are you seriously tempted by this cockamaime proposal?"

"You prepared to dismiss it that easily?"

"No problem—but then, I'm not at risk the way you are."

"Ramsey had a point."

"Nicole, forgive me, but this is no time to indulge your martyr complex. There are alternatives to the goals they describe; this one's just top of today's list. But I for one am not inclined to accept at face value something that puts you wholly at the mercy of a family of certifiable nutcases who bear you no love whatsoever."

"You think I am?"

"I think you're susceptible to certain kinds of enticements. I wouldn't be surprised if Clan Cobri has a regularly updated copy of your psych file, along with every other scrap of data they can lay hands on about you, and that Amelia's been told in copious detail precisely which buttons to push. I don't like her, I don't trust them, I am scared of this." She lightly rapped the tabletop with a knuckle, by a stack of data cartridges that had been left behind for them.

"That makes two of us."

"Three, actually," added Jenny, "for what it's worth."

Nicole looked Hana full in the face.

"I need your help," she said simply.

Hana responded with a shallow nod, followed by a slow smile, as though this was something she'd been waiting a long time to hear.

"Well," she said at last. "Canfield put the three of us together, let's see what we can make of that."

CHAPTER EIGHT

She doesn't understand the power of the waves or the terrible force of the undertow that's sweeping her steadily out to sea. She doesn't know how to swim, but blind instinct prompts her to make the right moves. In smooth water, she might have a fair chance. But the tide is still in full flood, its current is too strong, the wave action—from a storm raging far out of sight beyond the horizon, whose fury never touched this coast at all—far too severe, quickly sapping both strength and will. Time and again, she sinks beneath the waves, until she fights her way back to the surface. It's as though the water were a hunting pack—much like her own family—harrying and worrying at a healthy prey, wearing it down to the point where it simply hasn't the strength to resist. She still refuses to admit it, but she's face-to-face with her own mortality.

She flew a dozen *Swiftstar* sorties in the ten days after they achieved orbit around Faraway, and looking back on it hadn't felt more exhausted or more happy in her entire life. Colors and textures notwithstanding, sky was sky and ground was ground and she passed between them as though she'd been born to it.

The *Swift* surpassed even her expectations, handling the heavy lifting tests—which climaxed with a full load of cargo and then passengers—as easily as the initial shakedown flights. It was a relief to put aside the cares and concerns of the last week and concentrate on the welcome, familiar stress of flying.

She couldn't sleep the first night she spent dirtside. It was like sitting on the Throne in SecCom, with the ship charging up about her to hurl itself headlong across the stars, only more so. She lay on her bed for what seemed like hours, almost giddy with the excitement of being here, her eyes wide, senses preternaturally alert as she just *listened*. She'd left the windows open; in the far distance, she could hear voices and remembered another night back on Earth when she discovered— much to her chagrin—precisely how far noise traveled on the high desert in the dark. The stillness was disconcerting; in space, there was always sound—beginning with something as basic, and essential, as the ventilation system. There, silence was a warning.

That thought rolled her back to *Lamplighter* and she twisted on the bed and punched out the pillow.

Still, sleep wouldn't come, only now it was no longer from exhilaration. Which made her even more angry that this special moment had been ruined.

She swung herself up and cast about in the darkness for shorts and sneaks, pulling on a polo and a sweatshirt as she stepped outside. Like the High Mojave around Edwards, this plateau was lousy at retaining the day's warmth; the air had an edge to it that let her see her breath. She didn't mind. It was a welcome relief from the canned, perfectly controlled climate aboard *Constitution*.

There was no traffic this late, air or ground, not enough people on-planet, nor enough activity to justify round-the-clock operations over Faraway's thirty-one-hour day. The landing field was mostly shadow, decorated by the boundary lamps that lined the roads and aprons, plus the day-bright floodlights to illuminate some of the parking revetments in the far distance. She could pick out the *Swiftstar* without any trouble, and the thought came unbidden that her plane made a temptingly perfect target. On a mostly empty planet, there wasn't much need for security.

A skeleton staff was on duty; everyone else—locals and visitors both—were enjoying the town's hospitality. In many ways, Faraway was a resonant echo of life on the American frontier two centuries before, when long stretches of isolation were broken by the welcome arrival of a traveller from home. Starships were still the fastest and most efficient means of communication between systems, radio being limited by the speed of light. Messages sent wouldn't be received for decades, much less their replies. Yet, along the same line, because starships themselves were still relatively few and far between—and the territory they covered expanding exponentially in literally every direction—those visits were also comparatively infrequent. Even scheduled flights couldn't be guaranteed. A missed date could mean something ominous—as had happened twice since the colony's founding, ships vanishing en route without a trace. Or merely that the vessel involved had been diverted to more pressing duties.

Nicole thought while she stretched of all the elements of life she took for granted; even on the Moon, there was ready access to the latest releases in every aspect of the entertainment media: books, audio, video, computer. Not so on Faraway, or any of the other colonies. That was another reason for the starships' importance. They weren't required any longer for the necessities of life; Faraway was so well established it could survive on its own. They were like honeybees, enriching and revitalizing the plant with deposits of new and different pollen, broadening and deepening the cultural gene stock just as new immigrants did the biological.

In some ways, these visits were a lot harder on the starships' personnel. Only a comparative handful ever made it down to the surface, and that was generally restricted to the flight crews, plus various teams of mission specialists. There simply wasn't sufficient equipment to accommodate everyone. Which in turn formed the primary rationale for the *Swiftstar* project, to find a more economical means of transit from orbit to planet and back again. If the original Rockwell shuttle was envisioned as a space truck, *Swiftstar* was more along the lines of a bus—or better yet an off-road utility vehicle, as useful with passengers as cargo and intended to go pretty much anywhere.

She felt as much as heard the rustling whip of wings slapping the air behind her and flinched as an owl swooped after something small and scampering too far in the distance for Nicole to see clearly. She heard a squeak that ended too suddenly, and watched the owl climb, silhouetted against the midnight starscape. Evidently, she wasn't the only one thinking in terms of targets tonight.

Both rodents and predators were imports. Nobody was quite sure how the one got here, or rather would admit to the responsibility. The birds came later, in an attempt to establish a biological balance before the place was overrun. According to the biologists, the birds were adapting quite nicely to their new environment, and expanding their hunting activities to include some of the native population as well. What would come of that, and of reports that the rodents were beginning to inter-breed as well, no one was yet prepared to say. But quarantine protocols had been strengthened. Considerably.

She set herself a gentle pace to start, following the road away from her bivouac and towards the flight line—no sense risking foolish injuries by striking out cross-country in the dark. The planet had three moons, but none could compare with Earth's Luna; these were more of a piece, in size and orbit, with Mars' satellites Diemos and Phobos. They didn't have a significant effect on the planetary tides, and didn't cast a whole lot of light. They didn't have to, really; the stars did it for them.

She'd never seen so many from within an atmosphere, and in truth had never breathed air so pure and clean. The most pristine spot on Earth still reflected the effects of two centuries of rampant industrial development, even if she couldn't smell the pollution outright.

She caught a glimpse of movement impossibly high over-head and thought at first it was the owl again or perhaps a hawk. Then she grinned, as the shape swiftly occluded one star after another in a straight line movement; it was only the *Constitution*, far enough out that it took the better part of a quarter hour for the great starship to pass from horizon to horizon. She stopped watching after only a couple of minutes; she was more interested in the background. The only moment she counted as more impressive was her first deep-space EVA, aboard *Wanderer*, when she stepped out into open space way beyond Mars and saw nothing in almost any direction around her save the Universe.

She couldn't help herself: she threw her arms wide and let out a howl of purest delight, same as she had the day she soloed. She spun herself around so violently she lost her balance and sat down hard on her tailbone. From there, she thought nothing of toppling full length on her back and staring wide-eyed at the celestial sights, grinning all the while like the classic village idiot.

She loped along the main runway, a relaxed, steady gait that brought her from one end to the other in surprisingly short order and with no shortness of breath, despite the altitude, the plateau being almost a full klick above sea level. She turned to start back without a break—and at a faster speed—when she heard a sharp, high-pitched giggle from beyond one of the nearby dunes.

Her first instinct was to mind her own business and keep going, but the woman's voice was familiar, the male that answered—although the words were indistinguishable—very much so.

She picked her way cautiously up the slope. The sand was hard-packed to the consistency of concrete—one of the main reasons for laying out the field here—but the occasional weather cracks, just wide and deep enough to catch an unwary ankle and wickedly difficult to see in the dark, made for dangerous footing. She had no illusions about surprising the couple; even though she was approaching from downwind, in that naturally still manner she'd somehow absorbed from the Hal she'd known, she assumed Raqella would hear her. Probably pick up her scent as well.

Sure enough, the voices faded as she cleared the crest of the dune. Amy lay on her back, braced on both elbows, a miffed expression more than plain in the faint starlight. Raqella was facing the young woman, with his back deliberately to Nicole.

"Fancy meeting you here," was Nicole's opening line, though she sighed inside at how lame and parental that sounded.

Amy agreed with the thought.

"To me," she said, "it has a certain air of inevitability." Her subtext was clear, *get the hell out of our faces and leave us the hell alone.* Nicole wasn't about to. "Anything we can do for you, Major?" she asked, in open challenge.

"It's late," Nicole said. "Raqella's flying tomorrow."

"You're up."

"Only for as long as it'll take me to reach my room. And I won't be in the air."

"Do you question my capabilities, Shea-Pilot?" Raqella

demanded, features still in shadow as he trailed claw-tipped fingers along Amy's arm, making her shiver in delight.

"I require my personnel to be on a par with their equipment, if not better. If I have doubts about either, I'll get a replacement."

Suddenly he rose, in the swift, disconcertingly fluid motion common to all the Hal Nicole had known—the least graceful among them making their most graceful human counterparts seem like lead-footed sluggards by comparison, a stark and absolute contrast that never failed to infuriate her. He faced her at his full height, his stance giving Nicole a flash of memory to their confrontation on the San Diego waterfront. Nicole's body responded of its own accord, with minute adjustments of balance and bearing that cast a look of apprehension over Amy's features, the beginnings of a realization—and a fear— that matters were on the verge of slipping out of hand.

"You have no right to speak so to me, *Waryk sk'nai!*" Raqella spoke in Hal, using a term Nicole had never heard before. The tone was insulting, so she made sure to answer in English.

"I'm a Squadron Commander aboard the *Constitution,*" she told him deliberately, "and Project Manager for the *Swiftstar* test series. You're subordinate to me in both areas. *That* gives me the right. I think I know something of what you're both feeling tonight—hell"—she tried a small smile in an attempt to ease the mood, though her eyes never left the young Hal's—"it's why I'm out here myself. That's why I'm not making this an order, merely a suggestion. You show up in the morning ready to fly, all well and good."

She left the rest unsaid.

She thought about what Raqella had called her all the way back. It was a burr under her skull that refused all her attempts at banishment as she slowed first to a walk and then a stroll, and tried to lose herself once more in the natural wonders that surrounded her. The sneer and the body language were clues, indicating a secret he was privy to that she wasn't. But though she racked her memory, she couldn't find a way to take her past the next step.

It didn't get any better in quarters, as she hunkered on her bed, a mug of steaming tea in hand and a plate of fresh-baked cookies close by, to stare at the screen of her PortaComp while it flash-scanned the Hal dictionary she'd built up over the past five years.

"Sod," she muttered at long last, when yet another marginal lead—and at that, the best she'd been able to manage—crashed and burned.

Her head ached and her eyes felt like they were tucked snug into sandpaper-lined sockets. *A good thing* I'm *not flying tomorrow*, she told herself in disgust, *or I'd be nailed by my own regs.*

She thought of pouring another mug, but couldn't find the energy; instead, she gathered her comforter close about her and folded herself into the corner where bed met bureau, making a place for herself that was as much nest as cave.

There was no sense of falling asleep.

Her eyes popped wide, and closed just as quickly, as she tried to burrow her head beneath arm and covers in a desperate attempt to block out the sunlight streaming through her open curtains.

She was sore all over, as though she'd aged a lifetime overnight, and not simply from the miserable position she'd stuck herself into when she went to bed.

"I'll bet you have a story to tell," announced Jenny with disgustingly good cheer on the flight line as Nicole hobbled gingerly out of the jeep.

"And let me guess," was Nicole's reply, spaced between sips of tea, "you're just the one to listen."

"Is that an invitation, then?"

Nicole shrugged, narrowing her eyes behind the dark lenses of her RayBans as she took a preliminary look at the *Swiftstar*.

"Didn't see you at the party," Jenny said.

"Nope."

"Stayed to yourself, then?"

"How was it?"

Nicole started her walkaround inspection, Jenny obligingly following along behind. Nicole didn't ask about Raqella; she was late, so she assumed he was already here and running through the on-board checklist.

"The party? Not half bad, considering. Not in the class of a proper *ceildh* of course, but then what is?"

Nicole allowed herself a smile of agreement. Her mug was empty, so Jenny—staying true to her public role as team dog's-body—went to fetch a refill. She found Nicole on tiptoes atop the main undercarriage, glasses clenched between her teeth while she shined a flashlight into the recesses of the wheel well to examine the fittings.

"Can you really tell what's what by a gander at the outside?" Jenny asked.

"Can you tell what's what by tapping on my chest and feeling my wrists and ankles?"

"You'd never believe how much."

"Same applies here. As without, generally, so within. Not a stone guarantee, of course, but a fair indication nonetheless." She fiddled with a couple of fittings, satisfying herself they were snug and tight, and gave the tire an unconscious caress as she clambered down.

"Your first night on a new world. It must've been grand."

Nicole cocked an eyebrow, to question the abrupt change of subject. "Aren't *we* the traveling woman," she said. "Been this way before, have you?"

"Is that a joke? I'm so jazzed, I could fly without wings. I was just thinking, is all, that this is something you've been working towards your whole adult life."

"What's the old saying," Nicole said before she could stop herself, " 'be careful what you wish for'?"

"I've done all this, Shea-Pilot," Raqella called out from the boarding platform overhead.

"Good for you," Nicole muttered, though she knew the Hal would hear her, "but she's still *my* plane." Nicole was grateful for the interruption; she suspected Jenny felt otherwise.

"If you do not trust me to fly—!" He bridled, but she cut him off by striding to the base of the stairs and plugging her Pad into an I/O data port. A touch of the main menu called up the plane's status display, which told her that Raqella had been on-site since before sunrise; the preflight was complete, all systems checked out.

"He's very good," Jenny said. "A natural pilot, the instructors said in class."

"Yup," was Nicole's sole response as she handed Jenny the mug and climbed the stairs. He looked none the worse for his late night, and Nicole wondered sourly if he'd been to sleep at all.

"Mission profile?"

"Logged and loaded," he replied, properly professional. "Rendezvous with *Constitution*, return with one passenger module, two cargo. Total trip time projected at eleven hours. I can do it in less," he added.

"I'm sure. But we're not out to set any turnaround records."

"Or is it perhaps that you don't want anyone setting them but you."

She didn't rise to the bait; she went on as though he hadn't spoken. "Eleven hours brings you back in pretty near full daylight. I don't want a night approach, not yet, and I don't want a dusk approach at all. If processing looks like it'll take you past the operational window, you can come back in the morning; we'll adjust the rest of the schedule accordingly."

"A needless concern, Shea-Pilot. It won't happen."

"Fine. And you have your orders if it does."

"I never thought of you as being so cautious."

"Live and learn, hotshot. Have a good flight."

Jenny put her finger on his attitude as they drove across the field towards the terminal complex: "He doesn't like you much, does he?"

"So it would seem."

"Not the way he acted in class. To hear him talk, you were a step removed from deity. And besides, however he feels about you as a human, doesn't your status as a Hal demand his respect?"

"How much do you know about that?"

"There isn't much *to* know, actually. The odd magazine article—scholarly or scandalous—either way, depressingly superficial. All the books about the Contact and the Alliance are from our perspective; there's almost nothing in the public media about the Hal through their eyes. And the diplomatic evaluations, from our legation on s'N'dare, are still mostly classified."

"They're not that helpful, either."

"You've read them?"

"Gone them one better."

Jenny nodded understanding. "Your letters from Marshal Ciari."

"Thanks to his exposure to their Speaker virus, he has a unique insight into their culture. The primary effect was only temporary, the Hal flushed the bug out of his system as soon as we were safely rescued, but there are residual resonances. A widened perception."

"But that's not enough, is it?"

Nicole shook her head. "He's been sounding more and more frustrated. He said it's like looking through a pair of binoculars. The image is crisp and clear, but ultimately it's limited. You see only what the field of vision allows. For all the good it does you, what lies beyond might as well not even exist."

She made a face as they pulled up to the terminal. "I asked General Canfield to send him our flight schedule, I was sort of hoping there'd be a Courier waiting, with his latest letters."

"There was a Courier in orbit."

Couriers were small, unmanned, overpowered mail ships— lots of engine, lots of shielding, state-of-the-art guidance systems—capable of surviving stresses the much larger starships couldn't. One more set of links in the growing communications chain that bound the worlds together.

"But it's outbound, I'm afraid," Jenny continued, "this morning, for s'N'dare."

"Wish I'd known, damn it, I could've sent Ben a letter of my own. Maybe there's still time—!"

Unfortunately, there wasn't, as Nicole discovered upon entering the Flight Control Center at the Tower; the Courier had launched while she slept.

"We'll be here for near another fortnight yet," Jenny said hopefully. "There's plenty of time for something to turn up."

"True. And if not here, there's always Nieuwhome or Tiburon."

She caught sight of Amy, holding court across the room.

"That probably explains everything," she chuckled, with a jut of the chin in the young woman's general direction.

Jenny didn't get the reference, and said so.

"Why Raqella's so pissy. Probably comes of hanging about with Amelia. Last night, I sort of tripped over the pair of them canoodling out behind some dunes."

"Oh, dear."

"I've a feeling it may be early days yet for any interspecies romance—but try telling them!"

"Oh, *dear!*"

"Too prudish, was I?"

"Were you?"

Nicole gave it some thought, and finally shook her head, waving a greeting to Ch'ghan as she took a seat at her own dedicated console.

"It wasn't right," she said, "but I think that has more to do with his choice of partner than the act itself."

"I get the impression that feeling's mutual."

"Hmnh?"

"They *really* don't like you, the Cobris I mean."

"We've had our differences." Her tone signaled an end to that topic of conversation; Jenny obligingly took the hint. "Any news on *Lamplighter*?"

"Hana's taken herself off the planetary passenger rotation, if that's any indication."

"Only that she's working. Which I suppose is good. When she gets going full bore, she tends to lose track of externals. I should probably send you up with Raqella, to make sure she eats."

"I'd rather stay with you."

"My shadow regardless, eh? All right then, we'll pass word on to Ramsey; he should love playing baby-sitter. Send him an encrypted message, cc'd to Hana's buffer."

Movement caught Nicole's attention, and she glanced up automatically to behold Amy sauntering past—as always, as though she owned the place. As always, with fairly good reason. People may hate her guts, but they were always unfailingly polite, Nicole being one of the rare exceptions. Amy's father—Emmanuel, patriarch and founder of the empire—professed that was one of the things he respected most about Nicole, that she appeared utterly unimpressed by Cobri wealth and power. But she knew that was a sham. The only thing the Cobris respected was themselves; in actuality, they liked subservience. They tolerated her defiance because they had no choice, the cost of any response was too high.

Emmanuel, being the family template, merely accepted that reality with somewhat better grace than his daughter.

Who offered a smile that was mostly sneer as she went by, and a morning greeting.

"Howdy-howdy," she said, *"waryk sk'nai!"*

She must have practiced, the pronunciation was almost a match for Raqella's and Nicole knew Amy didn't have that great an ear for the language. Nicole had been expecting something like this, so it was no problem letting the barb slide; Ch'ghan's reaction was something altogether different. He swiveled in his seat as though someone had yanked him on a chain and while he kept his standard poker face, the sudden tension to his body told Nicole eloquently how shocked and upset he was. Out of nowhere came a flashback to early days on the ocean, she and some neighbor kids out for a day sail, when one of them mouthed off with a major-league profanity. None of the children had the slightest idea what the word meant, it was simply something they'd heard the grown-ups use. Nicole's mom was at the helm and she wasn't amused, as she gathered the youngsters into the cabin and explained that certain expressions were totally and absolutely inappropriate.

Then she went back on deck and nailed the crew—including Nicole's father—for setting bad examples.

Ch'ghan turned back to his own console and a telltale on Nicole's indicated he'd opened a secure channel to the *Swiftstar*, one even Nicole couldn't monitor. He spoke briefly, emphatically, and appeared no less angry when he signed off.

Nicole leaned over his shoulder, ostensibly on business, to keep this exchange private as well.

"So," she asked, "what's it mean?"

"A gutter expression, nothing more. Raqella will have better manners in future."

And that ended the discussion.

"There's an interesting theory making the rounds, about the Hal, y'know," said Jenny.

"Which is." Nicole was listening but her eyes never left Ch'ghan, who seemed totally absorbed in his own responsibilities. She used binoculars to monitor the *Swiftstar*'s progress as the spaceplane rolled smoothly along the ramp towards the end of the active runway, then called up current crew medical stats on her Pad. Raqella was within nominal specs but was just as clearly not a happy camper. She held up a hand to silence Jenny and opened a ComLink channel of her own.

"NASA zero-one," she said quietly, using the *Swift*'s official designation; it was called "*Sundowner*" only when she was aboard and in command. The Link was audio only; in full pressure suit, strapped tight into his seat, with his helmet visor hiding his face, there really wasn't much Raqella's picture could tell her.

"Yes, Shea-Pilot."

"How you doin'?"

"Obviously not well enough, else you would not be calling."

"I'm more interested in your evaluation, as Flight Commander."

"I am fine."

"Ch'ghan's your Controller, is that a problem?"

"No."

That, she knew, was as good as she was going to get from him. And a lot more than from Ch'ghan.

"Whatever's going on," she said, "it stays off my flight deck."

"Understood. Neither proficiency nor performance will be impaired in the slightest. If there is nothing more, Shea-Pilot"—there was, but she knew better than to press the point—"I will be on my way."

She watched the plane pivot at the end of the runway, the height of the landing gear giving the aircraft a deceptively delicate appearance. In less than a minute, it was lost to sight, even at the most extreme magnification of the monitor cameras, forcing her to follow its progress on a radar display.

That was when she finally turned her attention back to Jenny.

"You were saying?" she apologized.

"It was Marshal Ciari, started folks thinking along these lines, actually. Did you know that what we call Standard Hal translates remarkably well into English?"

"Try speaking it sometime."

"I have. I can't imagine how you manage an' still find yourself with a functional voice box. The sounds may be difficult to the extreme, but the linguistic structure itself meshes quite easily."

"So?"

"Doesn't work anywhere near as well if you try a straight translation to or from any other Terrestrial language—not French, nor Spanish nor Japanese nor Chinese, not German, not Russian. The dynamics quickly become so unwieldy that there's no real point in even making the attempt. Far simpler to translate into English and then to Hal, and vice versa. I'm not speaking simply about the words, mind you, but the thought processes behind them. Every aspect of the Hal language appears designed to interface with a *specific* Terrestrial counterpart."

"Makes sense, from a First Contact point of view. They were reaching out to us, remember; they knew we were here."

"But it also makes you wonder, doesn't it, what we may be missing?"

"Ben's binocular analogy, you mean?"

"Standard Hal's very polite; even its profanity has an appropriate English analog. Yet here's Raqella using a term so offensive it gets Ch'ghan visibly outraged. And though you're fluent in their language, even you haven't a hint as to its meaning."

"Ter*rif*fic," was all Nicole could find to say.

Starships kept a standard calendar, based on Earth's seasons, as a benchmark frame of reference—all too necessary, given the vagaries of outworld orbits—and the American elements of *Constitution*'s crew celebrated Thanksgiving during the transit to Nieuwhome. That visit was less than a week—they spent more time in the approach and departure phases than in actual planetary orbit—which suited all concerned. The settlers here, in this most populous of the existing colonies, were primarily Afrikaners, intent on establishing a homogeneously gene-pure society free of the elements that had overwhelmed their homeland back on Earth. They had the strictest immigration policies in human space, and—depressingly, Nicole thought— the longest waiting list of applicants.

She never saw the surface, save from a distance; none of the crew did. The closest they came was the Terminal Station that had been built at one of the planet's LaGrange points, half a million kilometers out, where it orbited the world like a natural moon. The staff was unfailingly polite, professional to the core, and made not the slightest attempt to hide how unwelcome they felt the starship's presence was. And unnecessary. Nieuwhome had two starships in service, one dedicated transport, one combat vessel, with another warship on order. It was abundantly clear that they considered this just the beginning. Whatever the future held, they were committed to surviving it on their own.

Tiburon, their third stop, was something different. Lush, where Faraway was Spartan; teeming with life, where the other world was bare. Much of the planet was jungle and explorers had come to discover—the hard way, of course—as well stocked with predators as prey. The surface stations were constructed like forts and more and more the fieldwork was being relegated to remote probes, directed from orbit. The test program planned here for the *Swiftstar* was significantly less extensive than had been the case on Faraway. Partly because there wasn't so much for it to do dirtside; mostly, though, to reduce the risk to the single prototype and its crew.

Which, Nicole suspected, meant primarily her.

The treat for the colonists was that the starship's arrival coincided with Christmas, and plans had been under way since before they departed Earth to make the visit appropriately special.

The ship had its own theater—listed on the original design specs as a secondary cargo bay until Hobby and his shakedown crew executed some modifications of their own to create a fairly impressive space that served equally and easily the demands of drama, dance, and concert. A casting call was posted for the crew's presentation of Handel's *Messiah*, but Nicole found to her chagrin that her voice wasn't quite good enough; no matter, it was loads more fun bellowing the "Hallelujah Chorus" from the audience than from onstage.

As part of their own contribution to the festivities, she and Jenny put together a set of Celtic songs, Jenny pulling lead vocals with a rich contralto while Nicole provided accompaniment on a borrowed guitar. They'd wanted Hana to join them but the one time they raised the point her response was so blunt and unequivocal that neither felt foolhardy enough to try again.

They offered help with her work, and that response was even nastier.

Amy was keeping a very low profile as well, as Hana put increasing demands on her time, calling the young woman whenever there was need, regardless of the day or hour, and not giving a damn if the circumstances proved somewhat inconvenient. Which happened on occasion, because Amy was playing the field with the ship's bachelors, enjoying as much of their company as she could manage. Good times were had by all, but she never dated the same man twice. Nicole couldn't help wondering how Raqella felt about *that*.

Nicole busied herself in work of her own, as the Hal's attempt to mate a warp module to the *Swiftstar* moved in swift progression from theoretical to actual. The three of them were civil, but whatever warmth there had been between them had cooled like a dying star.

Constitution was inbound to Tiburon, just past Transition down to Normal Space, the night of the Christmas concert. Nicole dressed with Hana's flair—almost in deliberate defiance of their argument weeks ago—and drew more than her share of raised eyebrows and admiring glances as a consequence. Strangely, she hardly seemed to notice and even less to care. Almost as though the person being complimented wasn't really her.

The first act closed with the "Hallelujah" but so much raw energy and good cheer was generated that nobody wanted to leave; the audience stood and clapped and cheered through a half-dozen curtain calls until at last the few cast members left onstage began an impromptu a cappella encore. The orchestra members left in the pit picked up the cue, almost as though this was a jam session, their enthusiasm quickly bringing choristers and musicians back onstage. It was a mess and it was glorious and when the doors finally opened, the lobby resounded with laughter and good cheer.

Tom Pasqua pressed a glass into Nicole's hand and she drained it in a few hearty swallows before realizing it was champagne. She hadn't eaten and the alcohol went straight to brain and nervous system, throwing her a tad off-balance and the room about her just as much out of focus. She couldn't help a giggle of surprise. She wasn't that easy a drunk; she knew she could cast aside the effects simply by focusing her concentration, but she didn't want to. It was a lovely evening and hours at least since she'd thought of anything unpleasant; she wanted the mood to last.

Even as she made the wish, she saw Jenny's glance shift past her shoulder and sensed before she looked around that it was Hana.

They hadn't seen much of each other for most of this leg of the flight. Hana was like that when she worked, a regime she'd established for herself flying long-haul interplanetary missions, playing the hermit while she worked through a problem to its conclusion. However much this structure worked for Hana, Nicole thought the price was too high. Her friend looked tired, the rigors of the spirit taken out on the flesh. Nicole had never seen her so carelessly dressed, a jeans, sneaks, and sweatshirt ensemble that had clearly been lived in for quite a while. As if the two of them had switched public personas.

"Now who's not taking care of herself," she said, too softly for Hana to hear over the surrounding hubbub. She should have known better.

Hana's mouth quirked, a ghost flash of humor so brief it was barely noticeable.

"We have to talk," was her reply.

"Where?" Nicole asked.

"If you'll excuse us," Hana said to Pasqua, and pointedly waited until he'd withdrawn. Then she looked around, again with a smile.

"I'd say right here. With all this crowd and the room's acoustics, there's too much ambient noise for any effective eavesdropping."

"Are you sure that's necessary?" from Jenny.

Hana ignored the question; Nicole knew, if it hadn't been, she wouldn't have mentioned it.

"I found a glitch," she said, after shifting the three of them towards a corner, making sure to keep her back to the room to mask her face from any possibility of lipreading. She collected three champagne flutes along the way, so that—to all appearances—they were simply enjoying the intermission.

"In the C^3 software?" Nicole asked.

Hana nodded. "It's buried deep, and the rewrites are so slight they're almost impossible to find."

" 'Rewrites'?"

"Scattered to hell and gone throughout the master program, seemingly at random. I've tagged about a dozen so far, across roughly ten million elements."

"That's well within the range of acceptable anomalies," Jenny said.

"Precisely. That's why the diagnostics sweeps overlooked them. Jenny, I wrote the program, I know what's supposed to be there; these go beyond the operational parameters. And their presence isn't an accident; someone put them there."

"Why? What do they do?"

Hana shrugged. "Dunno yet. The key is in the context, how these elements interact with the main body of the software. They're dormant now, of that I'm pretty certain; I've been trying to provoke a response every which way I know."

"Perhaps they're nonhostile then?"

"In just the time I've been examining the system, I've come across brand-new nodes. Nicole, this fucker's self-replicating; it's seeding itself throughout the whole Command structure. And *that*, Dr. Coy, is not an acceptable anomaly."

"I stand corrected." Despite the apology, Jenny hadn't really backed down a millimeter. Hana was impressed.

"We'll have to tell the Captain," Nicole said, "and pull the tertiary nexus."

Hana shook her head, violently. "*Big* mistake, Ace. We don't know where this comes from. Did it leave the factory flawed, or was it a corrupted upload, delivered before we left Earth? Was it introduced remotely or by someone aboard?"

"Doesn't matter. We're not cops. Our task was to identify the problem; Hobby has professionals to deal with it."

"Assuming he can be trusted."

"What d'you want from me, Hana? It's his ship, we got no one else to turn to. We haven't the status, the skill, or the personnel to run any kind of investigation ourselves, if that's where you're heading."

"Actually, where I'd like to be heading is to the nearest exit, so I can thumb a ride on the next flight home."

"At least your 'glitch' is confined to a backup system," Jenny suggested.

"You think so?" Hana countered. "Consider this analogous to looking for a cancer on a molecular level. Apply Ben Ciari's binocular analogy. We've come up with a series of infected nodes in a single organ. There's potential for more. Trouble is, we can't pull back for a panoramic view of the entire organism; we see everything there is to see in this search, but only a little bit at a time. If I'm right, we'll only have gross evidence of the disease's existence when it's too late and we're in the middle of an across-the-board catastrophic failure."

"There was free and full interaction between the C^3 systems before we left," Nicole echoed. "And the C^3 has access to every subordinate network aboard. We have to assume the other systems are at risk. If not already involved."

"If it were me," Hana said, "I'd have the core instructions— the Master Sleeper—hardwired into one of the mother boards."

"Surely," Jenny insisted, "that can be detected."

"Why? We're talking about commands written on an atomic level, gigabytes of ROM etched on a silicon wafer the size of my thumbnail. You keep it simple, you keep it quiet; nothing registers on any diagnostics scan because nothing wrong is happening. Until it gets its cue. One trigger sets off another, in a cascading sequence, each element building on the one before. It's a chain reaction, only of data. Next to nothing at first," she paused, thought, spoke a little faster. "There's the old story about the chess master and the King. Master beats the King, who offers any reward. Master asks for a grain of rice, to be doubled on every square of the chessboard. King thinks this is a hugely witty jest—except, by doubling and doubling and doubling, the master possessed all the rice in the kingdom before the board was half full. Same here. It's the cumulative effect we have to be afraid of.

"But not to worry," she told them, and even the slight quirky smile faded, "that's the good news."

"I had a feeling."

Hana took a long swallow of champagne to drain her glass, then switched it with Jenny, who hadn't touched a drop of hers.

"I've also reviewed *Lamplighter*. It works."

"How?"

"There are two stages—I've got to tell you, Nicole, old poppa Cobri must be choking on the irony. To think what his son was, to think what Alex could have been and then how easily Daddy dearest cast him aside."

"I do. Get on with it, Hana."

"Two stages, I said. The first is an initializing process, essentially, it's a marker, it gives the C^3 system you're mated to a beacon to anchor to. It also primes you for what's to follow."

"The second stage."

"Which is essentially as Amy described it."

"That's daft," Jenny said sharply. "You can no more integrate a starship's C^3 nexus into a living nervous system than you can a main line megavolt power cable into an average household grid. The body'd never stand the load. You'd burn up every neural circuit in an instant!"

"Which is precisely what happened when they tested it."

"What are you talking about, Hana?" Nicole demanded.

"I'll say this for the kid, she gave us everything. All her research, back to Alex's notes. She had computer models built based on his original data, but when she tried to apply their findings to a real-world system . . ."

"D'you mean a person?" Jenny asked, shocked.

"Not quite. There was no point. For the longest time, there was nothing to test. Each critical element of the network worked. The body was the hardware; the neural circuitry could be genetically modified to handle the data load. As well, biological software could be written to establish a gestalt link to shipboard electronics. But they couldn't find a way to bring them together. Every permutation they tried to run in Virtual blew up in their faces."

"Then Amy went back to Alex's notes."

"And found the answer," Nicole finished, in a flat, hard voice that was wholly unlike her. "But *why*, Hana? What makes me so unique to this project? Why am *I* so essential? Why the hell will this bloody *Lamplighter* work with me and no one else?"

Something changed behind Hana's eyes while Nicole was speaking, a look of sorrow that terrified Nicole, because she'd never seen anything like it before. Her hand began a movement of its own accord, until she consciously stopped herself, reaching up to comfort her friend. Instead, she clenched it into a fist, so tightly the tension ran up both arms and across her shoulders, pulling her back taut until she was standing at something like attention.

All this happened in the few awful seconds it took Hana to reply.

"Because," she said, "it's been done to you before."

CHAPTER NINE

*She cries for parents, siblings, for all the family she
left behind. She rages against the arrogance that
brought her here. She wants to be saved, knowing
that won't happen. She's so wrapped up in herself,
she doesn't notice the first tickling touch against
her foot. The second questioning caress makes her
flinch, gathering legs tight against her body. Which
makes a hash of her buoyancy and almost drowns
her, forcing her to drop them again so that she can
continue swimming. In her aching heart, though,
she exults, delighted at last to have a foe more to
her liking. The sea is like the wind, her natural
weapons are of no use against it. Whatever the ultimate outcome, even if the ocean claims her, at
least this will be a battle she can win. She can go
on to the Shadow with pride.*

She was running, that was memory.

She was walking, that was fact.

At least, insofar as her gown would allow. It was designed
for form not function; she couldn't manage anywhere near her
proper stride. She didn't care.

The theater lobby soared above her, five separate levels, each
with its own balcony overlooking the main floor courtyard. It
was an exercise in total indulgence, and that made it an
altogether human creation. She didn't see.

There were people all around her, families, couples, solos,
finishing intermission drinks and snacks, discussing work,
critiquing the performance, juggling relationships, chasing

after children who were chasing after other children, a setting as utterly normal as any on Earth itself. She didn't hear.

She threaded her way through them as though she were flying a racing slalom. Cut the corners as tightly as you dare but never *ever* touch.

She moved on instinct, eyes unfocused, inner vision set on a wholly different scene. To her, the people she passed, the deck she walked on, barely existed.

Out the entrance, into the access hallway beyond, take a pause for bearings, she knew she was running, she had to know where.

Her nostrils flared, with the remembered ozone snap of shock-wave blasters. Hal sound and smell, Hal weapon. And her arms tucked a little tighter to her body, as though she were wrapped once more in a TangleFoot web.

Then, she shook herself free of the images and started walking again, following her instinct.

She'd left Hana and Jenny abruptly and was thankful they weren't following; she wasn't fit company for friends, she was spoiling for a fight, barely on the edge of control. Those she passed sensed that, even if they didn't quite realize why, and gave her a wide berth.

"It's been done to you before."

The words rang in her head, another window opened in her memory, and she saw herself and Ben Ciari, bound up like mummies as they bobbled in the weightless air of the ship's corridor. Out of her frame of vision, the other direction, were Hana and Andrei Zhimyanov. Before her stood the Hal, Shavrin and Kymri, a clutch of security bods, plus a medtech whose name Nicole never learned. She held a scanner that she passed to her Captain, who swung it back and forth between Nicole and Ben. Nicole caught the reflection of its display screen on Shavrin's tunic, saw it flash gold when it was focused on her, gold mixed with scarlet when Shavrin aimed it at Ben.

The Hal dragged him away, and then Shavrin shot Nicole in the head.

"It's been done to you before."

She couldn't take a decent breath, had to force her perceptions back to reality and her body to behave. She'd come to a t-junction, where a short dead-end hallway led off the main corridor she'd been following. It was capped by a double-width, double-height hatch, which signified this as another of the cargo holds. But instead of the usual brace of restrictive warnings—text and sigils—there was only the legend GAR-DEN.

She fumbled in her bag for her CardEx and slid it through the door's access slot. With a pleasant chime, her presence was acknowledged and the hatch slid open.

Within was another indulgence, another compartment whose function had nothing whatsoever to do with the physical operation of the starship and yet—like the theater—pretty much everything to do with its emotional and psychological well-being. It was a standard bay, which made it roughly the same size as the theater, which in terms of raw space meant it was roughly huge. Hobby's designers had filled it accordingly.

Because they had more height to play with than floor space, they established a number of levels, linked by ramps and stairs and flying bridges. The ceiling was a lesser version of the overhead display used in both the Primary and Secondary Command Centers, programmed to run a natural day/night sequence; at the moment, it was pretty near the middle of the night and the fantasy sky was filled with stars, the view from Earth without the intervening screen of atmosphere to blur and distort the sight.

The holographic field extended down the walls as well, creating an equally spectacular wilderness vista in every direction. A brook followed the gentle slope of one platform, casting a small waterfall down to the main floor, which in turn created a stream that was wide enough at one point to require any who cared to ford to hop across a couple of conveniently placed stones. A couple of bowers had been built to provide some privacy—there were no trees, unfortunately, save those manifested as part of the background (which were spectacular)—and around them, separated by grass borders, flower beds that mixed Terrestrial blossoms with those brought back from other worlds. There was color here, and glorious scents, and the reality of growing things.

It was Jenny who'd found the Garden; she had a love for horticulture that surpassed Nicole's for sailing, to the extent that a couple of the latest additions to the collection were hers.

She said working here was the perfect way to relax and while Nicole couldn't buy that side of the argument, she also couldn't deny the chamber's attraction.

The Garden was quiet, the status board by the entrance indicating barely a dozen visitors. Nicole's name had automatically been added to the list when she entered. Instinctively, she swept the room, a spacer rule that had long since become as natural as breathing: know where everybody is around you, in case you have to move them in a hurry. Know all the exits, in case you have to use them.

There was a spicy cinnamon fragrance to the air that she recognized instantly, and evidence of new plantings just along the wall from where she stood. Her mouth turned down and she thought seriously of leaving—except that the fragrance, as always, was wondrous, and she couldn't think of anywhere else to go. There was no boat at hand, no ocean to sail it on.

Kymri'd had a few cuttings in his quarters back at Edwards, next door to her own house, and she'd taken care of them after his recall to s'N'dare. The individual flowers were impressive enough but the pictures she'd seen didn't do justice to the effect of a massed array, a vibrant mix of hot colors that fooled the eye into thinking the ground itself was painted with flame. It was a breed found only on the highlands of the southern continent of the Hal homeworld, in Shavrin's domain.

She pulled off her shoes and in stocking feet climbed the incline from the entrance, taking a ramp and a bridge up to the midlevel balcony by the waterfall. In the far distance, a youngster spun a Frisbee into the air, her playmate, a level below, squealing in delight as he raced to catch it.

She lay back, stretching full length on the grass, trying to lose herself in the sensual delight of the setting. She was glad to be alone.

"Ah, Christ," she groaned, and felt the sting of tears at the edges of her eyes and an icy hollowness deep in her chest, as though she'd been stabbed.

And she thought of *Maenaes't'whct'y'a*—the Void *Between*—where souls resided without honor, or Name, or even form.

She shook her head, telling herself that was wrong and then wondered why she bothered because those boundaries were blurring by the second. No less than the elements of her essential *self* they were intended to define.

She sensed an approaching presence, recognizing who it was from the way she walked.

Hana hunkered down beside her, close enough to reach while still maintaining a discreet distance.

"I won't bite," Nicole said.

"More's the pity."

"Will you stop!"

"What, Ace, you can't take a little banter?"

Silence followed. Hana took the opportunity to make herself more comfortable. Nicole lay with her arms covering her eyes, teetering on the edge of a good cry.

Hana recognized that and said, "You should let go."

"Easy for you to say."

"True. I don't have your image to uphold. You might feel better, though."

The tears came with surprising ease, as though all she'd been waiting for was permission.

"I didn't . . ." Hana began, "I didn't know how else to tell you."

"Yah."

"Nicole?" She felt Hana's hand on hers, a hesitant touch, that pulled away a few seconds later when she didn't respond.

"I could be wrong," Hana said.

"I think I'd beat you bloody if you were," Nicole said, "but you're not."

"Certain of that, are you?"

"That word Raqella called me . . . ?"

"*Waryk* something or other, the one we couldn't translate."

"*Waryk sk'nai.* Literally, it means 'unevolved.' The only references that come to mind are beasts that run on the ground. Old paths, old ways. In the Hal lexicon, it's an obscenity."

"What, you mean like calling one of us an ape?"

"It goes way beyond that, there are cultural resonances you wouldn't believe. I'm not sure I can explain."

"But you understand."

"Hardly. I may have exchanged binoculars for spectacles, but the optics are lousy. I see more, and not as well."

"They lied to you, Nicole. To us all."

"Looks like."

"How can you be so damn calm?"

"Calm?" The word emerged drained of all emotion because otherwise, Nicole would have shrieked it. "So tell me, Hana, what did you find?"

"Actually, it was a lot like looking for the C^3 software sleeper. Nothing quite as obvious as an extra set of chromosomes. The changes, in and of themselves, are inconsequential."

"But the cascading, cumulative effect . . ."

"Right. Devastating. I don't have access to Ciari's medical history, but I'll lay odds there's a similar pattern throughout his DNA. I haven't had the courage to take a look at mine.

"They tried to fix things, Nicole, to erase the genetic configuration they'd superimposed on your own. In your case, though, I think the structure was interlaced too tightly. It wouldn't all go away."

Nicole managed the faintest of chuckles. "Well, Ciari said I scored highest on that damn Hal scan."

"And they weren't kidding when they said you were too compatible for your own good. The problem was, they found out the hard way."

"So, my altered DNA is making me more receptive to whatever residual Speaker RNA is left over in my head. It has to be why I'm thinking in Hal terms, of Hal places." She wrapped her arms close about her head. "God, that dance with Raqella at the launch party. No wonder he was so spooked, that was *Hal* behavior."

"Most likely. It's analogous to writing over the memory drive in a computer. Theoretically, once you erase data, it's gone. Only that isn't always the case. You'll always have missed sectors, temporary files that didn't get the word, the command won't be as globally comprehensive as you assumed. And that's in a linearly configured data base. The mind's holographic, the imagery's physical as much as analytical."

"Activity triggers response."

"Flashbacks from your subconscious, that sort of thing."

"Ter*rif*ic! I still don't get it, though"—she levered herself up on her elbows and for the first time looked towards her friend—"Ciari exhibited physical manifestations of the genemod, even after the Hal flushed it from his system. Why didn't I, if the process took so much deeper with me?"

"It had time to *set* with him, to become part of his physicality. We got to figure, they knew they'd made a major mistake with you fairly quick off the mark and tried their best to rectify it. Fact is, Ace, in all sorts of little ways, you *are* different."

Nicole let herself collapse once more to the ground.

"And that's what Alex discovered."

"Hacking through your medicals. I got to hand it to the man; he was a neurotic asshole, but he was one of a kind. Right up there with Baumier and Feinman. I mean, Nicole, I never knew how good—and I mean *really* good—I was until I started going over his stuff. Brilliant doesn't begin to describe him."

"Still, Amy put things together."

"Only what was there to begin with. She followed Alex's lead, she doesn't have anywhere near the capability to expand on it. Alex played with electronics and software like it was a jazz improv; he made most of it up as he went along. Amy needs a score. She can replicate what he did, she can't make up anything new on her own.

"As a consequence, *Lamplighter* is a user-unique system. Your genetic structure's already primed to accept the interstitial overlay, and the extraordinary data base Alex built of you enabled him to custom configure software to match." Hana chuckled but without much humor. "That's what Amy's team's been doing for the better part of five years, trying to establish a similar base for other subjects."

"All they have to do is live in that effing telemetry skinsuit for as long as I did."

"Believe me, they tried. Believe me, they failed. Big time. Somewhere in there was the intuitive leap of genius that made the difference, but Amy can't see it and Alex didn't write it down. Probably because it seemed so obvious to him, the next natural step in the process."

"How about you? Could you find a way?"

Hana didn't answer, and Nicole found she couldn't bear to wait for her reply, didn't want to hear it when it finally came.

Instead, she said, "If the Hal couldn't erase the effects of their Speaker virus . . ."

"That could be a problem, all right. It certainly was for Alex at that point."

"You know there's no way in Hell I'm going to do this."

Hana nodded, but something in her face made Nicole sit straight up and face her.

"God *damn* it, are you saying I should?"

"I honestly don't know. There's no way to establish a partial interface. The process looks to be all or nothing. Even Virtual Reality can't do more than echo the expanse of sensory input, and there's no way to replicate how you'll deal with it."

"There's no fucking guarantee I *can* deal with it!"

"No, actually, there isn't. Though Alex's models . . ."

"Computer models are only as good as the baseline information, and you just said he was making most of that up as he went along!" By the time she finished, she was on her feet and nearly screaming, the force and fury of her voice turning heads throughout the Garden.

"Hei," her friend said simply, in Japanese.

Nicole stood stock-still for a long time after that, demanding a silence that Hana respected, while staring upward at the false sky as though searching there for her answer. Her feet were planted shoulder width apart, her body set for a fight, her fists were even clenched. She looked to Hana like someone who'd taken a flurry of brutal body blows and was ready to return the punishment.

At long last, without relaxing her stance, Nicole spoke in a flat and deliberately toneless voice.

"Can you work with this?"

"Based on the information at hand, no, not the way you need me to. I need access to the Hal records—to know precisely what they did to you and Ben. For that matter, to me and Andrei as well."

Nicole looked around.

"What d'you mean?" she demanded.

"What d'you think, Ace? Just because we haven't had any overt repercussions doesn't mean we were spared. The fact is, in big ways and small, we were *all* of us changed by our encounter with the Hal. Maybe that's why everyone wanted us kept on Earth, to keep us from finding out."

"Jesus."

"It's not a happy sitch, I agree. As far as *Lamplighter*'s concerned, there are a couple of hints in Alex's literature—not so much in the specific notes, but scattered through the body of his later work—that the system would always remain in place but command protocols might be possible that would enable you to shut down the linkages at will. Actually, something like that would have to be essential, to prevent any catastrophic event aboard ship from affecting you, or vice versa. But like I said, to have more than a ghost of a trail to follow, I have to see this from the Hal perspective."

"You want to ask 'em?"

"Nope. But I sure as hell mean to be there to see what happens when *you* do, Shavrin's-Child."

Nicole made a curious, partly dismissive face at the name. Hana responded with a genuine grin.

"Hey, Ace, think about it," she said cheerily, in anticipation of a great fight. "You maybe got juice with the Hal you never even dreamed of. Couldn't hurt to give it a try."

"Couldn't hurt at all." She sighed heavily. "Unlike me, right now, who seems to hurt all over. I feel pummeled."

"Can't imagine why."

"Bugger off, Murai."

Hana held up her hands in a placating gesture. "Enough, okay? Look, how 'bout we head home, wrap ourselves up in a quilt or three, brew something warm to drink, and pop something rude and mindless in the video. And, while we're at it, pass a note to Environmental Maintenance about the temperature in here—it's *freezing!*"

Nicole looked at her sharply, as those last words left a small cloud in the air.

"It *is* freezing," she echoed, looking at the residue of her own breath. There was more than an evening crispness to the air, it was actually cold. Then she felt the faintest of breezes stroke her cheek.

She looked over the edge of the platform, at the whole of the Garden, and saw the glitter of the first beginnings of hoarfrost on the grass. There was less sound from the brook as well; the water still flowed over the cataract, but ice was growing from the banks.

Suddenly she found her mouth stretching into a huge yawn

in an attempt to pull a decent breath into lungs hungry for air. Her feet were aching with cold, her bare arms not much better, and she blew into her cupped palms to keep them warm.

Hana was on her feet beside her.

"Systems failure," she said to Nicole, in horror.

"A bad one," Nicole agreed. "It's knocked out the environmental monitors. And the alarms as well."

"That's not possible."

"Look around you, Hana, it's happening. And we're losing air.

"Take the main floor," she went on, speaking in staccato gasps, "gather up everyone here, get 'em out the main hatch. I'll go high and check the platforms for stragglers."

Most seemed unaware of what was happening; the kids were still playing, enjoying themselves all the more because the ground had become suddenly slippery, while a couple strode towards the hatch, body language muttering about the chill.

"Do you have your PortaCamp?" Nicole asked as Hana stepped onto the ramp, hoping her friend could use it to interface with the starship's primary system to sound an alarm.

"In the flat, I didn't bring it with."

"Go then! I'll catch up! Soon as you're clear, flash Emergency Services and the Bridge." Even as Nicole spoke, she wondered if the leak was confined to just the Garden, and immediately thrust that speculation from her thoughts—if it wasn't, if more of the starship was compromised, they were all dead anyway, so what was the point worrying?

She found a couple packing their picnic basket on the next level, and sorting their clothes as well, clearly interrupted in the middle of a very romantic date. Nicole was panting as she reached them. The pressure, she guesstimated, was the equivalent of the Rocky Mountain highlands, along the Continental Divide.

"Downstairs, fast," she told them in a voice that brooked neither question nor argument, "we've got to get out! The compartment's decompressing."

The man started to protest but Nicole cut him off.

"I'm Major Shea," she snapped, hoping the rank would get their attention where the growing cold had failed.

The man's companion tugged at his arm. "She's an officer, Jake, she must know what she's talking about. Come *on!*"

As they left, Nicole heard a final word from the woman.

"I *told* you it was colder!"

She took a quick three-sixty from the lip of the platform, saw nobody else beside the small crowd at the distant exit. Yet even as she started to follow, something struck her as out of place. She tried to dismiss it as a natural consequence of oxygen starvation, lack of air mucking up her thought processes, but she couldn't shake the sense that she'd forgotten something important.

She looked again, cursing the fact that the Garden was in nocturnal mode, a deep midsummer twilight that provided illumination enough to see but not terribly well. Her lungs were aching from the strain and she felt giddy; it took an effort to keep an idiot grin off her face and after a while she stopped trying. In a way, this all seemed quite delightfully funny.

Lights. They were the key, something about lights, why couldn't she place it, place herself, maybe now was her chance, plant herself good and proper among the blossoms and hook up with Alex once and forever!

Movement caught her eye — one of the kids, coming towards her at a run. He tripped just before he reached her, crashing into her like a football tackle.

"What the hell," she gasped as she picked them both up.

"Major," he cried hoarsely, voice rubbed raw by his lungs' ever more desperate need for sustenance, overlaid with fright, "the door's locked, we can't get out!"

Nicole shoved her way through the crowd to the hatch. The auto function would have disabled itself automatically once the sensors detected the loss of pressure in the compartment, but by the same token it should have been sounding the most god-awful siren in the corridor beyond. She palmed the activation plate, punched in an override keycode, used her CardEx on the SlideLock.

"We tried everything," Hana told her quietly. "Both hatches."

"The manual crank?"

"Wheel's locked tight. Or jammed. I faked a call on the

intercom, that's why everyone's so calm, they think help's on the way. But that system's trash as well."

Nicole looked through the door's tiny window, to the airlock beyond, catching sight of the status board, the green of its telltales mute mockery of their situation, proclaiming the lie that all was well.

"For what it's worth," Hana said, "I don't think this is an accident."

Nicole didn't bother replying directly, but instead took another survey of the cavernous chamber.

"This was originally built as a cargo bay," she said, "double-hulled all around, airlocks at every exit. Designed," she added without irony, "to provide an extra measure of internal integrity in case of any accident. We could set off a bomb in here and nobody outside would know it."

Lights, she thought suddenly, making the connection at last, looking at the board once more, then at the crowd around her. *Thirteen lights, but only a dozen people; someone's still missing!*

"*Shit!*"

"What?" From Hana.

"We're short a body."

Tough luck, she told herself. The group had problems of its own, no time and less air to waste on a search for someone probably more dead now than alive. Didn't matter anyway, they'd all be dead themselves before long. *Stop it,* she snapped silently, *think!* Simulators, tests, everything she'd gone through since coming aboard, every moment of training leading up to it—wasn't there *something* in all that mess to help them?

A teasing wisp of memory prompted a look over everyone's heads up the slope of the main floor knoll.

"There's another way out, isn't there?"

Nicole shook her head. "I'm not sure." A silly little fact actually, an addendum to the original construction schematics she'd found while reading the *Constitution*'s history, so obscure it wasn't mentioned on the Master Plans.

Slimmest of hopes, nothing else to grasp.

There was a small cairn at the crest, bearing the initials of the men and women who'd built the Garden. The others huddling about her, close together for warmth and comfort, Nicole tried to find the switch she was more than half convinced didn't even exist, raging inside at the lack of sensation in her fingers, afraid she wouldn't even realize when she touched it.

She found an indentation at the base of the cairn, her numb hand pressed, and she heard an outcry from someone in the crowd at a hissing sound and the solid *thunk* of locking bolts pulling free. A sod-covered catch bar lifted out of the ground, to be grabbed by as many hands as could fit so the hatch it was fastened to could be hauled open. There was nothing pretty about the space below—it was bare and functional and utterly utilitarian.

"What is that?" someone demanded.

"Maintenance access," she gasped. "These work alleys are isolated from the main compartments; pressure loss out here shouldn't have any affect. It also runs on its own dedicated communications network. Find a CallBox, you should be able to sound an alarm."

"I thought that woman already did that," came from another man, meaning Hana.

"She did," Nicole said. "We do it again and again, as long as it takes, until we get an active response."

Not bothering a whit about ceremony, she hustled the people down the ladder—handing the two stuporous children down into waiting arms—then, instead of following, she reached aside to close the hatch shut.

"Nicole," cried Hana, lunging for her, "what are you doing?"

"One more left, remember?"

"It's too late, you haven't a chance, it's suicide!"

"Hana, I have to *try!*"

Another sweep of the meadow, then her eyes went to the only place the missing person could be—the topmost platform. The other thing she'd forgotten. No sense in recriminations, but she mentally kicked herself anyway. Then she began to climb.

She didn't see the body until she fell over it.

Fur, was her first thought as she hauled it close to her, *who even wears fur anymore, especially on the Frontier?* No need, really, in a spacecraft's controlled environment.

Then, she started laughing at the absurdity—*given what's happening,* she decided, *a coat of fur ain't such a dumb idea after all.* The effort left her silly and barely awake.

No more laughing, she told herself, quite sternly—which in turn almost provoked some more—*can't afford the air.*

With a snarl, because she'd found an adult, she heaved the bonelessly limp form to its feet. And just stood. Confused, totally lost, befuddled as a lifetime drunk, not knowing where to go or even what next to do. She felt so sleepy, fella here had the right idea, just curl up and give yourself over to the cold, nice cold, considerate and gentle cold, lulling you into the sleep from which you'll never waken.

"Sounds good to me," she breathed so faintly she couldn't even raise a cloud.

Giving up so easily, chided a familiar voice. *That's not the Nicole Shea I remember.*

She stared blearily, trying to fixate on a face to go with the words that sounded surprisingly close and clear in her mind.

"Wonderful," she said, "hallucinating."

The price you pay for not enough O_2 to breathe.

"You're dead, Cobri."

I'm not the only one, sweetheart. Difference is, I know it.

"Fuck you!"

Nice mouth.

"Fuck you, more!"

She settled her burden across her shoulders in a fireman's carry, baring teeth at how hard it was to bear the weight. That took almost all her strength; by the time she'd reached the next level she was too weak to go on and had to pause a while to catch her breath. Not that there was much left to catch, and she wondered (again in that damnably analytical part of herself) how close the Garden was to vacuum, and hoped she wouldn't make too much of a mess when her bodily fluids boiled. She could dimly see the knoll, it looked like it was at the bottom of an abyss, knew that was where she had to go, figured she could make it no problem, right up to the moment she stuck her leg out for another step and hit ice.

Her foot shot out from under her and she spun down hard on her back, scrabbling futilely for a handhold as she skidded along the slope carved for the stream before flying off into space.

It wasn't so far a fall but she landed badly, with the body she was carrying mostly on top of her. Something splintered high up in her shoulder, the pain skibbling across her back like cracks in a pane of glass, so sharp she gasped in shock and surprise. Which was a major mistake because she'd crashed through the surface of the pond and was mostly underwater. In a desperate reflex, she muscled herself onto the bank, sputtering and choking with such force that her vision went gray and the invisible bands about her chest tightened enough to bring a low moan of pain.

Stubbornly, though, she refused to black out, and hunkered instead to knees and then feet, balancing on her forearms like an ape. She decided to think of this as one last test—she put Alex Cobri's sneering, lovely, sarcastic face right in front of hers, filled her ears with his taunts, and used that as a goad, refusing to give him the satisfaction of seeing her fall and fail.

She caught hold of her charge and hauled him up beside her. She couldn't manage any more than that.

"This is stupid," she said calmly.

This is true.

Alex again. Some friends didn't know when to quit.

She was too tired to be insulting, so she smiled up at him instead, handsome man, breathtakingly so, with irresistibly lean, sleek lines, just like the boat he gave her.

The ocean stretched away from them on every side to the horizon, a following breeze pushing *Sundowner* powerfully through long, lazy swells under a sun that shone with delectable brilliance through a cobalt sky. She was lounging in the cockpit, tiller in one hand, main sheet in the other, the boat completely under control. He was striking a pose above her, fully aware of how much she liked what she saw and letting her know the feeling was reciprocated.

The wind shifted, and she trimmed sail and course ever so slightly to compensate, shivering at the sudden chill across bare shoulders, the flash of icy ocean spray on her skin. Something wriggled beneath her and she levered herself up slightly on her elbows—wondering why her hands looked so funny—letting her head loll forward so she could see better. Her belly had gone all fuzzy, wasn't that strange? It had grown eyes, too, that glowed with a faint, golden iridescence. She heard a voice, so faint she almost took it for her imagination, the tiniest of groans, and decided she must be hungry.

Food's over there, Red.

A new voice, right beside her, and she swung her head around—asking herself in the process why it felt as big and cumbersome as a wrecking ball, so massive that her neck seemed barely able to support it—to behold Ben Ciari. She wanted to reach out to him—his ponytail had grown, even as his hairline had begun to seriously recede from the temples creating a very dramatic widow's peak, and was far more salt than pepper, the color of mountain birch bark—but her hands were full with the boat. A wave broke hard over the prow of one of the catamaran's double hulls and drenched them both, making her shake her head violently to clear her vision. There was no sign of Alex.

"Shit, Ben, you better not be dead, too," she stammered, teeth chattering from the open-water chill.

I'll assume that means you're glad to see me.

The air was different, the sun darker than she was used to, the water like a rich burgundy wine, with red highlights instead of blue.

If you're hungry, Nicole, food's over yonder, Ciari said, pointing to a small mound, just up the beach from where they'd come ashore. It was a small bay at the foot of a towering escarpment that struck a resonant chord within Nicole but no specific tag. Virgin sand curved away from her on either side in a wide "U" that formed a spectacular natural harbor, and a fairly deep-water one as well, she realized, from the color of the sea. She could hear breakers thundering in the distance, out of sight beyond the point, but the waves here were significantly gentler, the shape of the bay creating a natural breakwater. An ideal refuge from any storm.

Her gaze returned to the cairn, and her eyes narrowed in confusion. Everything else was pristine sand and sun-stroked rock, yet that small hillock looked like it had been transplanted from the arctic tundra. Ice-rimed grass on grayed earth, with the sizzling glow of a flare perched on top. Damnedest McEats she'd ever seen, and decided she didn't like it, no way was she going near it, better to stay where she was and soak up some rays.

"No," she groaned, gritting her teeth and uttering a cry that was in no way human, pulled from a place within her heart she never dreamed existed. *"No!"*

She pushed with all her might and found herself once more on hands and knees. One hand grabbed hold of her companion while she rose the rest of the way; she almost fell again as he slipped in her grasp, thrown off-balance by the extreme shift in weight and the belated acknowledgment that he was as big as she and growing heavier by the minute. The beach was gone, the boat and its ghosts with it, she was back in the Garden. But one thing was different—the blinding brightness she'd enjoyed hadn't vanished with the hallucination—someone had dialed the lights up to full intensity.

In their glare, she noticed now that she'd grown fur, and thought, *This is* crazy!

A fine russet pelt that matched her hair, marked with intricate indigo designs, and the hair itself had grown into a thick leonine mane cascading across her back in a style no spacer would dare risk. She grew claws and fangs, her eyes blazing like fiery emeralds as the pupils elongated into vertical slits and the shapes of face and body changed until it only vaguely resembled what was considered human. But was, in basic, a match for the body cradled awkwardly in her mostly useless arms.

The slope was ridiculously easy, yet as far beyond her capabilities as the sheerest cliff on Everest. So she didn't bother walking. Instead, she let herself collapse full length and dragged herself to the top, gouging elbows and toes into the frozen ground, her companion wedged as best she could under one arm, as though she were making a water rescue. Each breath—so shallow and fast by now they were almost impossible to register—drove another acid-coated spear through her breast. She welcomed the pain, she thrived on it—if she could feel it, feel *anything,* she was still alive—used it to drive herself on, knowing that if she stopped now, and yielded to the shadows closing in around the periphery of her vision, she was done.

She grabbed for the flare, caught the post supporting it by mistake, flesh freezing instantly to the metal, tearing as she yanked her hand free. That knocked the flare from its perch, and she flailed with desperate clumsiness to bat it aside before she set herself afire. Wasn't 'til later that she figured there probably wasn't sufficient air to sustain combustion; the flare only functioned because it was a self-contained chemical reaction. She came away with some burns to add to her torn and bloody palm. No pain, though, she assumed that would come after, with a vengeance, when the numbness wore off.

Cairn, she needed the cairn, switch at base, where'd it go, why were they hiding it, no fair, refuse to come so far and lose, belated realization that she was lying on it, sneaky little bugger, playing tricks like that, fix you later sod, switch switch, seemed so simple last time, fingers moved last time, nerves transmitted sensation, maybe they still are, only the brain's given up on receiving them, too much trouble, systems shutting down, failing, she was failing, put to the test and found wanting, just as Canfield had feared and Nicole herself always known.

She hammered at the rock like a madwoman—fortunately, with so little strength that her hands were only bruised, not broken—sobbing her frustration and terror. Not knowing which was more awful, the thought of dying or surviving with a crippled brain.

Wasn't anyone in the airlock paying attention, couldn't they see her out here, why can't they open the frigging door, is that too much to ask? Someone turned on the lights, why not add some air as well?

She lay the palm of one hand over the fingers of the other and leaned her weight on it, hissing with imagined pain—in actuality, she didn't feel a thing—as the fingers snapped flat. Then, she shoved them under the cairn, grinning like a fool as she heard the activating click. She didn't bother with her hands, but hooked both elbows through the handle, putting the last of her strength into this effort, the counterbalanced hatch opening so smoothly and easily that she was sent sprawling halfway down the slope. Too stubborn to admit she was done, she wriggled right way 'round and hooked her companion. She found herself at the lip of the hatch, staring down into its inviting, empty depths. No sign of the others, they'd exited to what she prayed was safe haven. Her turn to follow. Come this far, no sense quitting now.

But her legs wouldn't work. Try as she might, scream as loud as she could inside her head, they didn't stir. She tried to twist her torso, use the open hatch as purchase to lever herself to a sitting position, so she could lower the two of them inside—there was a switch, a big, beautiful brute of a lever, outlined in glaring Day-Glo colors, all she had to do was pull and the compartment would flood with atmosphere, the hatch closing automatically behind her. Except she couldn't snag a handhold. Her muscles were spasming, no part of her body was paying the slightest attention to any of her commands and most of what she was thinking was dribbling into gibberish.

One more try—missed—then another—missed—then another, each attempt more widely uncontrolled and uncoordinated than the one before. Each also—without her realizing it—shifting her balance on the lip of the hatch, until, suddenly, she felt herself slip over the edge. She had time—and instinct—for a frantic grab that snagged her companion as well and yanked him with her as she fell.

This time, the impact was more than sufficient to smash her instantly and completely unconscious.

CHAPTER TEN

*She's yanked underwater so suddenly, there's no
time to grab a final breath. She bends double, to
slash with both hands at what holds her ankle. But
her claws make no imprint on the flesh and the
only blood that's drawn is hers, as the blow glances
off the tentacle, to rake her calf. Worse, another
ropy shape whips out of the darkness to catch her
arms and bind them and legs together. She has no
analog for the form that holds her, or the strength it
manifests; she'd always been a match for all but
the strongest of the family adults, yet her most
violent struggles here don't make the slightest
difference.*

She coughed herself awake—so hard she nearly pitched
herself off the bed—but when gentle hands reached for her
shoulders to push her back into place, she lashed out, with a
caterwauling wail. The hands jumped immediately away, and
she heard a word she didn't understand but which, from the
tone, she registered as a curse. That realization came after the
fact; at the moment, she was beyond coherent thought, acting
solely on primal instinct. Fortunately, that spasm of resistance
stole the last of her strength. Momentum left her with a
shoulder hanging off the edge of the bed, too weak to lift
herself up or offer more than feeble gestures as she was rolled
back into place. She was panting—shallow little gasps for
breath—because anything more felt like she was rubbing razor
wire up and down her throat. While two sets of hands pinned
her wrists, a set of fingers peeled back an eyelid; she tried to

twist her head away from the dazzling flash of light, but that too was more than she could manage.

A face moved into view, triggering the right set of switches inside her memory, and Nicole smiled wanly up at Jenny Coy.

"Water," Nicole tried to say, barely registering the thought, much less the sound—she wasn't even sure her lips had moved—and wondered why Jenny looked so startled. She assumed the other woman simply hadn't heard, and tried again, putting as much force into her voice as she was able.

Jenny said something in response, words of comfort Nicole assumed from the expression on her face, but nothing made any sense. The sounds were little more than gibberish. She could feel her body tense, the reaction echoed by the increased chirps and beeps of the bio-monitor out of sight overhead.

She tried sitting up, calling out to Hana, to Ramsey, but her skull felt like it was clamped in a vise of spikes, and she couldn't help another yowl of misery. Worse, even this slight movement set her perceptions to swaying as though her skull were mounted on a set of frictionless gimbals. The pain gathered itself about her face like a caul and then settled deep into her shoulders and arms and to her shame she found she couldn't help the burn of tears at the outer corners of her eyelids.

A cloth to her cheek gently pressed the wetness away, and she heard a familiar, welcome, gloriously comprehensible growl from the shadows.

"Isn't safe to leave you anywhere."

Speaking was hard, her teeth felt swollen and her jaw didn't fit properly together, but she managed.

"A knack, I guess. Come all this way to tell me that, did you?"

The growl deepened into a mostly subvocal rumble that was Kymri's unique blend of Hal and human laughter. Her own response was a weary groan.

Her eyes stayed closed, in part because that made it easier for her to cope with the pain but also because she was half afraid Kymri's presence was part of some other dream; and if it was, she wanted to prolong it as long as possible.

To her surprise, he said something in the same nonsense syllables she'd heard Jenny use. Her eyes opened sharply, closed again almost as quickly as she found the overhead light unbearably bright.

"What did you just say?" she demanded, creasing her eyelids just a little and using her loose hand as a sunshade. Her other arm was plugged into a brace of IV lines; moreover, there were telemetry telltales scattered across her body and both temples. It was a full spectrum Intensive Care setup, applied to only the most critical of cases, and once more the monitor broadcast her surging anxiety.

"Merely that you sound awful," Kymri told her softly.

"Then why the hell didn't you just say so in English." She'd begun a catalogue of her situation and could feel the puffball shape and weight of bandages where her hands rested on her thighs. She decided she wasn't up to asking details just yet. "May I have a drink, please? My throat's dry as the *W'kans'qtll*."

Jenny held a squeeze bottle close and pressed the straw between her lips. The water was laced with lemon and probably a whole brace of restoratives; Nicole didn't really care, beyond the fact that it tasted wonderful. Unfortunately, the drink also provoked another burst of coughing.

"Small wonder," she rasped to Kymri and Jenny after the spasm passed, "about how I sound. My throat feels like it's filled tight with barbed wire."

She was watching Jenny as she spoke, and knew from the first that her friend didn't understand a word. Jenny looked at Kymri, who spoke more gibberish and saw comprehension sweep across the younger woman's face. Nicole put her hand to her throat, and closed her eyes for what seemed a long time, ignoring the others while she set a random sequence of imagery cascading before her mind's eye. There was no rhyme or reason to this interior slide show; she was simply rummaging through the attic of her memory and seeing what was there, what she could put names to.

At that first scattershot glance, nothing seemed missing, nothing whatsoever wrong.

She wept. With grief. With rage. With a terror so stark it was almost palpable.

She called for Hana, aware—now that she was looking—of how natural that name should sound and yet how difficult it was to wrap her voice around it. When Kymri hesitated, Jenny appearing totally confused and unsure of what to do, thrown by the exotic pronunciation, Nicole lunged from the bed. Kymri caught her, as she knew he would, held her fast in a grip she doubted she could break even in the best of shape as she roared, *"Hana!"*

She called again, though not as loud or with anywhere near the force, because that was all the strain her voice could manage. The door to her cubicle popped wide and Hana Murai thundered in, a samurai ready for battle.

"Hana," she cried, *"help me!"*

She didn't need any translation to understand Hana's initial reaction; her friend rounded on the Hal ShipMaster with a vehemence that made him take a defensive step back. There was such raw fury in Hana's tone that Nicole's hands twitched in response, the biological triggering mechanism for claws she didn't possess.

The next line, Nicole understood; though the accent was rough and ready, nowhere near as proper as Nicole's own, Hana got the job done.

"You miserable, faithless son of a bitch," Hana snarled, "what have you done to her?!"

"Say that again," Nicole told her, amazed that her voice was steady "As you would to me, not him."

And Hana did so, using two distinctly different arrangements of nonsense noises.

Nicole shook her head.

"Save your breath," she said. "One was Japanese, yes?" Hana nodded; Nicole didn't ask, she didn't need to be told, about the other. That had to be English.

"You should rest, Shavrin's-Child," Kymri told her. "You were very lucky, no need to push that."

"Raqella," she asked.

"You know it was him you rescued?"

"Not that many Hal aboard to choose from. Ch'ghan's broader across the chest, built more like you."

She felt the faintest tickle of claws on the inside of her left wrist and with her next breath a wisp of cinnamon, and closed her eyes tight against a flood of associations, too many of which she recognized as being wholly alien yet all of them hers.

"I stand beside you," he said, "on your heart side."

Where else, she thought, and pondered a response that was as automatic as it was natural. She touched her own, far blunter nails to the inside of his wrist and offered a formal greeting.

"R'ch'ai."

"S'm'ch R'ai," he replied, and then, "Raqella has a room of his own, suffering the effects of his exposure somewhat more than you."

"That's a little hard to believe," Hana offered acidly. "And it strikes me, ShipMaster, you stand in a place to which you have no right."

Kymri made a shallow nod of acknowledgment, but before he stepped aside, he bent low, his mouth next to Nicole's ear and whispered something for her alone, in a High Speech she was certain none but they would understand.

"Trust me, Shavrin's-Child," he said, while she retained her most guileless poker face, "whatever comes. More than your life depends on that."

"What's happened," Nicole demanded of Hana, when she took his place and Nicole's free hand was well.

"Hard to explain," her friend replied, her frustration evident. "I'm not as fluent in Hal as Kymri ShipMaster is in English."

Jenny looked outraged as she faced off against Hana and Kymri. Nicole tried to make some sense of what she was saying, to discern at least a pattern to her words, but there was no music to them.

"She's upset," she said, stating the obvious.

"With reason," was Hana's retort.

Nicole wanted to say more, but she was too dry and her throat hurt.

"That's to be expected," Jenny told her through Hana, after she made the plaintive complaint. "Dehydration of the tissues in the airway, caused by the decreasing air pressure. And the fact you were screaming pretty loudly."

"Was I? Don't remember."

"Slight disruption in immediate short-term memory is consistent with this kind of event."

"What do you mean?" Hoarse as Nicole was, the flash of fear in her voice was unmistakable.

Jenny understood her concern. "Follow my finger, will you?"

She held it up before Nicole's face, a foot or so out, and moved it back and forth, up and down; Nicole had no trouble tracking or keeping it in focus.

"We'll be running additional tests to be sure, but I think they'll confirm the initial results: you weren't deprived of oxygen long enough for there to be any cerebral damage. Other than the mother of all headaches, of course." She offered up a smile to give the last observation a humorous twist, and Nicole made a wan and weary effort to return it.

"That obvious, is it?"

"The good news is, it'll pass."

"I'm so happy. When do I get to speak English again?"

"Yes, Kymri," added Hana pointedly, *"when?"*

"Answer me true, old lion," Nicole asked him, forcing her voice to remain calm and steady through sheer act of will, "was I infected with the Speaker genetic virus as well as Ben Ciari?"

"Yes."

Hana's hand tightened convulsively on Nicole's.

"To one extent or other," he continued, "you all were. There were too many unknowns, our computer models didn't apply; we were desperate, we had no way of knowing if the virus would work at all, much less who would be the best subject. You, Nicole, had the greatest potential, far too much of a good thing as it turned out. Your natural personality would have been overwhelmed, subsumed completely by its Hal counterpart—as Ciari's very nearly was. We aborted the procedure as soon as the danger became evident. But some mistakes are more easily done than undone."

"Why didn't you tell me?"

"Why didn't you tell *us?*" Hana added bitterly.

Kymri faced her, eye to eye across Nicole's bed. "In your case, Hana, and Dr. Zhimyanov's, there was no true need. In Nicole's"—a pause, and a sense to Nicole that this was a decision Kymri had disapproved of and fought—"we thought it best that she not know. That was the reason for your adoption," he told her, "to guarantee you—should the worst happen—a place among us."

"I'm not one of you!" she cried.

"More so than you might think, Shavrin's-Child."

"What does that mean?"

"This happens occasionally to Speakers," he told them all, pausing every so often to repeat himself in English for Jenny's benefit. "A traumatic shock scrambles the brain's circuitry, rearranges the patterns of Self. A Speaker is the repository of what you might call the institutional genetic memory of our race."

A Shaman, Nicole thought.

"What happens," he continued, "is that the walls between past and present become porous, the component aspects become intertwined, sometimes inextricably. There are no identities to contend with, it's not a question of absorbing past lives, but past life *experiences*. You are not your ancestors reborn, you have access to the signal events of their existence. You're unable to differentiate where you end and they begin; all are one.

"A school of philosophy among the Hal considers this a desirable attainment, a way of communing more completely with our history, and, they believe, our Creator."

Nicole caught sight of a plastic bracelet about her left wrist, idly lifted it into view. She lay her head back against her pillow, blinking rapidly as unexpected tears washed the surface of her eyes.

"Nicole," asked Hana in concern.

Nicole's acknowledgment was in as flat and toneless a voice as her Hal speech could manage. "That tag on my arm, Hana, what's written there, is that my name?"

"Yes. It's a standard hospital ID."

She took a deep breath, then another, filling her lungs until she could feel her ribs ache and then letting it out ever so slowly.

"They're squiggles," she said, but Hana didn't comprehend the Hal term she used. Nicole uttered a foul mental curse and threw in an alternative before Kymri could offer his own translation. "Shapes," she snapped. "They have no meaning. They're not even recognizable to me as letters. Like looking at

Hebrew or Cyrillic or Arabic or *kanji* for the first time." She smiled thinly, humorlessly, at a spot flash of memory. "Like how we felt aboard *Range Guide* the first time we saw Hal text."

"We'll have to run tests," Jenny said through Kymri, with hints of strain and concern about her eyes and mouth that spoke of far more history than simple years would indicate. "To determine the extent of this syndrome and whether its cause is psychological or organic."

"Can you fix it?" Nicole asked.

It was Kymri who answered.

"We tried."

She couldn't help staring. She stood alone in her bedroom, naked before her reflections being displayed on the VideoWall. There were three ScanCom sources, allowing her to see front and back simultaneously. Patterns had formed on her skin— "akin to stigmata," Jenny had said, caused by her body trying to adapt itself to the new image of herself being dictated by her mind—as though someone had taken a brush and drawn a trio of interweaving russet stripes down the length of her spine, in a design eerily reminiscent to Nicole of Celtic knotwork. Two began under each ear, just behind the knob of her jaw, the third at the base of her skull, just above her cranial hairline. They joined along the column of her neck, and branched once more where the curve of her spine was most pronounced, into three distinct double-knotted motifs, one fading away just past her coccyx, while the other two followed the hollow of her hips to her pubic bone. There were similar markings on the backs of each hand, wrapping around her wrists, and on her feet and ankles.

She'd seen them before, they were part of the vision of herself that came in dreams and hallucinations, the vision of Nicole as a Hal.

She stroked her fingertips along the frontal hip stripes, very lightly, to see if there was any difference in texture between the two shades of skin. Then, harder, she rub-rolled one hand across the other and back again. The change in her coloring was striking; she had no trouble acknowledging it as beautiful. From the first, she'd accepted this without question, as part of the natural order of her being. So much so, in fact, that when Jenny first brought it to her attention—while she was still in hospital—Nicole hadn't known what she was talking about. It wasn't until Hana thrust photos of herself under her nose that she finally understood—and even then the figure of herself that looked strange was the one in the pictures.

She'd been confined to quarters since being released from hospital; Hobby had no practical choice in that regard, everyone—Nicole most of all—knew there was no way she could function effectively in her present state. *At least*, she thought, and not for the first time, *aboard a human vessel.*

There was a lot to get used to, very little of it pleasant. She could manage food, but only by substantially ignoring the taste and texture. She was too angry to turn to Kymri for dishes from the Hal stores, and Hana and Jenny too tactful to attempt preparing anything themselves. Videos she found boring—it wasn't simply being unable to comprehend any dialogue, the physical action itself, the actors' behavior, often made no sense—and music had become disturbingly hard to listen to. That shook her far more than losing her language, because it was one of the means she and her *Wanderer* crew had used initially to expand and enrich their contact with the Hal aboard *Range Guide.* She tried her guitar one night, delighted at first when her fingers remembered all the right moves and she found herself launching into one of her favorite pieces. Moments later, Hana had to tackle her to keep her from smashing the instrument against the nearest wall. She'd struggled like a crazy person, lashing out with words and fists, giving her friend a spectacular black eye for her trouble as Hana buried her on the couch until the outburst passed.

True, her body could play, but the sounds it made gave her ears no pleasure.

Clothes, too, presented a problem and here she had to turn to the Hal for help. Nothing of her own looked right, felt right. Not uniforms, nor casual attire. To no one's surprise, Kymri produced a traveling bag outfitted specifically for Nicole. She hadn't said a word when he offered it, but for the first time in days felt decently dressed.

She'd asked Jenny about the stigmata when they'd first appeared, darkening by the day until they were the same black with red highlights as her hair. Mainly to discern, if possible, what else might be in store for her.

"Don't think you'll grow fangs or claws, if that's any help," the young Scot had said, in cheery Highland gallows humor that provoked a snort of agreement from Hana (who as usual was translating).

"I am suitably reassured," was Nicole's deadpan rejoinder.

"Stating the obvious," Hana went on seriously, "the mind executes absolute control over the body's systems. That's one of the governing principles of yoga. We can adapt quite remarkably to external environmental realities. In your case, the dynamic catalyst is internal. How far it'll go, how long it'll last"—she shook her head—"I've no idea."

"Some help you are," Nicole had told her.

"I feel like a freak," she said flatly, to her reflection. And heard the silent rejoinder in her thoughts: *Get used to it, Ace, you are a freak.*

She found herself a pair of loose shorts and a pullover shirt. They were natural fiber, as were all Hal clothes, combining the durable comfort of soft cotton with the elegance of silk. The cut was full, the idea being to look as attractive as possible without sacrificing any ease of movement. She grimaced ruefully at memories of herself, snugged into outfits that on occasion were cut as tight as skin; she knew how good she looked, how good they made her feel at the time, yet now just the thought made her shudder with distaste. For the Hal, probably because the designs of their bodies and their fur made those bodies as much a part of their costume as the clothes that adorned them, sensuality was a far more essential aspect of social presentation than simply looking sexy.

Another smile, no sadness in this one at all but eager anticipation, as she scrabbled through her traveling LockBox for the mail disks Ben Ciari had sent her from the Hal homeworld, s'N'dare. Even after better than five years, he was still considered essential personnel, but she suspected from his letters that he'd stay on no matter what, regardless of his official status. Thanks to the Speaker virus—and here, her expression twisted momentarily into something dangerous, her eyes flashing an anger she wasn't bothering to hide—he, like she, had a unique insight into Hal society. Which in turn sparked an insatiable fascination.

His first letters were basically a travelogue, written in Hal of course; he told her the reason was to hone her own knowledge and facility with the language, but Nicole had decided from the start that it was really to drive her nuts. He would video some and write others, using the classically oriented Trade Tongue—their equivalent of Standard English—and then a growing number of street dialects, forcing her to learn to read and write. He told her initially about the world, the people, the sights and smells and sounds, painting a mural in words and pictures that would make up for her not being there in person. She couldn't wait now to compare his descriptions with the actual reality; that was why she wanted to look over her mail, to refresh her memory.

Yet, as she shuffled the deck of plastic squares, letting her fingers and blind fate do the choosing, she found herself thinking about his most recent communiqués. There hadn't been as many of late—and her brow furrowed as she realized "of late" meant the better part of a year. She'd been so caught up in her own work, and the attendant neuroses, that she hadn't paid more than superficial attention. He'd apparently gotten himself hooked on Hal philosophy; the last letter had been so thick with allegory and folk tales that had neither meaning nor resonance for her that she gave up trying to read it. Instead, she skimmed for any sign of something comprehensible and seriously contemplated forwarding a note to Judith Canfield recommending a psychiatric evaluation for Ciari.

Now, she thought she understood some of what he must have been going through.

Be interesting, she noted to herself as she tucked a disk into the appropriate I/O slot, *to see what I think of those stories now.*

She never got the chance. The entire Wall popped to life, presenting a panoramic image of *Sundowner* hurling itself through a phalanx of Pacific swells. The camera was mounted on a fantail stanchion, the lens encompassing virtually the same field of view as the human eye. In the foreground, in the cockpit, was Nicole, bundled into a suit of foul-weather gear; she took a wave head on with a terrific crash that sent spray cascading the length of the hull. The boat was groaning under the pressure of wind and water, but handling the strain with ease, as was its Master, Nicole's ear-to-ear grin visible even in partial profile.

For Nicole, watching this playback, there was no such excitement and not a hint of the joy. Only an awful, atavistic terror that sent her reeling across the room, stumbling over furniture, scrambling across the bed, uncaring that her nails were tearing the sheets in a frantic desperation she didn't understand and couldn't control. She was howling, a noise neither human nor Hal, yet stark in its presentation of an absolute and all-embracing fear.

The reaction was so fast, so physical, that there was no way for her rational self to reassert control before she tumbled into a ball and tucked herself as tightly as could be managed into the farthest corner of the room. She screamed to herself that there was nothing to be afraid of, that she was safe aboard a *starship* for God's sake, that she was reacting to a damn *image*! Not to mention one representing a memory that she cherished.

Didn't matter. All she could see, all she could sense, was the fearful immensity of the ocean.

"How do you feel?" Jenny asked, much later, in the common room of their suite, while Nicole nursed a steaming mug of tea and the hangover induced by the cocktail of sedatives Jenny had spray-shot into her arm.

Nicole offered a wan smile in return and gently corrected the doctor's pronunciation.

"Fine," was her reply, although that was a concept with many meanings for the Hal, ranging from "fine," as in "I'm ready and able to hunt," to "I'm still alive and breathing." Nicole chose the latter, though she still had her doubts.

Her scream had been heard, of course. As Hana noted acerbically afterward, all the way to the Bridge. When the door to her bedroom had opened, she'd sprang for it, ready to kill any who blocked her way. Ramsey Sheridan caught the full brunt of her panicked charge, managing to wrap his arms about her legs as he went down, to keep her from going any farther. It had taken three more people to hold her still enough for Jenny to administer the tranquilizer and even then Nicole was so jazzed on adrenaline that she never wholly lost consciousness.

"How crazy am I?" she asked Jenny, staring down at her tea and wishing there were leaves at the bottom of the cup to tell her the answer.

Jenny touched her hand and, when Nicole looked up, spread her arms in what Nicole recognized—after some thought—as a gesture of helplessness.

"I'm sorry," Jenny said, "I don't understand."

Nicole nodded—another consciously remembered gesture, not common to the Hal—while Jenny was mastering the basics of Trade Tongue in surprisingly short order, she was still at fundamentally the phrase book level of communications. With all the attendant limitations. Even if she'd understood Nicole's question, she didn't have fluency enough to convey any sort of effective reply. And this wasn't something Nicole wanted fed through an interpreter.

She felt a blind surge of frustration, so great an urge to strike out—at something, *anything*—that she flexed a hand to extrude her claws. She caught herself then, and closed the hand into a fist, watching how naturally the fingers folded over while noting at the same time that the gesture felt utterly wrong.

She loved the sea, as much as she did the sky. She'd grown up surrounded by water on Nantucket—and quailed within at the image—she'd learned to sail as soon as she could walk. All the memories were there; in that sense, nothing about her had changed. Only the way she related to them. The *her* she saw today in her mind's eye had no place in those scenes, creating a growing schism that threatened to shatter her like a poorly cut diamond.

"For what it's worth," she heard and swiveled on her chair to see Hana framed in the doorway of her room, "I'd say pretty fucking crazy."

Nicole made an acknowledging bow of the head, a tilt and change, with a follow-through of the hands that signified acceptance and agreement. She'd learned early on—simply from observation—that communication between Hal was as much contingent on body language as the spoken word, but there was no comparison between that intellectual awareness and actual physical *being*. Life for them was a constant dance, with crucial information conveyed by the inflection of a hand, the set of their torso. Reversing perspectives had made plain to her how limited interaction with humanity was for them. She saw it now with Hana, her stance painting the subtext of her words in broad, almost garish brushstrokes, where a Hal would have presented a far more complex symphony.

"We need to talk," she said, and Hana stepped aside for Nicole to pass by into her room.

One hallmark about spacers was that they were invariably tidy, a place for everything, everything in its place. The reason being that they had to know where to find things, in a hurry, and not always under the best of circumstances. That attitude Nicole learned on a racing sailboat, long before the Air Force. With Hana, it was always a struggle. Being Pacific bicoastal— Japan to California—the natural order of one society was constantly at war with the equally passionate and ingrained chaos of the other.

California was in the ascendency, that was immediately clear from the clutter. Hana hadn't picked up in days and was probably sleeping in her clothes.

Nicole kept her feelings off her face but to her surprise, Hana picked up on her reaction anyway.

"Don't start," she said, "I know it's a mess." There was no apology in what she said; she was merely acknowledging a state of being.

"You've gotten very good," Nicole told her, looking now to see how her friend was presenting herself, and recognizing what she'd missed before, that Hana was deliberately exaggerating the link between body and speech, presenting herself as the equivalent of a loudmouthed New York Mama or the classic Ugly American *tourista* so that anyone dealing with her would perceive only the cliché.

Hana strode past Nicole, permitting herself a small smile of delight to show how pleased she was with the compliment. Her desk was thick with hardware, three portable CPU modules mated to a pair of flatscreen displays. None of it was tied into the ship, not even via a direct power cord.

"I've got the room screened," she told Nicole as she took her seat. "Anyone taking a peek will see and hear the pair of us talking about what you've been going through"—a humorless smile from Hana, echoed by Nicole—"thick with the appropriate existential angst. I think there's even a good cry in there somewhere. And, in case they get truly anal, I patched in a bioscan profile to match the scene. Our telemetry will be wholly and completely consistent with the pictures."

"Suppose they just drill a hole in the wall?"

"So sue me, Ace. I did my best."

"This is a lot of trouble, Hana."

"No argument. We're *in* a lot of trouble. These computers"—she waved an arm over the desk—"are mine. I cut the chips, built the motherboards, designed a proprietary operating language. User specific to me alone."

"Power?"

"If I wanted to patent the little suckers, I'd be set for life." She shrugged. "Maybe I will, we get out of this."

"Think we won't?"

"I have questions, fearless leader."

"Not half so many as me, I bet. This in aid of what we were talking about in the Garden?"

Hana nodded, the shallowest inclination of the head. *Being very careful*, Nicole thought. *I suppose this is where devouring a lifetime of espionage fiction in books and films finally pays off. Sort of. I should be so lucky.*

Nicole decided to follow Hana's lead.

"Should I assume there's more involved than what you told me?"

Not even a nod this time, just a flicker in the eyes.

"Am I going to like it?"

"Depends on the context."

Nicole sighed, making it obvious in order to buy herself a little time for thought.

"I'm going with Kymri," she said at last, when the silence between them grew long.

"That's absurd."

"Why?"

"I don't give a damn about the scrambled circuitry in your head, woman, you're not Hal."

Nicole quietly arched her neck to present Hana a better view of the pattern on her throat, and raised a hand as well.

"Don't flash your stripes at me, Nicole." Hana sprang to her feet, pacing the floor with a controlled and furious intensity that would have done a Hal proud. "They don't cut shit with me, not a bit of it! That's surface, a cosmetic adjustment; soon as your head's straight, they'll fade."

"That doesn't matter. This is something I *have* to do."

"It's fucking *politics*, Nicole." Hana spaced her words with bitter, incremental pauses, as though firing a sequential volley. "Shavrin fucked you. She fucked us all. We don't owe her a blessed thing. Least of all your life."

"I have no life," Nicole replied patiently, "until this is straightened out. I can learn English, Hana." *I hope*, she thought, because her early attempts were not encouraging. "But I'll always remain an outsider in my own head. The contexts, the resonances, the *being* of my humanity will always remain alien to me. I can't explain it any better, I only know it's true. I have to resolve the schism in myself, and that means taking on the Hal part of me in its totality.

"And yes"—she raised a hand to head off another outburst from her friend—"that's only part of it. I have a place in Hal society. What I may have assumed before, I understand now, more completely than I can say. I have obligations"—and the term she used was one closest to the Japanese *giri*, Hana's reaction telling her she'd caught the specific reference—"that must be fulfilled. That *must* be fulfilled." With emphasis both verbal and physical, understated but unmistakable.

"I for one think Shavrin could do with a little disgrace."

"We need her where she is."

"Or what, Nicole, the whole damn Treaty goes south? I think it's a little late for that."

"Tell that to the clowns who tried to shoot us down."

"Well," Hana said, offering a gesture with her hands to echo her wholly human nod as she reluctantly conceded the point, "at least you'll have me to cover your back."

"I'm counting on that. Only from a distance."

Hana looked at her sharply, her silent question as obvious as it was demanding.

"I'm going in alone," Nicole told her. "I want you to stay here."

"The hell you say! You need me."

"Agreed. But if I have you by my side—where everyone

expects to see you, by the way—then we have no one to make sure things are okay here aboard the *Constitution*. Or keep tabs on Ch'ghan."

"You think he's part of this?"

"I prefer to hope not. I'd rather be certain. Raqella has the same obligations waiting for him that I do, and he's injured besides. They're sending him home. And I can't think of a better test bed for you than *Sundowner*."

"*Starswift*," Hana corrected automatically.

Nicole started a negative gesture with her hands, then stopped herself, set her jaw ever so slightly and deliberately shook her head. It wasn't a comfortable gesture and she could see how disconcerted Hana looked watching.

"What?" Nicole asked, and then tried humor. "Didn't I do it right?"

"It looked funny," Hana said lamely. "Like it does every time I see a Hal try the same thing. It's artificial, isolated from the physical language of the rest of the body."

"At last," Nicole sighed with a sad smile, "my dear friend gets the bloody point.

"Between us," she continued, "I want the ship to have its own private call sign."

"Understood. Who's with you when you're down there? From our side, I mean."

"Jenny Coy. Kymri."

"He's Hal!"

"I trust him."

"More fool you, Shea."

"I need his voice. Jenny doesn't speak the language."

"There's Ben Ciari." She saw something in Nicole's expression. "What?"

"I don't know really. A deliberate ambiguity in Kymri's responses."

"And you have the nerve to tell me you *trust* him?" In frustration, Hana shifted to Japanese and cut loose in wholly incomprehensible fury. Nicole waited patiently for the verbal storm to pass, reaching into her bag while she did for a small box buried at the bottom.

"As much as I do you, yes," she said finally, carefully choosing the most personally intimate form of the pronoun. It was partly a test—the phrasing was the far more sophisticated High Speech, rather than the Hal Trade Tongue—to gauge the breadth of Hana's knowledge.

No nod in response, nor words, but a gesture of acceptance that was wholly Hal.

Nicole stood before Hana, cradling the small box in cupped hands. Even in the indirect and neutered light of the room, the dark, polished wood gleamed with a marvelous richness that created the illusion of an ocean's unfathomable depths. Hana seated herself on the corner of her bed, watching with a quizzical but interested eye.

"This is wholly improper," Nicole said, and the casual observer might be forgiven for assuming she was talking to herself. "There's a ceremony."

"The *chn'chywa*," Hana guessed.

"You are *very* good. Yes, the *chn'chywa*. The way Kymri explained it to me"—and Nicole trembled ever so lightly as she flushed with remembered heat and smelt once again the intoxicating fragrance of a jungle—"it's a bonding. To Hearth and Family. Those of blood on one level. And on another, those who reside in the Household of the Heart."

"I'm sorry, Nicole, I won't do this. I won't have it. I want no part of that fuzzy bitch." Hana spoke with intentional disrespect. Nicole ignored it.

"Too late. We're all part of her, like it or not. This isn't about Shavrin, it's about *me*. The linkage with the House is through me, the Bonding is between *us*."

With a fluid grace that seemed so natural a part of her it was impossible to recall that it didn't exist a few short weeks before, Nicole went to her knees before Hana, making a deep obeisance until her bow touched her forehead to the floor. As she came up, eyes still downcast, she held the small box before her, open now for Hana's view.

The other woman had gasped at the sleek elegance of Nicole's movement; she gasped again at the piece of pure wrought silver she beheld.

It was an earring, a single pendant gemstone wrapped in a Celtic knot.

"Lapis," Hana breathed, not yet daring to touch the piece of jewelry.

"Lunar lapis," Nicole acknowledged. "Found the piece myself. And mined the raw silver."

"And the frame?"

"From my cousin Kit, on Skye."

"How long you been planning this, Ace?"

"The gift," Nicole subvocalized the questing *chirrup* that was what passed among the Hal for a shrug, "awhile. The context, well I'm afraid that's wholly improvised."

She still hadn't looked up from the floor, although every part of her shrieked its demand for a sense of Hana's reaction. Nothing was forthcoming though, neither in word nor gesture.

Nicole was shaking inside, furious with herself for this sudden flash of weakness. She closed her eyes tight, determined to reassert control by any means necessary. When she came back to herself, Hana was on her feet.

"I don't know what comes next," Nicole heard, in a voice as soft as her own.

Again, with that same infernal grace, Nicole rolled to her feet. Hana had placed the gem on her right ear, matching the position of the single stud Nicole wore in her own.

"Me, neither," was Nicole's reply. "Like I said, I'm making this up as I go along."

She held her hands out, palms upward. Hana took the cue, and placed hers over Nicole's, so that their fingernails lightly touched the skin on the inside of each wrist, right over the blood vessels. Then, each woman reached for the other's neck, again the barest touch atop jugular and carotid. No big deal, for human hands, with their blunt, square-cut nails. But Hal fingers were tipped with claws and even though they were mostly for show these days, the old memories remained. This was the greeting that said, *I place my life in your hands, to give or take as you desire.*

They broke apart, as if by command. Hands to sides, with a body's width between them.

"I have to go," Nicole said.

Hana's voice made her pause at the door. "Be careful," she said.

Jenny was thankfully gone from the common room; there was no one to see Nicole stride through the shadows to her own

room and slip inside. The lights brightened automatically, as
the internal sensors marked her entrance.

She stood with her back to the closed door, taking deep,
gulping breaths, as though she'd just run a mile sprint, or come
up from nearly drowning. The last image opened her eyes wide
in a proto-panic she quashed with such ruthlessness that her
teeth set in a snarl.

She couldn't help wondering if this was how Shavrin felt, all
those years ago on the Moon, when she named Nicole as her
daughter. The difference being that Nicole hadn't a clue back
then of the ramifications of the Hal's act. No such luck with
Hana. Both of them knew full well the depth of the commit-
ment offered. The piece of lapis was etched with Nicole's
personal sigil, and the cartouche of the Bond between them;
wearing it, Hana could follow her anywhere in Hal society. No
door could be closed to her. In effect, she was Nicole.

She growled in amusement, the sound not so rich to her ears
as it should be, and making her throat hurt besides. Shavrin
would not be amused when she found out what Nicole had
done.

As if Nicole really gave a damn anymore.

On impulse, she crossed the room in quick, long-limbed
strides, to grab her guitar off its rack. She sat on the bed,
holding the instrument awkwardly, wondering if this was a
mistake, debating whether or not to return it to its place. The
door was locked. Even if Hana used the override, she wouldn't
be able to stop Nicole from smashing it this time.

She strummed a chord, experiencing again that awful duality
of consciousness that told her it was in tune but that the sound
it made was most unpleasant.

She took a deep, calming breath and just sat there. She would
play or she wouldn't; either way, it would be what felt most
right.

Her fingers twitched on the strings, hesitated, began again.
Not random strumming but the opening chords of a song. Not
classical, either, it was raw and passionate rock'n'roll.

She grinned. Lila Cheney's *HighFlight*. The music that came
to her most often when she was stressed, pushing herself and
her machine *way* beyond the outside of the envelope.

Her grin widened, at the recognition of a wholly human response to wholly human pleasure.

The words came.

The accent was a little odd and Nicole's voice as rough as it had ever been—she had a lot of talents, with skills to match, but singing wasn't one of them—but the words were English.

When she slept that night, the guitar snug in her arms and a smile on her face, there were no dreams.

CHAPTER ELEVEN

*She's drawn deep, to where she can no longer
make out the shimmer of sunlight on water surface.
Her lungs burn, pain such as she's never before
felt. She opens her mouth a final time, putting the
last of breath and—she believes—life into a
hunter's cry, to let the Shadow know that while she
may have been defeated, she has not surrendered.*

"What do you mean he's disappeared?"

Nicole was so angry, there was no room left in her for
excitement. She appeared to tower over the Hal Majordomo
who'd been sent to greet her, and she deliberately used all the
aspects of language—words, tone, gesture, the set of her
body—to convey her fury in no uncertain terms.

In a way, this was the perfect ending to a perfect trip, almost
something that should have been expected. The latest wrinkle
in Murphy's Law. Relations between human and Hal had
become increasingly strained ever since Kymri had informed
Captain Hobby that Nicole's presence was required on s'N'dare.
Of all the Hal Nicole had met, Kymri had proved most adept at
conveying and comprehending the fullest range of human
expression; in effect, he was the Hal equivalent of Ben Ciari.
Not a Speaker, but in many respects just as useful.

In his meeting with Hobby and Ramsey Sheridan, he was
polite to the point of diffidence. He was also adamant. Nicole
chose to sit very quietly in her own chair, watching the scene
unfold from as unobtrusive a vantage point as possible. She
still couldn't understand what was being said—the exchange

was in English and that language was still lost to her, despite her earlier breakthrough with Lila's song—and had trouble reading human physical expression, so she contented herself with watching Kymri. He kept himself under splendid control but she was able to read nuances of response, elements only a Hal would notice, that told her as effectively as a running commentary how things were going.

Not well, that became clear from the start. Neither Hobby nor Sheridan were prepared to let her go, even in the face of Nicole's own request for transfer. They had ample evidence she wasn't in her right mind, they felt, which made them wonder if this entire situation wasn't some form of mind-control coercion. She had to concede them that point, it was something she'd wondered more than a little herself.

It was Sheridan who dropped the bombshell, a question that changed the tenor of the room so completely that Nicole had felt compelled to ask for a direct translation. After that, matters got a trifle more complicated, since Kymri had to relay what was said to him, to her, and then her replies back to the two men. The advantage to everyone was that there was suddenly a built-in grace period, allowing them all time to consider what had been said—and what was to be said in response—before actually speaking.

"I may be missing something," Ramsey'd said, with a pointed look towards Nicole and then back to Kymri, fixing the Hal in a glare of such naked hostility that hackles immediately twitched on the back of Kymri's neck, his body stiffening ever so slightly into a fighting posture. This was way beyond a challenge. Though Ramsey's tone was conversational it was as if he'd reached across the table to punch Kymri in the mouth.

"You're telling us," he continued, "that Major Shea's condition is a form of psychological discontinuity that occasionally occurs in Hal Speakers who suffer some grave traumatic shock, either physical or psychic in nature."

"Yes," Kymri replied. He knew full well where this was leading, as did Nicole, but there was no way to head it off. She suspected Ramsey also knew the truth; this was to put it on the official record.

"But it was my understanding, and General Canfield's as well, that only Marshal Ciari of the *Wanderer* crew was infected with the Speaker genetic engineering virus." He paused, but when Kymri made no comment, went on in that same gentle, deadly manner. "Were we mistaken, Kymri?"

The omission of any honorific was another calculated insult. Any other Hal sitting in Kymri's place—save perhaps the Liege of his Clan, Shavrin herself—would have been at Ramsey's throat. These were the kinds of affronts only blood could settle. And Ramsey knew that—*Heaven knows I've given enough briefings on the subject,* Nicole thought, and wondered if this deliberate provocation was another kind of test, Ramsey's way of taking Kymri's measure.

"We did what was necessary, Sheridan-Colonel, for the success of our mission and the survival of *both* crews," a hint of emphasis. "My government was informed. As was yours." A second flash of emphasis, making clear: *Don't lay this on my people, pal, your guys made the exact same decision.* "We have nothing to hide," he finished.

Nicole couldn't help herself. To her, his lie was so blatant that she simply had to react. It wasn't much, a flash of the eyes, a grunt from the bottom of her throat, probably incomprehensible to the two men. Kymri chose not to notice.

Kymri's original plan had been to transfer Nicole to the Hal cruiser that had brought him from s'N'dare to Nieuwhome. Hobby flat out refused, a decision seconded by Ramsey. They sent a Courier missile back to Earth, with a full report encrypted for the President and a request for complete instructions to be waiting when the *Constitution* reached Hal home space. No reply meant no Nicole, both officers making plain that they considered any comments or entreaties she made on the subject totally suspect.

When they'd arrived in the Hal home system, two days ago, they had their answer, brought out on another starship and hand-delivered by its CO.

The *Constitution* was directed to a parking orbit at one of s'N'dare's two open L-5 points. No one needed to be told that their position placed them within the firing arcs of the two giant stations bracketing them from the neighboring LaGrange loci. They were targeted from the surface as well.

"The locals don't seem too pleased to see us," Hobby remarked idly from his seat on the Bridge.

Nicole was standing by him, having come to bid farewell before her descent to the surface. She felt as uncomfortable as hell, but she'd made a point of wearing her Air Force flight suit.

"With respect, Hobby-Captain," she said, through Hana, "haven't we given them reason?"

The starship had downshifted from warp at battle stations, establishing a combat defense radius of a million klicks for the initial approach. Anything coming closer than the Moon's distance from the Earth would be considered hostile.

The Hal home system wasn't as symmetrical as ours; where Earth and its fellow planets were arranged pretty much along the same dynamic plane, these worlds followed much more varied orbital tracks. In fact, the next planet closest to the sun followed a wildly eccentric path that took it across the plane of the ecliptic at a significant angle. Hobby's intent was to slingshot *Constitution* past this world on his way to s'N'dare; that way, if he decided to abort his insertion, they had a potential Runway trajectory that held nothing but clear space.

The Hal had other ideas. The *Constitution* was told to follow established vectors and procedures. No threat was made; that hadn't been necessary. Every sensor on the starship registered the beginnings of their collective response.

A Hal starship winked out of the warp Shadow close enough to set off every critical proximity alarm on the Bridge, and proceeded to take station in the *Constitution*'s path, just beyond Hobby's defense perimeter and between them and the planet they were aiming for. Thing was, it was traveling a hair slower than its Terrestrial counterpart, so that the *Constitution* was gradually overtaking it. There was no danger of a collision— unless somebody made the decision to intentionally cause one—but it was only a matter of time before the Hal ship violated Hobby's directive.

"Touchy," noted Hana.

"Oh, really," Nicole responded. "How many Hal ships you see gallivanting unescorted around the Sol System, *hmnh*?

"Hobby-Captain," she told him, as always through Hana, "you can't do this. They won't back down in their own front yard, any more than you would!"

"Major," he replied, "you have no place on my Bridge. Stand aside, or return to your quarters."

The Hal cruiser crossed the line, and Hobby contracted his perimeter. When it crossed again a few hours later, he contracted it again. But he didn't modify his course.

"This is insane," Nicole breathed as she watched a secondary window in the panoramic rooftop display overlay a targeting grid atop the schematic silhouette of the Hal starcraft.

"Wonder what's so special about that world," Hana mused aloud. "The Hal are putting out so much ECM clutter that we haven't been able to manage even a marginal scan."

"From this distance, we wouldn't get anything worth the effort anyway."

"Precisely. So why are they going to so much trouble?"

"We're in their face, big time, Hana. They don't like it. Damn it," she snarled, mostly to herself, in frustration, *"damn it!"*

"New contact in the Sky," announced Commander Rossmore from his station. "Downshifting out of warp, and blue-shifting to our velocity. IFF flash, with confirmed transponder return; it's one of ours!"

That had been the ship from Earth. The Courier matched trajectories and its commander shuttled over to deliver the letters. Handwritten, sealed in wax. With a typed, secondary copy so there would be no misunderstanding whatsoever.

At last, Hobby called off his game of Chicken and gave the orders to resume a standard approach. He stood down from battle stations and dropped his defense perimeter.

The Hal ship paced them the whole way, until the *Constitution* had reached its final "mooring" about s'N'dare.

The Ambassador was apoplectic, so much so—thanks to a blistering audience at the Foreign Ministry—that he couldn't bring himself to speak to Hobby. He didn't even come up from the surface to greet them. He let his Chargé d'Affaires do that.

She was brusque to the point of brutality, the situation not helped by the fact that her primary allegiance was to the United Nations, while Hobby's—and the *Constitution*'s—was to the United States. For once, Nicole was thankful for her ignorance; she just waited as patiently as she could for the noise to subside, on the assumption their attention would turn to her eventually. Hana wasn't present, they'd agreed on that beforehand and kept their good-byes private; when Nicole left the Bridge as the ship assumed its final station, Hana had gone her own way. Jenny stayed close, looking more nervous by the moment. Nicole empathized; at least she knew the language, the people, the culture. Jenny was jumping blind.

To Nicole's amazement—though, when she sat back and considered, she realized it made perfect sense—there was one additional passenger for the surface waiting at the sally port: Amelia Cobri.

"You're not getting away from me that easily, Shea-Pilot," she told Nicole with a superior smirk that was more fitting to the girl Nicole remembered from five years before. She spoke in passable Trade Tongue.

Can't blame me for trying, Nicole thought in reply, but said, "Do you have permission, Amelia Cobri-Child, or do you simply assume—as always—that no one will dare stop you?"

Amy actually laughed, in genuine amusement, which Nicole found disconcerting.

"I'm glad to see you haven't lost your sense of humor, Shea-Pilot," she said, "even though it's still pretty lame." She directed a superior sneer at Jenny. "Dumped one slant shadow for a younger model, I see."

Jenny knew a cut when she heard one, and had enough Trade to catch the reference, but said absolutely nothing.

"Actually," Nicole used the most neutral phrasing and tone, taking care not to reveal how angry Amy'd made her, "Flight Lieutenant Coy is here under orders. As am I." *What's your excuse, kid?*

Again, Nicole found herself taken aback, when Amy looked suddenly abashed, as if realizing how cruel she'd been.

"Raqella asked me to come," she said in a small voice, the closest Nicole sensed she would ever come to an outright apology.

"You took good care of him," Nicole acknowledged. In fact, Amy hadn't left his side during the whole of his convalescence.

"Someone had to," Amy said. "Ship staff didn't have a clue and Ch'ghan couldn't be bothered."

"You knew how to treat him?" Nicole was curious, although she was pretty sure of the answer. Amy confirmed it.

"I had access to briefing disks."

"Whose?"

The smile this time was pure triumph.

"All of 'em."

"Even mine?"

"Early on," Amy confessed. "If the data went into any form of Network, I got a copy. Until the last couple 'a years, when Ciari began having the disks hand-shipped; that's when I was frozen out. Didn't much mind by then, he was spiraling *way* off his loop. Sad case."

"Too esoteric for you?"

Amy looked up at her with that eerie assessing directness so reminiscent of her father.

"Straight translation is useless without the cultural context," she said. "I had the words; without the social and anthropological referents, I hadn't a clue what they meant."

"Pity. I have the referents, those damn letters are *still* a mystery."

Which wasn't altogether true, of course; it merely meant that Nicole was still in the process of puzzling them out.

A *Constitution* shuttle carried them from the starship to Agarast'ya, the station ahead of them. The Hal took over from there.

Nicole was on the ground, and in her residence, in time to view a moderately spectacular sunset.

She thought she'd be more impressed, but it didn't measure up to the moments stored in her memory. Didn't even come close.

The first thing she'd done on arrival was place a call to Ben Ciari, fuming when she got his VoiceMail. She demanded to know where he was. At dusk, the Hal Majordomo arrived with the answer, and she decided to lose her temper.

She was no longer in her flight suit; she'd ditched that outfit the moment she was alone in her suite. She'd called Ciari from the bath, luxuriating in a tub that was longer than she was and which held enough water to allow her to float. When company rang at the door, assuming it was him, she pulled on a caftanlike robe that managed to be as artfully suggestive as it was dauntingly modest. The room was candlelit, with drinks on ice and hors d'oeuvres set on the coffee table. For effect, Nicole had donned her own pendant silver earring, Hal silver wrapped around a *fireheart* crystal, emblematic of her place in Shavrin's Household. It was the first thing the Hal saw when she ushered him inside and to Nicole's eyes, the Majordomo immediately looked a step removed from sick. The Terran Chargé was with him, presenting nowhere near as hostile a front as she had earlier aboard the *Constitution*.

"What do you mean," Nicole repeated, after a command to the house computer to increase the level of interior illumination. As the system obliged, she snuffed out the candles with short, sharp puffs of air, each a punctuation to her anger. "Marshal Ciari's disappeared?"

The Chargé struggled with workmanlike Trade Tongue.

"Gone missing, yes," she said, "we believe so."

"Aren't you sure?" Her face was to the Terran woman, but her focus was on the Hal.

"It's difficult to say. He's been spending so much time alone, buried in the Archives, roaming the countryside. He'd be out of touch for days at a time, as though he'd set himself the task of exploring the entire planet all by himself."

"You allowed this?" Nicole demanded of the Hal.

"He is a Speaker, Shea-Pilot."

I'm living with the residual effects of the virus, she reminded herself, *he had it full force.* And remembered the two of them grappling in the airlock of Shavrin's starship, Ciari desperate to hurl himself into the battle, to avenge the souls of the slain Hal, she just as determined to stop him. The Hal had done their best to counteract the effects of the virus, with him as with her, but a significant residue remained with Ciari. Most strongly evident in his carriage and manner, the way he presented his physical being. The son of a bitch had broken her heart with envy, he'd become so graceful. Now, she saw the same moves in herself and feared the day when that would fade and leave her the way she was.

He's known from the start how the Hal relate to Speakers, she thought further, *that was one of the reasons he was assigned here, to give us as comprehensive a view as possible of their society. He was our means of looking at them from the inside-out. But he had an agenda of his own. He knew he wouldn't be challenged, by either side.*

"Have you considered hostile action," she asked. "My test vehicle was attacked in near Earth space; perhaps Ciari-Marshal was similarly assaulted here?"

The Chargé turned a querying look on the Majordomo, who assured both women that the matter was being looked into.

Nicole shifted to High Tongue.

"Why are you lying?" she demanded.

"Because, daughter, *I* told him to."

All eyes save Nicole's went immediately to the doorway, and the new arrival. Nicole deliberately took a breath to compose herself, and another and another, before making a slow pivot—just as she had so many years before, floating in zero gravity, on the *Range Guide*'s command deck—towards her foster mother, the Clan Lord Shavrin.

She hadn't changed much. A head shorter than Nicole, and slighter in the body, yet possessed of such an innate presence that she seemed the young woman's equal and far more. She carried herself as someone who'd earned the right and responsibility of command, with a calm self-assurance that Nicole had seen before only in Judith Canfield. Shavrin's base coat was silver, patterned in indigo, with markings of stark, pure simplicity. She wore her hair longer than Nicole remembered from their first encounter—somehow that hadn't registered as effectively on the holos she'd seen since—and dressed far more elegantly. The gown was formal, creating an impression of power and authority that would be noticed immediately from across a ballroom. Or a Council Chamber. Her eyes were dark and hooded. Shavrin was keeping her true thoughts close to herself.

The Majordomo made a formal obeisance, echoed by a bow from the Chargé. Their gestures made Nicole stand all the straighter.

There was a brief exchange between the two diplomats and they attempted as graceful an exit as could be quickly managed. Neither woman paid the slightest attention.

They stood like samurai, awaiting the signal to draw swords, knowing the cue would destroy them both.

Shavrin finally broke the silence.

"Do you know what you have done?"

"I know what *you've* done," Nicole replied with equal deliberation.

Shavrin looked suddenly away, and Nicole caught the flash of an earring from her left ear. A pendant *fireheart* that a second, closer look revealed was a twin for her own. Shavrin caught the glance and her hand twitched in a gesture of acknowledgment.

"Yes," she said, "they are a set. From my mother to me, from her mother to her, and so on, it's said to the birth of our line. A fair piece, I'll grant, but probably not that far. One stone during life, the other after."

"Why?" was all Nicole could bring herself to say, in a ghost of a voice that was hardly there. "Do you mean for me to take your place?"

"Would matters were so simple." Shavrin crossed the room in big commanding strides, taking charge of the space the way she did any situation, and poured herself a drink. Custom and etiquette required that she ask Nicole's permission; that she didn't was a measure of how upset she was.

"You are comfortable here," Shavrin asked belatedly. "Your needs have been attended to?"

"Hard to say, Mother-Lord," and Nicole saw Shavrin bristle at the intimate honorific, "since my first request was to see Ben Ciari. He's gone *Harach't'nyn,* hasn't he?"

"As shall you, youngling," answered a new voice, and Nicole didn't attempt to hide her annoyance at how easily people seemed able to intrude upon her privacy.

This Hal was big, even by human standards, taller than Nicole and much broader; where Shavrin was lithe power, he was raw brute force, the kind of elemental battering ram you turn loose on wayward mountain ranges. He was a blond, head to toe in rippling shades of tawny gold that most reminded Nicole of a mountain lion; he had no natural markings and affected no cosmetic ones. He was as handsome as he was majestic, knew it, and used both assets to full advantage. Unlike Shavrin, he was casually dressed, loose slacks and sandals, a wraparound tunic and a jacket, wearing a cloisonné pin on his lapel emblazoned with his coat of arms instead of the full, formal chain of office.

"Forgive my trespass, *domna,*" he said to Nicole, showing a hint of teeth, "but your door was ajar." She didn't believe that for a moment and resolved immediately to install a set of locks of her own. Maybe two.

She recognized the emblem on his pin, this was the Lord President of the Council of Clans.

He steepled his hands, chest high, with the tips of his claws barely touching, and inclined his body forward into a slight bow. It was a deliberately awkward stance and left him momentarily vulnerable to attack.

"R'ch'ai," he told her. The formal statement of trust, warrior to warrior. *By entering your home, I do you the honor of placing my life in your hands.* "I am M'gtur."

She responded in kind, and held out her own hands, palms upward. She felt a pinprick as he grasped his hands about her wrists—she couldn't close hers around his, they were too massive—the claw point of each forefinger had broken her skin, right above the big vein. His grip tightened; she knew from the first that she couldn't break his hold and so didn't try.

He made a sharp, *huff*-ing outrush of breath and again flashed fighting teeth in grudging approval as he let her go. There was a sharp tang to his scent, a fragrance Nicole had no name for, that made her blood run hot and cold at the same time. The Hal in her suddenly hungry, the human recognizing itself as prey.

"You are what you seem," he acknowledged, "yet you cannot be. I can fault the wisdom of Shavrin's decision, but not her choice."

He had hunter's eyes, like Ciari only more so, but there was something deep within, tucked away so far in the back that Nicole hoped she was imagining it, a hint that the hunt itself was nothing without the kill. He held her gaze a few moments more, as though daring her to make some response. Two came to mind, each equally strong, to flee and to strike out at him. When she did neither, he finally turned his gaze to Shavrin, leaving Nicole to wonder if she'd passed *this* test, and how many more there'd be to follow?

"You are determined in your purpose," he demanded of Shavrin. Before replying, she made a hand sign to Nicole, who obediently folded herself to her knees, touching her forehead to the floor in a posture of total submission.

"She is my daughter," Shavrin said simply. Of course it was anything but. In a foster-oriented society like the Hal, where family can have a score of meanings and cover a multitude of relationships, the word she'd used specifically referred to the issue of her body as well as her blood. She had bound Nicole as close to her as any biological child, and the earring Nicole wore meant she stood closer to her than any of them.

"She is OutWorld." There was no analog for the concept in High Speech, he had to use Trade Tongue. But he spoke with a spitting snarl that made his feelings plain.

"She is Blood," was Shavrin's calmly implacable reply. Nicole wanted—desperately—to stand up for herself, but she knew she had no right. Until she celebrated her own *Harach't'nyn*—the ceremonial coming of age, a walkabout to mark the transition from the four-footed way to the two—she had no place in a dialogue between Elders. To a great extent, she didn't even exist.

"Then what must be, shall be." Shavrin must have made a gesture of protest; Nicole heard nothing from her, but M'gtur responded as if she'd spoken aloud. "In this youngling's case more than any, the spirit of the Way is not sufficient, the letter must be observed."

"For the first time in a score of generations," Shavrin scoffed.

"That will change, you have my pledge on it."

"You'd have us crawl, old man, after we've learned to fly."

"Crawl, fly, whatever, gracious lady, I would have us remain *us*."

"In the ways that matter, nothing has changed."

"To you. But I have a different vision of which ways . . . matter. Prepare your daughter, Shavrin"—and the term M'gtur used was a world apart from Shavrin's, implying only the most superficial relationship, the kind used for a creature one step removed from a pet—"she will walk her road once the Terrans have departed."

Nicole felt the breeze of his passing and again the heady mix of atavistic fear combined with an equally powerful instinctive desire to leap for his throat. She kept her head down, thankful Shavrin couldn't see her own bared teeth, and struggled to regain what was left of her composure.

"Damn," she heard in Trade. And then a grumpy, "Get up, Nicole. We're alone, there's no need for protocol."

Nicole started a sleek athletic rise to her feet, as a Hal would, then stopped herself and defiantly unfolded a slow stiff leg at a time.

"How very human of you," Shavrin acknowledged.

"It's an effort to remember sometimes."

"I was afraid of that."

"But you couldn't warn me?"

"There was nothing to be done on Earth, child."

"Don't call me that!"

They locked eyes. Shavrin blinked.

"I would rather have you tormented by dreams," the Hal Chieftain said, "than run the risk you face here. I am half-tempted to put you on your ship and send you home."

"M'gtur would have your heart."

"Dear one, he means to have *both* our hearts. He may yet, too, before we're done."

"Unless you get his first?"

"No. Regrettably. He may have a head as thick and impenetrable to new ways as the planetary crust but he's also an honorable foe. He'll take all that's due him from a victory, but he'll also accept defeat with becoming grace. Behind him, though, are those with less scruples."

"Sounds like home."

Shavrin took a seat at a small table on the terrace, with its view of the city beyond, and motioned for Nicole to do the same. There was a bowl of fruit, which Nicole offered to the older Hal, slicing her selection and laying it attractively on a plate before sitting herself.

"You look surprised," she said to Shavrin.

"Kymri's report didn't do you justice."

"I'm just doing what I find comes naturally."

"I did not want this to happen, Nicole. I wish I could say I would have done anything to prevent it, or that I will do anything to cure it."

"You don't need to justify anything, Shavrin. I'm angry, yes, but I understand." Nicole didn't want to sit, every aspect of her being—Hal *and* human—demanded some form of physical expression for her agitation, but she forced herself to stay where she was, at attention in her chair, with hands folded politely behind her on the table. "I've never liked being lied to. Lately, that's all anyone seems to be doing. Not the most pleasant revelation for someone who thought her society was built on a foundation of trust.

"You never answered my question, Shavrin," she finished suddenly, "*has* Ben gone walkabout?"

"To be honest"—and there was no irony, intentional or otherwise, in her use of the phrase—"no one is sure. Only that he is gone. The indication in his notes and belongings—and his behavior—are that such is indeed the case."

"And you haven't a clue where?"

"Nicole," she said with some asperity, "try finding a lone man wandering through the wilderness of your own world."

"Can I help?"

Shavrin's gesture was negative, and not to be questioned.

"You may not," she said flatly.

"I beg your pardon?"

"You are my daughter. The Lord of the Council of Clans has accepted that. Until you face your own *Harach't'nyn,* you may not be human. In all ways and all things—publicly, as an absolute necessity, but I would prefer in private as well—you must be Hal."

"I have oaths that supersede this insanity, Shavrin."

"I do not ask you to betray them." *Yet,* Nicole thought.

"And afterward," she wondered aloud.

"Like any Hal, you will be free to choose your own trail. My hope is, the experience will restore the balance within yourself."

"I'll still have the memories."

"But not as the dominant aspect of your personality."

Nicole broke from the table and took a stand by the balcony, eyes slitted against the golden sun, as she let a wayward afternoon breeze cool the bare skin of her shoulders. In the distance, diamonds of blinding light flashed off the curved crest of the metropolitan arcology's primary hemisphere.

"I want to hit something," she said. "A response," she continued, with a sidelong look towards Shavrin, "from both sides of my skull."

"Restrain yourself," was her Chieftain's acid reply. "You don't have the equipment for an alley fight."

Shavrin rose to her feet. "We may never find Ciari-Marshal," she said.

Nicole turned to face her. "You think he's dead."

"The disservice we did you was nothing compared to what was done him. Five of your years and more have given you a mental cushion that allowed the Hal aspect of your self to integrate wholly with its human counterpart. The asset is, you are one being; the liability, you may never be the being you were. In Ciari's case, there was no such equivalent, gradual evolution—more like, instead, a violent overthrow. We were able to effect a successful counterrevolution, but it still left him struggling to cope with the aftereffects of the experience."

"You raped us, only with me you managed to turn it into a successful seduction."

"Call it what you will, I would do it again. Perhaps we would have been kinder to leave well enough alone with Ciari and let his Hal persona claim complete ascendancy."

"Perhaps I should have let him go, you mean, so he could've died with the rest of those bastards when we blew the raider base to atoms?"

"We both have our mistakes to live with, Nicole . . ."

"Fuck you!" Neither High Speech nor Trade, the expletive popped out in English. Her hands were clenched, her stance as wholly human as it was aggressive.

"Your presence is required at certain diplomatic functions," Shavrin said in that special way parents have to warn off their children from doing something fundamentally stupid. "A schedule has been posted to your buffer. M'gtur's pronouncement to the contrary, be prepared for your Ordeal at any time. Once you embark on that sacred path, Nicole, you are alone. Neither I nor Kymri, nor any friends, human or Hal, may help you."

"I'll be ready."

"This is such a goddamned, fucking *pain*," she cried, without a care who heard her.

Then, she sank down onto her haunches and wrapped her arms about her knees, holding the pose for the better part of a minute before rolling backward onto her butt and then her back, flopping arms and legs out full length. Since the sun was still a good half hour below the horizon, all that did was make her cold, and she pulled herself grumpily up to a sitting position.

Jenny was more sensibly dressed, in thermal sweatpants and a long-sleeve RAF pullover. Nicole favored shorts and though she wore a long-sleeve sweatshirt, she wished for an extra layer like her friend. It was the Hal equivalent of spring, and while the days were delightfully warm, the nights could be bitter.

They weren't jogging so much as hiking with speed, blazing trails along the ridge line above Nicole's house, following a different route every morning and seeing where it would lead them in an hour before they began to circle back home. The escarpment was Shavrin's territory—each of the major Clans had their own piece of turf overlooking the city proper, as well as all manner of residences within, from apartments to palaces. The city had one key function—much like Geneva in the days of the League of Nations, or Washington—the governance of the community. In this case, the whole of the Hal Federacy, a concordance of rival Households as reluctantly bound together by the headlong advances of technology as were the nations of the Earth. And as uncomfortable about it. That had been made plain to Nicole the night after her arrival, when she'd been formally presented to Shavrin's nearest and dearest.

Everything had gone passably well—some wouldn't speak to her, some were fascinated by the freak, most did their best to endure the situation, with only Kymri and Raqella (of all people) relating to her as friend and kinsman—until some bravo from one of the more remote septs decided to see what she was made of. The attack was ferocious, but she recognized from the start that it was a bluff; problem was, they were all nearly undone by his state of drunkenness. He misjudged both distance and timing and a swipe of the hand intended to miss by the merest fraction of a millimeter instead drew blood. There was instant shock and consternation—mixed with a fair dollop of admiration at how Nicole had stood her ground and later bore what had to be considerable pain. The incident earned her a measure of respect. It also resulted in Jenny's summons to the estate, to look after Nicole's wound.

Nicole was glad to see another friendly face, even if neither of them could speak the other's language. Hana was still struggling with Trade and Nicole's grasp of English had proved limited to that one outburst to Shavrin.

"That's probably why they let us hang together without supervision," she groused further. "They know we can't make bloody *sense* out of each other!"

The view was even more spectacular than from her balcony, presenting an unobstructed panorama that swept across the whole of the valley, encompassing the city and the lake far beyond. One of the odd aspects of s'N'dare was its lack of surface water. There were ice caps, north and south—although precious little visible evidence of recent glaciation—and a number of large lakes. No seas or oceans, though, and none of the lakes were exceptionally deep. Indeed, they appeared more like rivers that had overflowed their banks to form perpetual floodplains. The bulk of the planetary water appeared to come from underground sources, either freestanding or in aquifers.

The city sprawled along the slopes of this modest highland range, following a design philosophy that preferred a horizontal orientation to a vertical one. The highest structures were the central arcologies, one dedicated to government operations, another to business, another to commerce. The Hal didn't mind commuting to work—considering the sophistication of their computer and communications technologies, that often meant simply strolling from one room in the house to another—but they were absolutely insistent on having a space to call their own. An individual habitat and land to put it on.

By nature and inclination, they were solo creatures, with a passion that the American Libertarians of the last century would have admired. They understood the advantage of acting in concert, but made sure to always guarantee the rights of each member of that group. That's why they called themselves a Federacy: each belonged to the whole as a matter of personal choice. It was their privilege to walk away at any time; it was the group's responsibility to be sufficiently aware of the needs and concerns of the individual, and responsive to them, that they would never feel the need.

Hence, the evolution of the Speaker concept, a class of mediator/facilitators, beholden to none, bred and trained to bring an objective eye to any dispute and settle it to the best workable advantage of all concerned.

Nicole caught a flash of movement overhead, and spotted the triangle wedge of a hang glider riding the dawn thermals. It was still twilight where she stood, but as she stared she saw another glint of sun off the polished metal spars. She knew as well there'd be morning sail races on the flats close by the lakeshore, young Hal aboard wheel-equipped roadboards, horrifying their elders by playing so close to the water's edge.

She found herself suddenly thinking of Raqella, thankful that she'd been in a wholly human frame of mind when he'd dunked her in the ocean back in—and suddenly she paused, her face ghost pale as she groped for the right name, with a shiver that had nothing to do with the predawn chill.

"San Diego," she said, the Hal shape to the words making them incomprehensible. She focused all her will, gritting her teeth, clenching her fists 'til they were as white as her face beneath its tan, and tried again, *"San Diego!"*

She still spoke with an accent, but at least it came out right. Or so she assumed from Jenny's reaction.

"San Diego?" the young Scot queried. Which forced Nicole to wave off further questions. It was too complicated to explain, even if Jenny could understand.

Blessed earth, Nicole thought, *he was waiting for me out on the pier. On a bay that opened into blue water ocean. He must have been terrified.* For no Hal she knew had ever gone out on a boat. Even Kymri, on the one occasion he'd yielded to Nicole's invitations to visit the beach, hadn't stepped off the porch of the friend's house they'd stayed at, and for the duration looked ready to bolt for high ground at the merest provocation.

She couldn't help a small smile then, at the memory of one of Ciari's later letters, when he related how he'd scandalized the Terran diplomatic community and almost caused a crisis in Council by taking a sailboard out onto the lake. Raqella, she recalled, had been one of the few to follow him, more as a matter of pride than anything else. Anything a Terran could do, these young Hal were determined to do better.

With one exception. She knew, whatever the provocation, she'd never voluntarily get a Hal out on blue water. The oceans were the cradle of life, you didn't trespass on the front doorstep of God.

Eminently sensible, she agreed to herself, *except that s'N'dare doesn't have any deep water oceans to speak of.*

She did a three-sixty pivot, scanning the horizon without a clue as to what she was looking for; Jenny picked up on her sudden agitation and stepped close, only to spring back, tucking her hands back close to her body as Nicole visibly flinched.

"I'm sorry," Jenny said.

Nicole offered a placating wave and replied, "Not your fault." But then she had to hunt for an appropriately simple phrase in Trade when her colloquial response went right over the other woman's head.

"I must learn better. More quickly." Jenny was just as frustrated as Nicole. Unfortunately, it wasn't merely a matter of learning the words; the pronunciation was an integral element in their true meaning. Sibilants for her were fine, it was the gutturals—with clicks and swallowed glottal stops and all manner of growls, fully half of which were subvocal grace notes—that caused the problems. The point of Trade was to craft a dialect of Hal that both races could manage to speak and comprehend with a modicum of ease. Nicole suspected it was also to deny humans the full richness and eloquence, not simply of the Hal language, but of their society. Like learning to write Japanese as a phonetic expression of speech, without ever tackling the challenge of *kanji*.

Something still didn't feel right, as Nicole took another circle from her vantage point. In her mind, beyond and below any level of conscious awareness, tied into her physical memory of smell and sight and taste, was a sense of what this world should be. Only it didn't quite fit.

There was a crease of light at the distant horizon, so bright and sudden it made her blink, and in that fractional amount of time the sun leapt a full diameter into the sky.

"Dawn," she said. And, knowing Jenny wouldn't understand what she was saying, pointed towards the house. "We've got a long day ahead, Jenny. Time to go."

She had no warning. A movement right at the corner of her eye came simultaneously with a reflexive collapse onto her back and a cry of alarm from Jenny. As Nicole hit the ground, she kicked off one leg, propelling herself onto her stomach and from there into a combat crouch, while her assailant—perceived in blurred passing as a grown Hal, dressed in casual hunting attire—rolled out of one attack and right into another. She met him in midleap, going with the flow of his charge and adding to it some impetus of her own as she pitched him over her shoulder. She spun after him, low to the ground, one leg extended to scythe his out from under him. Unfortunately, he'd anticipated this move and was ready with a counter of his own that dropped her hard enough to leave her momentarily breathless.

Before the scrap could proceed any further, though, Jenny blindsided the Hal with a hard football tackle. Her follow-through was a strike to the throat that would have done some serious damage had it connected, but Nicole launched herself at her friend, knocking Jenny aside and catching the brunt of the blow on her own shoulder.

Jenny was aghast at having hurt Nicole, but also totally confused about the situation, as the Hal called out to her in English, holding his hands up to further allay any concerns about his intentions. Nicole lay where she fell, concentrating on the modest black hole of pain where Jenny'd nailed her. For all her modest stature and demeanor, the woman could *hit*.

She said as much to Kymri as he helped her sit up. He obliged them both with two-way translation. For all that Jenny was a third-generation Highlander, there were those—mostly summer people, from the lowlands or below the border in England—who looked askance at the immigrant Scots and sometimes came to the islands looking for trouble. While there were always plenty of friends to come to her aid, she preferred to stand up for herself. First rule she'd learned was that once something starts, go in with all you've got and finish it fast.

"I feel fortunate," said Kymri with a chuckle as he rubbed Nicole's aching shoulder.

"You should. If she'd connected, we'd be waiting for an emergency Medivac."

"That would have put something of a crimp in my plans."

"Which are," Nicole wondered, with more of a bite than she'd intended.

"I asked you to trust me, Shavrin's-Child . . ."

"You did. I do. Don't push it."

Sensing a sharpening in the mood, Jenny motioned Kymri away and probed the soreness. It hurt enough to provoke a visible reaction.

"Nothing's broken," she told Nicole through Kymri. "But you should have a lovely bruise."

Nicole growled unenthusiastically as Jenny said something else to Kymri.

"The good doctor wants a reason for my presence here," he passed on to Nicole.

"Makes two of us, old lion."

"I missed our old sparring sessions. I wanted to see if you'd lost any of your edge."

"Truth and half truth."

He looked uncomfortable as he faced out towards the city, one arm tucked protectively against his side where he'd been shot a half-dozen years before. Nicole thought at first he was looking at the city, but the angle of his gaze was wrong, a shade too high and off to the side, as though at something up in the sky.

"Have I?" she prompted. "Lost my edge?"

He coughed amusement, with a silent promise to put the question aside until their next encounter.

"You didn't hear me coming," he said at last.

"You missed," was her quiet riposte.

"Take a cue from your companion," he told her seriously. "Not every duel will be in fun."

"That a warning, or a challenge?"

"You have been summoned before a committee of the Council," he said. "An informal gathering, somewhere between a conversation and an interrogation."

"They want to see the elephant." She deliberately chose a human metaphor. The thought that had come instinctively to mind was, *They want to see how the cub walks.* On two feet or four. Everything about the Hal came back to that, the demarcation between their evolutionary ancestors and themselves, as though the transition were of recent memory. That, and their relationship with the ocean.

Kymri wasn't amused.

"I understand your need to be human, Shavrin's-Child," he told her.

"I *am* human," again, with that extra sharpness.

"Not today. And not until you've faced your *Harach't'nyn*."

"I *know* all that, Kymri, Shavrin made it very plain."

"Listen to her. Listen to *me*. There is more at stake than you know."

"But not so much that anyone'll bother to tell me."

"Save your anger, child."

"Save your breath, Kymri. I know how to behave. I won't disgrace the side."

They faced off a minute longer, and Kymri looked as though there was something else he wanted to say. But he needed an opening from Nicole, some sense that his words wouldn't fall on hostile ears, and she wasn't in the giving mood. So he stalked away in anger that came from deep within and had nothing really to do with her or the specifics of the moment. And it was suddenly her turn—in a breathtaking reversal of roles—to want to run after him, reach out, offer a companion's hand. The human in her actually took a first step . . .

. . . but the Hal, sensibly, held her back. Because in his black mood, Kymri would have most probably reacted from the heart, with a physical expression for his fury. Nicole, being a friend, would have taken the blow. Being human, her body would have paid the price.

CHAPTER TWELVE

She's on shore again, sprawled belly-down, with water from a receding wave tickling her belly as it wriggles and races down the shallow incline. She coughs for so long and so hard she's sure she'll tear her insides out. As it is, the spasms are so violent each delicious breath comes with its own pain. She doesn't care. The marvel is that she has breaths to take and pain to be felt. She rolls onto her back, squinting her eyes against the sun-sparkle off the waters, not at all sure what she's searching for. She sits through the remainder of the day and the night that follows, stirring only to keep her distance from the next high tide. Certain as she watches and waits that she is being watched in turn by an intelligence and a curiosity that puts hers to shame.

Over the next few days, Nicole had cause more than once to think back over that conversation with Kymri and reflect on his innate gift for understatement.

Her encounter with the Council was indeed something more than a conversation, but only fractionally less than a full-court interrogation. Not every duel, she was reminded, was fought with physical weapons.

They came at her every which way, and wholly on their schedule—which meant whenever they felt the mood, whether day or night, in public circumstances or the most intensely private. She was quizzed on matters of protocol and etiquette, on history, on behavior. At last—as reward or another test, she wasn't quite sure—Nicole was flown halfway across the continent, to be Witness at a Bonding of two members of

Shavrin's *Range Guide* crew. One of the pair stirred a memory, though Nicole had to be reminded of his name, but she drew a complete blank on the mate. The feast lasted through the night and while Nicole restricted herself to the most innocuous of refreshment, the mood was so riotously infectious that she was as jazzed as anyone by the time morning came. So, when the suggestion was made that all present—still able to walk, that is—embark on a ritual Hunt, she found herself as enthusiastically eager as the rest.

Somehow, she found herself on point, stumbling along a mist-draped woodland trail, dimly recollecting that the honor had come to her after a highly embellished—and ridiculously juiced—retelling of the battle between the remnants of her *Wanderer* crew and Shavrin's, and the raiders who'd seized *Range Guide.* Of how Nicole, armed with a crossbow—as she was now—had gone out alone against the raiders' commander, a renegade Air Force officer named Daniel Morgan, who carried one of the Hal rifle blasters, a directed energy weapon capable of effortlessly punching holes through battleship armor. The footing was awful, the light worse, casting everything in degrees of shadow, with no hard edges to be found in this forest except by tripping over them.

After a couple of awkward staggers and one legitimate tumble, Nicole tucked herself up under the trunk of the nearest, biggest tree to take stock of herself and the situation. Thinking about Morgan sobered her up, always did, it took hardly any effort at all to remember the ozone stink in the station's stale air from the blaster's discharge, or the way its beam lit up the darkness like a searchlight from Hell.

She sat very still and listened to the forest around her. There was a lot less noise than she expected, especially from such a crowd of drunken revelers.

Ideal circumstances for an accident, she thought, using her fingers in the darkness to check the action on her bow, *assuming I'm not being paranoid.*

According to Hana, there was still nothing to report concerning the decompression of the Garden. Rose Guthrie's teams were no closer to solving the mystery than when they started, which was generating some serious heat from the Bridge. In no way was Hobby prepared to accept any sort of major failure aboard his vessel, much less one that remained inexplicable. As far as Hana was concerned, though, it was of a piece with the *Swiftstar* ambush in Earth orbit. Clearly, someone had strung an extraordinarily sophisticated software chain to disable all the relevant systems—it was far too comprehensive a crash to be coincidence or accident, that had been assumed from the start—but they were kamikaze commands that self-destructed upon activation. No evidence left to lead investigators to the perp; none, in fact, to indicate that anything amiss had even happened.

A tremendous crash erupted so close at hand Nicole nearly jumped out of her skin, something charging through the brush that was so big and powerful it didn't care who heard. Her startled brain immediately—instinctively—put a name to the noise: *p'm'taie*, a four-footed omnivore, sort of an adolescent elephant with the agility of a mountain goat and the disposition of a great white shark, possessed of enough brain to make its tusks and brute strength truly dangerous.

The Bonding party had been hunting smaller game, if there'd been even a hint of a *p'm'taie* in the vicinity they'd have stayed close to the lodge. Common wisdom held that the *p'm'taie* were as eager for Hal trophies as the other way round. The unassailable fact was that the ratio of slain over the generations was pretty much 1:1.

She had an arrow nocked, a half dozen in the quiver clipped against one hip, plus a knife. For all the good they'd do her, she knew she might as well be wholly unarmed, and she glanced upward to see if her tree could be climbed. Problem with that was, what to do if the *p'm'taie* decided to knock it down? That too had happened over the years.

Then, the decision was made for her by a hoarse scream, too close at hand to be ignored. She found a shallow ravine just beyond her tree—by nearly pitching herself headlong into it—and scrambled along the edge, following the noise of the fight, hoping that would mask any sound of her approach because there was no way she could move fast *and* silently.

She heard another outcry, this of defiance, a different voice than the one she'd heard before, and the basso grunting of the beast. Below her feet, the ravine deepened and widened, forming an oblong bowl-shaped depression that gave the *p'm'taie* plenty of room to maneuver. A Hal was backed hard against the wall, under a lip that prevented her from climbing any higher, with only the length of a spear between her and the beast. She was still yelling but the animal didn't appear to mind; both knew the only possible outcome.

Nicole had an emergency lamp clipped to her belt. Quickly she strapped it onto an overhanging branch, angling the lens as best she could and ready to sell her soul for some duct tape—which prompted a wild grin, because if she was making that kind of offer, then a rifle blaster would be by far the more practical request. The Hal was jabbing at the beast, as though trying to provoke an attack; Nicole remembered the other voice she'd heard and realized the woman was trying to protect someone else. Her hope had to be that she could keep the *p'm'taie* occupied long enough to attract the other hunters and thereby save her companion.

Sorry, kiddo, Nicole thought as she finished her work, *I'm afraid I'm all you've got.*

She put a bolt in her teeth, and centered the cross hairs of her scope on the animal's side. She had no illusions about this shot, it was basically to catch the beast's attention. She pulled the trigger.

With a roiling cry that was as fearsome as its appearance, the *p'm'taie* wheeled away from the Hal. It was faster than Nicole had expected but how fast became brutally apparent when it lashed out suddenly with both hind legs, breaking the woman's spear in two and catching her full in the chest to hurl her back against the wall of the ravine. She went down like someone body-slammed by a truck, and Nicole flicked both switches on her lamp.

Instantly the ravine was flooded with million-candlepower blue-white light. At the same time a piercing siren savaged what remained of the predawn stillness. As if that wasn't enough, Nicole knew that "Mayday" transponder signals would be flashing on at least a score of receivers—and for once she was sincerely thankful for her special status among the Hal. All she had to do now was survive until rescue arrived.

She stayed in the shadows behind the beam, scooting sideways along the lip of the ravine while the *p'm'taie* shook its massive head and blinked disturbingly large and aware eyes to try to restore its vision. A head-on shot was useless, the beast was too heavily protected by folds of leathery skin that were the functional equivalent of armor. Her bow didn't have force enough to punch its bolt through its skull.

The *p'm'taie* went for the lamp, the sheer power of its forward momentum sufficient to drive it almost all the way up the slope of the ravine. It tried to leap but here its strength and size turned into a liability; so much dirt had been churned up that the beast couldn't find decent footing. Again and again, it hurled itself at the wall—Nicole assumed it was trying to uproot the tree or shake the lamp loose—but she'd fastened it more securely than that. From its actions, she also deduced that the siren was causing the beast more annoyance than the light.

It turned back toward the fallen Hal, still crumpled across the way, and made a deliberate show of preparing to charge. Too deliberate a pause, too much of a display, it was daring her to respond and letting her know the full price if she didn't.

When it made its move, Nicole put her second bolt into the *p'm'taie*'s thigh, as close to the joint as she could place it. The beast stumbled, as though that leg had been lassoed out from under it. She took off herself as soon as she fired, scuttling back the way she came, so that when it went for where she'd been she had another clear shot at its flank. That bolt went into the hip hollow where hind leg joined the torso.

She hadn't counted on the *p'm'taie*'s terrifying speed. From a standing start, it wheeled and leapt, and only a reflexive panic spasm backward—a reaction that would have done a startled kitten proud—saved Nicole as it crashed onto the lip of the ridge where she'd been hiding.

It howled its fury and frustration, forelegs holding it in place while its rear hoofs tried to find sufficient purchase to kick it all the way over the top. Nicole had no illusions about her fate if it was successful, and for a moment was tempted to run. No sense wasting an arrow with a head shot, that would only make the creature madder.

Then, suddenly, it tumbled backward. She scrambled forward—aware of the risk she was running but also just as positive the beast wasn't faking—as it toppled off-balance, onto its side, onto its back. She fired without consciously aiming, a bolt to the lower belly, but it recovered its feet before she could nock another arrow. Common sense demanded that she withdraw to the cover of the trees and cede the beast the next move, but she couldn't take the risk it would go for the fallen Hal. It wasn't moving as easily as before, as it took a stance facing her, and she wondered if her second shot had done some damage. She took a few steps along the lip of the ravine, and the *p'm'taie* did a little crab step to keep its head towards her. She went back the other direction; it did the same. Its head was down, its lungs working like some giant bellows, each exhalation making little depressions in the earth beneath its lowered nostrils.

It bared its fangs in a ritual challenge and Nicole knew she was marked. The fight had become personal and the *p'm'taie* wasn't going to quit until one of them was dead.

Without warning, it doubled back up the ravine. She barely had time for a snap shot—that missed—as it disappeared around the bend and then heard a tremendous noise, partly the cries of the beast as it made its ultimate effort, partly the consequences to the local flora. The next sound was the snapping of the tree she'd used to hold her lamp as the *p'm'taie* hit it with full force. The light spun crazily as the tree fell into the ravine but Nicole wasn't there to watch. She was running for her life, praying there was enough of the predawn quasi-light for her to see her way. Not that it mattered much. The *p'm'taie* was not only faster, even wounded as it was, it could bull its way through the obstacles Nicole was forced to duck around. With each step, it gained.

The ground disappeared from underfoot and Nicole cried out as she pitched into space. She made a hard pratfall onto a modest slope and cascaded full length to the bottom. Her clothes were torn by the impact, probably her skin, too, but she wasn't really interested in either as she fumbled for her bow and remaining arrows. The *p'm'taie* thundered off the edge, same as she had, but with a leap that took it well over Nicole's head; bad mistake, because it gave her another shot at its belly and then her last bolt into its already bloody flank before it could face her once more.

She crab-scuttled back up the slope, looking for a way out, finding nothing, hardly aware of her more immediate surroundings until a pair of infant tusks scored her forearm and another set jabbed at her back. A roar from the animal was answered by a chorus of falsetto *peeps* from the den behind Nicole, and with only a marginal awareness of what she was doing, she grabbed for the shape nearest her, catching it by the scruff of the neck and covering its throat with the honed blade of her knife.

Whatever sounds the *p'm'taie* had made thus far were nothing compared to those Nicole heard now. Hardly surprising, when a mother sees her babies threatened. Nicole's teeth were chattering and she moved the knife a little clear of the baby so as not to inadvertently cut it. She could make out four shadowy humps in the opening to the den, plus the one in her grasp, and assumed they had to be fairly newborn because of their size.

Terriffic, she thought sourly, and wondered what was taking everyone so long to come to her damn rescue. One of the other babies made a lunge for her arm—quick strike, quick retreat—and she hissed as it drew more blood. *Nervy little buggers*, she thought in admiration, and then noticed there weren't as many lumps as there'd been a glance before. She couldn't keep constant watch, not with Mom to consider, but when another slash caught her attention she saw only the one baby left. The others had withdrawn deep into the den, probably far out of her reach.

Shit, she thought in one language, and then, *O blessed water*, in the other. The kid would keep coming at her until she let its sibling go, which was all Mom was waiting for. Or, just as ominously, Mom might decide to hazard—even sacrifice—the life of one baby to protect the rest. Either way, Nicole had no more time.

She sensed a movement, dropped her knife, grabbed for the kid coming in for another attack, aware that Mom was charging, forcing her to a stop as Nicole came up with both infants wriggling in her hands.

The *p'm'taie* uttered a shriek pitched so high into the upper register it made Nicole want to scream. At the same time, it was so close—hardly a couple of its body lengths away—that she could feel the gusting stench of every breath.

"Back," she said, in a fairly impressive snarl of her own. *"Back off, Mama!"*

The babies were upset, as were their siblings in the den.

Mama looked ready to trample Nicole to sludge but at the same time she didn't want to risk her offspring. Nicole knew the stalemate couldn't last much longer, she could feel blood flowing down her arm from the baby's gashes, she simply didn't have the strength to hold them.

She pitched the babies, in an underhand toss up over the top of the bank behind her. In the same movement, she hurled herself in the opposite direction, following the wall of the ravine. She figured she had about five steps, tops, before Mama nailed her, but the freight train passed her by as the *p'm'taie* went for her babies first.

As she rounded the bend and came into the light field of her lamp, she caught sight of a shape hammered into the ground, broken and disemboweled. Up ahead was the fallen Hal. Nobody else.

Deep ocean take you all, she snarled silently, *where* are *you?*

She didn't know she could run so fast or move with such flawless abandon. She marked her launch point and target, hit each perfectly, put herself onto the bank above the Hal as though the leap had been rehearsed. She anchored herself on an exposed root, then reached to her full extension for the Hal. As she caught the woman by the collar, she heard a sharp *crunch*ing sound and both light and siren went out.

The *p'm'taie* waited until she looked up before lifting its hoof from the shattered lamp and stepping delicately aside.

Aw hell, she cried to herself. And then, aloud, in asperity, "What'd you do, Mama, creep up on us on bleeding tiptoe?" She could've sworn the creature laughed in response.

Hobson's choice. If Nicole broke and ran, chances were the animal wouldn't follow, not and leave its babies unprotected. But the Hal below would die for it. Assuming she wasn't dead already. If Nicole stayed to defend her, that would probably condemn them both.

Even as the alternatives presented themselves, Nicole knew it was no contest. She measured the distance to the woman's broken spear, and then rolled off the top of the bank to grab hold of it.

No words, no bravado, she braced herself as best she could and looked the animal in the eye.

A flare burst overhead, its effect muted against the lightening sky, and in the near distance voices could be heard calling Nicole's name. Near enough to avenge, possibly, but not to save. Nicole didn't take her eyes off her foe.

The *p'm'taie* took a deliberate look up at the falling, guttering flare, then towards the sound of the other hunters, and Nicole had a sudden chilling sense of the carnage that would ensue should each encounter the other. It squared off against her once more, but didn't charge.

Instead, it turned away, trotting up the ravine to its den.

Nicole sank down onto the ground, unwilling to wholly relax her vigil, unable to accept that the duel was over and that she had somehow survived.

"Shea Shavrin's-Daughter," came from close beside her, in a voice just this thready side of consciousness.

"I'm here. You're alive. We're safe."

"Why did it leave?" There was pain in the woman's voice, but mostly wonderment.

Nicole was about to answer when the thought struck her that she might be the only one to know about the babies. And with that realization, she decided to keep it that way.

"Damned if I know," she said.

The local physician spoke of scars won in honorable battle but Nicole would hear none of it and an emergency summons went out for Jenny Coy.

Kymri arrived with her but immediately went into conference with the Lords Councilor who'd brought her here. Nicole didn't pay any attention, she had a more pressing engagement—with the young Hal she'd rescued.

Her name was Sirat's'ai, and she was first cousin to Matai, the Hal Speaker who was Nicole's friend and who she was forced to kill six years ago. The skin patterning—which is what most Terrans used as the means of telling Hal apart—was totally different, it was the facial structure that marked them as biological family. She was big for her age, as a glance at her stats told Nicole just how young she was, in the first blush of adolescence. *Probably her first Hunt,* Nicole thought.

She wasn't in Intensive Care, thanks in some measure to youthful resilience, but the wounds she'd suffered would be a fair while healing. A multitude of broken ribs, two of which had punctured and collapsed a lung, comprised the bulk of the damage. She was tagged into a brace of medical scanners, with numbers towards the low end of the acceptable range. Her appearance echoed the telemetry; her skin looked sort of collapsed on the bone, as if all the cushioning fat—of which the Hal invariably had little to begin with, being by nature an infuriatingly lean species—had drained away, and there was no sheen to her fur. There was a purplish undercast to her skin tone that extended across her breast, above the bandages wrapped snugly about her rib cage, and up over one shoulder.

"Nice bruise," Nicole muttered softly.

Sirat's'ai's eyelids flickered as the woman groaned acknowledgment. Her breaths were shallow, with a beat between every one, as though each was a conscious decision, accompanied by an effort that left her exhausted.

"Does it hurt?"

Another groan, plus a tightening of the lids.

"Can I get you anything for the pain?"

"Not pain, really." Her voice was, impossibly, even less powerful than the night they'd met. "More of an ache. And I'm injected to the legal limit. Don't see how they can call this 'flying.' Me, I feel positively leaden. Suppose I should be thankful I *can* feel. Considering my brother's position."

At that, Nicole leaned forward, to speak in a hard, commanding tone.

"Stop it, Sirat's'ai. None of us knew that *p'm'taie* was out there; *none* of us were equipped with the proper weapons to fight it."

"And that excuses all fault, Shea Shavrin's-Daughter?"

"There is no fault. Bad fortune, perhaps, but nothing more. I saw your brother's body, Sira. He was right on top of her den. At that distance, under those circumstances, I doubt even a rifle blaster would have made any difference for him. He died with honor. You survived with honor."

"Thanks to you. There is *alach'n'an* between us, a debt of blood. You will have Heart Right to the *p'm'taie* when I claim my just vengeance."

"*Alach'n'yn*, you mean? Blood price."

Sira weakly bared her fangs.

"One on one, you and the *p'm'taie*? You've nothing to prove, girl; one or the other of you—maybe even both—will be slaughtered to no good purpose."

"I do not expect you to understand our ways . . ." she began, but Nicole gruffly cut her off.

"I am a Speaker, Sirat's'ai, and Heir to Shavrin," and Nicole shot her wrists out from the cuffs of her jacket to flash the markings on her lower arms. "I know more of your ways than you can possibly imagine." She shifted gears at that point, turning to the formal dialect that Speakers used during Arbitrations. "You claim blood price on the *p'm'taie* for the life of your brother . . ."

"Blood must answer for blood," Sira cried as passionately as she was able.

"Not always so," Nicole said. "The *alach'n'an* is owed, not to me, but to the *p'm'taie*. Yes, I stood between you, but it still could have slain us both and escaped long before help arrived. It chose not to."

"Out of respect for your prowess!"

"Who knows? What matters, though, is that *it* made the choice to walk away. The life you hold, you owe to the one who spared it."

Sira blinked rapidly, masking her eyes behind their nictating membrane, features twisting into an expression of such grief that Nicole wanted to reach out to her. Instead, she sat more straightly in her chair, gathering about herself as formal and remote a demeanor as she could manage, reaching to an image of her own mother laying down the law after Nicole had broken curfew during exam week in junior high. Comparatively, she was pretty much the same age back then as Sira was now. She'd been racing all day (with permission) and was having so much fun hanging out with the crew and their sailing buddies afterward that she deliberately lost track of the time. She'd never dreamed her mother had such anger in her; Siobhan Shea didn't raise her voice, or her hand, to her eldest when Nicole finally returned home, but made it abundantly plain that Nicole was never to break these rules again. That was the last she would ever speak of the moment; trust had been betrayed once, it was Nicole's responsibility to earn it back.

The next day, of course, Nicole learned the reason: a classmate, raped and murdered by an off-islander. There hadn't been an immediate ident on the body so when the word went out, Siobhan had feared it was Nicole.

"It isn't fair," Sira sobbed.

"What blood the *p'm'taie* had to offer has already been shed. No good will come of more. Let it go, Sirat's'ai."

"Do you command, Shavrin's-Daughter?"

Half smile and bared foreteeth, her wry response a blend of human and Hal. "Is that the Speaker's way, Sira? I offer the resolution I think is just and appropriate. Yours is the choice, whether or not to take it."

She stroked her palm gently up the girl's forehead, smoothing her hair on the pillow. "Grow wise, little lion," she said, "that you may grow older. Now get some sleep, I've kept you too long, and you've a lot of mending to do."

Nicole made her way stiffly back to her suite and then onto the balcony overlooking the forest valley, her own bumps and bruises making themselves more and more felt with each passing hour. It was a lovely view, and she'd been assured time and again by the staff of the lodge that she was high enough above the ground to be guaranteed safe. Having seen a *p'm'taie* in action, Nicole wasn't anywhere near so sanguine, but she also didn't think she had anything to fear. If she and "Mama" met again, and somehow she sensed they never would, it would be for a fair fight.

When Kymri found her, she was happily ensconced on a day bed, basking in the rays of the lowering sun.

"Scouts report that the immediate vicinity is clear," he told her and Jenny both, sequentially.

"So they said before," was Nicole's reply.

"So I understand."

"So—either they're not very good at their job . . ."

He lifted her bandaged arm gently, prompting a warning cough from Jenny.

"Very small wounds," he noted.

"From very small tusks."

He understood. "That's probably why they missed her. A pregnant mother, or one nursing newborns, isn't about to attract attention."

"I hope she got away."

"If she hadn't, we'd have heard by now."

"I'm glad. There's been enough bloodshed."

"We come from predator stock, Nicole. Hunting is in our nature. And when the prey is very much our equal . . ."

"I put six arrows into her, Kymri," Nicole marveled, "all solid hits. Hardly made a difference."

"You were very lucky, Nicole."

"Tell me about it. I saw the boy's body."

"You saved his sister." The term he used meant birth siblings, not fosterlings.

"Tell me, Kymri, how strong was the faction that wanted to view *us* as prey? A challenge to be overcome, a foe to be conquered?"

He looked down at her, all humor gone from eyes and features.

"Wrong tense," he said simply. " '*Is* the faction' is the more applicable query. As with your kind, too strong to be ignored but not enough to make policy. We are hunters, yes, and warriors of necessity. But we don't have the racial taste for wholesale organized annihilation that you appear to."

"Is that why you came to make friends, because you're afraid of us?"

"Among us, conflict is resolved . . . *personally*. The fate of a Household, or a Clan, or even the entire race, is entrusted to a single individual, to stand surrogate for all the rest."

"And you all buy into that? Everyone accepts the outcome, no matter what?"

"Why do you ask me, Nicole, when you can find the cultural bases for your answers in your own memory?"

"I find them, Kymri. I accept them. They make perfect sense and none whatsoever. The cognitive dissonance makes me nuts."

"Because you're still looking through human eyes, Nicole"—he knelt down beside her, putting his face almost level with hers—"the inner music must be in harmony—heart, soul, mind, body—if you are to survive the *Harach't'nyn*, there can be no such dissonance. All this"—and he opened his arm as though to encompass the lodge but Nicole knew he meant the interrogation of the past weeks and that yet to come—"is for show. The Challenge Quest is the only test that matters."

"Does every Hal pass?"

Kymri straightened to his full height and turned away. There was a long pause before he answered and even then, he chose his words carefully. "That's a question time and custom has rendered somewhat . . . moot. We *are* evolved, that is a fact of birth, so the Challenge Quest is generally considered the celebration of an accomplished fact. A symbol more than a reality."

"But not for all."

"No," he continued, with that same deliberation. "Some look on the Challenge as a means of returning to the traditional heritage of our people."

"You don't approve?"

"Each must make their own choice, that is the most fundamental tenet of our society."

"And likewise bear responsibility for the consequences."

"It is not simply a physical ordeal, and those other aspects cannot easily be described. You seek the origins of our very being, you stand naked—to the core of your essence—before the face of God."

"What happens when you fail, Kymri?"

"I had a friend. We had flown together, fought together, there were blood bonds between us, the *alach'n'an*. We were as close as two Hal can be. It was his choice to accept the Challenge, my responsibility as his *sidi'n'an chai* to cover his back."

"And?" she prompted when he fell silent. There were early evening clouds scudding across the sun, bringing a cool breeze that made Nicole wish for a jersey to go over her gauze blouse.

"Whatever he sought was not what he found. Something broke inside him, that neither physician nor Speaker could heal. He withdrew into himself, beyond the point where I—or anyone—could reach."

"He died?"

"Physically, no. I still visit, from time to time, but there's no real point anymore. He takes no notice. In all the ways that matter, he's been dead for years."

"You were there with him, Kymri, what did you see?"

He leaned on the railing, again with that fixed stare off into the sky. Nicole filed the angle in her memory, resolving to take a look herself after sunset, but she already had a fair suspicion what she'd find.

"Nothing."

"At all?"

"The world as it is." He bared teeth in a particularly humorless Hal grin. "The curse—or perhaps blessing, who's to say—of no imagination."

"You never went back on your own?"

"It's a singular experience, Shavrin's-Daughter. If God isn't of a mind to chat, why press the point?"

"Is that what's in store for me?"

"I don't know. Truly. You could ask every living Hal who's walked the Path. Or consult every Speaker with the memory of a forebear who has. It wouldn't mean a blessed thing. The experience is unique, for *we* are all unique—or at least, so we like to think—you, I'm afraid, far more than any."

She stepped to his side and laid a hand ever so lightly on his. He looked at her sharply, her approach and the gesture had caught him off-guard, and she caught a sense deep within his eyes of a lifelong regret, the ache of a wound that had never really healed, for him as for his friend. She began to speak, but he placed his fingers gently on her lips, to stop her voice. She leaned against him instead, drawing from the warmth that radiated through his close-cropped fur. After a time, he put his arm about her shoulders and drew her closer still.

Then, it was his turn to follow her gaze, as the sunglow finally faded from the heavens and the first of the twilight stars came into view. He wasn't surprised, he also wasn't happy, as they stared at the twinkling planet.

"It's at aphelion, I'm told," Nicole commented, as though making idle conversation. The evening breeze was off the forest, rich with wondrous, myriad scents—but not the ones she was looking for. "Making its closest orbital approach to s'N'dare."

He said nothing, but from the whisper of tension beneath his skin, Nicole knew he wanted to change the subject; at the same time, she marveled at his self-control, which allowed so little overt awareness of his feelings. A casual onlooker—or even a ferociously interested one, like Jenny, watching with inscrutable patience from her chair—wouldn't have known anything was amiss.

"A formal dinner has been scheduled to mark the departure of the *Constitution*," he said, as though she hadn't spoken. "You will sit by Shavrin's right hand."

"As you require, Kymri ShipMaster."

"I'd put you *on* that bloody starship, if I could."

"If you tried, I'm not sure I'd fight you."

"You'll be returning home with me, tonight."

"No."

Her refusal didn't register at first. When it did, Kymri dropped his arm and took a step away from her, to say, dumbly, "Your pardon, Shavrin's-Daughter?"

"You heard."

"That is unacceptable."

"I am done with the Council, Kymri. With respect, I am done with you. And my foster mother. And all her damnable machinations. I am tired and I hurt and I would like some time to myself."

"Nicole, you have responsibilities . . ."

She cocked a jaundiced eye his way. "You really think so? As far as that aspect of my being here is concerned, you and I both know I'm just a distraction. More in the way than not. That may change after the *Harach't'nyn*, but then, isn't that the point? You said it yourself, Kymri, *that* is the test that matters."

"The rest does matter, Nicole. How well—or poorly—you do beforehand builds the context within which the Challenge will be judged."

"Fine. I'm willing to stand on what I've said and done 'til now."

"Very well then," he said, although he conceded nothing. "I assume you have other plans?"

"Ben Ciari has a place along the Saudakar Range. He said it's very private."

Kymri looked amused. "He has a Hal gift for understatement. The only safe way in or out is by air. There is a walking trail, but that is *p'm'taie* country."

"He sent video. To me, it's the perfect place to hide out."

"How do you propose to travel there?"

"I was hoping some friend might give me a lift."

"Ah."

"Otherwise, I'll take my life in my own hands and hike it."

"M'gtur won't be happy."

"Then he can hike in after me."

She fixed him with a gaze that was as disconcertingly level as it was fierce, both qualities Kymri recognized in her the moment they first met. She was daring him to call her bluff—for bluff it was. All he had to do was appeal to Shavrin; for all her defiance, with all that was at stake, Nicole wouldn't refuse a direct command.

"Be on the ramp at dawn," he said. "And pack warmly. Where you're going, the world hasn't heard yet that the season's turned."

The flight out had been on an executive Jumper, outfitted with the plush luxury the Lord Councilors took for granted. It was a breathtaking ride, as the hypersonic RamScoop whisked them to the edge of space and halfway around the world in barely an hour.

This was something altogether different. Very low, very slow, in a V/STOL bush plane built more for reliability than comfort. The wings were short and exceptionally broad—with triple-slotted flaps to provide maximum lift and maneuverability—the whole assemblage mounted on gimbals that allowed the engines to rotate through ninety degrees, thereby giving the aircraft the mated capabilities of a fixed wing vehicle and a helicopter.

Kymri was pilot, Nicole beside him, with Jenny on the jump seat behind and between them. Nicole was familiar with the aircraft, she'd honed her skills aboard *Constitution* in Virtual Reality simulations. Only to discover yet again the perceptual gulf that still existed between facsimile and the real thing. She'd learned to fly by the manual; now, she was leavening and embroidering those instructions with experience. And reminded once more how the first major technological breakthrough for the Hal had been flight.

They watched the birds from their high-country dens and worked to find artificial ways to make up for the natural gifts they lacked. They discovered the ball by watching boulders cascade down the mountain slopes in an avalanche, and from that observation—with a bit of work and some inspirational deduction—came the wheel. Useful to help with hauling loads, but as far as transport went not for much else. The Hal themselves could move faster unencumbered than they could pulling a cart. And there were no animals with speed better suited for domestication than prey. That was on the ground. The air proved to be a wholly different arena.

They made their way smoothly along the mountains after leaving the lodge, gradually building altitude until they were well clear of the peaks. Then Kymri turned west, paralleling the sun across the northern hemisphere, from highlands to fertile lowlands to the next major range. As this new line of peaks came into view, it was quickly clear to Nicole that here was much older and more elemental terrain than what she'd seen previously. There was a strange but essential harmony to most of the continental landscape that was missing here.

She was flying the aircraft, Kymri having turned over the controls with the stern injunction to call him in case of the slightest trouble, while he repaired to the cabin for a nap. They were on the third leg of their flight, after two refueling stops. The air was clear and smooth, visibility all but unlimited, with nothing to worry about on any panel displays.

Jenny had clambered into Kymri's chair, visibly impressed—as she had been from the start—by the panorama.

She touched Nicole's arm. Then, plainly frustrated at the language barrier, Jenny spread an expansive hand across the window.

"Very impressive view," Nicole agreed. "Been like that all day. Shouldn't be much longer now, though," she went on, even though aware that Jenny didn't have the slightest notion what she was saying. She indicated the nav screen. "This"— tapping a dot within a square one grid ring inbound from the edge of the image—"Ciari. Where we're going." She indicated her watch, then held up three fingers, hoping her friend would understand she meant three hours.

This only seemed to increase Jenny's exasperation.

"You could save us all a lot of bother by asking Kymri to translate," Nicole told her, fatigue and aches in rude places inspiring some of the same emotions in return.

"Kymri," she repeated, with a poked finger back towards the main cabin for emphasis. "Help. You. Speak. Me."

Jenny shook her head violently, the vehemence of her reaction and the subsequent set to her jaw clearly indicating her opposition to that idea. She scrabbled in her bag for her PortaComp, punched up a program, showed it to Nicole.

The first image was a spectacular shot of the Grand Tetons, above Jackson Hole.

Jenny pointed to the display, then at the window, and said emphatically in Trade, "Same!"

Then she twisted in her seat to point to the way they'd come, "*Not* same!"

Nicole couldn't fathom her meaning. *What are we talking here, Jenny,* she thought. *Not basic geology, am I right, something as obvious as mountains are different from plains.* She rolled a hand, prompting Jenny to continue. But before the woman did, she snuck a glance into the cabin, to check on Kymri.

Next came a scroll of images on her comp's display, beginning with an old tintype that showed the construction of New York's Central Park; a tap on the small keyboard advanced the presentation to the next picture, an overhead panorama of the finished project. Followed by Tokyo's famed Akasaka Gardens, in progress and after completion. The "Mona Lisa" Gardens on the Moon. She presented a score of images, but try as she might Nicole couldn't discern any linkage between them.

Jenny shook the computer at her, slapping the display—which now showed the *Constitution's* Garden—and said emphatically, "Same!"

She slapped the screen again, then the canopy, indicating the land leading up to the continental divide, to say just as assertively, *"Same!"*

She looked hopefully at Nicole, who for the life of her couldn't make the connection. There was a tremble from the aeroplane, like going over a line of speed bumps, as they encountered the leading edge of some light high mountain atmospheric chop. Nicole scanned the panel, then the panoramic vista beyond. The sky was still mostly clear, there looked to be nothing to worry about from the weather.

She sensed Kymri's quiet approach, and wondered suddenly whether he'd been feigning sleep. His expression gave no sign as he and Jenny exchanged places, the look he offered her as bland as hers was searching. Nicole let him take the controls and slumped in her seat, letting her eyes droop half-closed so she could replay Jenny's pictures in her mind's eye. Again, there were no resonant associations.

Yet the answer was blindingly obvious to Jenny, she thought. And the image came to her of the ambush in near-Earth space, during the *Sundowner* test, when all their calls for help went unanswered because the computers that oversaw the orbital communications systems had been programmed not to hear them. *Am I blind to what she's telling me,* she thought further, biting her lower lip in worry, *because it's in my nature not to see?*

Which, in turn, presented the larger question, right in her face: *What* is *my nature now? I know who I am—but what does that* mean*?*

She took a deep breath, her lungs filling reflexively to their full capacity, and held it, before finally letting go in a deliberately controlled exhalation. Because she had a sudden sense—a teetering glimpse into the Abyss—of *Maenaes't'whct'y'a,* the Void Between. And a terrible insight into its true meaning—to be neither one thing nor another, not four-footed, not two. Too evolved to return to the hunting pack, yet not enough to take her place among those for whom such concepts as Honor and Name had meaning. A part of neither world, forever apart from both.

"The scents are wrong," she said, standing on the balcony overlooking the lake and taking in the glorious smells of the forest at twilight. The breeze was stiffer out on the water; what only stirred the branches where she stood was creating little wave caps in the distance.

The lake alone made this setting markedly different from any other she'd seen since her arrival—in person or Virtual—it was a glacial trough, a valley filled by the runoff from a massive ice field farther along the range. Five klicks wide and nearly twenty-five long, it was probably the only body of water on the entire planet with any sort of decent depth.

Except for the clearing where Ciari had built his house, and laid out a landing pad for air transport, the trees marched all the way down to the water's edge. Kymri didn't ask to stay, though Nicole knew he wanted to. Once he'd off-loaded their gear, and made sure they had sufficient supplies in storage, he was on his way.

Nicole was out of the house immediately, knowing it was a rotten thing to leave Jenny with the unpacking, wishing she could have come here wholly on her own. That was an aspect of herself, she knew, where human and Hal were a match. The friends she made, the relationships that thrived, were invariably long distance. Even now, her best friend was aboard *Constitution*, and her newest, she couldn't effectively talk to. She never thought of that as a problem — mostly, she figured it as a major asset. Whatever came her way, she had to be able to cope on her own. Backups had their place, but *she* was the aeroplane driver.

Ciari was cut from that same mold.

She blinked, and realized that she had stopped her stroll a good twenty meters from the shoreline. She took a step forward, and had to stop again as her heartbeat picked up speed. She knew the symptoms, she'd heard them from a sailing buddy describing how he felt on the Observation Deck of the Millennium Tower, with only a pane of safety glass between him and a quarter-mile freefall. Intellectually, there was no danger; the man knew that. Didn't matter a damn, because emotionally he was just as certain that the window would blow out the moment he touched it.

She forced another step, and another, refusing to yield to a surge of anxiety that seemed to be increasing at an exponential rate. She knelt, going to hand and knees on the damp earth, and stared at the water lapping darkly just out of reach. She tried to fill her mind with memories of coastal scenes, but that didn't help much. Almost the opposite in fact, making her feel as if she were playing Russian roulette and added another bullet to the cylinder with every spin. She kept telling herself there was nothing to be afraid of, there was nothing in the lake that could possibly harm her — *Goddammit*, she raged, *I'm a sailor as much as a pilot, I bloody* love *to swim* — to no avail. She'd never felt her heart beat so fast, and feared that if she stayed much longer it would explode.

She stabbed an arm forward in a convulsive gesture, deliberately throwing herself off-balance, so that her hand landed in the water. And threw herself away so violently it was as though she'd just received a high-voltage shock.

"Ow," she said, stating the obvious, hoping to head off the pain with a stab at humor. Every nerve in her body felt like it had been strung out to the limit and tied into pretzel knots.

"So much," she breathed, "for catlike reflexes."

She placed both palms on her face, then pulled her left hand for a look. There was hardly any natural light left, dusk having almost totally given way to true night, but the water on her hand was a deliciously cool antidote to her flushed skin.

She rolled up to a sitting position, ignoring the cascade of protests that came from each joint and muscle in turn as it was called into play. Then, pushed forward—noting that while she still felt anxious, it was with nowhere near the previous intensity—to crouch at the water's edge, where she cupped her hands under the surface and properly splashed her face.

Didn't taste like home.

No reason why it should, she thought with a laugh. And then realized that she hadn't meant the Earth.

The stars were out, free she realized for the first time of the light pollution that dimmed the sight of them in the city.

Automatically, she looked for the benchmark stars, but nothing was quite where it was supposed to be.

She stood erect to her full height, putting her back to the water—ignoring the part of her shrieking that this was something no sane Hal would *ever* do—to gaze at the trees and remember her initial comment upon landing.

She picked her way up the path, noting now what she'd missed before, that Ciari had laid a walk all the way down to the shore. From the breadth of the passage, and the way the stones had been set into the ground, it was one he'd used frequently.

Interesting. In some ways, he was far more overtly Hal than she, yet he deliberately built himself a house by deep water, in a place no Hal could conveniently reach. And made a point of giving himself easy access to the lake.

Jenny was in an easy chair, reading, when Nicole came in. She watched, saying nothing, while Nicole found and rummaged through her bag, and came up with the PortaComp. Then, of course, Nicole's intentions unraveled completely— because, while she knew what she wanted, it was etched in her mind like cut crystal, she had no way to express it through an English language keyboard. The letters simply made no sense.

Ciari had sent plenty of video on his hideaway, so she was fairly familiar with the layout. His study was upstairs, and she quickly got hold of a pad and pencil, making another notation as she did that there was an awful lot of paper about, but precious little electronics. Not many books. Pity. She was ready to kill for a decent, and accessible, astronomical atlas. Her foot snagged and she almost fell; she untangled the trapeze harness from her foot and tossed it onto the most convenient chair, muttering about the uncharacteristic clutter. Ciari couldn't bear to live this way in space, how could he stand it on the ground? The answer of course was obvious: *to make it difficult for anyone to find anything, or know what's important even when you saw it.* Poe's "Purloined Letter," hide everything in plain sight. *Still*, she thought, as she rejoined Jenny before the living room's stone hearth and its cheerily blazing fire, *a man should take better care of his sailing rig. Treat a p-suit that way, you've signed your death warrant.*

She slapped her pad onto the coffee table and began to sketch. One globe showing the continents of North and South America. Beside it, another globe marked with visible canals. Above each, the appropriate astronomical symbol for Earth and Mars, respectively. Nicole pointed to one, then the other.

"Not same," she said to Jenny, repeating Jenny's words from their flight.

Next, she added what she hoped was a recognizable rendition of a factory between the two, with a couple of earth movers for emphasis. She pointed to the Earth, then the equipment, then Mars.

"Same?" she asked. One plus one equals . . . ?

Jenny hazarded a nod, then hurriedly repeated her answer aloud.

Okay, Nicole thought, as always these days unconsciously calling on Hal metaphors, *good thermals, we're flying with a lot of life.*

Then, she pointed to the machines she'd drawn, and waved both arms wide to encompass everything around them.

"Same," Jenny answered very quietly.

Nicole had to search for the word, because it had no analog in either Trade or High Speech, which meant forcing herself to consciously shift internal gears and try to look at things from a purely human perspective. It made her head hurt. It also made her angry. The information was there, but she only seemed able to access it in dribs and drabs that never stayed with her for very long. And possessing it gave no guarantees that she'd be able to express herself properly. She rolled the syllables around her mouth, working tongue and jaw in silence until she was sure she had the proper form.

"Terraform," she said.

CHAPTER THIRTEEN

She knew from the moment she awoke that she was on another planet.

She knew just as certainly that she had come *home*.

She was lying on the padded floor of a domed habitat large enough to hold her and not much else. From the initial muzziness of her thoughts and the octogenarian stiffness in her bones she suspected that she'd been unconscious quite a while and that she'd been drugged. She looked for some key memories, hoping for a clue to when she'd been taken, but all that came to her was some blurred imagery from Ciari's cabin.

She sat bolt upright then, ignoring the disorientation and borderline nausea that accompanied the sudden movement.

"Jenny," she cried, grappling desperately with a silverfish image of shadow-cloaked figures in the night, marginally backlit by the fire's embers. Jenny stretched out on the couch, unmoving, Nicole herself lunging across the upper floor study, from desk to stairs, catching a partial stunshot that threw her stumble-tumbling off the landing, cries of alarm from below as she fell.

She gingerly touched her forehead, a bit above the close-cropped hairline, to find the bump almost gone.

She looked around for something to wear, but nothing came immediately to view and she didn't have the mental energy yet to go hunting. Again with that sick sense of being an old woman, she pushed herself upright and hobbled the few short steps out the entrance.

A meadow. Grasslands one way, forest the other, her first outside breath filling her lungs with the lush cinnamon spice she always associated with the Hal. This world had to be a little bigger than s'N'dare, its core more dense, the difference in gravity was perceptible enough to be noticed. The air was richer, too. There was sky weather on s'N'dare; here was water weather as well.

She stood clear of the tent to get a better view of the trees and couldn't help a grin of familiarity from years back. The "getting to know you" phase of *Wanderer*'s First Contact with Shavrin's ship. The four Terrans had found themselves in a huge environmental holography suite, capable of generating all-encompassing, three-dimensional illusions. The Hal had shown them a travelogue of their world, scattered scenes from nature. Nothing of their society, no clue as to where each image was in a planetary context, or the planet within a galactic one. They simply wanted to see how their "guests" would react to these new experiences, as individuals and members of a group.

One of the locales had been a forest. Very old growth and vaguely deciduous, most akin to the woodlands of the Pacific Northwest, only there was nothing she could recall from Earth that remotely compared with this. The reality was even more impressive.

A skirling breeze raised goose bumps on her bare skin and she ducked back inside the tent to see what had been left her. All she found was a knife, a big blade, single-edged hunter, with a scabbard and a belt. There was a carafe of water, anchored to the floor, and an equally small dispenser of survival rations. She treated herself to a couple of drinks, noting sourly that the cups were ridiculously disposable; one barely survived a refill. Not a hope of using them to carry liquid any distance. The biscuits could travel, but the dispenser would only release a couple at a time. If she read the timer correctly, she'd be fed four times a day.

She opened the flap once more and hunkered down in the doorway, to view the morning and ponder her situation.

This was the *Harach't'nyn*. She could go or stay. If she stayed, there was shelter and sustenance to keep her healthy until the Overlords came for her. From the size of the food packets and their container, probably three days.

Her gaze fell to her forearms, which she'd sort of naturally crossed atop her knees, and their elegant interlacing of stripes. She lightly stroked them with her fingertips.

Stay, and all this was for nothing.

Did that justify the alternative? This was primarily a Spirit Walk, and the benchmarks came from racial memory, focused through ancestral teachings. Each supplicant followed their own instincts, and interpretations of what they'd learned, trusting both to show them the True Way. Ideally, the walk-about would bring her to the Memorial Mount of Shavrin's Clan, a place Nicole had visited before, in Virtual and her dreams. But she could just as easily be lost, and she had nothing to sustain her but her own devices.

She gave a little shrug. On one level, this was nothing more than a somewhat extreme survival exercise, and she had no doubt she could ace it.

Then she heard the cry.

From behind, and well in the distance, carried on the wind together with a ghost of a scent that had her on her feet in an instant, knife in hand, body taut to its full length as she craned for the faintest sight of whatever had called.

There was another cry, a little louder but perceptibly more urgent—not so much that the caller was any closer but that he was very much aware of her, and making her aware of him.

Of its own accord, the blade flashed in the sunlight and the pommel hammered down on her hand where it clutched the apex of the domed habitat, catching her right across the knuckles. She yelped, as much in startlement as actual pain, but enough of both to shock her back to her senses. She was gulping air, her heart racing, her body felt as though a brushfire had been lit beneath her skin. She flushed again, even more deeply, grabbing the tent frame in both hands as though it were an anchor and she a vessel being swept towards a rocky shore by some swift and terrible tide. Her eyes were wide and wild; she felt ice in her lungs and butterflies farther down, embarrassingly aware that her nipples had grown visibly, almost painfully erect.

"Blessed Maker," she started to say, but stopped herself with the first syllable, teeth chattering with the aftermath of one emotional extreme and the stress of another just beginning as she turned to the dormant parts of her.

"Jesus," she said, her Hal accent giving the words an exotic twist. Nonetheless, she spoke in English. Deliberately. Defiantly. Using this as another anchor to keep her from sure destruction. "Mary and Joseph. *Christ!*"

That last was a shout.

She didn't feel right standing erect. She wanted to be closer to the ground; four-footed was the proper way to hunt.

She narrowed her gaze, in response to a shifting shadow far along the tree line.

He was watching, with all requisite patience, waiting for her to acknowledge his entreaty. His mottled coloring provided superb camouflage, yet she had no problem picking him out, thanks to the same instinct that was trying to drive her towards him.

She had to get out of here—but which way?

Terrific, she thought. *This whole experience depends on me trusting my instincts.* Only those instincts were flashing her cues she didn't dare take.

But I'm more *than Hal. At least, I hope I am. How about seeing where* those *instincts lead.*

She swept the field, the hackles of her neck—hell, her whole scalp—prickling with the awareness of the silent watcher, wondering if he'd follow, partly hoping that he would. Wanting to fight him off, but not so hard that . . .

"Stop it!" she cried, deliberately putting herself back on the Academy parade ground and using the voice staff drill instructors use on unwary cadets who should know better.

She took another hefty drink before she went and finished the last of her biscuit ration. Then she struck out for high ground.

Can't figure where to go, she told herself as she strode for the shadows of the woods, *until you have a decent sense where you are.*

And just as suddenly, a biting rejoinder, that to her surprise prompted a chuckle of wry amusement.

Fucked is where I am, actually.

She wanted to move fast, but she was breaking trail and learned quickly that her bare feet weren't made for this kind of travel. It seemed like every step, no matter how careful, found her a new set of nettles or brambles or stones. Under the forest canopy, the air grew significantly warmer as the day progressed, and the undergrowth didn't permit much of a breeze to counteract it. She could hear the air moving way up-top, stirring crowns and high branches, but around her all was still and steamy. The water she'd drunk soon burst free as perspiration, making her slick and sticky, and annoyingly attractive for the local insect life.

Here, Hal memory came to her aid, as she hunted up a *t'agua* bush and crushed the berries on her skin, smearing a film over all the skin she could reach. They looked good to eat, too, but a faint touch of juice on the tip of her lip reminded her why they weren't. Some animals thrived on them; the Hal didn't number among them.

She kept pushing upslope, walking mostly, but occasionally forced to climb, and gathering a growing collection of aches and scrapes along the way. Days were longer than on Earth, all the more so since the vegetation told her this land rode the leading edge of summer, but that still didn't mean she had time to waste. Sooner rather than later she'd have to find shelter, and sustenance. She thought more than once of going back to the tent but dismissed the idea out of hand. She'd seen no sign of the creature from the meadow, but likewise had no doubts that he was following. She still wasn't ready to trust herself if they met face-to-face, and she didn't think her knife would be sufficient to protect her.

For some reason—and that prompted a grim (and altogether human) chuckle—the more she thought about him, the more disturbingly familiar he seemed. The shape of his head, the way he held himself, they struck resonances she couldn't explain, and she grumbled a hopeless wish for a pair of binoculars.

Eventually, the sun having quartered the sky, she reached the crest of the escarpment. The ridge line continued to climb and she decided to follow it, since the forest was still too thickly wooded to get any bearings. Underfoot, loamy earth gave way more and more to scattered boulders, where wind and erosion had worn away the soil down to bedrock. She could walk more easily and so picked up her pace, scanning the way ahead through the thinning trees. The trunks were smaller, shorter, evidence of a harder struggle for survival.

The end, when it came, was breathtaking. She emerged onto a massive outcropping of stone that jutted off into space like a promontory. Below, a couple of hundred meters down a steeply climbable drop, she saw a twisting river valley fed in part by a waterfall from the stream she'd seen in her meadow. The sun was to her right, easily halfway to the horizon, which meant she was looking south. A glance farther east showed her a coastline, with dark water visible beyond.

She bared teeth—her appreciation for this moment wholly Hal—because she knew now precisely where she was, and what was expected of her.

She wasn't aware, as this revelation cascaded through her thoughts, that she'd sunk down into a crouch, legs folding double to put knees on a level with a back that she was unconsciously elongating, hands gripping the rock before her as naturally as if she'd been born to run this way. She flexed a set of fingers, and her mind filled in the proper sound of claws skimming the bare rock.

The proximity alarm saved her, a nerve-scrambling siren most often described as the "car alarm from Hell," sounding off barely ten meters along the crest and spooking her so badly she nearly flung herself off the precipice.

She wasn't the only one scared. The beast from the meadow—which *had* been following and had begun at last to make his move—uttered a howl that mixed fright and defiance, bursting from the shadow of the trees and onto the promontory in a challenge stance.

Nicole was splayed flat on the sun-baked stone, her knife pinned unreachably underneath her, staring in terrified astonishment at the sight the animal presented. The body fur was longer, but that was a minor cosmetic variation; the shape of the legs was different and the proportions between them and the arms as well. Stood to reason, quadruped orientation versus bipedal. But beyond that, she could have been looking at a Hal.

On the whole, he was bigger than most of the males she'd seen, broader in the shoulders and thighs, the legs built to push him hard and fast and she suspected for a good long time. Most of the motive power clearly came from them, the arms were for balance and direction. The fingers didn't appear as articulate as a bipedal Hal's, but there was an opposable thumb and the capacity for independent movement was confirmed when he grasped a rock and tossed it towards the sound. His base coat was a dark chestnut, splashed with mottled orange, ideal autumnal camouflage.

His head twitched marginally towards her, as though acknowledging her presence, and she caught a glimpse of hazel-gold eyes. He had no tail, and on closer inspection both eyes and ears were larger than on the bipedal Hal—*All the better,* she supposed, *for hunting.* He growled, only the noise was laced thick with subvocals intended just for her that made it as much an invitation as it was a warning for whatever was sounding the alarm.

Immediately into her head popped the correct response and she clenched her teeth to keep it there. With slow, deliberate movements, she pushed herself up enough to clear her knife. Then, praying to every deity that came to mind, she uttered a warning of her own.

It wasn't much compared to his. No matter the desire, human throats weren't designed to produce the same variety and depth of aural resonances. He turned his gaze to her, full-on, the expression of questioning confusion so eloquent that for a moment she couldn't respond. He tossed a quick, wary glance towards the siren, and reached a hand to her, emphasizing the gesture with a little half step towards the cover of the trees.

Again, she repeated the warning, attempting a subvocalized refusal of her own. She did not want him, she would not go.

He roared, the sound so powerful, coming without the slightest warning, that Nicole was on her feet in an instant, one leg bent, the other braced, ready to stand fast or move as the attack warranted, one arm out to ward off any blow while the other held her knife at the ready. She met his gaze with a determination as grim and indefatigable as his own.

He looked hurt.

But he left.

She wanted to collapse, as fatigue replaced the empowering rush of adrenaline to the point of utter exhaustion. Instead, she straightened to her full height, her back protesting mightily at the strains she'd put it through, and picked her way along the rock until she came to the source of the alarm.

It was an armored pressure suit. Twice the size of a big man, it was designed to take an awesome amount of punishment, both natural and man-made—radiation, solid impacts, heat, directed energy, the works. Any doubts as to its origin were banished when she rubbed the scorched surface over the left breast and uncovered the etched shield of a United States Marshal.

It was empty, of course, nobody home, its wearer long gone. She flipped the locking latches on the helmet, lifted it off with a moderate effort, and silenced the alarm. Then, she began releasing the body clips as well. It was late, she was tired, and she didn't want to find out the hard way that her four-footed paramour maybe wasn't inclined to take no for an answer.

Inside the torso, she found a carryall with her name on it, a leftover of the *Wanderer* mission she and Ciari had shared together. She set it down beside the suit and climbed in, to find the fit a great deal more snug on the inside that she expected.

You modified the suit, Ben, she thought, as she struggled with the Popeye-sized arms—and their infuriatingly stubby fingers—to close the shell. She shifted the carryall under her butt—with apologies to herself if there was anything breakable inside—and lastly seated the helmet properly on its neck ring. Internal systems sensed the presence of an occupant and popped back on-line the moment the circuit was closed.

"Ident please," she heard Ciari say, in English and High Hal. It was good to hear his voice.

"Nicole, Ben," she replied.

"Voiceprint confirmed. Biostats confirmed. Identification accepted. Internal unit systems active." She didn't want to consider the fate of anyone who *wasn't* approved trying to spend any time in here. Automatically, she checked the air and saw that the suit was bleeding off an external shunt. Made perfect sense: why draw on finite reserves when there's breathable atmosphere available?

She wanted to sleep but she was too tired, in that special state where everything functioned but nothing really worked. She could speak, but Heaven knew whether or not the words would make any sense. Walk, but probably run into things.

"Why am I not surprised to find this?" she asked rhetorically.

She didn't need to wonder how he got here. Only one effective way to traverse solar distances unnoticed, especially when the worlds themselves were in such close proximity as s'N'dare and this. A Solar Sailboat, a solo life-support module tethered to a silver polymer sail, to catch the energy wind streaming from the sun, very much like riding a current of air. Not a very fast means of travel, but the wind never died and over time it was possible to build up a respectable velocity. Add to that the advantage of traveling down the solar gravity well and this became an eminently feasible trip. If you ignored the risk of something going wrong, a fouled line, a tear in the sail, some failure of capsule support systems, an error in navigation. In this kind of circumstance, there was no margin for error. Screw up a reading or a computation, mis-enter a coordinate, and you could be all by yourself in the Big Dark, without sufficient supplies to get home. Certainly, you could call for help, but that would mean you'd never get this opportunity again. The Hal would be ready for it, then.

Precisely the kind of challenge Ben Ciari thrived on.

But how'd he get down? A capsule with shielding enough to survive reentry would also survive impact. And probably be noticed on the way down. And if the capsule bore the brunt of the atmospheric friction, why was the suit so scored.

The suit was rich with the smell of him. She assumed he'd lived in it for the entire flight, which meant that he had to have cleaned it after landing. For that, she was sincerely grateful. The scent of Hal cinnamon added a welcome texture and she suddenly found herself blinking back tears. She blinked harder, stretching her lids as wide as they'd open to clear her eyes, because there wasn't enough play within the suit for her to wriggle an arm free to wipe them clean. Her eyes burned from the moisture and the salt made her skin sting a little; blurred her vision a little, too, but it was getting on past sunset and she didn't mind taking a pass on the sights for tonight.

She hadn't seen him—to touch him—in better than six years, since their last farewells on the Moon, when he left to help establish Earth's Embassy on s'N'dare. She'd wondered all along how she'd feel when they met again—they'd crammed more passion into less time than she'd ever thought possible, perhaps because both had known it wasn't meant to last—but if she was expecting anything wildly dramatic, it wasn't happening. Yet.

"Sorry, Marshal," she muttered, "that damn cat got a better rise out of me."

She didn't want to think about that, so she turned her focus back to Ciari and the problem of crossing the last leg from sky to ground. Most pressure suits maintained their environment from a separate backpack; this one had a shaped torso, with integral life support, all self-contained. Provided better security but it was murder to deal with in case of a malfunction. Even then, he'd put in extra padding.

"You madman," she said full-voiced in disbelief. "You bloody, suicidal lunatic!"

There was only one answer. Skim the top of the atmosphere with the capsule, along a meteoric trajectory—hitting enough air to slow down some but not so much that the capsule would initiate its own insertion. The slingshot effect on the flyby would most likely send the module off on some unplottably wild-ass trajectory—knowing Ciari, Nicole bet it was a long loop the rest of the way down the well and into the sun. In the meanwhile, he simply bailed out.

There was no suit made to provide a controlled freefall descent into an atmosphere. It wasn't simply a matter of the heat to deal with, but raw speed as well, and the absolute need to reduce orbital velocity to something that a floatwing or even a paraglide chute could handle.

Had to be a *balut*. Essentially an inflatable heat shield, to protect you from reentry friction and provide active deceleration. It was called a SCRAM scenario, for getting survivors down from a low-orbit accident. Without proper optics, anyone watching from the ground would most likely assume that a chunk had broken off the core meteor and wouldn't think twice about it. When a thing looks like a duck and quacks like a duck and even floats like a duck, who expects it to be a hawk in disguise?

"That got you here, Ben," she said. "And obviously, you were expecting me to follow. But where have you gone since?"

She slept more easily than she had in ages and when she dreamed of water, she was sailing.

That led her back to Ciari's house by the lake, and the harness she'd tripped over. A trapeze harness. For a man who'd never sailed a day in his life.

She opened her eyes to morning twilight, the eastern sky

glowing but still the better part of an hour to go before she saw the sun.

She asked the suit for a proximity scan and was thankful for a negative response. Next, on impulse, she inquired about incoming messages, but again came up empty.

She cracked her helmet, then the torso latches, and clambered stiffly into open air. The morning chill made her shiver and her breath visible as she started for the trees to relieve herself, with a last-minute grab for her knife. She was prepared to rely on the proximity alarm but it never hurt to be extra careful.

Afterward, she hunkered down over the carryall, to see what Ciari had left her. Clothes, bless his heart, an eclectic mix of human sensibility and Hal style. She pulled on underwear before continuing her exploration, then came up with a pair of military-cut trousers, socks, and hiking sneaks. Lightweight but rugged. Short-sleeve polo shirt went over her sleeveless singlet, then a long-sleeved bush shirt over that. Bandannas for throat and forehead, another knife, a collapsible canteen, and a carton of rations. Essentially, a standard SAR survival pack. Then, at the bottom, a major surprise: a set of sailing gear. Bathing suit, light shorts, boat sneaks, a foul-weather pullover, gloves. It wasn't new, either, it was hers.

She stood straight and looked east, past the shore to the sunrise horizon, but there was nothing to see but the smooth, unbroken line of ocean. She knew what was out there, a good fifty miles across the water, the Memorial Mount of Shavrin's Clan, atop a bluff that towered over three hundred meters above the coast. The only way a Hal would reach it would be to follow the near shore until the bay narrowed and shallowed enough to provide a decent ford. A long hike, and a formidable one, through some ferociously rough country, especially once she reached the other side.

That was her Quest, the route of her *Harach't'nyn*. A route that kept her within sight of the ocean nearly the whole way but never brought her close to it save for one point. Always she came up against this fundamental dichotomy, this association with the ocean combined with a fundamental aversion to it. A race who apparently transplanted itself completely from a world with seas to one that they intentionally designed to have virtually none.

What the hell are you so afraid of, Kymri? she asked silently. Ciari and she had both been dosed with the heritage DNA of the same Speaker, only Ciari's awareness was always more surface than hers. She knew how his mind worked, in fair measure because he'd taught hers to think the same way. He'd be asking these same questions. The search for true answers had brought him here. With a specific intent. Not to follow the traditional *Harach't'nyn,* but to strike out on one uniquely his own.

She zipped the carryall closed and proceeded to do the same with the suit. Spacer's Rules—always leave equipment as though you're going to need it yourself. But before sealing the helmet once more, she initialized the Homer Beacon. There were two frequencies. Broad Band, designed to make the most amount of noise over the widest possible frequency spectrum, and Security. Designed so that its signal was virtually impossible to trace to the source—unless it heard the proper, coded response—this was for use in hostile territory, so that only your own people would know where you were. Nicole chose the latter, and took a pocket transmitter with her, slaved to the main unit. If the right people found the suit, they could also find her. Another traveling beacon was already gone from its slot; Ciari was plotting along the same wavelength.

There were some fairly evident trails, leading along the ridge line, a couple back into the woods, but she went the other direction, over the edge and down the rock face. It was as steep as it looked from up-top, but nowhere near as hairy a climb as she'd feared. She let her body set the pace, curious to see what sort of rhythm it would fall into. She saw no sign, felt no sense, of the Hal male—for that was how she'd come to think of him—she'd run another proximity scan just to be sure. At the same time, she didn't have anything approaching yesterday's dramatic physical responses to the thought of him. That intrigued her, and she filed the observation away for later study.

The valley was more open, thanks in part to the fast-flowing stream. Another curiosity—Hal had no problem with high-country cataracts, with water that came from rock and was in a major hurry to get somewhere else. They even had a taste for freshwater fish, and had taken to the Terran art of fly-casting like they'd invented it.

She paused, head cocking quizzically to the side, as though listening to some silent tune. In quick movements, she stripped to the skin and strode forward to the water, grimacing at the shock of the cold around her ankles. It was as if entering the stream had calved her, like an iceberg or a diamond cracking in two. Part of her watched with an anthropologist's excited dispassion as she moved her hands and arms and body over the surface in a simple but elegant dance; she was singing as well, a gentle croon that mothers sing to their young, telling of the leap the crawling child must make to become a walking adult. Yet somehow, the same song had resonances for the race as well, reaching back to the moment where four feet gave way to two. The water that sustained the world also sustained the Hal, the two casting a tidal cadence that all were bound to. She plunged her hands deep into the soft earth; they came up coated with rich, dark mud and she stroked fingers across temples, cheeks, plunging down the long column of her throat and out over her breasts. She was on her knees, the rushing water at hip level as she faced upstream. She had a sense of her flesh dissolving, the river bursting the walls of her blood vessels and racing headlong through her system. She was aflame within and without, her blood molten, the sun beating on her upraised face, filling her eyes with glorious light even through closed eyelids.

She could barely walk as she staggered ashore, unsure her body could bear her weight, working and wiping her eyes to restore at least a semblance of sight. She let herself sprawl on the smooth-pebbled riverbed—dry now since the spring floods had receded—allowing the cool stone to counteract the extraordinary heat radiating off her skin.

This was a Young Female's Mystery, for someone more than a girl, not yet a blooded woman. By rights, Nicole should have sung it over a decade before, but because this was all new to her, she was experiencing all at once the benchmark moments of a lifetime.

She filled her canteen and treated herself to an early lunch, water and biscuits, as tasteless as they were nourishing.

She was starting to get dressed again when she realized she'd drawn patterns all over her front. It was hard to make sense of them—she couldn't get a proper view from this close and upside down—there were crossbars and swirls, arrows on the collarbones and the stiff feel of dried mud on her face.

She only had that moment to look, because the moment the mud dried, it powdered at the touch or even the smallest movement of her body, leaving no sign that it had ever been.

The day was warming quickly, and she confined herself to sneaks, trousers, and singlet before pressing on. The rest went into her carryall.

She followed the river for as long as it seemed to be heading her towards the sea, then struck out cross-country when it turned meanderingly away. The forest was giving way to grasslands, a stretch of coastal prairie that she remembered from her dream. Then, she'd come from far behind her, the interior mountains that compared to the escarpment she'd just descended the way a DC-3 did to a 747. Or better yet, her *Sundowner* spaceplane to the *Constitution*.

Thinking of the ship prompted thoughts of Hana, and a surge of longing that was wholly her own. It was like being apart from the other half of her self, the one person in whom she had absolute faith. She wanted a proper dance suddenly. Loud, driving music, rippling lights creating a cascading rainbow over a dance floor big enough for them to have room to strut their stuff. Clothes to die for and men to make the offer. Passion and energy, as raw and untamed as mountain lightning.

"That, Ancestors of my adopted House," she cried aloud, full-voiced, "is *my* mystery!"

Right at sunset, with half the sky painted in streaks of flame, came a flash from beyond the top of the world, which prompted a smile of recognition from Nicole, watching for stars. She heard or saw nothing unexpected afterward, and filed that moment away with all the rest, tucking herself in for what she hoped would be a dreamless night.

She was nervous at first, without the suit. Through the day, she'd seen sign of the four-footed Hal, and long-distance glimpses of the creatures themselves, singly and in what she assumed were family groupings. A couple of times, she modified her trek slightly to accommodate them, erring on the

side of caution and allowing as wide a berth as was practicable.
But they showed no interest in her.

She found a burial platform, crudely constructed, as savaged
by the elements as the body it supported, which had long ago
been reduced to bones. Gifts had been left, to provide sustenance and amusement in the Hereafter, and the structure
arranged to allow the body a view towards the sea, still out of
sight in the distance beyond the last line of coastal hills.

Before dawn, the world still dark, the sky overhead decorated like a velvet cloth splashed with all the diamonds that
ever were, Nicole faced another Mystery as the Ancestors came
to answer the implicit challenge of her call.

She didn't think it was a dream, there was too much
physicality. Her body ached from the way it was lying on
unyielding ground, her innards were all growly from her stingy
diet. She heard her breath, in spaced, deliberate *huffs*, and felt
the pounding in her chest—her heart seemed determined to
announce the fact of her continued existence with every
thunderous beat—but nothing beyond that. The night was still.
No breeze to stir air or grass, nothing making even a ghost of
a move—*nobody* wanted to draw attention to themselves, it
seemed. All were content to leave that role to Nicole.

Her visitors didn't know what to make of her, these forebears
of Shavrin's House, an attitude she shared completely. Spectral
forms hovering around her, temptingly close enough to
reach—she kept her hands to herself—as though waiting for a
cue.

It came from a spunky girl half Nicole's age and barely
two-thirds her size. Tall for her own era, most likely, but not
even close anymore. She strode forward like she owned the
place, striking a ballsy, cock o' the walk stance that made plain
she was ready to follow Nicole to any club she named. She was
such a firecracker that Nicole couldn't help bursting out loud
with a laugh.

The noise startled the ghosts, it wasn't a Hal response, nor
anything they could relate to from the catalogue of their
collective experience. The girl, though, she took it in stride and
tried to shape her mouth to match Nicole's smile. She knew it
didn't quite work—too different an arrangement of facial
muscles—so she tried the laugh instead. This time, it was

Nicole's turn to jump. She hadn't expected the ghost could talk. The exchange of tit for tat eased the mood somewhat; she saw a subtle volley of teeth that signaled their approval.

The girl moved forward, back, forward again, then side-stepped with a languorous, inviting grace that drew Nicole around after her as though they were linked by a tether. Nicole rose to her feet, the girl going big-eyed at the size differential, and Nicole felt like a fumble-footed hulk by comparison. After a few more moments, though, she no longer cared. All she had eyes and thoughts and feelings for was the girl and their dance.

The other ghosts took positions in a great circle around them, the combined glow of their bodies giving light enough to see—not that the girl needed any. As for Nicole, it didn't really help. She couldn't watch the ground and the girl and after a couple of stumbles—the second nearly planting her full length on her face—she locked in on her partner. In tone and structure, this most reminded her of the Memorial Service aboard *Range Guide*. There was music all around, none of it heard, but rather felt—in the pulsing of the blood, the pounding of the heart, the slice of arms through air, the slap of feet on earth.

There was a distinct progression to the dance. Comparatively slow to start, gradually integrating Nicole into the choreographic structure the girl was establishing. Then, a progressive escalation in the complexity of the movements and the speed of their execution. The girl flashed around Nicole like a dervish, every gesture, every expression, a dare to the human woman to catch her. Try as she might, Nicole always fell short. Desire—no matter how fundamental and heartfelt—couldn't change her physiology.

So, since she couldn't win on the girl's terms, she threw down a gauntlet of her own. She called up memories of music from where they lived inside her soul and cast them loose.

The girl watched until she had a sense of the dynamic idiom, and then she joined in with a vengeance.

The more they moved, the more their movements began to match, as two solos merged into a duet. Each drew on elements of the other's style, using whatever worked to craft a whole that was increasingly more than the sum of its parts. There was no sense of fatigue, even though Nicole knew she'd been going flat out since they started, and even less of effort. Once again, she asked herself if this was a dream.

Only problem there, she thought in response, *is that if this is a flipping dream, shouldn't all this come easier?*

Features blurred around her, a vague awareness that her ghosts had begun to join the Hal, as if the energy she was throwing off was somehow shaping itself into tangible form. The girl's features shifted, quicksilver, to Alex, to Paul DaCuhna—bringing a surge of moisture to Nicole's eyes, momentary tightness in her chest, reminder of grief and friend long buried, so much so that she tripped a step—to Ben Ciari. With him glowed a surge of worry, a prayer that he still be alive. At the last, joyously, Hana. Here, Nicole cast care and caution aside, letting go with a freedom she'd never allow herself before living beings. She still thought of this as fantasy—dream at best, hallucination at worst—which made things all right.

She was so transported by the sheer, glorious rapture of the scene that she never felt the girl's first strike. Or the second or the third. She was vaguely cognizant of her slipping close and then away, of arms and hand flashing faster than Nicole's mind could follow. Something presented itself as increasingly not right, but the ongoing momentum of the dance, its rhythms so fundamental and overpowering, meant that she had to take a calculated mental step back to survey the setting. That, too, caused its own moment of dislocation, leading to a fatal lag between realization and response.

The girl was no longer spectral, and her companions nowhere near benign. Her glowing body had turned a deep ebony—Nicole's mind registering colors even though the massed star and ghost-light rendered the hilltop in shades of chiaroscuro black and white—the only silver aspect of her was her hair. Eyes of the deepest blue Nicole had ever seen, to put the ultimate sapphire to shame. A pattern of silver stripes down the spine and branching over the curve of the hips, echoed by cuffs over the wrists. All interlaced, reminding Nicole of the Celtic-type knotwork decorating her own body. At the same time, Nicole's color had faded, flesh edging towards insubstantial, silver where the girl was dark, dark where she was silver, the sole difference being that Nicole was fire-toned where she was earth.

She saw the hand, but it was as though Nicole had become the ghost. She moved reflexively to block the attack, yet somehow she missed. A myriad of excuses instantly presented themselves, anything to deny what her eyes actually saw—the girl's solid hand passing through both of Nicole's. Claws crossed her line of vision, so light a caress that Nicole didn't believe she'd even been touched. Then, heat. Eating its way inward, top to bottom across her face. Nicole's mouth opening to scream but no sound emerging because there was no air to activate her vocal cords, because diaphragm and lungs and cords, all the active, physical elements of being had no substance. She was less than smoke, held together by no more than force of will.

It was enough.

She knew that Abyss, she'd seen oblivion up-close, in friends and strangers.

Awareness splintered, presenting her more views of more realities than she wanted to handle, like being stuck on a Virtual Prismatic Moebius loop, perceptions fractaling into the mental equivalent of an insect's eyes, only each image was different. She relaxed, letting the ride carry her through, sensing the girl approaching for the coup de grace and trusting that she'd find the way to parry it.

A thousand thousand messages, threading neatly by as though they were humming along the ultimate freeway, telling her each in its own way that all was well. Sense of wholeness, power unimaginable, politely restrained. A friendly presence, unaware that Nicole was watching. Desire to move, to flee, to be free, thwarted by shackles binding her to the ground. Simply dealt with, by diverting a car off the freeway, passing it on to a neighboring loop—all this happening in blips of time so small the measurement had no meaning—and the manacles popped open.

The girl was closer, but Nicole still wasn't ready to respond. She needed power. And found it within her greater self.

Nicole bared teeth, mixing human humor at last with Hal, and when the claws arrived to bleed her dry, she was no longer there.

The girl hurled herself at Nicole, without pause, without restraint, in a killing frenzy that nothing living should have stood against. Only Nicole wasn't quite alive at that point—or perhaps was so much more so. Each attack failed. And with each failure, a little more of the balance was redressed.

Until Nicole and the girl faced each other alone atop the knoll, each returned to the state they were in when they began, one woman, one specter.

The girl laughed a very human laugh and said in English, "Not too terribly shabby, Shea!"

Nicole bowed—but not too much for only a fool takes that great a risk after a blood duel—eyes downcast but hands ready to parry any betrayal. There was nothing tinny or misformed about her voice, her Hal was as perfect as the girl's English.

"You have done my soul more honor than I know my soul can bear."

"Damn straight."

"Are you a ghost?"

"Aren't we all?"

"Is this a dream?"

"Isn't everything?"

Nicole looked around, and grabbed her head as that simple gesture set the entire Universe tumbling off its axis. The world was gone, the ghosts were gone, about her were nothing but the stars and somehow she could see them all, whether they were before her eyes or not. She wasn't afraid because she knew Hana was with her, watching her back as she'd asked.

She thought she heard Hana's voice, which wasn't possible, and then she heard Raqella's, which shouldn't have been . . .

. . . and opened her eyes—real eyes at long last, for which she breathed a hearty sigh of relief—and had to close them again, right away, until her pupils contracted sufficiently to accept the glare of morning.

Raqella was crouched before her, but she'd been levered up at an angle, with someone else supporting her shoulders and head. She felt the curve of breasts on the top of her scalp and spoke the first name that came to voice.

"Hana?"

"You wish," in fluent Trade, but with a bad accent Nicole recognized immediately.

"Amy," she said, and hazarded another try with her eyes. Better. Not great, but well within her ability to cope—especially since she was damned if she'd show any weakness to the girl.

"Raqella," she said, taking a decent look at him, "what are you staring at?"

Her first panicked thought was that she'd become a ghost—and for those seconds her head filled with the stories told by her relatives in the Western Isles of fairy mounds and the prices paid by feckless, foolish mortals with the temerity to challenge a dance with the eternal Sidhe—but then he held up a mirror and she saw it was actually something worse.

Vivid slash lines slanted leftward in a straight diagonal from the crown of her forehead, over eyes and cheeks, to her jaw. *In heraldic terms,* she thought absurdly, *a* Bar Sinister—*but to complement my* fireheart *pendant, or oppose it?* Only they didn't stop there. She pulled her singlet out from her body, staring down to see they continued across her collarbone and then the bicep of her left arm, the lowest band just touching the inside of her elbow.

"You're not surprised to see us," Amy said, a bit petulantly.

"Not quite. I'm surprised to see *you.*" Nicole wasn't much interested in chitchat; she had too many questions about these markings. But the answers could come only from Raqella and she could see that he wasn't yet ready to be pressed. She also wanted some time to restore her own equilibrium. A quick inventory of the rest of her showed that the stripes were the only alteration.

"I saw a reflection from the top of the atmosphere at sunset. Perfect location and track for a HALA insertion." HALA was High Altitude, Low Approach, considered a combat reentry. Make the initial transition from orbit at the end of the day, where the friction plume was partly masked by the natural colors of the sunset. Pace the sunset as you drop to the deck, attacking the Terminator, beginning far out to sea on a progressive angle that forced anyone trying to spot you from ahead to essentially stare right into the sun. By the time you reach land, you're low enough and slow enough that you don't cast a significant heat or light signature against the dusk sky. It wasn't considered a practicable maneuver for anything as large as a shuttle or hypersonic spaceplane, but preliminary studies had been done with much smaller lifting bodies.

"It was Raqella's idea," Amy said, with an evident pride that caught Nicole's attention.

Nicole was impressed and said so. The Hal appreciated the maneuver, and their equipment was much better suited to it; the one drawback was the necessity for a long overwater flight.

"It had the virtue of being something no Hal in their right mind would consider," he said, but with an air of distraction that made plain his attention was on other things.

"We figured you could use some backup," Amy told her. "Evidently, we weren't the only ones," she finished, fingering the strap of Nicole's carryall.

"Isn't this breaking the rules?" Nicole asked Raqella.

"If so, we are not alone."

"You mean, the *Harach't'nyn* doesn't begin with a kidnapping?" Nicole feigned astonishment. Raqella looked sourly offended, Amy amused.

"You have Amy to thank for us finding out as quickly as we did," said Raqella.

"How so?"

Amy picked up the story, after popping a quick smile to the young Hal for his compliment. "Jenny Coy was left at Ciari's lodge, no com gear, no way to travel, presumably incommunicado. You'd made plain you wanted to be alone, the assumption must have been that you wouldn't be missed until the formal farewell bash for the *Constitution*. Even then, your absence would be covered by telling a simple truth, that you were on your ritual walkabout. That puts Shavrin in a neat box. She sounds any alarm, she compromises the test; 'cause we all know neither Hobby nor Sheridan's gonna stand by when they think you're being seriously skunked."

"They'll assume foul play."

"What assumptions, hotshot," Amy chided, "there's been foul play from the start."

"Did you eat or drink anything upon waking?" Raqella asked, as serious as Amy was being playfully conversational.

"Of course."

His response was a profanity so foul, it made both women stare in astonishment.

"Drugged?" Nicole asked him.

"To make you susceptible to certain bands of pheromones."

"So that if a local male came calling, I'd be inclined to answer?"

"It happens—only to Speakers and then very rarely. It's considered one of their private mysteries, something to do with their genetic linkage to all their previous generations . . ."

Nicole held up a hand to forestall any further explanation. She could fill in the rest for herself. She felt her face grow warm with the memory of the emotions she'd felt only a couple of days before. She decided not to think of what might have happened had she proven more susceptible.

"So what happened," she demanded. "What brought you both here?"

"Ciari'd map-marked Ranger and Rescue stations," Amy replied. "Jen was ready to hoof her way out to one . . ."

"Any credible opposition would have thought of that, even allowing for the fact it's *p'm'taie* range."

Raqella gestured agreement. "The com systems on the network are all intact, but our suspicions are that the emergency frequencies were monitored. More to the point, the nearest station to Ciari-Marshal's habitat is inactive for scheduled maintenance, and the next was recently destroyed by natural causes."

"Yeah, right," said Amy, leavening her Trade Tongue with a colloquial English structure that Nicole had to struggle to follow, "but you gotta figure, their main assumption was that the critters would take care of her."

"The *p'm'taie* are intensely territorial at the best of times," Raqella echoed. "You yourself have seen what they are like with newborn young. The odds of Jenny-Physician's survival on such a trek would have been slim to nonexistent."

"But you got there first."

Amy shrugged and for the first time looked intensely uncomfortable. The moment she spoke, Nicole knew why, as both women were reminded of the history between them that neither wanted to confront.

"Your tag bounced off my scans," she said simply.

Nicole's voice went so flat, so suddenly, that Raqella took a protective step forward, poising himself to leap between the two.

"You've been monitoring me?" *You arrogant little shit,* was the snarled thought that finished the sentence.

"You're a valuable asset," the girl flashed back with equal vigor, as ready to stand her ground as Nicole was to reduce it to scorched earth. "With the investment I've got in you, and all that's riding on it, damn straight I kept tabs on you."

"You don't have the right—"

"Spare me your talk of rights, Nicole, okay? One way or the other we're all of us wrapped up by forces bigger than ourselves, defining the roles we have to play. We all do shitty things, we've all had shit things done to us, so what? Grow up and get a life! Tell me what matters more, okay, that I had a string on you or that I used it to watch your back?"

That's today, bright eyes, Nicole thought, *but tomorrow you could switch that helping hand for a knife.*

"That how you found me here?"

"We followed an SAR Homer, to Ciari's suit, then to you."

"How'd you get across from s'N'dare?"

"We caught a lift, okay?" Nicole didn't ask more; she could see in Amy's eyes that these were all the answers on this subject she was going to get.

"Did you fly seeker orbits before your insertion?" she asked Raqella.

"Too dangerous. There are defensive scanners in orbit and on the ground; we came straight in. I knew where to look," he confessed.

"Because you've been here before."

His eyes hooded as he looked towards the coast, then to his left along it.

"Shavrin wanted my hide, she was so angry. Kymri argued for assignment to Earth instead."

"Why the anger?"

"This is meant only for Speakers nowadays, Nicole. We are presented our past, our heritage, at face value. What we are, we are told and we believe, we have always been."

"You think something different?"

"That is what I came to learn. Also"—and he made a shy twist of the fingers to complement the wryness of his tone—

"in my arrogance, I felt that what Kymri did, I would do better."

"And did you? Learn," she prompted, at his hesitation.

"A truth, yes."

"Which was," she let her growing exasperation show.

"*My* truth, Shea Shavrin's-Daughter. Yours, you must face for yourself."

"Is that what this is all about?" She didn't have to indicate her new markings to tell them that was what she meant, and she didn't try to hide the mix of fear and rage in her voice.

Raqella looked genuinely perplexed as he reached a tentative couple of fingers over to trace the line of these new markings. She wanted to flinch as they crossed her eyes—and she had a sudden sense memory, so achingly vivid she lost her breath as though she'd been punched, of Shavrin's fingers tracing the same path during their first meeting, aboard *Range Guide*.

"It is something I have never seen," he said, cognizant of her anxiety and shifting hands to her shoulders to steady her, the concern on his face echoed (to Nicole's surprise) on Amy's, "or heard of." Next, he tried what passed from him for a joke. "But then, my ignorance in both regards covers a whole world of territory."

"Ghosts came to me in the night, Raqella. I danced with them—no," she paused, reconsidering her memories, "only with one. A woman. Sable fur with a silver crest and blue eyes."

Raqella had no help for her. "I am not the one to tell this to," he said. "Better to try Shavrin herself, or perhaps M'gtur. Or another Speaker."

"M'gtur?" Amy was openly contemptuous of that suggestion. "What makes you think the head of the opposition's going to give a straight answer?"

"We don't know he's part of this."

"Oh, really, Nicole? You got a better candidate? He's against you, against the Alliance, and he has the clout in-house to pull all the necessary elements together."

"Suspicions aren't proof."

"And platitudes, missy, won't save your ass." She knew Nicole wanted to slap her and took a stance that dared the older, taller woman to try.

Nicole ignored the temptation and followed Raqella's gaze. "You think there's anyone waiting up ahead, on the assumption the drug didn't do its job?"

"'S what I'd do, in their place," Amy offered.

"Me, too," Nicole agreed. "What about Shavrin and Kymri, are they likely to send anyone after me?"

"However badly this was begun," Raqella replied, "the *Harach't'nyn* must be seen through to the end. I know Shavrin is deathly afraid—she blames herself for much of this, so much so that she still holds herself obligated to the blood price she offered you."

"I released her from that debt."

"You may have said so, but she chose not to heed you. She says you have always been closer to the Void than you know. She believes this is the only way your inner balance can be restored."

"This applies to Ciari as well."

"Not so much, I think."

"I can handle what happens to me"—ignoring Amy's scoffing comment from the background—"but the important thing is finding Ciari."

"You got any peeps from your Homer," Amy asked, and when Nicole responded in the negative, "we got zip on ours."

"Then we presume—since we're both cast from the same mold"—she was watching Amy out of the corner of an eye, but the only response her words provoked was a level gaze back at her—"that we'd both head in substantially the same direction."

Raqella pointed them parallel to the coast, as Nicole had sensed he would. She had other ideas.

The little transceivers were line-of-sight units, designed to broadcast to airborne searchers—as the parent unit was meant to reach to orbit—and the country was too hilly for it to be effective over any decent range. The others grumbled—Raqella protested outright—but she pressed on towards the coast.

They reached it late in the day, after cresting the last of the phalanx hills that formed a natural breakwater to the ocean beyond, just as the great cliffs did on the far side of the giant estuary. The first thing Nicole noticed was a marked drop in temperature, the warm sunlight leavened by a chill offshore breeze picking up strength as the day waned. Raqella was visibly disturbed by the sight of so much water, which provoked a gentle reminder from Nicole about the weekend in San Diego.

He groaned at the memory, choosing an intentionally human response. "Do you know how drunk I was that whole time?"

"Enough to allow you to walk out onto a floating dock and shove me in."

"You won't tell Shavrin."

The thought had never occurred to her, but she saw instantly what effect it would have.

"She wouldn't be amused, would she?"

"She'd have me skin myself and hand over my own heart in the bargain. I must have been insane, that's the only way I can explain it."

"You made up for it on the *Sundowner* test flight."

"Hardly. It was Ch'ghan's place to speak; he'd seen the same intelligence reports as me, I'll never understand why he held silent."

The Homer beeped, demanding attention.

The signal led them down to the edge of the shore, and a narrow but deep arroyo set well above the highest tide line but with fairly easy access to the beach. It was one of a series of winding defiles that lined the hills like grooves cut into the face of an old man, places where the land had folded from crustal shifts, brought about by the never-ending expansion and contraction of the surface from tectonic pressure deep within.

The natural expression of a living world, Nicole thought, and chuckled at the contrast between the rough-and-tumble features of this planet, the arroyos worn deep over the aeons of rain and perhaps the ebb and flow of much stronger and higher tides, and those of s'N'dare. *One face wears the cares and experiences of its life,* she continued, *and the other's the product of plastic surgery. Much prettier to look at but nowhere near as interesting. This place proclaims its history for all to see; the other denies it.*

The Homer didn't lead them to Ciari—Nicole had suspected all along it wouldn't—it led them to his boat.

CHAPTER FOURTEEN

Once he heard Nicole's intentions, Raqella was so angry, so upset, he wanted to carry her bodily away from shore. He didn't care a damn for Ciari's plans, he wasn't interested in her explanations, he thought she'd lost her mind and said so. Often. More and more loudly, as though brute volume would succeed where reason and logic continued to fail.

The tide turned towards the end of the afternoon and Nicole spent as much of the evening as there was light to see watching it progress across the beachfront. She didn't recognize the lie of the land but the movement of the water itself struck a resonant chord with her basic dream. She remembered the warmth of rock under back, sun on her face, the sudden shock of water—the desperate, doomed race for shore, the sick horror of being swept out to sea. Moments that touched both sides of her double self, fears the human could relate to as fearfully as Hal.

"Doesn't look so tough," noted Amy, overplaying the exertion of clambering up the dune. "There isn't much of a surf 'til the water comes in close," but from that point on, the ocean hammered the beach with combers that would give the most experienced and eager surfer pause. This was a tidal race that put Newfoundland's Bay of Fundy to shame, with a water rise that Nicole calculated at nearly twenty meters.

"You hump the boat out midway," Amy was saying, "maybe onto one of those sandbars, and float it when the leading edge of the tide goes by. Water enough to sail on without getting busted to bits."

"Good analysis," Nicole said, "as far as it goes. The real trouble's a lot farther out. Something I spotted when we came over the last line of hills. The flats give way to a reef, out where the shallows drop off to deep water. That surf's even bigger."

"Double your pleasure," the girl hummed, "double your fun . . ."

"That's what makes this so nasty. The reef acts as a barrier, holding back the gradual flow of water, until enough pressure builds up to pop it over the top in a great big surge. Then, everything comes hard and fast. A legitimate tidal wave.

"I've got to cross the flat before the tide turns. Ideally, float the boat over the reef while it's still ebbing, when all the water factors are in my favor. At the very latest, when it's just starting to return, before the wave action has time to build."

"Kymri won't consider this, even for you, but I could come with. It's a helluva load to carry, you could use another back."

Nicole gave her a long, searching look. They were both mostly in darkness, the last swirling shades of dusk casting their features more as suggestions than reality, defining them by degrees of shadow. The offer sounded genuine, but she couldn't help thinking, *Why? To trip me up and push me under until I drown?*

Amy must have been on the same wavelength, because Nicole was sure she'd offered the girl no other clue to her reactions.

"No reason to be scared, Nikki-Tikki-Tavi," she said in a casually matter-of-fact way that only partially masked a bitter undertone. Nicole caught the thread of anger, but also realized it wasn't directed at her. "Cobris never take direct action, you of all people should know that. Always through surrogates, always with cutouts to protect the home office."

"I feel so reassured."

"Your Marshal brought a boat," Amy said, to change the subject. "Why didn't he use it?"

"He did. All the equipment's been properly stowed, but there are also signs of use. I think he tried, maybe more than once, and gave up."

"That's not like him, is it?"

"Quite the contrary. If he quit, it's because of something he couldn't beat—almost certainly something he didn't anticipate . . ."

"And you're determined to follow in his footsteps."

Nicole gestured a silent yes.

"So much for your precious walkabout."

"Where do you get off judging me, girl?"

"I could ask the same in return, y'know?"

"I have the right."

The mood was changing, as quickly, as markedly, as inexorably, as the tide, the words—for all that they were still soft-spoken—taking on barbed edges intended to cut.

"What, you figure I owe blood price for my brother, Nicole?"

"No. That one's between you and Alex's ghost. Or better yet, you and your father, since he's the one made you what you are."

Amy stared as if she'd been slapped.

"The debt you owe me—*girl*"—and Nicole's voice had grown softer still, without a shred of gentleness, flattening to razor keenness—"is for Paolo DaCuhna and Chagay Shomron and Cat Garcia."

"Your Air Force renegade, Morgan, did them, Nicole."

"And who put him in business, Amy? Who deserves the real blame, the chess pieces that do the dirty work or the hand that moves them?"

"They were just games." The sentence had all the underlying passion of a full-throated scream, yet Amy spoke it almost as a throwaway, as though she didn't dare give true voice to her emotions. She turned bodily away from Nicole and fixed her gaze at the newly risen moon, the first of three they would see during the night.

Nicole wasn't aware of any time passing, yet somehow the moon was a measurable distance up the sky before she replied.

"People died, Amy."

She heard a rude sniff of dismissal, a rebuke for stating the blindingly obvious, but realized as well that Amy was crying.

"Like I was supposed to care," the girl said. "They weren't friends, they weren't even people I knew! I saw opportunity, I took it. Most natural thing in the world.

"I am what my daddy made me," she said suddenly and looked Nicole in the face, her eyes glowing a dull, dusky red as they reflected the moonlight. "How long have you known?"

"Since you were a kid. Since Alex."

"I hated him, I couldn't help it. He was my rival. I knew he was brilliant, in ways I could never hope to be. But more than that, he was *natural!*"

Now teeth flashed, in a self-mocking smirk. "Poor Daddy," the savagery of her tone trashing the overt sympathy of the words, "he could alter all the physical parameters, lengthen the legs, shape the line, smooth out the cosmetic rough edges, he could make me the best version of 'him' money could buy, only just different enough so's nobody would notice. But that was the limit. With a clone, he could only improve on what already existed, he couldn't introduce anything new into the mix. Alex's gifts came from somewhere outside.

"You know, Alex's mom had herself a hysterectomy after I was born?" Nicole could only shake her head. "She'd made her contribution to the Cause, she didn't want any more Cobris knock-knock-knocking on her door. Can't say I blame her. 'Cause the first thing I thought of after Alex"—a pause, and Nicole knew Amy was referring to her brother's death—"was to try again, consider Alex's life the Beta Test cycle of the Mode One wetware, fix the glitches with the second release. Keep trying 'til I get it right." Her voice broke as she finished, "Just like my old man.

"That's why I was so crazy," Amy said, "that day you came to visit the house on Staten Island." The images were burned into Nicole's memory and popped into view as clearly as the Hal ghosts the night before. She saw herself striding through the foyer, ignoring the increasingly strident and out of control cries of the teenaged girl on her top-floor landing high overhead. "You killed my brother," Amy had shrieked, until her voice splintered like breaking oak, leaving it with an incongruously husky quality she still possessed, *"you killed my brother!"*

"I'd just found out, about Alex's mom.

"Antigone's got nothing on me, y'know. I'm a fucking Greek tragedy, three thousand years too late."

"And you tell *me* to get a life?"

Amy actually grinned, and the thought came to Nicole of Persephone, looking for release from Hades, wanting to stay as much as she yearned to go. "We're a matched set, you and me. Both as much the product of the genegineer's splicer as nature."

"I'm not Alex, Amy."

"Yeah? Well, you're not Nicole anymore, either. Just like I'm not my daddy."

She launched well before dawn, using the light of the other two moons to see by.

"Since there's no sign of Ciari near his boat"—they'd ranged as far afield as they could the previous afternoon in an unsuccessful attempt to find either the man or some indication of his trail—"we have to assume he's gone ahead on foot. Your job," she told her companions, "is to find him."

"Assuming he's following the profile of the *Harach't'nyn*," Amy offered.

"Each in our own way, that's what we're both doing. Who knows, kiddo, maybe even you, too."

"Shea Shavrin's-Daughter," Raqella was more impassioned than she'd ever seen him, going so far as to stand between her and the shore, putting his back to open water (which no sane Hal would ever do), as he made his plea, "must I beg you not to do this?"

When she said nothing, he cried, "It is *madness!*"

"No argument," she conceded.

"But you will go forth nonetheless."

"Ciari isn't a precipitate man, Raqella. None of this was done on impulse. His dreams—like mine, I suspect—led him to the sea. I have to know why."

"Must I sing your soul skyward from the Memorial Mount?"

"If it comes to that, I hope you'll do me proud."

He had a lot more to say—and Nicole suddenly sensed his intent was to keep her occupied until she missed the tide, reasoning (rightly) that she wouldn't embark on a night sail on unfamiliar waters aboard an unfamiliar craft—but Amy cut him off.

"Yo, Rocky, waste of breath."

He wasn't pleased with her interruption but she wasn't fazed in the slightest by his reaction.

"Save the snarls, guy," she said tolerantly, "for anyone we meet along the path."

She shooed Raqella up the dune face and when she caught Nicole looking at her strangely, she demanded, "What?"

"Nothing."

"Oh. *That*. Every so often, I see it in people, this thing they can't quite figure about me, how come I'm just a kid but I have such a force of command."

"Manuel must have been some piece of work when he was young."

"Who knows? Everyone tells stories, your guess is as good as mine how much embroidery goes on to get in good with the boss." She indicated the bundle stretching back from Nicole's feet. "That gonna be good enough to get you where you're going?"

"Depends on what that means, doesn't it? Out to sea, yeah, no problem."

"And after that you're where you love it best."

Nicole looked questioningly, not sure what the girl meant. Amy sounded surprised, as though she considered the answer too obvious for words.

"On your own," she said.

The catamaran was a masterpiece of design and engineering. Six meters long by two and a half wide, molded out of a polyfiber laminate that was as strong as steel yet light enough for a single person to manhandle, its heaviest components were the sails and tackle. Ciari'd done the skunk work, putting her together, and when Nicole did her own check, she saw he'd done well.

She stuffed her hiking gear into the carryall and stood naked atop the dune, flesh goose-bumping from the perpetual breeze.

Raqella was right, she *was* insane. The water was no place for Hal—she was trembling, and no longer from the cold.

She closed her eyes and put herself back on the quay of the San Diego Yacht Club, letting the distant rush of the waves stand in for the duller slap of surface water on the pilings. There was more salt to the air of memory as she filled her inner view with the image of that first sight of *Sundowner* at her moorings. The boat Alex had rescued from the breaker's yard and lovingly restored, just as she had her own beloved Beech Baron.

The sea was as much a part of her as the sky, twin facings of the same coin. She took tight hold of that thought, as though it were the last lifeline between her and the Void, and opened her eyes.

The clothes she'd worn on land had been mostly Hal; not so what she pulled from the carryall, marveling as she did how Ciari had managed to get ahold of them. Single-piece racing maillot went on first, followed by a pair of shorts and a polo. Boat sneaks and her foul-weather pullover, with mountain shades, gloves, and a baseball hat to complete the ensemble. Lastly came the harness, pulled snug against her backside and snap-shackled securely at the front. All her gear from home. She wriggled inside her skin, the clothes provoking a multitude of conflicting emotions, as welcome and familiar as they felt uncomfortable.

"Enough," she said flatly, stifling a debate that only action would truly end. Her stomach twisted into a Gordian knot. She'd never felt such fear—and she wasn't yet on the bloody *beach!*

"I said, *enough!*"

She slung the tow rope over a shoulder and put a double wrap of line around her left hand. Then, she began to pull.

She'd marked the route to follow, down the shallow slope of sand to where erosion had created a channel that still had water in it. She had a rough moment at the high water mark, especially once the water began soaking through her shoes, but she pressed on regardless, a step at a time, occupying her thoughts with a review of all she'd ever learned about handling a Cat.

It was a couple of klicks to the reef—the last stretch wading waist deep in the tidal outflow—and by the time she reached it she was moderately exhausted. She couldn't for the life of her figure how Ciari had brought the Cat down from the highlands and admired him all the more for that success. She was bumped and bruised from the effort of keeping the Cat in tow; its low mass and shallow draft made it a ferociously lively boat, susceptible to every shift in wind and water, until at last she was yanked off her feet and dunked. Her fear became a palpable thing, then, as she floundered like a novice, forgetting everything she'd ever learned on Earth, remembering only what was Hal, and believing she'd been buried alive in a medium that couldn't be properly fought.

She wasn't sure how she reached the surface, only that when her senses finally cleared, she was draped over a pontoon, with the stench of vomit in her face and the sight of it on the canvas platform. Even as she watched, she heaved again, the convulsion worse than being punched in the belly. And followed that with a fit of sobbing that was a long time passing.

There was a lot less water when she finally straightened to her full height, resisting an instinct—only slightly less powerful—to scamper for the high ground on all fours. Resisting as well a far more analytical assessment that prompted essentially the same course of action.

Her hope had been to reach the reef while it was still substantially underwater. But she'd lost too much time for that. It stretched before her like a squatly massive seawall, as far away on either side as she could see, a far more spectacular sight in the night than during daylight. All three moons were down and in the hour or so left before the eastern sky would begin to herald the approaching sun, the creatures whose chitinous bodies formed the living fabric of the reef set up a tremendous light show as they were exposed to the air. Ripples of color cascaded before her in sheets and rainbow streamers like an aquatic aurora borealis. Despite her misery, Nicole couldn't help but be impressed by the never-ending display.

She had as far to go as she had come, a klick for sure and more likely the better part of a mile. The sensible play would be to wait for the next tide—which for her purposes would be tomorrow night. But she couldn't guarantee for herself which ghosts would be waiting for her on shore, any more than she could what she'd do after a day staring at the water with the Hal aspects of her in ascendancy. Coming this far was a supreme act of will; she wasn't sure she had it in her to try again.

She tried to pick a path between the segments of the coral array, but the openings were too narrow, too winding; they left her unable to manage the boat behind. She picked a likely foothold, crossed some mental fingers, and pushed.

Next, making sure she was safely braced, she began to haul on her tow rope. The twin keels made an awful noise as she dragged the Cat on top with her, but the laminate wouldn't even show scratches from the passage. Nicole herself would probably come out in worse shape.

She quickly found that while the light beneath her feet was beautiful, it was as much hindrance as help. There was residual water left in the gaps between the coral plates, as well as pools on their mostly flat surfaces; they caught the flashes, refracted them, scrambling her perspective and perceptions. She found it painfully reminiscent of being in flat calm under a midday sun, where each little reflection was a dagger made of diamond, punching one pinpoint hole after another in her vision until she was dazzled blind. Solution then would be to simply don her shades. Not a practical option in the dark.

She could hear the surf, and used that as an anchor, thankful that the sound of waves was much the same as on Earth, even if the water itself looked sometimes like burgundy and others like arterial blood. But hearing and actually reaching it were a pair of widely separated concepts.

She felt the faintest change in the quality of the air and searched around herself for a couple of minutes before finally registering that the stars weren't as brilliant as when last she'd looked, before she'd started across the reef. The reason was clear in the east, a roseate glow right on the horizon. She dropped her line and left the Cat to scout ahead a ways, to see if there was any easier approach. She went farther than she should, all the way in fact to the edge of the reef, and it was like standing on a scawall with the full force of the ocean hammering against its face, sending up curtains of spray as it attempted to tear down what the little creatures so patiently and laboriously built up over the aeons. Eventually, she knew, the reef would grow high enough to put it continually above sea level. Sand would build up on top, a line of true barrier islands would begin to form. The water behind her might form a lagoon, or be trapped to form a lake, or simply be flushed out altogether so that the continent itself would expand a little farther.

A comber swept in, a rogue wave substantially larger than its fellows, cresting over the top of the reef where the others still fell short. Nicole saw it coming and was already backtracking when it hit. The water struck like a hearty shove to the body, and as she struggled to keep her feet a sneaker landed on a newly established outcropping that immediately gave under her weight.

She yelped as she fell, from surprise, and stayed flat while a second wave followed the example of the first. The tide was turning, with far more speed and violence than she had anticipated.

She scrambled up and hurried back to the Cat, grabbing the towline with redoubled effort. The approaching sunrise was muting the light show from the coral, but there wasn't yet sufficient illumination overhead to make up for it. She wanted to surge forward, Hell for leather, desperately worried that she wouldn't clear the reef before the waves started crashing full force onto it. She'd seen divers and swimmers unwary enough to be hammered like that, after being snared by the swirling, fiercely antagonistic currents set up by water action through the multihollowed structure of reef. Difficult enough to pull someone out of that maelstrom, impossible to fight free on your own. Instead, she forced herself to take her time and properly pick her path. She wore solid shoes, but nothing short of an armored combat sole would be proof against a spike through the foot. Even if she missed impaling herself, a gash could prove equally deadly. The reef was a living organism, but the true danger came from the vast panoply of microorganisms that made their home in the warm and fertile shallows. Any cut was virtually assured of infection. Nicole knew that the rules of Terran eco-biology might not apply here but she had nothing else to go on, since the Hal dealt with the sea by ignoring it. Best bet, she decided from the first, was to play things safe and assume the worst.

She was ready to collapse when she dropped the towline a final time, with the sun a full diameter above the horizon, sending her shadow stretching ten or twenty times her height along the wet, shimmery crest of the reef.

She didn't have the time.

She secured the line—she was damned if, after all this body-busting effort, she was going to have it snag on some coral and hang her up—and checked her carryall to make sure it was lashed tight as well.

The wind was to her back, a stiff breeze that worked on the water in concert with the last of the ebbing tide to flatten the wave action. She wondered if Ciari had gotten this far and saw no reason to be ashamed of him for calling it quits.

She stood at the aft crossbar of the trampoline platform and stretched forward, body and arm to full extension, to catch the jib sheet. A series of hearty tugs raised the sail two thirds of the way up its track, and she tied it off on a handy mainstay. She scanned the rest of her lines a final time, as she would the panel of a spacecraft just before launch, knowing that she'd done her job properly from the start but always remaining careful enough to make certain.

Then, her body acting seemingly of its own accord, she lifted her head and roared a challenge, as primal as the setting and the moment. She had a stroboscopic image of the Hal from her dream, the ghost who'd marked her, uttering the same cry as she was yanked beneath the waves.

She hurled herself forward, putting her shoulder to the trampoline frame and heaving with every ounce of strength.

The Cat launched itself off the reef and immediately caught the crest of an incoming comber. Nicole leapt aboard and shot the rudder into place, straddling the tiller, pinning it between her knees to point the twin bows into the approaching swells at an angle of forty-five degrees. In the same motion, she grabbed for the main sheet and hauled like a madwoman, jamming the line between a pair of lockjaws and shoving the boom out to better catch the following breeze. Both main and jib fluttered in the wind, neither fully raised, she'd take the time to neaten things up after she cleared the surf—*if* she cleared the surf.

She hit another wave and spat water from her mouth, aware that she had the damnedest grin on her face and a laugh of exultation every bit as rich as the challenge cry she'd uttered minutes before. Now—finally—all that was Hal in her huddled deep in its cave and let the human claim ascendancy.

In quick, practiced moves, she shackled her harness to the trapeze, although it wasn't time yet to hike herself out off a pontoon. She hauled the jib sheet until it was tight and tied it off, then repeated the process with the main. The Cat was riding more easily as it slowly fought clear of the reef and cresting combers gave way to rolling swells.

Nicole turned the bows farther away from land, checking the telltales atop the mast—fluttering strips of tape that indicated the wind's direction and speed—as she put herself on a broad reach.

She held her course through the early morning, while the breeze stayed firm, watching the shore dwindle in her wake until all she could make out were the coastal hills and the mountains far beyond. There was no stress to this kind of sailing, it was mainly a matter of getting her boat and herself properly tidy. She had donned both hat and glasses and was happily centered in ways she hadn't felt since leaving Earth.

She had no MapMaker, no nav aids of any kind save a compass that was integral to the mast. Hopefully, she wouldn't be out long enough or far enough to need them; though the Cat handled superbly, it wasn't equipped for voyages of any duration. Ciari had chosen himself a day sailor, probably for the fact that it didn't look much like a boat more than its practicality.

To check the trapeze, she swung the Cat closer to the wind, gradually hiking herself out on the upwind pontoon as the boat picked up speed. The pontoon beneath her lifted from the water, and she leaned back, counterbalancing the force of the breeze with her own weight, serving the same function here that a lead keel did on a big single hull like *Sundowner*. She didn't press for the max, Cats being notoriously easy to flip. She had few doubts about being able to right the boat if it did indeed capsize, but there was no one to offer assistance if anything went seriously wrong. As well, she didn't know what lived beneath the local waves—save for that one awesome monstrosity she'd seen during the *Range Guide* travelogue—and had no desire to learn about them the hard way.

She moderated her course, deciding to push on a bit farther before beginning her sweep across the mouth of the huge estuary towards Shavrin's Memorial Mount. She felt a twinge as she swung inboard and breathed a heartfelt curse when she bent her leg double to see why.

"Look what I missed in all the excitement," she told herself aloud. "Ter*rif*fic!"

It was a long surface slash along the meat of the calf, deep enough so that it was still showing blood. Now that she was actually looking at the wound, she suddenly felt the sting of salt water in the cut and felt the residual pain, both from the injury itself and the subsequent use she'd put to the leg. There were some lesser scratches as well, and a shredded tear up one seam of her shorts that left them dramatically shredded almost to the hip.

She scrabbled in her carryall for a medical kit, and expended almost the whole tube of antibiotic lathering the slash and the attendant abrasions. She had no tape, or bandages big enough—not that they'd be much use, considering that water was breaking pretty much continuously over the trampoline— so she settled for tying her bandannas around her shin to hold the wound as closed as possible. Beyond that, she had to hope her blood would clot with its usual enthusiasm and efficiency.

She could guess when it happened, when the big wave decked her—which meant she'd been humping across the reef, floundering in pools and channels, with an open wound.

"Hey," she said hopefully, "it's another world. Who's to say the neighborhood microbes have the slightest interest in out of town visitors?"

By midday, she was becalmed, in that hellish slot of time when land- and sea-based breezes canceled each other out, creating swirling cyclonic eddies of no use to any sailor, or not a puff of wind at all. She was out of sight of land in all directions and her leg had begun to resemble something out of an old *Popeye* cartoon.

It was hot to the touch, but then so was every other exposed surface, the sun's intensity muted only slightly by a veil of high-altitude clouds. It didn't hurt, for which she was unbelievably grateful. It also couldn't be moved worth a damn, neither at knee nor ankle, and it seemed to weigh as much as the rest of her. It looked like a sausage, in the process of being nuked in a microwave to the point of bursting.

"Well," she said matter-of-factly, "this seemed like a good idea at the time."

She lolled on the trampoline, aware that she should be watching the water for the telltale shadows that indicated an approaching gust. But what was the point? Sure, she'd forge ahead, blaze new trails, cross far horizons, behold sights none of her kind had ever seen before. It's what she always wanted. To hurl herself across the stars, to be all the things her parents' generation could only dream of.

"Beat that, Mom," she said with deep and abiding satisfaction. Then she frowned, wondering where that thought had come from. Or rather the resentment behind it.

The thought was too much effort, the products of her head had suddenly each grown as heavy as her leg, and so she let it slip from her fingers. She felt the main sheet start to follow and convulsively tightened her grip. The Cat was drifting, propelled by tidal action. Nicole had no idea of the local currents but she'd been beating against the inbound tide since she launched; if the sun's position was any indication, the tide had to be nearly full. Once it turned, she'd be in the position of being swept out to sea, which she didn't want—although she was finding it increasingly harder to care one way or the other. By the same token, the deepening afternoon should bring with it a decent wind.

Her knee was numb. She trailed a rope end up from her ankle but for all the sensation, she might as well have been stroking the pontoon.

She felt desperately thirsty but allowed herself only a single swallow. Sick, she was; stupid, she was determined not to be.

It was just getting to be such an effort simply to hold up her head!

She couldn't tell about her color. The value of the Hal sun red-shifted everything a step, which made the warm colors appear richer than they were. Sallow flesh looked healthy and healthy skin downright glowed. In her case, Nicole figured she was radiating a heat signature that would attract a decent hotdog missile.

She narrowed her eyes, shifting position awkwardly on the cloth trampoline and scrabbling at her glasses, trying to unhook the semicircular mountain frames from her ears and get them off so she could see better, the lens having been degraded by caked sea scunge.

There'd been a stir in the water, off in the distance, hope flaring that it might be a wayward zephyr, then fading as the surface settled back to sparkly stillness.

She wondered about Raqella and Amy, and Ciari, but mostly she found herself thinking of the silver-haired Hal. All along, she'd been trying to place what seemed so familiar about her. For some reason, with her faculties at their literal worst, Nicole made the connection. She looked and moved mostly like the male Nicole had seen, yet she stood. She made the effort to relate to everything—people, environment, situations—from two legs.

She'd seen enough of the local Hal to conclude that they were intelligent. They reasoned, they used tools, there was evidence of both. Yet they remained random hunter-gatherers, as though at some point the race had reached some evolutionary crossroads and they were the ones who chose to stay behind. She knew she was on the right track, but there were too many gaps in the line of dominoes, still too many places where she had to make a frantic leap to keep them falling in sequence. She was dancing the same dervish fandango she had a long time past with Amy—rueful noise, meant to be a laugh, possibly not as she considered the propriety of such a lively image in her present state—with all these pieces scattered before her but no sense of the structure to build from them. Because here, as with Amy, the answer had to be so far beyond common experience as to be almost outlandish.

"Oh, goody"—with a dangerously giddy giggle, wonderfully impressed with herself for the impending revelation— "they're all clones."

The water beneath the Cat changed color.

It was dark for a time, then light, then dark for a very long time, then light again. Nicole stared stupidly, head plopped over the edge of the trampoline, all thought of driving her boat cast away by this latest curiosity. Try as she might, she couldn't find an explanation for this either. There was certainly nothing soaring past upstairs to generate such a shadow.

She was still trying to puzzle things out when the first questing tentacle—a little thing, hardly thicker than a finger— plipped into the air to touch her right between the eyes.

She felt herself tumbling, one of those madcap testosterone stunts, where you find yourself and a clutch of likewise nutcases heaving bodily out the back of a perfectly good aeroplane a dozen klicks above the ground, with a FastPak of O_2 and an acrobatic chute to bring you to a safe landing. Problem with skydiving, she always felt, was that it was essentially a one-way ride. No matter what you tried, all you could do was modify your rate of descent; you never actually went back *up*. A primal rush to be sure, but that would only take

a body so far. That was why she preferred riding something
with wings, it gave a body alternatives.

Only consolation here was that there was no more sense that
she was cooking beneath her skin. Delightfully cool, it was,
akin to fresh sheets of top-quality cotton.

She could feel a wind now, a tickling caress across every
centimeter of her body, charged particles hurtling outward from
their star, yet at the same time she felt enfolded in a primordial
element, not a faint sensation—like the other—but more of an
embrace.

She'd calved before, cracking into parts Hal and human, and
felt it happening again, a duality of vision that told her she was
sick, she was well, she was alone, she was with Hana, she was
lost, she knew precisely where she was, she was helpless, she
was acting.

She wanted to scream, but none of her broken selves had any
means to give her desire voice.

Sound rippled through her, a basso profundo thrum of such
low frequency that she didn't perceive it as noise. Rather, it was
something far beyond that frame of reference; the only analogy
she could apply was the memory of standing on the Visitor's
Gallery at Canaveral when a shuttle launched. The motors
generated such raging power that even kilometers from the
gantry, the sound of them possessed palpable physical force.
She'd stood closer still, at Edwards, for a static test firing of the
main engines for her spaceplane. It was as though her body had
become the world and been cast into a period of perpetual
earthquakes.

But if those were her benchmarks, they were wholly inad-
equate to encompass what she felt now as the sonic pulses beat
through her.

At the same time, with curious dispassion melded to a giddy
and near overwhelming effervescence, she found a scale to
measure it.

Stop, she tried to say, to all the splintered parts of her, as the
pain from without was matched by that within.

The latest pulse was the last.

Questing fingers now, sliding under clothes, over skin,
following the triple strand tattoo left by her ghost. Perhaps it
was the sensation of actual contact—flesh on flesh—that

sparked a vague awareness in her, shunting circuits together to finally build a proper sequence of perceptions. She struggled—feebly to begin with, but gathering strength with each flailing roundhouse swipe of arms and legs—to reorient herself. There was a burning in her chest that demanded immediate attention. She knew the signs well, she was short of air, and her eyes opened wide and focused as she realized that she was drowning.

Through all her gyrations, the little tentacle had never lost its hold on her skin. She fumbled hands towards it, gave as hearty a yank as she could manage (not very) to break its hold. It came free without resistance, but she had no cause of exultation, because something of her went with it, a glittery intertwined strand that radiated energy so bright it was like a little lamp in the deeps. She wanted to howl, she recognized what this was the instant she saw it, the miraculously tangled double-helix of her own DNA, the biological foundation of her very being.

More tentacles, wrapping her as securely as a mummy, their moves incredibly swift—as though through vacuum—while hers were doddering in comparison. She was the alien here, in every sense, no part of her equipped to survive in this environment. But that reality proved quickly subject to change as other tentacles, a veritable nest of them, too many to count, so fine they made the one that initially tagged her appear a tree trunk by comparison, descended on the helix strands like tiny sharks to a banquet.

Before her eyes, all the delicate dots of light that were *her* were gobbled up and carried away. She felt the essence of Self begin to follow, flesh and spirit exploding into bubbles, as though she were some Virtual creation being banished with a wicked special effect. The fabric of her body had no more substance or cohesion than the bubbles of air that marked her descent, and they hurried as quickly away.

She was nothing. Yet—*impossible*, she shouted double-voiced in Hal and English, mostly to prove to herself that she still could—she still *was*. Aware of nothing save her own thoughts, and struck with that realization by a plaintive wonder, *Am I dead, then? Is this the way oblivion comes?* The Hal in her wanted a fight, Nicole hungered for answers.

She flexed her tail, adjusting depth with a modest tilt of her flukes to slide beneath a thermocline to a level where her sonar could range more effectively afield. Eyes weren't much use so she left them closed, the better to scan the rest of the incoming data. Sky above, three hard strokes to the air she needed to breathe, but no necessity for that for a good long while. Emptiness below—and she rolled into a double somersault, to the right and over her nose—to offer a focused *ping* just to be sure. That explained the deep-water wave action so close inshore; the entire estuary formed the crest of a magnificent abyssal canyon, as though the continent itself were some giant seamount, the open air summit of a vast plateau. She burbled delightedly, still a little fried from fever toxins, at the concept that this might be a variant of Conan Doyle's *Lost World*, only for fishies!

Then, she got a return from her lateral pulses and that notion didn't seem anywhere near so silly. She was being paced, the same as an interceptor flight would their bogie, a pair off her quarter, another pair behind. The flankers were at her level, the followers above and below. The data was fuzzy, as though they generated their own interference, the only thing she was sure of was size; they put the great whales to shame, and made her feel very tiny indeed.

She unleashed a series of sonic pulses, a symphony of information—everything she could relate about her situation and her escort—even though she knew from her first instant of awareness that there were no others of her kind to hear. There were songs in this blood sea, but none that she'd ever heard or could easily understand.

That done, she made her break. Pivot and dive, an air-combat maneuver so extreme it would have torn vehicle and pilot to bits had she tried it in the sky. Doubled back at an angle, to pull her escort into hurried turns to follow, perhaps force a collision. At the very least scramble their seeker pulses until she could put some scrambling layers between them.

She hadn't given a thought to what she'd do after that, she merely wanted to get away. But proximity alarms popped throughout her brain and she had to pull up short as something she wanted to register as the side of a mountain rose up before her, forcing her to hurriedly recalibrate all her conceptions of size among these strange creatures. This was to the others as they were to her. She saw tentacles reaching for her and bolted once again, only this time there was nowhere to go. Every course she took, every maneuver attempted, no matter how blindingly fast, found a tentacle to block her way, hemming her in more and more tightly.

Again, she felt that lightest of taps in the center of her forehead; again, she felt the essence drawn out of her, eyes too poorly positioned this time to actually see the glowing strand of DNA, but knowing what was to come and offering a keen of utter distress as her glorious physicality dissolved.

Eyes opened, body stirred to move hands into field of view, cry of joy to see arms and legs, all the requisite parts of proper memory. Then, a frantic collapse onto the bobbling surface of the trampoline, fingers clutching frantically at the frame bars as she scanned the horizon but saw only the strange Not-Ground that refused to bear her weight (another part of Self provided the label "water," which she accepted and integrated without question). At first, she thought it like the water of home, but a trial taste proved it foul to the taste, dangerous to drink.

Wind ruffled wet fur, making her shiver despite the radiance of the sun. She attempted to sit up, to take better stock of her situation, but each move of hers created an equivalent motion in the platform she was lying on, and she quickly dropped as flat and still as she could, so she wouldn't be pitched over the side. She yowled dismay, irritation more than actual distress. Strangeness abounded, but she as yet had no doubts about her ability to cope.

By trial and error, she gradually accustomed herself to safe movement aboard the tiny craft, hampered by the terrible reflection off the surface that forced her to protect her sight by sliding her nictitating membranes closed. She was still able to see, but it was like peering through a curtain of heavy gauze (never a moment's consideration of the origin of the analogy, or what gauze might be; if it came from her own thoughts, it was part of her *self* and consequently nothing that need worry her).

She prowled every inch of the trampoline, extending herself along the narrow pontoons to see what they were—a neat feat of logistics, that, since she was equally determined not to get herself wet—and finally hunkering herself at the foot of the mast to stare upward at the loosely flapping sails.

She reached an arm, then the other, her expression changing to one of puzzlement. She looked down at herself, as though examining how her legs were folded. The next time, she reached, she extended the motion along her entire body, steadying herself with a hand around the mast while she pushed as high as she could manage on tiptoes. Her hand still fell far short of the top of the mast.

She settled onto her feet, but stayed erect. This stance felt more natural. The Cat stirred and to keep her balance she caught a line, yelping with surprise as it gave in her grasp; at the same time, the big sail rose a bit on its track. She peered more closely at the lines, pulling the first one again and letting it go, watching the equivalent movement of the sail. She tried them all in turn, very cautiously, as though they were critters with teeth, just waiting for the chance to bite. With meticulous patience, she traced every line and experimented with them—a tug here, an ease there—learning gradually how the various elements fit together. She watched the wind and water, seeing how the action of the one was reflected on the other. She found out about the tiller the hard way, by the bar banging sharply into her ankles. Pulling it back and forth, she discovered, altered the heading of the boat. In the process came the observation that her direction materially affected how the sails filled with air. That, in turn, altered the movement of the boat itself through the water. When the wind came from in front, the sails flapped uselessly and not much happened. After struggling to turn her heading, she got better results.

The wind curled across her shoulders to fill the sails and she heard the burble of water along the length of the pontoons as she picked up speed. Now that she was going somewhere, she needed somewhere to go.

Joy turned marginally pensive, her gaze shifting from masthead to horizon and some clue to an answer. Her inattention proved costly, as the air seemed to pause for breath, the sails flapping in confusion, demanding to be filled. She looked around trying to find some new breeze, the Cat falling off even more, broadside to the swells, putting her at the mercy of the wave action. The surging up-and-down motion went straight to her stomach and added to her distractions. Nothing stayed still or level and the harder she struggled for control—of her body, of the boat—the more it was torn from her grasp.

The wind finished her. It caught the sails hard, pushing the boom to the limit of its travel and sending the Cat skidding in a shallow diagonal along the down slope of a comber, more like a surfboard than a boat. She tried to put the stern to the breeze, but the elements were in opposition; the more she tried to go one way, the harder she was pushed back, so that when she crested the next swell she was broadside to both wind and water.

When the last gust caught her at the crest, there was nothing to counterbalance it. She was on the wrong side of the trampoline, with the upwind pontoon riding high. In a heartbeat, the Cat tumbled and she was in the water.

She was calm, her universe ordered and correct, the sum and substance of her DNA projected before her like the starscape of a nebula. She expanded the perspective until the molecular gaps were an arm's length apart, then moved among them for a closer look. At the same time, she was aware of all the other myriad aspects of her existence—in that way people are constantly and automatically aware of their bodies—yet saw no need to consider anything directly unless there was a problem. She moved with an easy effort; there was nothing within the range of her perceptions to concern her; Hana—her sole companion—was fine. No problems anywhere.

She wished she had a comparison strand . . .

. . . and one appeared, neatly labeled, from her personnel file, taken prior to the *Wanderer* launch. Even at a glance, she saw there were differences, but she'd known there would be. She grinned at the thought of how temptingly easy it would be to reach out and pluck the proper structure from one image and restore it to the other.

Even as she watched, gossamer streamers intruded from the boundaries of her vision, snake-wriggling towards her display with a speed and purpose that telegraphed danger. She tried to banish the images, but that system crashed. Called for a defensive array to protect them, only to see the snakes pass through as if they didn't exist. She attempted direct intervention, but as many strands had come for her as the helixes, binding her too tightly to move, to breathe. She tried to cry out to Hana—a warning, a call for help—but they filled her mouth, her nose, covering her eyes to blind her and stopping her ears to make her deaf. She felt a tremendous weight, had a vision of the great creature she'd encountered as a dolphin.

Why are you doing this, she tried to say, but thoughts were becoming as impossible as speech, all the corners of her mind invaded, overwhelmed by the tentacles of energy.

Again, there was that awful sense of dissolution, not the absolute cut-off transition to sleep, but something more horribly gradual. All the boxes of her memory were being shaken out, the contents stolen away, stripping her naked in ways she'd never imagined, reducing her to component parts as a conscious being the same way they had as a physical one.

She stood her ground until the last, struggling to hold on to what was left her, only to have it collapse in her grasp. She wanted to cry—defiance, denial, a demand for vengeance, a final plea for mercy—but the words lost meaning and then the concepts themselves. She was aware of *being*—but that could have been merely a forlorn hope, since she had no sensoral input to substantiate it—she was aware

she was nothing

She surfaced too fast, without any sense of place, to thunk her head soundly on a pontoon. Instinctively—with a fervent cry of *"ow"*—she tried to wrap herself around any part of the Cat that was available to grasp and in that same stumbling movement attempt to get her face above the surface.

Her opening breath was mostly water. While the salt content wasn't a match for Earth's oceans, there was still sufficient to make her gag spectacularly. She couldn't let the coughing last, she needed air too badly, so she consciously broke it off to grab a breath. The pattern went on a few minutes, a serious bout of coughing, then a mighty gasp, followed by more coughing.

Sodden—*Within as well as without*, she decided, *waterlogged to the effing core*—she reached the trampoline on the third try, and let the sun evaporate the upper half of her while the bottom drained back into the sea. The sun was on the horizon and she assumed it was sunset until it moved up the sky. She wouldn't put it past the critters she'd encountered to be able to alter time, but decided the far more sensible answer was that she'd been out for one or more days.

Belatedly, she noticed that she could feel her right leg. And move it as well, she discovered as she struggled for a look. The swelling had gone down significantly, so much so that her bandannas had slipped down to the ankle—*Damn thing looks positively normal*, she thought. The effort of taking that look cost her dear and she collapsed onto her side, tucked into a fetal curl, most conscious of an ache within that had nothing to do with her sore diaphragm and salt-scored lungs. A joyous sadness was her first impression, a sad joy the second, the fact that she was weeping her third.

She looked at the sea, saw faint movements in the distance that told her the air was beginning to stir, turned her attention to her boat. Paused with a memory that had no place and bundled her jacket over her head for a better view of torso and arms. She put her hands tentatively to her face, but the only hair she felt was what she'd grown up with. She wore the ghost marks—as she'd come to think of them—visible across her shoulder and winding down her arm to merge with the pattern on her hand as neatly as if she'd been born this way. Her right hand, though, was clean, no more stigmata. She couldn't see her features but assumed that what was on her arm still extended across her face, and didn't want to check the marks on her hips.

Aside from that, she felt like herself.

If only, she thought, *I knew what the devil* that *means.*

Reality—what a (mutable) concept.

She laughed, taking great and unrestrained pleasure in that basic *human* sound, while at the same time the physical expression accompanying it was as pure as Hal could be.

"Hullo," she tried. English in concept and execution. Then, to be a brat, she announced, *"Konichi wa."* And, to finish, a greeting in Trade.

She took another long look around for a sign of wind, decided it was an acceptable risk to leave the sails full, and sat herself down on the aft pipe of the trampoline. She was cross-legged, at a relaxed attention, and while she appeared to be looking towards the horizon her gaze was actually directed inward.

"Whoever you are," she said, choosing to speak in English, though the sentiments were as old as her adopted race, speaking with a relaxed formality that felt right and appropriate for the moment, "Great Old Ones, I thank you for my life. There is no debt between us but a Bond. You are part of what I am, what I have been and yearn to become. Honor have you brought me, honor shall I offer in return."

She had to confess, the phrasing worked more eloquently in Hal, but hoped it was the thought that mattered. She saw no sign that she'd been heard but likewise had no doubt the Old Ones were listening.

No wonder the Hal have always been spooked by the sea, she noted to herself, *if This is what lives here. Especially since the deep-water drop-off is so close inshore and so bloody steep. I wonder how many Hal simply . . . vanished over the aeons before They found one not only capable of listening to Them but of handling what she was told.*

She thought of sharks, and a theory she'd read once that since the species seemed to suffer virtually no effects of age, there could be specimens with phenomenal life spans. The giggle hope, of course—a staple of the supermarket tabloids, along with the Loch Ness monster—being that there might be one out there who dated back to the Pliocene. Jurassic shark, big enough to sink ocean liners. Given the size of the creatures she'd seen here, and the tremendous *gravitas* she felt from them, that didn't seem like much of a joke.

She had no explanation for what happened but that didn't bother her, and resolved to offer a small monograph to the Clarke Institute in Sri Lanka about how the technology of a truly advanced extraterrestrial species really *was* akin to magic.

The mainsail rattled, a glance confirming an approaching gust, with more beyond. She tightened up her lines and reattached herself to the trapeze.

The Old Ones left her close to the far shore of the estuary, and the sun was still fairly high when the cliffs hove into view. She had far less trouble with the approach than her launch, because she knew the lie of this land from her sessions in Virtual. Ages ago, part of the cliff wall had collapsed, creating a natural cove—accessible only at low tide—that was the only safe landing along this entire stretch of coast. The drawback was, once in the cove there was no way she could beat her way out; that'd be a challenge for a keel-equipped boat. In the shadow of the giant cliffs, throwing herself into the wind—the worst sailing aspect of a catamaran—she'd never make it. Once the tide came in, she'd be treading water in gale-force surf.

My final test, she told herself, and found a scrap of memory from her ghost that this was where she'd found herself ashore.

It was why this spot was the Memorial Mount of Shavrin's Clan, it was where they learned to walk.

She was sorry to leave the Cat on the tiny beach, after such good service, but she didn't have time to break it down, and couldn't manage carrying it anyway. She stripped it of usable line, not knowing what she might need, and a bunch of quick release shackles to double as improvised carabiners. There was a path—and she couldn't help wondering if its presence was wholly natural . . .

She shouldered her carryall and attacked the cliff, climbing some bits, walking others, making steady headway as the shore disappeared beneath her and the Cat consigned to the deep.

She reached the top near sunset.

She knew she wasn't going to get to the tocsin in time to sound the ritual farewell, but wasn't about to press herself. Dusk was significantly degrading visibility and the footing was still sufficiently treacherous that she couldn't afford to take stupid risks.

The view was a wonder to behold. Sky was fire, sea blood, the land substantial enough to endure the assaults of both the other elements. Nicole had always associated the Hal's natural cinnamon scent with their high mountain origins—probably because it most reminded her of the Colorado ranges that nestled the Air Force Academy—but now she realized it was fundamentally a sea smell. Belonging to the Old Ones.

She was so startled by the sound of the great tocsin that she almost lost her balance. With desperate inelegance, she plastered herself against the slightly canted cliff wall, praying for stable handholds and willing herself to be wholly unaffected by gravity.

She heard a man's voice begin the ritual farewell to the sun—and with it, farewell to the ghosts of friends recently departed, or a remembrance to those of longer passage—and stayed where she was, stifling a shout of raw delight while she gathered wits and balance for the final ascent, as well as allowing him to complete the ceremony undisturbed.

She was just starting the last few steps when Ben Ciari called out her name, as one of the honored dead.

CHAPTER FIFTEEN

She wanted to cry out but some blessed instinct inspired her to stealth instead. She'd always believed him alive, because of a sense bordering on certainty that she'd know when he wasn't, even on Earth. Their Speaker selves had been cast from the same template; they were more than twins, the Hal in them were virtual clones—and Amy's parting words came back to her from the bluff across the estuary: *"We're a matched set, you and me . . ."*

Nicole wondered then if the girl felt as angry as she at this violation. It was only with conscious effort that she could differentiate between one aspect and the other; in the normal course of life, she couldn't honestly say which were the parts she'd been born with and which had been grafted on, both felt totally natural. Which gave rise to another set of gnawing anxieties—what else within her was a falsehood, and what would be changed next? Worst of all, if past did indeed prove prologue, how would she ever know? There was no master file that was primally, essentially Her, pristine and uncorrupted, allowing her to shave clean all these new prisms and restore herself to the way she began.

Stop it, she told herself severely, deliberately choosing English and a cadence of attack derived from Judith Canfield. *You've found a balance, why're you acting like some ground-hugging pudknocker and trying to upset it? Where's the sense in bitching about what can't be changed, Shea, make do with what you've got!*

We're all *the products of what we're made of*, she thought, a fraction more rationally, *I just have the benefit of a little more hands-on attention.*

It wasn't meant to be funny, but she barely stifled a burble of laughter that would have surely given her away.

Something about Ciari's voice, something about the situation, felt *wrong*—and that, she knew, was an instinct learned from him. Just as she'd know his fate, so would he be aware of hers. So there had to be a reason for his lie.

"Very impressive, Marshal," she heard from a new voice, also in English. "Close my eyes and I'd almost mistake you for a Fuzzy."

Do it, Nicole taunted, *that'll be all the opening he needs!* Ciari said nothing, did nothing, which told her he wasn't facing a solo. While she had light enough to see, she scoped her head back and forth, trying to fix the layout of the cliff in her mind, and possibly find a lateral path. At the same time, she strained her ears for any available scrap of information.

Silent as a ghost, was her watchword, without a shred of irony. She didn't need a downward glance to remind her how close she was to becoming one. She needed more than simple hand- and footholds; ideally, she had to find somewhere to rest her carryall, so she could get at the knives tucked deep inside.

"You don't like the locals so much, cock, how come you're workin' with 'em?"

Nicole bit back a snarl. The words were shaken by the stiffening sunset breeze but still recognizably Amy Cobri.

"The enemy of my enemy is my friend, Ms. Cobri. Oldest dictum in the Book of Tactics."

"Puh-lease." Nicole couldn't believe the raw contempt the girl applied to those two syllables. "Is that as original as this gets?"

She heard the sharp retort of a gun and shoved a clenched fist between her teeth to choke back any outcry. Whatever happened to Amy, there was Ciari to consider, and hopefully Raqella as well.

"You don't know how long I've wanted to do that," the man said, with real satisfaction. From the strength his voice carried, Nicole placed him closer to her than he'd been earlier, probably speaking to Ciari.

"Knew a guy once," Amy said, her own voice suddenly thin and reedy with pain, "couldn't hit the mouth of a two-inch pipe from two inches out. He teach you how to shoot, Rossmore?"

Shit, from Nicole, Constitution's *Exec!*

"With a mouth like yours, Ms. Cobri," said the Commander, "you must really want to hurt before you die."

"You allow this?" Nicole heard from Raqella in Hal, an undertone of strain telling her he'd been hurt as well.

"Speak English, furboy," Rossmore told him.

"Gee, Commander," from Amy, "you figure the locals might conspire behind your back?"

"You have allied yourself with the New Order," Ch'ghan replied to Raqella, in his thick accent. "You have denied your people, betrayed your heritage. Why should you be granted the honor in death you have so willingly cast aside in life?"

Nicole had to take a look. She'd goosed herself around the edge of the headland, thankful the cliff was showing the effects of centuries of weather. What appeared dauntingly sheer from afar was a lot more broken up close, textured by the wind to allow good purchase. It was still a brutal climb, though, and she had precious few reserves when she started. Her leg worried her most of all. True, the swelling was gone, although the scar was as distinct and livid in its own way as her tattoos, but the wound was far from fully healed. It wasn't happy with the effort she was demanding and what had been a dull annoyance most of the afternoon had begun to seriously hurt. There was a growing fragility about her leg, a sense that each step would be the one where it folded, so much so that she couldn't help favoring it. Which, in turn, threw off her balance, creating an instability she could ill afford, on the ridge and especially in a fight.

She tried to give the leg a rest, taking most of her weight on her hands and pushing off her left foot, moving smoothly and oh so slowly along the shadows thrown by an outcropping where the cliff looked as though it had been folded back on itself. Unfortunately, the darkness that masked her presence also made the opposition hard to spot. Ciari hadn't moved from his position by the tocsin, almost at the lip of the headland. There were a couple of huddled shapes across the way that she assumed were Raqella and Amy. Rossmore stood between Ciari and the kids, closer to them than the Marshal—*Sensible placement,* she thought, *allows him to nail them and still have time to drop Ben before he can cover the distance.* That left

Ch'ghan, and with him she saw a pair of backup bruisers, one from each race. Both carried rifles, and while she couldn't see details Nicole had no doubt the Hal held a blaster, the same kind of weapon Daniel Morgan had used to hunt her on his asteroid.

She closed her eyes as she lowered herself below the crest, and saw a corridor lit like a passage out of Hell with the fireflash of the beam. Morgan was at a junction, the halls fanning away from him like the spokes of a wheel. He was scorching each in turn, he didn't give a damn who was in his sights—friend or foe—so long as he burned her for sure. She couldn't outrun the beam; she'd ducked into a Primary tunnel that cut a straight line all the way through the rock, she couldn't even be guaranteed another intersection for better than a hundred meters.

She had no choice. She charged him. She killed him.

Ciari had been Law Officer on that *Wanderer* mission. He was a Senior U.S. Marshal. Facing violent death—and, on occasion, dealing it—came with the job. It wasn't why she'd come to the High Frontier; she'd told him that with all the vehemence she could muster; she refused to allow him to remake her in his image. Yet those lessons had saved her life. She hoped they were about to again.

Suddenly the rock swayed. She tightened her grip reflexively, her initial fear that an earthquake had struck the coast, and the cliff begun to tumble into the sea.

But it wasn't the world swinging wild, like a runaway fun fair ride, merely her perceptions of it. She stared, wide-eyed at the granite in front of her face and wailed deep inside as it appeared to dissolve into a view of stars.

Initial orientation was ridiculously easy. There were a half-dozen main sequence benchmarks in immediate view, not even counting the Hal sun, off to the left and a little below. Her perspective was above the plane of the ecliptic and a quick glance ahead gave her the position of the third of the system along her line of flight. At the same time, she was equally aware of all the other worlds—with an equally clear picture of them—to the sides and behind, above and below. Her focus was forward, her vision was all-encompassing.

She couldn't help but be impressed, and said so, profanely.

"Nice mouth," Hana told her.

"If you could see with my eyes, lady, you'd speak my dialogue. How can I be here, I'm holding on to a rock."

"Don't worry about the details. You want to bring us down?"

"Very much so."

She had the world now, and for a few moments could only behold the wonder of it. She'd thought the *Constitution*'s overhead Bridge Master Display was magnificent, but there was no comparison. As she watched, the globe expanded to fill her whole field of vision. At the same time, her gaze encompassed an expanse and variety of perceptions that part of her accepted as perfectly normal while the rest simply stared goggle-eyed, struck too dumb to even comment.

"I can't stay here," she said. "Hana, if there's a way, cut me loose, before I fall off that frigging cliff."

It was like a story from the *Arabian Nights*, she was Mistress and Genie all in one, her every wish her own command.

She found the night very dark and very still, the twilight breeze slackened, the stars overhead unchallenged by the reflected glow off any of the planet's three moons. Her nails were cracked, fingertips torn enough to draw blood, and she saw faint gouges in the rock where she'd clawed for an anchorage. She flexed her hands, one at a time, noting the stiffness brought on by extreme tension—no worse in her extremities than any other part of her, she was the living embodiment of soreness—but otherwise she was okay. Except for the leg. When she tried to lift it, it was as though strands of barbed wire had been stretched beneath her skin, sending a surge of pain throughout her body that made her want to be sick.

She wondered how long she'd been out—trying not to think at all about where she'd been—cocked ear and eye to try to once more place everybody.

Something slapped her backside, like the lash of a whip, a sting more than an actual hurt, the surprise was what made her yip.

Perceptions splintered. She found herself staring at the world along parallel tracks of vision, the same dual perspective she'd have in a cockpit, with one eye on reality and the other following all the data on her heads-up display. She catalogued

the sensation as a scanning field, with more to come—
sensations akin to finding herself in a swarm of hungry
gnats—as her position was triangulated and locked. The
probes originated from sentry remotes, mostly because she was
crossing an automated defense perimeter, and were satisfied by
the clearance she offered in return. Thus far, she was alone in
the sky; she knew that was about to change.

She heard a shuffling step, cautious as it approached the
edge, wished for dark clothes as a flashlight was switched on.

"Mir't'zach?" called Ch'ghan.

"I heard something."

The Hal translated for Rossmore.

"What are we waiting for, Ch'ghan?" he demanded.

"Dr. Murai, actually," was the reply. "A great deal of my
life's work is bound up with the *Swiftstar*."

Your *name for it, you faithless slug,* Nicole snarled. *She's*
Sundowner *now and always will be!*

"I would like to salvage it," he finished, "if I can. Dr. Murai
is not a combat pilot. She will do the sensible thing—
especially with the lives of her friends at stake—and surren-
der."

Nicole thought nothing. Her smile said it all.

The beam swept over her and she hoped at first missed—but
it had caught the corner of her carryall and that brought it back.
She was already moving by then, swinging the bag off her
shoulder, catching the strap on her hand; when the Hal sentry
hove into view above her, she let fly.

She had no illusions about the throw doing any harm. The
bag held clothes, she'd do more damage in a pillow fight; her
goal was a halfways decent distraction.

He flinched, expecting something heavier, his hands automatically batting it aside. But turning them on the bag meant
releasing his hold on his gun, which was all the opening she
was going to get.

Her leg made her want to scream and so she did, but what
emerged was a cry of war not pain as she lunged up over the
crest to hook ahold of the blaster rifle. It was a heavy
gun—way too big for shooting people, was her instant
assessment, until she remembered the approaching spaceplane—and he'd looped his bandoleer over his shoulders so

they'd bear the bulk of the strain. When she tugged, her intent to disarm him and possibly gain the weapon for herself, he came with it. The ground canted steeply as it approached the edge and Nicole gave the sentry too much momentum to be stopped with a single step. He took one, another, the third would do the trick, and he was already twisting his body to bring the barrel to bear when his foot planted itself on empty air.

Nicole was already diving the other direction, so she didn't see the Hal's face in the split second before he began to fall, when he realized what she'd done. He scrambled for balance, in an explosion of movements more appropriate to a cartoon character, but there was nothing in reach to grab hold of and nothing for him to offer but a scream.

For some reason, he pulled the trigger. The gun was at its highest setting, because it was intended to punch holes in a spacecraft and at a pretty fair distance. The beam gouged a monster slice out of the rock—had Nicole not scrambled when she did, it probably would have claimed her, too—then shot skyward. Her *other* eyes spotted the signature, as it topped out at better than fifty kay, and was thankful she didn't have that to deal with, while at the same time wondering if there were any more.

He tumbled as he fell, the blaster carving afterimages on the retinas of those who watched, as it cut a swath seaward through the air, leaving the stench of ozone in its wake the way fireworks do the smell of cordite. It cut into the water with only slightly less force. The beam was tremendously focused, its cohesion only marginally affected by the heavier medium, and Nicole realized with horror that it would cut all the way to the bottom. And through anything in its path.

"No," she cried, holding herself responsible, "no no no no no no *no!*"

The sentry completed his first tumble—with more than enough distance ahead to allow another full revolution—and the beam struck the cliff once more, with force enough to shake it bottom to top. The fire struck a seam, where the apparently solid frontage had buckled ever so slightly under the ocean's unrelenting assault. The solar heat ignited the pocket of air, causing the equivalent of a small mountain to burst outward, as

though all the skyscrapers in Manhattan had been piled atop
one another and then pushed over.

The blaster was obliterated with the Hal who held it, in a
heartbeat, while the reverberations of the avalanche seemed to
go on endlessly.

They were nothing compared to the awful cry that came
from beyond the horizon. From this height, Nicole figured the
distance at a hundred kay, minimum, better than fifty miles, a
sound of such transcendent grief and rage that she was
hammered to her knees.

It was too dark still to properly see closer inshore, but again
there was no missing the rush of water as something huge
broached the surface, and more of the great creatures took up
the lament.

Rossmore's bully-boy made the mistake of going for Nicole.
He was Navy, she assumed SEAL—their Sea, Air and Land
commandos—and a burst from his autofire would cut her in
half. Not as fancy a death as from the blaster but just as final.
She was God's Gift as a target, even without his laser and
infrared and enhanced optical NightVision sights. He didn't
even bother aiming, he simply brought the gun up to fire from
the hip.

Amy hit him with a rock. Right between the shoulder blades,
with as hard a throw as she could manage. Which, given her
physical template and the effort she'd made over the years to
hone it to near perfection, was very hard indeed. The man
couldn't help but react, and from the way he favored his left
arm, Nicole hoped enthusiastically that the girl had broken
some bones. The second his eyes were off her, she hurled
herself at him in a low post tackle that turned him horizontal in
midair.

Hurt as he was, the man was a pro. He caught her with a
roundhouse kick right as he hit the ground, that bowled her
over onto her back. His rifle got lost in the confusion. The noise
was rapidly becoming unbearable, a cacophony of atonal
foghorns, creating the same effect as a multitude of Nosferatus
scraping their ancient, clawed fingernails across an infinite
number of blackboards. The sound was pitched across the
entire length of the audio spectrum, above and below perceptible human—or Hal—frequencies. It made Nicole want to

shriek in sympathetic pain at the same time as it threatened to shake her to bits on a molecular level.

My God, she cried in her mind, because that was the only level left on which she could make herself heard, knowing as she did that the deity she called to lived as much in the deep water as the heart of the sky, *how many did that blaster kill? Who did it kill?*

A lance of horror went through her, as deadly as the real thing, at the image of the Great Old One, who had taken her and shaped her as He had Shavrin's ancestor—Nicole's ghost Hal—all those untold generations before, split nearly in two across the whole of his impossible length.

The SEAL came up with a roundhouse kick meant to crack her skull. She flattened under the blow and planted the sole of her own foot (the good one) full in his backside. He rolled on impact, taking care to recover well short of the edge—he wasn't about to follow his Hal comrade—a knife in each hand, weaving an intricate, intertwining web, blades clashing sparks as he struck them together and advanced on her. They leapt for her alone or in tandem, strikes meant to harry more than slay, to tempt her into a response extreme enough to leave her vulnerable. Nicole backpedaled as fast as she was able, desperately searching for room to maneuver or better yet a weapon, but her leg wasn't up to the demands she was making and she stumble stepped, allowing him close enough to draw blood. He took delight in cutting her tattooed arm, three fresh scarlet slashes to complement the black, plus one across the opposite ribs. He was showing off, confidence in his own skill making him increasingly contemptuous of hers.

She switched tracks with his next attack, letting her Hal side run the show—and spun away from his blades with a balletic grace that masked an equally remarkable speed. Now, he was off-balance—for no more than a heartbeat, too little time for it to register on those watching—as she pivoted on her good leg, using the other for a hook. It was too obvious a move to actually trip him up, his own reactions were too good for that, but she forced him to jump aside, shifting the impetus of the duel back towards her.

As she fought, part of her was looking for her companions—noting that Amy and Raqella were effectively out of action, that

Ciari was doing nothing but stare at Rossmore, that the Commander was torn between wanting to help his man and the certainty of what would happen the moment he relaxed his guard. Of Ch'ghan, she had no sign, and wondered if that meant he was coming after her.

There were no more games in the SEAL, no more flash to his approach. The moment he was close enough for a blade to reach her, she was dead. She considered taking a hit, in order to get close enough to do him some major harm, but rejected the idea just as quickly. Any wound he inflicted would be as near fatal as made no difference and he had the advantage of height and bulk. At her best, in a fair fight, she probably couldn't hurt him worth noticing. The only reason she'd lasted this long was his ignorance of Hal combat techniques, and he was adapting most impressively.

But she had better eyesight, especially with only starlight to see by. She pitched herself away from him at a sharp angle, came up with a rock and hurled it, in a fair copy of Amy's throw. The SEAL had learned from that mistake, he slapped the projectile aside. All she'd wanted was that little distraction, and she used it to charge Rossmore.

It was a perfect blindside. He was so intent on Ciari that he never saw her coming, and the SEAL's warning served only to startle him. He was flattened while his mind was still trying to focus on the threat. She wasn't interested in him, though, heaving herself bodily away from the obvious target— Rossmore's fallen pistol—just as one of the SEAL's knives ricocheted off the stone. If she'd grabbed for the gun, it would have hit her dead center in the back. Instead, it was Raqella who caught up the blade as it landed close by. Amy held him down, and rightly; he was no match for the trained knife-fighter.

Besides, Nicole had her own plan.

Without a glance, wishing for a portion of the holographic perspective she seemed to enjoy during her recent interludes with Hana, she sensed him close behind her and gaining. She put on a last burst of speed, scooping up the mallet a fraction of a second ahead of a sweeping blade, and let go a roundhouse swing against the tocsin.

The bell was as wide across as she was tall and better than

three times her height; she struck it far more strongly than Ciari had earlier—those were taps by comparison—and the sound that followed was as much felt as heard.

The SEAL was as close as she, but she knew what to expect. The gong was deafening but she ignored the new lances of pain and let fly a second blow. Without a pause, as the man bellowed and clutched his ears in a vain attempt to shut out this new and louder noise, she came around the bell and swung for him.

The mallet caught him smack on the point of an elbow and she had the satisfaction of hearing bones break. He plucked the knife from his now-useless hand and made a stab for her. But she was already pirouetting away from that thrust, reversing her grip to strike him on the breastbone, hard enough to stagger him. Again, with that impossible speed, she spun the mallet yet again and hammered its head full into his midsection. He doubled over, poleaxed, gasping for air as the shock of the blow paralyzed his diaphragm.

She wanted to hit him again—Hell, she wanted to pound the man until he was nothing but a smear, standing him as surrogate for the fallen Hal gunman, to pay for the slain Old One—but there was no need. Beyond vengeance. And she was neither that cold- nor that hot-blooded, no matter *what* had been done to her.

She felt warmth on her back, a wicked tingle on her belly, and understood immediately. *Sundowner*. Dayside approach, to burn off all the necessary speed and altitude before crossing the Terminator where such a fire trail would be easily seen. Everyone knew she was coming, but she saw no reason to make it easy for them.

She blinked herself back to the Mount, to find Rossmore on his feet. He wasn't the athlete or the fighter his SEAL was—that's why the bruiser was along—and he had one hand clutching a handkerchief to a cut Nicole had somehow torn in his scalp. It was the other hand, though, that concerned her. The one with the gun to Amy's chest. She hadn't heard a shot but from the way Raqella lay sprawled she knew instantly one had been fired.

"Is this really necessary?" she asked, locking aside the surge of grief. "C'mon, Commander, you kill her, you kill yourself."

"You think I'm not patriot enough—*man* enough—to die

for a cause I believe in?" was his retort. No boast in the statement, merely a cool presentation of a fact so obvious it might as well be a natural law.

"Is that how this has to end?"

He gave a thin smile and she knew he was a pilot who missed the killing fields.

"Not really. Why don't you take her place?"

Ciari's hand closed on her arm, her head jerking around in surprise at this first acknowledgment of her presence.

"Out of the question," he said for her ears alone. He was standing behind her, oriented out to sea, and she sensed rather than saw the gun masked from Rossmore's sight by both their bodies.

"*Now* you help?" she demanded, with mock incredulity. "And *this* is what you offer?"

"Every teacher likes to see their star pupil in action, don't'cha know?"

"I need him alive," she said quickly, in Hal undertone, hoping her words weren't being overwhelmed by the dirge resonating ever more loudly from the ocean. "I think something's been done to the *Constitution*."

"I'll only have the one shot, Nicole."

"Leave him to me." She looked him full in the eye as she said this. She'd been so much younger—in ways that had nothing to do with the six years difference in her physical age from then 'til now—when last they'd been together. The gulf between them—in experience, in the maturity that comes with command—was as much an abyss as the ocean trench leading out of the estuary below. The changes he saw had nothing to do with the markings on her skin, or the first scattering of silver on the autumnal fire of her hair.

"Your call, then."

She stayed directly between Ciari and Rossmore as she strode slowly forward, adding a limp that was only slightly exaggerated. She didn't want to risk him taking a shot at the Marshal. By the same token, she was also telling Rossmore what was in store if he chose to turn his gun on her.

"What do you hope to accomplish here, Rossmore?"

"*Commander* Rossmore, Major. I earned my rank. No one

made me a gift out of some perverted notion of feminist 'sisterhood.' "

She almost lost it then and there. It had been a half century since the full integration of the military services—with women finally getting their shot at combat roles—and Nicole thought history alone would have justified the decision.

He took her by the shirtfront, bundling the material inside a tight fist and lifting, so she was forced to go up on tiptoes. The barrel of his Beretta he tucked snug and secure under the shelf of her jaw. He was stronger than she thought.

"This is the end, Shea," he said. "Only fitting, don't you think? Your life and your precious Alliance, lost in the same action."

"You're wrong."

"You're stalling." Again, that killer ace smile. "There's no rescue coming, girl. There's been a SpaceCap in orbit since your arrival, on the off chance Murai would sortie the *Swiftstar* . . ."

"*Sundowner*," she corrected automatically.

"What?"

"My plane. It's *Sundowner*."

"It's not *your* anything, bitch. But since that qualifies as a last request, I see no harm in humoring you. Full details of what Shavrin did to you *Wanderer* survivors have been flashed to the *Constitution*; that's why Hobby's pulling out, he feels his position has been compromised and that he's alone, in potentially hostile space. He won't put his ship at risk."

"You're his XO, won't you be missed?"

"Who do you think uncovered the critical information? At great risk and very possibly the loss of his own life."

"So. You get to go home the hero. Congratulations. I'm one woman, we're a crew of four. People may be horrified but ultimately our fate won't make that much difference."

"True. But coupled with the destruction of NASA's premier starship . . ."

"Son of a bitch, that's your *crew!*" Hobby was the plank owner of the starcraft, he'd been slated for command since its inception, but Nicole knew that Rossmore had been beside him almost the entire way.

"This is war," he said simply, as though it explained everything.

At which point, as timely as if she'd been waiting for a cue, *Sundowner* ripped down off the distant mountains—approaching from the land, where Rossmore had been expecting her from the sea—as though the plane had suddenly metamorphosed into a ground-attack platform. The flyby was below Mach—but not by much—and speed and mass combined with an obscenely low altitude to create a brutal assault on all the senses that sent everyone diving for cover. It was pure reflex, probably dating back to the time when humanity was small enough—and raptors sufficiently large—that we qualified as prey. Something came at you hard and fast from the sky, you hugged the dirt.

Rossmore still had his gun, but as he hurried to bring it to bear, Raqella managed to wrap both arms around one of the man's legs and drive the blade he held into the meat of midthigh. Rossmore screamed, his cry as suddenly choked off by the blow Nicole delivered to his Adam's apple. The way he fell left his front unprotected and she stomped hard on his solar plexus, driving what air remained from his lungs with an audible *woof!* The coup de grace was a straight fist to the face, short and sweet, with the force of a piston.

She plucked the gun from his nerveless fingers, spared the time for a quick, glancing exam of Amy and Raqella—*Too much blood,* she thought, *from both of them*—the alternate channel in her skull immediately swinging *Sundowner* back towards the promontory, ignoring the returns from the surface-scanning radar as the plane passed over the estuary, and what was being displayed on the ultra-res full-spectrum monitors. Another fast check told her the gun had nearly a full magazine and a round in the chamber. No sign though of Ch'ghan.

"Shea Shavrin's-Daughter . . ."

"Not now, Rocky. Got work to do. Rest quiet, boy, you need the strength."

"What has happened? What is . . . happening?"

"I'm not altogether sure," which was as significant a lie as it was the unvarnished truth. He recognized it as both but thankfully didn't press the point. He had the will but no more reserves.

"Ch'ghan," she called, and after a momentary pause that brought her no reply, *"Ch'ghan! Show yourself, damn you!"*

"Here." Ciari, not the Hal. "I think you'd better see this, Nicole."

He was standing by the tocsin.

There was better light now, under the glow of the primary moon—once the twin secondaries added their reflections, it would be like appearing in a classic black and white movie, with everything fairly visible but bleached of perceptible color. Beyond the tocsin, the ground started a shallow slope for another thirty-odd meters to the actual lip of the headland. That stretch was considered off-limits, mostly because of the wind; it wouldn't take much to scoop an unwary visitor right off the edge.

But that's where Ch'ghan stood, so close that Nicole didn't even consider going out to join him.

He was staring at the sea and when Nicole followed the general direction of his gaze, she understood why. And thought of Kymri.

She must have spoken his name aloud, because she prompted a question from Ciari.

"Something he told me," she replied. "About how, on his own walkabout, nothing happened. His best friend—his *sidi'chai*—lost his mind, but for Kymri it was just a wilderness stroll. I asked him why he didn't try again. He said, the way he put it to me, 'When you ring the bell and God doesn't answer the door, why push your luck?' Oh, Ben—what, when He does answer, if you blow His head off?"

There was no water to be seen, beyond the immediate inshore swell. Only massive bodies, the smallest Nicole could measure—and here she drew on data developed from *Sundowner*'s brief flyover, not a conscious request, she simply had the need and the answer popped out, same as with any memory—on the order of an ocean liner. She thought of submarines, great, cylindrical tubes of black on black, trailing tentacles that could be double the body length and more, crushing together as though they were commuters on a rush-hour subway platform. But a better analogy came to mind, from her grandfather's day, the funeral of Robert Kennedy. Gramp stood on the viewing line at St. Patrick's in New York, one among the multitude, from before dawn to well into the afternoon, patiently waiting his turn to pay his last respects to the murdered man.

"Where's your wings?" Ciari asked quietly, speaking English deliberately and colloquially to pull her from her reverie.

"Ten minutes. Downwind leg along the coast to get beyond the worst of that lot"—she indicated the sea creatures—"then base leg to bring her over land, final to us. Just dirtied the flight profile, deploying flaps and gear. There's a flat stretch behind the promontory, should be enough for a short field touch-down."

"Can we get off after?"

She shrugged and deadpanned, "Never know 'til we try."

"Ter*rif*ic," he said, matching her affectation perfectly. "Might be prudent to put some distance between us and them."

"Kids can't be moved."

"I know."

She gave him the same look as when she'd gone to confront Rossmore. "I won't leave them," she said, ending any discussion. The pronoun encompassed both the wounded young folk and the critters beyond.

"What about the *Constitution*?"

"Hana found an anomalous line in the tertiary operating software . . ."

"A *line*? In the second-level *backup*?"

"She wrote the program, Ben, stands to reason she'd notice any glitches. But actually, it was a Guardian Sequence that raised the initial flag. Disappeared after that. If it *is* sabotage, some kind of stealth virus . . ."

"Have to be, to get around the safeguards on a starship."

She nodded, but continued as if he hadn't interrupted. ". . . then the logical point of attack is Transition. Degrade the warp field, the ship simply disappears, with nothing left but a trail of scattered molecules the better part of a light-year long."

"Nicole, I understand the need for respect . . ."

"No, Ben, I don't think you do. I started a crash call to the *Constitution* before touching atmosphere. It's a long way and we're on the wrong side of the planet, but they should hear."

"And do what?"

"Hopefully, light off the Runway until they have a better sense of the situation."

"Suppose they assume it's a trap? What d'you mean, *you* sent?"

"Long story." She looked at him. "You were on the water, you'd gotten that far, why'd you quit?"

He sniffed ruefully. "You'd'a been proud, Shea. I spent a year in Virtual turning myself into a sailor. Practiced when I could on my lake. Had to be careful there, though, in case I was under observation. I got her out to the reef . . ." His voice trailed off.

"I almost turned back then, myself. I wouldn't wish that kind of launch on my worst enemy."

He sounded surprised and the reason made her want to throttle him, inappropriate though the sentiment was under the circumstances. "That wasn't any problem at all."

"So what then?"

"The wave action," he explained. "The swell. I got sick."

"Seasick?"

"First time on a boat. In Virtual I had pictures of what to expect, but actually *feeling* the motion, that's a whole different ship to fly. I couldn't stop puking."

"Happens."

"I tried. I couldn't hack it, so I headed back. Came over the reef at high, pretty much sailed right in, then trolled around waiting for the water to recede. Beached the Cat, tidied her up, tucked her away with the Homer so—once you showed—you could find her."

"And did the rest on foot. Any revelations?"

"Nothing to compare with yours, evidently—*my God!*" He finished in the smallest whisper.

They'd brought the Great Old One at last to the surface and even at that great distance, in the stark glow of the single moon, the awful wound was plain to see. It was as though someone had gutted Him, opening Him to the heart—yet Nicole was certain He still lived.

"I think those tentacles reach all the way to shore," Ciari murmured. Even as he spoke, the creatures nestled close around their Elder began shunting Him forward.

"Nicole," Ciari said, taking gentle hold of a sleeve.

"Go," she told him, finishing his thought but putting her own twist on it. "Go to the others."

"I won't leave you."

"You have no place here, Ben." For emphasis, she stripped off her savaged shirt, followed in quick movement by shorts and swimsuit, to stand naked in the moonglow. Her skin was pale as alabaster, she seemed at a glance more statue than living woman; all her markings—the stigmata, the triad stripes, the dried blood of her wounds—registered as black. She looked wild and fierce, neither Hal nor human, something more formidable than both. Even Ciari felt himself taken aback by the sight of her, the quintessential Huntress, the Questing Soul.

"Nicole"—his voice was barely audible, made hoarse by the depth and complexity of emotions—"what have they done to you?"

"My words exactly," she replied with a gentleness to balance his horror, "on *Range Guide*, do you remember, a long, long time ago?

"See to the others, Ben, do that for me, please. I'll be fine."

He didn't move until she was halfway to the edge, and even then his first impulse was to follow. He could hear the sound of *Sundowner*'s motors, heralding its approach to landing; he was tempted to scoop her up and carry her bodily into the plane. He didn't need a closer vantage point to confirm that the mortally wounded creature's tentacles were dragging themselves laboriously up the face of the cliff. And had no doubts they'd be long enough to reach the top.

But Nicole put her faith in that creature, as she had in Ciari; he didn't know about them, but he had to trust her.

That was actually a lot more equanimity than Nicole herself felt as she padded silently up beside Ch'ghan, allowing herself an inner smile at the incongruity of being stark naked save for her sneaks.

The Hal had a fixed stare on his face, that of a man who'd never believed the stories told of the Burning Bush until one day he'd torn a shrub out of his garden earth to have it blaze to life in his hand.

"There is where you come from," Nicole said pitilessly. "The beasts in the hills, the ones that look like Hal, they're what you once were."

He paid no attention, she wasn't even sure he heard. She pressed on regardless.

"Until *she* fell in the ocean . . ." A shape was taking form before them, floating on open air, Nicole's ghost and Shavrin's ancestor. ". . . and He taught her how to stand on two legs, where she'd run on four."

She wondered suddenly if that was why Speakers were invariably female, if the sexual resonance somehow made the cross-species interface more compatible.

"You're not the dominant species on this world, Ch'ghan," she told him. "You're their adopted children."

With a squall of fury, leavened with heartbroken despair—a cry that spoke of ultimate loss—the Hal rounded on her; he had barbed combat tips on his claws and his hands were already moving to cut her open at throat and belly. Nicole had no time to defend herself, he was so quick; she hardly had time to register the attack—even though she was expecting it, watching for it. She had a sense of movement from him, a response from the ghost—a lunge forward to intercept the blows with her own insubstantial body—but nothing beyond that. Not pain, not blood, no sensation of contact at all—because there'd been none. Ch'ghan had been caught in midstrike, by tentacles around wrists and neck, torso and legs, pinning him as expertly as Nicole herself had been underwater.

"No!" Nicole cried, thinking he was about to be carried over the edge.

Then, she stepped back—physically and mentally—and took a look around herself. (At the same time, her alternate perception—the part of herself just throttling back on the engines after touchdown on the flat behind the headland proper—gave her a panoramic overview of the scene. She saw Hana leaping from the main hatch, MediKit in hand, and wondered about the rough and ready bandage wrapped diagonally across her friend's torso and shoulder; she saw herself and Ch'ghan and other things besides that told her the ghosts had a tangible presence. And, of course, the Great Old One's multitude of limbs, wrapping themselves around the entire brow of the cliff as He pulled himself the last stretch to the top, the last of His life pouring out of Him in an obscene cataract.)

She felt the ground groan with the phenomenal weight of

Him, and a geological stress analysis immediately confirmed her unspoken apprehension. The cliff had already taken a heavy hit from the blaster. The Old One's exertions were adding geometrically to the instability .

"Get to *Sundowner*," she said, her words transmitted from the plane to Hana's headset. "Everything here could let go at any minute."

"I'm not leaving you!" Hana cried, and Nicole heard the words from a tinny distance in her ears and with full-throated passion in her thoughts.

"You'll do as you're bloody told, Murai. I got no time to argue. This thing starts to crumble, you dust-off, no waiting, no arguments." Hana got the message, as Nicole's other self saw her and Ciari gather up the wounded. Rossmore and his fallen SEAL, they'd leave for last.

Ch'ghan's eyes had opened so wide, they looked about to pop from their sockets, and she thought at first he was being squashed. His mouth was at its full extension as well, as though uttering the most awful scream imaginable, though Nicole heard not a sound from him.

The Old One had cleared the crest, to gaze at His murderer with an eye that was as big as a barn. He just had the one, the other had been caught by the blaster beam.

All the ghosts had materialized as well, Speakers from every generation across the whole of Hal history.

"That's how You keep tabs on Your creations, isn't it?" Nicole spoke in hushed tones, the way she would in a cathedral. She'd always considered herself religious — it was hard to find an astronaut who wasn't, even among the confirmed atheists, space inspired too great and fundamental a sense of wonder — it was the established hierarchies that gave her trouble. But this moment went far beyond any experience, and all her prejudices. The paradigm for her life was her boat — and her plane — forms and structures that she could materially affect, and ultimately control, functioning in an environment over which she had very little. She couldn't alter wind and water, any more than she could dictate the circumstances of birth and upbringing, or forestall her death. Within those parameters, though, she had what she considered an unlimited scope of operations.

Now, staring into that ancient eye, trying to relate the mayfly span of her own being to His unimaginably older existence, she found both icons in the grip of a monster hurricane, being blown helter-skelter into new seas and skies. The neatly ordered structures were long gone, and the storm was tearing at her foundation.

At the same time, she understood how much harder these same realizations must be for Ch'ghan.

"Forgive me," she heard from him, hardly spoken words at all, but an exhalation given the barest possible coherent shape. He used the most formal expression. A child begging its parent, who was also the Lord of the Clan.

The little ghost passed through Nicole—not with a shiver, as she'd expected from all the stories she'd ever read or heard, but a faint flush of heat—to take a stand before Ch'ghan, the marks on her face and shoulder and left arm growing as distinct as the identical ones she'd made on Nicole.

"*Arach'n'yn,*" Nicole said in the same archaic ritual dialect, the judgment coming to her in the same manner as data from *Sundowner*, manifesting on demand as natural thought. "Blood price, Ch'ghan. Is owned and must be paid."

To his credit, he didn't flinch; he scarcely could have expected less. The surprise came when the tentacles let him loose. Nicole was still within easy reach, but he knew better than to try for her. The Speaker ghosts had taken up position in a rough semicircle, allowing a fair expanse on the brow of the headland for what was to come.

Nicole couldn't help a glance skyward. The SpaceCap Rossmore spoke of had been faked out by *Sundowner*'s landside approach. There was a fair chance they weren't even aware of the plane's landing. But that window was rapidly closing. She was using a passive sweep, because active scans would only telegraph her position, and knew that the moment the opposition appeared, *Sundowner* had to go.

Yet she knew as well, to the core of her being, that her place was here.

The little ghost began her dance, but with none of the wild abandon she'd displayed the night she and Nicole were together. The opening steps were a challenge, and Ch'ghan responded in kind. His claws were manufactured, the ghost's a natural part of her; Nicole was hard-pressed to say which were the more deadly. Ch'ghan didn't know what to expect, whether his claws could hurt her or hers, him. He decided to take the opening lunge.

They were out of direct line of sight from *Sundowner*, so Nicole had only her eyes to see with—although the data was being digitally transcribed for later playback and analysis—and the initial flurry of moves proved too fast to follow. When the two separated, Ch'ghan was clutching his chest. The ghost had caught him with a full hand, in a sweeping diagonal slash that should have been a brutal wound. Only he was unmarked.

The ghost hadn't been so lucky. He'd cut her as well, opening a gash off the curve of a hip. Nicole hissed with the pain, and lifted a bloody palm from her own skin. A look passed between her and the little ghost—complemented by a snarl of delight from Ch'ghan as he took note of the sympathetic bond between the two women—just as Nicole provided the ghost's anchor to reality, so was harm done her reflected in Nicole.

Screw this, she thought. *If my ass is on the line, I'm going to fight for it myself!*

But a small tentacle touched her ever so lightly on the shoulder, as it had on the Cat when it tapped her between the eyes, a gentle beseeching that she stay her ground.

There was a dullness to the Old One's eye and while the tentacles had lost none of their strength—that she could see—Nicole knew they couldn't hold much longer.

She felt a tickle on the edge of her perceptions, and quickly closed all *Sundowner*'s scanning windows, willing the plane to become electronically invisible. It was only a stopgap measure. A few minutes closer and the SpaceCap fighters would see all they needed to with optical.

She stroked the little tentacle, it was warm to the touch. The much larger one that stretched behind her like a fallen, rubbery redwood was as cold as the stone.

Ch'ghan was enjoying himself. As a blade fighter, there was no comparison between him and the SEAL—who'd been pretty much the best Nicole had ever seen—but he was still poetry in motion, almost admirable if it weren't for the consequence of every successful strike.

He hit the ghost a half-dozen times to her one, mixing claw slashes with a random blow. Those appeared to have an impact on the ghost, she staggered or fell as though actually struck. It was only the cuts that carried over.

Ch'ghan went for the ghost's eyes—Nicole couldn't help a cry of protest, thinking she was to be blinded—and nearly lost one of his own instead. That made him more wary, but no less confident. Yet, even as Nicole watched, the tone of the duel began to alter. Ch'ghan had lost none of his quickness, his reactions and attacks were as focused and precise as ever. But none of them landed. In turn, the ghost began to have more and more of an effect. It was much like the duel between her and Nicole; the more she connected, the more solid she became, while Ch'ghan increasingly took on the aspects of a spirit.

It was becoming clear to Nicole that she was driving him as well, away from the edge of the cliff and the Old One, and towards the sentry line of Speakers. It was also clear that Ch'ghan was losing vitality along with substance. There was no longer a crisp economy to his movements; he was increasingly reminding her of a punch-drunk fighter, sloppy of action and slow of thought. This was new; so far as she could recall, her duel with the ghost had actually gotten more intense as it progressed, each inspiring the other to greater efforts and achievements.

Ch'ghan swung for the ghost, a flailing roundhouse that was far mightier in presentation than any potential impact, and which the ghost should have avoided with ease. Instead, she let it connect.

It passed through her as if she wasn't there—or rather, as if *Ch'ghan* wasn't. The inertia of the swing pitched Ch'ghan off his feet. He recovered as an old man would, befuddled and confused by events beyond comprehension. He kept trying to stand, and managed to get partway a couple of times, but it struck Nicole that he seemed less and less aware of how to make his legs work that way. She saw that before her stood an evolutionary crossroads, demarking the boundary between what was and was to be. Somehow, all that the ghost had taken from Ch'ghan had placed her more firmly on one side of the line, and cast him irrevocably to the other.

The tentacle left her shoulder and tried to reach towards

Ch'ghan, but it hadn't the strength. Nicole picked it up, using all her force of will to make a gift of some of the warmth left in her own body. Pulling the thing wasn't as simple as she'd first thought. Regardless of girth, the tentacle's length was another matter, making it as hard to handle as a fire hose. She tried not to hurt it but she also couldn't find a way to keep from dragging it across the rock—until the ghost (who now appeared as substantial as Nicole herself) came to help.

Proximity to Ch'ghan seemed to revitalize the tentacle, and it stirred from the two women's grasp to touch the crown of Ch'ghan's forehead, as it had Nicole's—and, she knew, the ghost's—and draw forth the glittery helix of the Hal's DNA.

Nicole's companion drew her away, their place taken by the line of Speakers. Each in turn lashed out at the helix strand with their claws, casting some elements free, scrambling others, savaging the glorious molecular mosaic beyond conceivable repair.

Nicole had never witnessed so terrible a sentence, as Ch'ghan was stripped methodically of all he was, all he had ever been, all he would ever be. Not simply in a personal sense, but a genetic one as well. As each Speaker executed her aspect of the sentence, they faded to nothingness. And with them went that much more of the Old One's life.

Ch'ghan had been almost fully erect when they began, somehow he'd managed to regain his feet. He was on his belly when they finished, legs tucked underneath in a position they weren't biologically designed for, hands curled uselessly before him. Physically, he was unchanged, but in all the intangible aspects that differentiated him from a beast, Ch'ghan was no more. He would never understand why he couldn't run as fast or jump as high, why his joints would always hurt, what the bloody, broken stumps that had once been fingers were for.

He would live alone, and probably not for very long, because the winters here could be cruel and he wasn't equipped to fight them. Nicole wondered if the Old One had left him any shred of awareness of what he had been and immediately looked away, so she wouldn't have to see the answer.

She and the ghost were alone on the headland with the Old One, and she knew these were the last moments of a promethean life.

The ghost offered a lopsided grin that didn't look at all correct on a Hal face and yet also was irritatingly familiar until Nicole realized it was her own.

She tapped Nicole on the arm, a peremptory, commanding gesture that was the faintest forebear of Shavrin's own manner, and pointed towards the waiting plane. Past time for Nicole to go. Her other self confirmed that, tagging a flight of three cresting the upper atmosphere, matching the configurations to the attack group that came after them on Earth. Too far away still for target acquisition by either side.

As Nicole glanced away, the ghost stepped forward, Nicole crying out as she felt a sudden twisting sensation within herself—an icy heat that blazed through her like an erupting solar flare yet left a refreshing coolness in its wake—and beheld the ghost (now once more a ghost in every respect) emerging through her skin to take a stand before her.

Nicole looked at herself and saw that all the wounds Ch'ghan had inflicted were gone. By the same token, the stripes were more a part of her than ever.

She blinked her eyes and in that moment became the only living, sentient being on the headland.

She knew she had to leave, but had one more responsibility to fulfill before she did.

The mallet didn't seem as heavy when she lifted it, or perhaps it was that she felt whole in ways she hadn't known she was missing. And for the first time in her life.

She swung the mallet once around, then twice, to settle the heft of it and build up a greater velocity, before finally sending it crashing against the side of the tocsin. The resounding gong shook her to the core; nothing she'd heard before came even remotely close. She hit it again. And again, each stroke more powerful than the preceding.

She was weeping, as she had when she faced this moment with Paolo DaCuhna, as she would when the time came for her parents, for Judith Canfield and Shavrin, for any one of the friends waiting for her on *Sundowner*. Even Amy, she had to concede—and, with a small flash of insight, realized the girl wouldn't be returning to Earth. She'd reached a crossroads of her own, with Raqella and Nicole both, she'd found a definition of life and being that transcended the limiting parameters laid down by her father. Or, in the girl's favorite phrase, "Hey, why serve in Hell, when you can rule in Heaven, y'know?"

In its own way, the silence was as complete and all-enfolding as the chimes had been. It lasted for as long as the resonance of those three strokes.

She felt the response before she actually heard it, as a faint vibration under her fingertips where they lay lightly on the tocsin. She had no sense of the meaning, or even that it was a song, she'd have to live the Old One's lifetime to comprehend that Mystery. Ch'ghan couldn't bear it, he scampered off the headland, uttering howls of dismay that intensified when he encountered *Sundowner* blocking his path. He hadn't a clue what it was, there were no circuits in his brain that applied labels to things, only that it was strange and he didn't like it and he had to run away. Which he did.

Nicole followed at a walk. Not to prove a point, but because that was the rhythm called for by the song. She never looked back, because some moments aren't meant to be witnessed in that way, as great cracks appeared in the brow of the headland. The weight of the Old One combined with the resonance of the song to finish the work begun by the blaster shot. There was another tremendous noise—that should have drowned out the song, but didn't even come close—the sound of rock *tearing*, and monstrous chunks of stone tumbled away, so large that anyone watching would have to swear they were moving in slow motion. It was impossible to conceive of anything so big possessing speed.

The tocsin remained, but where its dais ended, so too did the land, in a vertical wall so sheer it might have been carved by a stone mason. The cliff bottomed out in a jumbled scree of slabs, some of whom would be considered fair-sized mountains in their own right. The entire face of the headland was changed and Nicole knew that over succeeding generations—which for the Old Ones could well be measured in geological terms—it would be shaped further, into a fitting memorial for their fallen Elder.

"Something to see," she told herself.

She found Hana waiting at the ramp, with a flight suit and her leather jacket. Her friend was wearing the pendant earring Nicole had made her.

"Nobody ever listens to me," Nicole sighed, with a shake of the head.

"And miss all this fun? Perish the thought. Like the look, though."

"You're welcome to it, anytime."

Hana turned serious, while Nicole struggled to pull pants over shoes. "Jenny's aboard *Constitution*. We seem to be locked out of their transceiver net, I'm not even getting an acknowledgment of our carrier pattern."

"They lit the Runway yet?"

"Working on it. And we got the bogies to contend with."

"We'll run wavetop underneath 'em. Even if they spot our signature against the ground clutter, the angle will be too extreme to come after us. If they're Hal, they won't shoot over water, that's blasphemy. We'll cut behind 'em, and initiate our climb. They'll wait to complete their orbit to stage the intercept."

"You sound pretty sure, Ace."

"Hey, if I'm wrong, we'll adapt."

Hana held out the *fireheart* pendant. Nicole hung it from her earlobe, then donned her jacket. Both elements felt right. Hana led the way up the ramp, Nicole right on her heels as the farside engines cycled to speed.

"Ben didn't cut it, did he?" Hana asked, at the top.

"He was alone. I had help."

Hana sat right seat on the flight deck, but both knew that when all this was over, it would be Kymri's place if he wanted it. Hana's was the chair behind Nicole, where she could cover her back. And Jenny's a row behind, where she could look after them all, in her own way. Ciari was already plugged into the weapons console. He'd always be welcome, it would always be for a visit. As for the kids, Raqella and Amy had decisions of their own to make, paths a'plenty to choose. For the moment, they were stuck following Nicole's. What came after was up to them.

She didn't look back as *Sundowner* rotated, clearing the cliff line mere seconds after leaving the ground. Nicole eased the yoke forward and pressed gently on the rudder pedals to send the spaceplane into a looping dive out to sea. She stabilized at a hundred meters, ready to drop to thirty if she had to, and cranked the revs until she was a hair below Mach.

"No turb," she commented, "I'm impressed."

"The ground is where we live, the sky is our home." Raqella weakly offered the oldest Hal proverb, from the seat he'd been securely buckled into, right beside Amy.

"Well, kids," Nicole said, and the pronoun applied to their species as much as themselves. "Past time, I say, we made us a home of our own."

She opened the throttles to their stops and with a madcap laugh started *Sundowner* climbing, the ship responding as if this were the cue it had been waiting for.

Above them, the sky was clear, all the way to the stars.